YOU BELONG TO ME

YOU BELONG TO ME

Samantha Hayes

CENTURY

Century
20 Vauxhall Bridge Road
London SW1V 2SA

Century is part of the Penguin Random House group of companies
whose addresses can be found at global.penguinrandomhouse.com.

Penguin
Random House
UK

First published by Century in 2015

www.randomhouse.co.uk

A CIP catalogue record for this book
is available from the British Library.

ISBN 9781780893396

Printed and bound by Clays Ltd, St Ives Plc

MIX
Paper from
responsible sources
FSC
www.fsc.org   FSC® C018179

Penguin Random House is committed to a sustainable future
for our business, our readers and our planet. This book is
made from Forest Stewardship Council® certified paper.

For Audrey, and for Jo-Jo.
Always loved and remembered.

Acknowledgements

It's such a pleasure to mention everyone involved with my book when I come to the end of the writing process, and every thank-you here is heartfelt and genuine. So many skills and talents are poured into turning my words into the book you're holding, it's quite humbling to know how many wonderful and creative people are behind me.

So huge thanks, gratitude, and love to my brilliant editors, Selina Walker and Georgina Hawtrey-Woore, to Philippa Cotton and Sarah Ridley for 'getting me out there' (and getting me out of pickles), Dan Balado for eagle-eyes and good spirits, Richard Ogle for yet another stunning cover, Andrew Sauerwine and Vincent Kelleher for all your hard work, and sincere thanks to *everyone* at Cornerstone involved with my books – I really appreciate everything you do.

As ever, love and thanks to my dear agent, Oli Munson, and all the fabulous team at AM Heath, including Jennifer Custer, Hélène Ferey, Vickie Dillon. And grateful thanks, too, to all at Blake Friedmann, as well as the many foreign teams around the world for spreading my books far and wide.

I'd also like to thank the real Bethany Adams for allowing me to borrow her name for a good cause. The beauty, talent, and lovely voice are real, but any similarities end there!

Finally, love to all my family, especially to Ben, Polly and Lucy, and to Terry for your support.

YOU BELONG TO ME

Prologue

February 2014

It's freezing. But I don't care.

The frosty air wraps around my bare shoulders as I leave my house, touching me, loving me, caressing me with its icy burn. Waking me up, dragging me back from the terror of you.

For the first time in a year, I feel free.

It's been a month since I saw you or heard from you, sensed you ten paces behind me as I walked to the shops, took Lilly to nursery. A month since you last watched me sleeping, or phoned me in the dead of night, and a month since I received the last gift in the post – a framed photograph of us in Cornwall when you took me away.

I still have everything, you know, even though all I want to do is burn it all. They told me to keep the stuff, make a log of everything that happened. I did, but of course you found it and destroyed it, threatening me next time I saw you. Even when I had the locks changed, you still found a way in.

I walk along the icy pavement, wobbling in my new silver heels, wriggling down my short skirt. I bought myself a new outfit as a treat – a celebration of my freedom. I'm off to meet my sister. Off to have fun. Let my hair down. Have a few drinks. All without you. I've finally got the message through. *Leave me alone.*

The thought makes my throat close up. Makes my heart forget how to beat right. You'd be so cross if you saw me looking like this.

I walk on, catching the bus just before it leaves. I feel confident. Happy. Alive. Lilly is with Mum, and I'm staying at my sister's place tonight, so even if you go to mine, I won't be there.

Like I said. I am free.

I get off the bus, and a couple of guys call out to me, make lewd comments and noises. I don't mind, because it's not you. I almost like it. I catch sight of myself in a shop window. I look good with my hair up. This top leaves little to the imagination, but that's what I want – I want everyone to wonder about me, to admire me, to see freedom written all over my body.

Going up the steps to the club round the corner, I stumble sideways, hurt my ankle. I rub it, and when I see the tattoo, you're back with me of course. But the appointment is booked to have it removed.

Inside, the club is loud, noisy, pulsing. It's already stuffed full, even though it's not quite midnight. The music thumps through me, the bass line shocking every cell of me alive. I can't see Sally, but she's always late. But then

I feel my phone vibrating in my clutch bag. It's a text from her.

So sorry, Alex. Cracking headache. Next week? Sal xx

Immediately I blame you, think you've got to her. Paid her off to spoil my night, even though I know my own sister would never do that.

After everything, I feel wretched. I was looking forward to letting my hair down. Forgetting about you.

I buy a double vodka and knock it back. I get hit on at the bar by a bloke, so go to the loos to escape. I lean against the basin, crying. Ten minutes later, when I leave the club, the doorman says something to me, but I don't hear him. I stand on the top step, breathing in the cold night air again. I'll be OK, I tell myself. I've had worse.

For ages, I try to flag down a taxi, but it's so cold tonight, they're all taken. One slows and I think he's going to stop, but he just kerb-crawls past, looking me up and down. Probably wondering if I'm a hooker.

'Sod you,' I say under my breath, deciding to walk if there are no buses at the stop. I'm shivering, wishing I'd brought a coat. But at least I can feel, I think gratefully. At least I'm *alive*.

The bus pulls away just as I run up to it. It's not been my night. I kick off my shoes and hook them on my fingers. The frosted pavement feels oddly good against my toes – as if it's scorching hot, not cold. There's a short cut to my place, and it's all well lit apart from a passage cut through about two hundred metres long.

You can do it, I tell myself. *There's nothing to be scared of any more.*

I head off the quick way home, kicking up a pace. Feeling sorry for myself, I'm going to make hot chocolate and watch a movie until I fall asleep. The luxury will be that you're not there.

But suddenly I stop and turn round. I thought I heard someone. Someone close.

I sigh out a breath. There's no one there – no one apart from a group of boys smoking outside a pub.

I walk on, feeling anxious. I take my phone from my clutch and switch the camera to face me, holding it so I can see behind. Of course, you're not there. All I can see is a couple with a dog, another young woman walking by herself. The boys are in the distance now.

There – what was that? *Who* was that? I take a photograph, hoping to catch you out, but I don't. You are not in my picture when I check.

But I swear I saw you – your square shoulders, your pointy features, your quick legs.

I hear my breath, short and rasping, as I leave the lit-up street, heading down the alleyway. I can smell my own fear.

Oh God, oh God, I say in little icy shots. Why the hell did I come this way? But if I turn back now, it'll take me twice as long, and I just want to get home. I just want to see Lilly again.

My bare feet sting on the rough cobbles. Any light from the street has fallen away, and I'm closed in on either side by tumble-down garages, old cars, crooked fences and stretches of brick wall. There's only one way out, and that's straight on.

I stop suddenly and swing round.

'Who's there?'

I swear I saw a man's figure – *you!* – duck into a dark corner. I swear I saw the plume of your breath.

I half run, half walk, stepping on something sharp, hopping in agony. I begin to cry.

I tried to tell them about you, told the police you were poison, and that you'd stop at nothing to get what you wanted. *Me.* But they said they couldn't do anything, suggested I should get better locks and a personal alarm. 'Until he actually strikes,' they said, 'we can't prove he's done anything wrong.'

It's as I'm bending down to pick something from my foot that I feel the first blow. A bitter crack to the back of my head. At first, I don't realise I've been hit.

Then I drop down, rolling over, twisting in agony. I scream out your name as the hands come down on my neck.

I can't see straight. I try to scream again, but now there's blood in my mouth and more pain.

Pain everywhere, lashing at me as I'm hit and hit and kicked and spat on.

I'm writhing and wriggling, thrashing out, but it's useless. As my throat closes up, I try not to cry. Try not to give you the satisfaction of seeing me broken. Finally.

After what seems like for ever, I feel myself getting

weaker, feel myself losing hold on life. Everything hurts as I'm choked to my last breath.

You never really left me at all, did you? Even when you weren't there, you were still polluting my mind; still going to be my last thought.

At last, I stop struggling. I have no more fight or screams left in me. It's all over. I stare up to the sky, ignoring the angry, silhouetted face between me and the stars. It's as if I'm gazing right into heaven.

'*Jimmy!*' I yell out one more time, disgusted with myself that the last thing I say is your name.

1

I step out into the heat and bustle of the ever-busy street, leaving the sanctuary and safety of the small hotel. I've been hiding for nearly six months now, but I still can't help glancing over my shoulder to check I'm not being followed. Old habits are hard to break.

Nothing's happened since I ran away, but I've had to be cautious. I can't shake the feeling that he's waiting for me on every street corner, logging each move I make, photographing whatever I do with a leer spread across his sallow face. My ears still ring with the sound of his footsteps clicking close behind me. My skin still prickles from the brush of his lips on my neck.

Satisfied I'm alone, I press on, drawing deep breaths of humid air as I reach the crowded market. I even allow myself a small smile: maybe today will be different. It's as if something is finally shifting inside me. It's time to move on, to let go of the fears that have strangled me for so long.

You're safe, I repeat in my head, pushing through the crowds. *He doesn't know where you are.*

It's already hot, even though it's still early. I burrow between the canopied stalls selling fresh green herbs, colourful ground spices, and seeds piled up in giant baskets. I glance around, breathing in the rainbow of smells, wondering if there's a spice I haven't yet cooked with in the dense heat of Raksha's tiny kitchen, or if there's a new type of incense to try on Bhanu's tempting stall.

I stop, breathing in deeply again, scanning the colourful scene, hoping I'll find an explanation for my more positive mood.

When I arrived in India, the markets were almost too vibrant to look at for more than a moment. I was alone and depressed, frightened, barely able to cope. Now, it's as if my eyes have acclimatised to the hot-headed pinks, the bitter yellows and luscious oranges, as if my ears have become immune to the constant rattle and thrum of Delhi life.

But it doesn't take much for the bad memories to flood back, forcing me to stop what I'm doing, work through the migraine-like pain of everything that happened.

Last night, it was triggered by something a customer said to Raksha. Instantly, I was back at the Sengar Gow restaurant on a drizzly Birmingham street – the chipped paint, the maroon flocked wallpaper, the wailing background music of a lone sitar, some men fetching curries after a session at the pub.

It was all so real, as if I was back there again. With *him*.

I felt the sting of his grip around my wrist, remembered

the stoic expression I forced as I pretended everything was OK. The way he frog-marched me out to the car and locked me in it for the rest of the night. Later, he apologised, told me he loved me.

I rub my wrists, and an assortment of Indian bracelets jangle up and down my arms as I continue on my way again. Perhaps today's not so different after all.

Suddenly I'm shoved sideways, stumbling and gasping as someone bumps into me. My heart bangs loudly as a woman's apology rings out in Hindi. She glances back, smiling, the bright bandage of her cerise sari making her caramel skin appear almost edible.

The memory has put me on edge.

I press on along Chandni Chowk, weaving through the dense market, watching as the people go about their Monday morning business. My job is to buy spices, fruit and vegetables according to Raksha's precise list.

Soon her little hotel will be tingling with the scent of green cardamom and fenugreek, tamarind chutney and aloo pakoras, chickpea and mango curry, along with a bubbling pot of spicy sambhar as she prepares the evening meal for the fourteen guests currently staying at the Bestluck Hotel, Chandni Chowk Road, Delhi – my home for the last few months.

My lips spread into a smile – the first in ages – as I pull the shopping list from my pocket.

That's it, I think, suddenly realising what's changed. This strange, colourful, sensory overload of a place almost feels like *home*.

'*Ee-zee*,' comes a voice in strained English. A skinny boy in his early teens thrashes past me on a rusty bicycle, frantically ringing his bell. The slightly bent front wheel clanks with every rotation.

'Mees Ee-*zee*,' he cries again, leaving a trail of dust behind him.

I laugh and call out to him, but my voice is soaked up by the crowds. I see him waving at me as if I've been a local all my life. It almost feels as if I have, I realise, relishing the new feeling.

The sun is slowly breaking over the top of the messy buildings that form the backdrop of Chandni Chowk. It warms my neck where I've scooped up and tamed my hair in a clip. What I'm experiencing, I realise gratefully, are the first shoots of normality.

'Mees Eezee over here!'

The bicycle circles me again. Some feat within the constraints of the stalls, the myriad bodies jostling for food.

Javesh, the young bellboy from Bestluck, skids to a stop beside me. His hair is thick and black and plastered sideways across the wide expanse of his bony forehead.

A second later, I see a man approaching me with a purposeful stride. My heart inflames, suddenly switching from a steady beat to a frightened arrhythmia.

'She here! Mees Eezee over here, meester!' Javesh sings, his hand outstretched towards the stranger.

Without taking his eyes off me, the man pushes some coins into the boy's palm.

I back away, inwardly cursing myself for being so foolish.

Why did I believe for one minute, for one *second*, I would ever be safe?

'Wait,' the man says in a deep English accent.

His eyes are piercing blue and his hair the darkest brown, making him a suspicious blend from first sight. His skin is pale with no trace of a tan.

'I'm glad to have caught you,' he says again with an extra breath between the words.

It could be a laugh, but my default settings tell me it's because he's been hunting me, chasing me through the busy market, and it's his anticipation and exhilaration spilling out.

I'm unable to speak so I just look him up and down, the fear showing in my eyes. He's about my age, tall and lean. I continue to back away.

'Please, don't look so worried,' he says kindly. His face cracks into a smile and his hand comes out – perhaps an offer to shake, perhaps an attempt to grab me.

I turn and run, immediately stumbling and crashing into a stall. A second later, I'm lying in a basket of nutmeg, the woody nuggets spilling out around me. Again his hand is there, reaching out.

'The boy helped me find you. He told me you'd be at the market.'

When I don't take his hand, he steps back with a disappointed expression. The stall owner is yelling at me for ruining his display. I can't understand everything he says, but offer him an apology as I haul myself out of the basket.

'I'm staying at the hotel. I've seen you there,' the Englishman says.

It's then that a vague spark of recognition kicks in and I begin to relax.

'Bestluck?' I say, feeling a bit stupid. I brush myself down. My white trousers are streaked with ochre dust.

'Yeah, Bestluck,' he says with a laugh. 'I didn't mean to scare you.'

'God, I'm sorry,' I say, stepping away from the stall – partly to escape the owner's wrath, and partly in case I have to make a run for it. In six months, no one has claimed to have 'seen me', and certainly no one's made a point of seeking me out.

'What do you want?' It comes out harshly, but there's a lot at stake.

'To give you this.' He holds out an envelope. 'A courier delivered it to the hotel just after you'd left, saying it was urgent. He didn't wait. Young Javesh said he could find anyone for a few rupees, especially an *Eengleesh* girl,' he says with a laugh. 'I was going for a walk, so I offered to help.'

The man's face breaks into a grin. It's the kind of smile that's a hug, a therapy session and a promise, all in one.

I look away.

'How did you know I'd gone to the market?'

He laughs gently. 'Javesh said that Raksha sends you to buy vegetables at this time every day.' The man looks down at me as if I am some rare species he's just discovered.

I think highly of Raksha – she's big and loud and colourful. She saved my life, and I love her.

'Well, thank you for going to so much trouble,' I say, eyeing the envelope warily. It's only just occurred to me that a courier delivering something to Bestluck with my name on it is extremely worrying news. No one knows where I am.

I take the envelope. There is no address on it, just my name printed in a small black typeface.

'My name is Owen Brandrick, by the way,' he says, proffering his hand again.

Reluctantly, I shake it, though my eyes are still fixed on the envelope.

'Mees Eezee, Mees *Ee-zee*!' Javesh is back, circling us on his bike.

My mouth opens to say something, but nothing comes out. He's making me dizzy, as if he and everything around me aren't real, leaving me alone in a dark and unfamiliar place.

I shake my head, trying to be rational.

I'm being stupid. I'm perfectly safe and there's no cause for alarm.

Letters begin to arrive when you've lived somewhere for a while. It's probably junk mail, or perhaps something that Raksha signed me up for. I don't want to dwell on why it was delivered by a courier.

Whatever's going on, I mustn't show him that I'm upset. He's a guest at the hotel, after all. The back of my hand swipes across my top lip, dragging away the build-up of sweat. It must be thirty-five, thirty-six degrees and it's not even eight a.m. yet. My mouth is dry.

'I'm being rude,' I say, even though it feels as if I'm about to pass out. 'My name is Isabel – Izzy for short.'

'Javesh made sure I knew that,' he says with that same laugh, making me feel silly. '*Mees Eezee*,' he mimics with a broad grin. I look away again, but for a different reason this time.

'He's a good boy,' I manage to say in my most normal voice. 'And besides, you've already seen me at the hotel,' I add in a joking way, even though the words actually fill me with dread.

I've been watching you, Belle. Keeping you in clear sight.

'Well, nice to meet you,' Owen says casually. He turns to leave, and for some reason I suddenly feel disappointed.

'Wait,' I say. Javesh makes a whooping noise somewhere nearby, causing a flicker of a smile on my face. 'Are you walking back to Bestluck?'

'Not immediately,' he says. 'I'm having one last breakfast at Papa Raj's. They serve the best tea and nashta. I'm heading home to England tomorrow.'

'Oh.'

My disappointment is way bigger than the single syllable. Something inside me twinges as I slip my finger inside the flap of the envelope, staring at him as I break the crispy seal, gnawing through the paper at its crease.

'Bye, then,' he says with a flick of his hand.

I watch as he walks away.

'If you fancy some company,' I call out, 'I could join you.' I hold up my empty basket. 'After I've delivered Raksha's groceries I'll have an hour spare.'

It's a lie, but I'm sure Raksha will allow me a little grace before I have to clean the bedrooms. I worked extra hours yesterday and she's a fair boss.

Owen stops and turns back to me again, squinting from the sun. His eyes flick between my face and the letter as I remove it from the envelope. 'I'd like that,' he says, again with that same grin.

He's the first person I've approached or spoken to in ages, unless it's to ask for their dinner order, or to see if they'd like a top-up of tea. As I unfold the letter and read, I force my best smile to bloom, showing him I'd also like that. But then, as I skim down the words, drinking in the news, my eyes stretch wide in disbelief and my hand covers my mouth.

Then the world goes completely black as I fall to the ground.

2

The GP listens as I explain what's wrong. Rain drives down the old pane of the sash window behind her, distracting me. The sky is an inky black now that we've put the clocks back. The doctor doesn't write anything down, rather focuses on me as I weave my way around why I'm actually here.

'How long has the insomnia been a problem, Lorraine?' Dr Lewis asks. She pushes a loose clump of hair that's fallen from her thick ponytail back behind her ear.

I tell her that as I haven't slept properly in ages, I'm too tired to know precisely. But my mind is wandering again, second-guessing her exact age as a distraction from telling her why I'm here. I study the soft wrinkles beneath her eyes, mentally comparing them to my own.

Mine are deeper, I conclude. Hammered in, rather than having developed gracefully over time.

'Anyway, it's been long enough to make me feel like—' I'd get away with it at work, surrounded mostly by male detectives, immersed in the gravity of a big case where language, however vile, gets swallowed up by things far worse.

But Kelly Lewis doesn't deserve a foul mouth. She got me through both my difficult pregnancies and has looked after my family for nearly two decades. It's not her fault I feel like shit.

'Long enough to make me feel a bit rubbish, if I'm honest.' I'm staring at my lap now, watching as the fingers of one hand dig into the skin of the other. Then I let out a big sigh. It's instead of crying.

'The thing is,' she says, 'lack of sleep affects all areas of your life and—'

'My appetite's shot to pieces,' I cut in, again skirting the real issue. 'And I'm . . .'

'Go on, Lorraine. It's fine.'

I lift my head, looking her in the eye. *She's a doctor. Just tell her. She can help you.*

'I've been getting heart palpitations,' I say. It's true, but not what I was building up to. 'And I seem so . . .'

'Anxious?'

I nod and shrug. 'God, anyone would think you were a doctor or something.' I laugh – what I always do when I'm emotionally backed into a corner.

Dr Lewis smiles, turning to her computer. She scans through my history. 'Not allergic to anything, are you?'

'Penicillin,' I tell her flatly. Is that it? Is she just going to dish out a prescription and send me on my way?

'OK,' she says, clicking off the screen and standing up.

'Let's give you the once-over. Go behind the screen and take off your top. You can leave your bra on.'

I do as I'm told, while Dr Lewis, who has examined every part of me over the years, washes her hands and hunts for her stethoscope.

I make sure I'm lying down flat on my back before she sees me. That way the rubbish I've been scoffing when I do get a chance to eat – the takeaway food, the pastries on offer in the department, the snatched burgers at lunchtime – settles inwards at my waist rather than rolling over the top of my black work trousers.

I'm sure it's nothing a few runs with Adam won't sort out.

'I'm just so tired all the time . . .' I say out loud, though not meaning to. My head sinks gratefully into the pillow.

'What's that?' she says, appearing round the screen, smiling. She's holding the flat disc of the stethoscope between her hands to warm it up.

'Oh, nothing,' I say, feeling something of a failure. I'm sure most people manage to fit work and family into their lives, so why can't I?

My heart gathers thrust again at the exact moment Dr Lewis puts the stethoscope to my chest.

'Sit up, Lorraine,' she says with a frown. Her hand is on my elbow, helping me up.

I should just tell her what's happened, what's been going on.

'Lean forward,' she continues, putting the instrument against my back. Then she's in front of me again, staring at the ceiling as she listens. After this, she takes my blood pressure, frowning at the reading.

'Will I live to the end of the week?' I ask. 'The super will kill me if I don't get the reports to him.' Another laugh and that's it. My pathetic attempt at telling her.

'You will,' she says kindly, easing me down on to my back again. 'Sorry if my hands are cold,' she adds, gently palpating my tummy.

I feel a surge of something in my chest, making my heart race again, as she pauses over one particular area.

'You'll be *fine*,' she says as if she's read my mind, sitting me up again. 'But I am going to send you to get a Holter monitor fitted to record what your heart gets up to over a longer period. You'll have to wear it for twenty-four hours. It's just a precaution.'

'What, so I have to go to the hospital twice in two days?' I feel my palms start to sweat.

'Yes,' she says again. 'You can get dressed now.'

Dr Lewis goes round the other side of the screen.

'But what about work?' I say. 'I can't possibly take time off.'

I slide off the examination couch and swipe my white blouse off the chair. One of the sleeves has become tangled within itself and won't come out. I suddenly feel like ripping it off.

'I think that's exactly what you need to do, if I'm honest,' Dr Lewis says from across the room. 'Take time off,' she adds, as if I don't understand.

'Oh no . . . no . . .' I say, shaking my head.

I emerge from behind the screen with my blouse half on and unbuttoned. My hair has fallen from its clip, and I can feel my cheeks burning. She simply doesn't understand. I fumble with the buttons, forcing them through the holes with shaking fingers.

'I think you've . . .' Dr Lewis is looking at my blouse. 'You've done them up the wrong . . .'

Annoyed, I turn to the mirror on the wall beside the door. 'See?' I say. 'I can't even do up a shirt right.'

'Sit down again, Lorraine,' she says gently.

I do as I'm told, preparing for a telling off.

'I'm sorry,' I say. 'It's just that . . .'

'Go on.'

'Things are difficult at work.'

Keep quiet, I tell myself. My eyes fill with tears.

'Because you're not sleeping?' she asks.

'Like I said, I'm tired.' I bite my lip.

'I can give you a prescription,' she says, turning back to her computer. A moment later, the printer is spewing out a small green form. She hands it to me. 'Something to help you sleep.'

I stare at the paper. 'Temazepam?' I take the prescription, but then I fold my hands around it, crumpling it up. I shove it in my bag anyway. 'I don't need *sleeping* pills, Kelly,' I say, leaning in. My shoulders are up around my ears and it feels as if I haven't breathed properly in ages. 'I need *staying awake* pills.'

It's then that her hand comes out, pressing down upon

22

mine as I grip the edge of the desk, closing around my white knuckles. That simple act of kindness, even after I've rejected her good intentions, is enough to send me over the edge. I hang my head as the hot tears drop on to my trousers.

'God, sorry,' I say, trying not to snivel.

Detective Inspector Lorraine Fisher does not bloody cry!

Dr Lewis passes me a box of tissues. I blow my nose and wipe beneath my eyes, anticipating mascara streaks. Not that I had time to put on much make-up this morning. The world was a dark and dismal place at six a.m., and glamour wasn't top of my priorities.

I take a deep breath.

'There were two murder cases earlier this year,' I tell her, sniffing, hoping she'll understand how frustrated I am. 'The first was a young woman who'd complained of being stalked before she was killed. You probably saw it on the news.' What the news didn't report is how little evidence we have; how, ever since, we've been working pretty much on gut instinct alone.

'Yes, yes I remember,' she says.

My stomach clenches. Dr Lewis doesn't need to know that I was involved with the complaint made by the dead woman, that Alexandra Stanford approached me for help, that we chatted about her situation. And she doesn't need to know that I made some choices, some wrong choices, that likely led to her death.

Alexandra was discovered beaten to death and strangled

in an alley a few weeks after I'd sent her away, telling her there was nothing we could do to help her.

It's she who keeps me awake at night, I want to tell my doctor – Alexandra's ghostly grey face, twisted from fear, re-animating from death, talking to me through sweat-soaked dreams, leering over my bed and torturing me into consciousness. For hours I lie there, shaking, sweating, thinking about her, how I should have helped her, listened to her. Waiting for morning, watching as the orange glow of the streetlights bleeds from behind the curtains, my eyes prickling and dry from tiredness.

But no, I don't tell Dr Lewis any of that.

'And another woman was murdered not long after,' I say, almost matter-of-factly. Another dearth of evidence, I think – perhaps attributable to the low media profile we maintained, but no one wanted a panic. Eight months on, it's still causing the department – *me* – problems.

I feel as if I'm being crushed by a weight – the weight of the cases, the pressure to make an arrest. I'm certain the two are linked; others in the department believe this too. We just can't prove it.

'That's really tough, Lorraine,' Dr Lewis replies, because there isn't much else she can say.

'No staying awake pills on offer then?' I ask flippantly, standing up. I reach for my jacket, slinging it over my arm.

Dr Lewis shakes her head, pulling a pained expression. 'No, but I really think you should—'

'I understand,' I say, holding up a hand and turning to leave.

'You'll get a letter about the heart monitor soon, Lorraine,' she calls out before I close the door.

What I really want to say back is that I'm not certain my heart can be repaired.

3

'Isabel, can you hear me? Are you OK?'

There's a hand on my head, stroking my hair. For a second, it's comforting, but then I feel afraid – no, *terrified*. I don't have the strength to push it away. Every nerve in my body is raw, every muscle weak – even the air on my face hurts. I'm lying on my back and I don't know why.

'You passed out,' a man's voice above me says.

There's a pain in my head and I daren't open my eyes.

'What happened?' someone else asks, then I realise it's me.

'Mees *Eezee*, you OK?'

That voice I know. I turn my head sideways and see the face of a young Indian boy.

'Javesh.'

He's squatting down beside me with a worried expression. It's then I realise I'm on the ground. The smell of dirt, the rotting vegetables from yesterday's market mashed up by ten thousand footsteps, the residue of spices, the stench of the gutter, it all wafts up around me.

'Are you able to stand?'

And then I focus on him – the man with bright blue eyes and swathes of dark curly hair. My mind suddenly joins the dots between leaving Bestluck, walking through the market, a stranger approaching and, finally, reading the letter before blacking out.

'Where is it?' I ask, feeling around with my hand.

'I have it safe,' the man says kindly. He eases a hand under my shoulder and tries to sit me up. He is strong and his fresh cologne is a welcome relief to the stink around me. 'Up you come.'

Suddenly I am sitting, and then, as if I'm levitating, I'm standing, leaning against him.

'You fainted,' he tells me.

I touch my head. 'There must be some mistake . . . the letter . . .' If I say the words out loud, it will make them real. 'Sorry,' I continue vaguely. 'I'm not making sense, and I've forgotten your name.'

'Owen,' he reminds me, while keeping hold of me. The white linen of his short-sleeved shirt feels comforting against the bare skin of my shoulder. 'Owen Brandrick.'

'And you're staying at Bestluck?'

'Only for one more night,' he tells me. 'I'll take you back to the hotel, if you like. You need to lie down. Raksha can call for the doctor.'

'I don't need a doctor,' I say. 'I have to get the groceries.'

I spot my basket lying on its side and pull away from him. As I reach for it, I stumble, but Owen catches me before I fall. There are people everywhere, pushing and

27

shoving, the bright colours searing the backs of my eyes, the noises shooting pain through my head.

'I need a glass of water,' I say. 'Can we go and sit somewhere?'

Owen instructs Javesh to return to Bestluck to get a message to Raksha, telling her that I will be late, but not to worry. The boy holds out his hand for a coin, then pedals away furiously on his bicycle, his bell ringing repeatedly to part the crowds.

'I'll be fine,' I tell Owen. 'I just need a moment.'

I'm certain there's been a mistake. That letter can't have been for me. I need to sit beneath a fan for ten minutes, compose myself. A glass of water, a rest, and I'll be on my way. That good feeling will return and I will get on with my job, my life. My *new* life.

Papa Raj's is dark and breezy and thick with the scent of incense and bubbling spices. Long bench seats stacked with colourful cushions line one side of the room, while jewelled mirrors of all sizes cover the walls.

In the middle of the popular tea house are low brass tables with floor mats, and it's at one of these we sit, me with my knees drawn up to my chest, while Owen sits cross-legged, his sand-coloured shorts rising above his knees.

'It's my favourite place,' he says, looking around as we sip chai. 'I've been coming here nearly every day to work.'

He's staring at me, waiting patiently in case I want to

explain about the letter. But I just nod. I can't get the words out of my mind, let alone tell him. As long as I'm the only one who knows, then maybe it won't be true.

'Here, take this in case I forget,' he says, handing me back the envelope.

I stare at it.

'Don't you want it?'

My shaking hand slowly reaches out to take it as it dawns on me that my theory about it being a mistake is full of holes. Other people know the words in this letter too – the person who typed them for a start, plus several others in the British High Commission, and countless people back in England. In fact, it's likely I'm the last of many to know the news.

'They're dead,' I say suddenly. I feel light-headed when I think of the other name in the letter.

Owen frowns and pours more tea into our little glasses. 'I'm so sorry if there's been bad news.'

I take the letter out of the envelope, forcing myself to read it again. I take it slowly this time, walking my eyes over the words, noticing each punctuation mark in case I misread something, as if a comma could make all the difference – at least make *him* not have been a part of it.

But it's still the same. They're still dead, and *his* name is still there.

'My parents,' I say, placing the letter on the table. One corner of the paper wicks up a drop of spilled tea. 'They were killed.'

Owen drags a hand down his chin. I don't know this

man, and he doesn't know me, but for a few moments there's a connection, as if he's my husband, or a relative, or a lifelong friend, and we're both sharing this tragedy. It's actually a comfort to have him here.

'I am deeply sorry,' he says. His cheeks briefly tinge red, just above the light stubble grazing his jaw. 'Does it say how it happened?'

'A car crash,' I say, trying to block the driver of the car from my mind.

Something is firing up inside me. I recognise it. The shutters have come down and, one by one, emotional barricades are ring-fencing me. It is a familiar process.

'It happened a month ago. They've not been able to find me.' I bow my head in a display of sheer regret. If I hadn't run away, if I hadn't disappeared so comprehensively, things would have been different and they wouldn't be dead.

'May I?' Owen asks, reaching out for the letter.

'Go ahead.'

Perhaps he'll be able to pick up on something I missed, something that means it's not actually Mr and Mrs John and Ingrid Moore who are dead, rather that they are still happy and healthy, living in their neat semi-detached house in Birmingham and going about their everyday business. But then, I'd have ruined their lives one way or another.

Owen places the letter on the table. He reaches over and dabs my cheeks with a tissue.

'You're crying,' he says softly.

30

'A car crash,' I say incredulously. 'This letter tells me nothing. I have so many questions and . . . and . . .'

But there's only one thing I really want to know. Why were my parents in a car with *him*?

Owen points to the letterhead. 'There's a number you can call, look,' he says. 'Here in Delhi. I'm sure they'll be able to help with more information.'

The thought of phoning anyone after six months in hiding feels as unnatural as breathing underwater. 'Maybe,' I lie, knowing I won't be able to face it. Not yet, anyway.

'Who is Felix Darwin?' Owen asks, peering at the letter again.

It's like lightning striking directly overhead. For a moment, I can't speak; can't answer. I've not heard that name spoken out loud in so long. My headache kicks up a gear, and I hate that it actually sounds softer than I'd remembered; almost attractive, as if everyone with a name like that must be decent.

It means lucky, he once told me.

'Just someone I used to know.'

I fight the sick as it rises up my throat. I promised myself I would never have to talk about him again, never have to think about him or say his name as long as I lived. Never have to explain to anyone what he put me through, what he drove me to.

'It says here that he was driving,' Owen says, frowning. 'But it doesn't say if he survived or not.'

*

31

Raksha fusses around me like a clucky old hen, her sari slipping off her shoulder until she roughly pulls it round her wide waist, tucking it in. She settles me in a wicker chair on the back terrace of Bestluck with a jug of water and limes, saying things I don't understand.

Javesh comes hurtling outside, exclaiming that he has bought the vegetables on my behalf.

'I save the day, Raksha,' he sings out. 'Mees Eezee not well, so I buy the food and save everyone from starving. Thees is surely warranting a pay rise!'

Javesh's bare feet scuff about on the dusty coral-coloured tiles until Raksha reaches out to clip him around the head. She narrowly misses as he darts away with a laugh.

'Go and put the vegetables in the kitchen before they rot, stupid boy,' she says in a thick Indian accent. With many guests from the UK and America, her English is good.

Javesh dashes off obediently.

'I'm so sorry to cause all this trouble,' I say.

I sip the water and the limes open up my constricted throat, soothing my head. I still feel numb, especially now the news has been baked in by the relentless sun. Even the little quadrangle at the back of the hotel is heavy with hot, wet air. It's usually the place to go for a corner of shade, somewhere to escape with a fan and a cold drink when I've finished my work, but today it feels oppressive and dangerous.

'Mr Brandrick told me your sad news,' Raksha says, squatting in front of me. Her head rocks from side to side.

'You must go home at once, Isabel,' she continues. 'You must go and pay your last respects to your parents.'

Owen is sitting in the chair beside me, a calm and unobtrusive presence. 'Is there someone you can contact for help?' he asks. 'Do you have family or friends in Delhi to arrange flights for you?'

They don't understand. They have no idea that, however much I want to go home, however much the desire to find out what happened to Mum and Dad rages inside me, I simply can't.

'I don't know,' is all I manage while staring at a terracotta urn containing a dried-up shrub.

My vagueness encourages Owen to press on. I know he's only trying to help, but he doesn't know the first thing about my life, has no idea of what going home means. And I can't possibly tell him.

'Why don't you call the British High Commission? Raksha will let you use the phone, or you can borrow my mobile. They'll be able to offer assistance and give you more information about . . .'

Owen's voice fades to the buzz of a mosquito, the incessant rush of a waterfall, or the drone of an annoying moped speeding the streets. Raksha continues to fuss around me, bringing me the dirty telephone handset from Bestluck's reception desk, along with a couple of dubious-looking pills that she says will help.

I don't take either.

'Or, if you tell me where you'll be flying to, I could possibly sort arrangements,' Owen finishes. 'Isabel?'

I look across at him. I'd have thought him handsome once – the way his eyes slant slightly upwards, topping off high cheekbones and a strong jaw. If I hadn't just learned that my parents had been killed, if I wasn't still so nervous after everything that's happened, I'd like to get to know him. Perhaps talk over coffee or share a meal. I've not had company for a long time – not even a quick chat with a half-familiar face at the market. I simply haven't allowed it. It's not been part of my agenda.

I shrug, making a pained face, which prompts Owen to slide the letter from my fingers and take his phone from his pocket. He goes down the wooden steps into the centre of the shady quadrangle.

'Don't you worry. Mr Brandrick a good man. He will help you,' Raksha says, fanning me with a newspaper. She glances over at him, then back to me.

'Thank you,' I say meekly.

In the background, I am aware of Owen's calm voice.

'Will you put me through to someone who can help, then . . . yes, of course . . . no, she can't come to the phone . . . the reference number on the letter is DH14-3784 . . . I'll hold, thanks.'

I think of my parents – the gleam of my mother's always-neat hair, the ever-increasing hunch of my father's once-square shoulders as his sixties gave way to seventy. I wasn't there to see his special birthday celebration in June. I wonder if he had a party, but quickly decide no, of course he didn't. His only daughter had gone missing a month earlier. I should think he had the most wretched birthday ever. They had no idea where I was, and if they informed the police, they've not found me.

'Are you certain?' Owen says loudly. He's coming back up the wooden veranda steps, looking at me expectantly. 'That's official, is it?' He nods, scuffing his feet, and says goodbye.

He puts his phone back in his pocket and comes over to me. 'There's a glimmer of good news,' he says, squatting down beside me. 'The driver of the car survived.'

My heart shrinks within my chest, and my breathing slows. I nod resignedly, realising that he'd never die, never let go. The car could have exploded into a fireball or plunged a thousand feet into the ocean, and he'd still survive. Still be waiting for me.

'Listen,' says Owen. 'You're obviously in no fit state to make plans. I'm flying to Birmingham tomorrow and I'd be happy to escort you to the airport to catch whichever flight you need.'

Slowly, I look up at him. He thinks I'm going back. He doesn't understand. No one does, and no one ever will.

'Birmingham?' I say with a tinge of irony.

'It's where I live,' Owen says. 'Which airport do you need? I can book a flight for you.'

I don't speak, don't tell him that it was once my home city too, and I certainly don't tell him about *that* place, the place from which I fled.

Instead, I watch as Owen's mouth moves, trying to help me. I don't hear the words coming out; don't feel the warmth of his hand as he gently touches my arm. Rather, in the distance somewhere, I hear music – the soft twang of discordant strings accompanied by a steady beat. The beat of my heart, perhaps, as it tries to cling to something familiar.

Birmingham, I want to tell Owen. Where I met Felix, where everything turned bad.

I angle my head away from him. I feel the heave of my stomach as it tries to rid me of the toxic memories. How do I explain to him that the moment I set foot on UK soil, the second I go back, my life will be over for good?

'There's more news about the driver,' I hear Owen say solemnly. 'Isabel, listen to me.' He takes hold of my wrists firmly, making me flinch. 'The woman from the High Commission told me that Felix Darwin is still in hospital. I'm so sorry, but he is paralysed from the waist down. She said he's in a coma and on life support.'

Slowly, my head inches back round to Owen. This stranger from the market, this man who until now I'd only glimpsed around the hotel, has just given me life-changing news.

He holds out a glass of water. My mouth is so dry.

'I'm sorry, what did you say?' My heart is beating a thousand times a minute, hardly daring to hope.

'I hate to have to tell you,' he says. 'But apparently he was very badly injured.'

I want to laugh. He's trying to break it to me gently, when really he needn't. Amid all the wretchedness, this development is worthy of screaming from the rooftop.

I look him in the eye. 'He's paralysed and in a coma?'

Owen nods back solemnly. 'That's what they said, yes.'

The sounds of the sitars and the mosquitoes and the speeding mopeds grow louder as Delhi closes in around me. I gulp down the water, wondering if I'll ever get used to not looking over my shoulder.

Surely, I think, he can't hurt me now?

4

I arrive home to an empty house, feeling the first flicker of unease as I light the living-room gas fire. I go round closing the curtains.

It's not in my heart exactly, more a throbbing around it; a nagging feeling that sweeps from my core and out to my fingertips. At first I think it's because I'm cold, exhausted, but then I realise it's more than that.

In the kitchen, I fill the kettle, wondering what time Stella will be home. I already know that Adam won't be back until ten at least, and Grace is—

'Shit!' I say, dropping the kettle lid into the sink.

I grab the calendar off the wall and stare at it, not even certain of today's date. My eyes quickly scan the scribbled happenings of my family's life, searching for something that will make the feeling go away.

'Oh bloody hell, *Grace*,' I say when I see it written in my own handwriting. I was meant to fetch her, but I completely forgot. I pull my phone from my bag to see if she's called, but there's nothing on the screen. I dial her number, but it connects straight to her message service. 'God, I'm so sorry, I'm so sorry,' I mumble, cursing my overloaded brain. If I hadn't gone to the doctor's, I'd have remembered to fetch her.

I put my coat back on, grabbing my bag and keys. I'm over an hour late picking her up. She's been away with her netball team, taking part in a two-day tournament in Brighton.

'She's old enough to look after herself,' I tell myself on the journey to the sports centre where the coach was dropping them off. 'She'll be absolutely fine.'

I try to calm myself, but the throbbing in my chest won't go away.

'Bloody netball,' I curse through a laugh, in case it helps the tension. It doesn't.

I growl from frustration when the traffic halts yet again at a set of lights. I'm not used to feeling like this, as though there's an ever-lowering ceiling pressing down on me.

It was after I saw Alexandra's body lying at the scene back in February, the same once-alive body that had asked me – no, *begged* me – for help, that this all began. I tried to forget it, forced myself to move on. God knows, I've seen enough bodies in my time, but this has never happened before, these feelings of guilt. They've been brewing ever since.

Stuck in a stationary queue, I call Grace's number again. I leave another message, but suspect her phone's battery is probably dead. Several hours Facebooking and listening to music on the long coach journey would have killed it in no time.

I pull into the car park of the sports centre. It's dark and there's nothing but the bleak façade of the corrugated metal building where the team trains three times a week, and the sea of empty tarmac spread around it. At one end of the building a single light glows orange, highlighting the drizzle that's just started. The area is completely deserted – no coach or crowd of girls in games kits, no members of staff, no other parents chatting while their daughters gather their bags from the coach's hold.

I flick the wiper switch to clear the windscreen in case I'm mistaken, but there's still no one there. I'm now an hour and a half late, and I can already hear Grace telling me off. We've always had a rule that she should wait for her lift, never leave the arranged spot.

I get out of the car and run over to the sports centre, pulling up my collar against the rain.

'Grace?' I call out, in case she's sheltering somewhere. My voice sounds weak, swallowed up by the emptiness of the place. 'Are you here?'

But the small sheltered area in front of the glass entrance is dark and empty. I rattle the doors in case she's inside, although I can see clearly the whole centre has been locked up for the night. There are no lights on at all.

I turn back towards the empty car park and my heart begins to kick up another gear. I feel it in my throat, along with an uncomfortable pressure in my head. Quickly, I walk back towards my car, scanning the perimeter of the property, shielding my eyes from the rain. It's surrounded on three sides by tall trees and a scrubby thicket of undergrowth. I pray she didn't take a shortcut through to the main road.

'Grace!' I call out again.

If she'd decided to walk home in disgust at having been forgotten, she'd probably have taken the route I just drove. Although if her phone was dead then she wouldn't be able to call me or have a map and—

'Oh stop it!' I say to myself, getting back in the car. 'She'll have got a lift with someone else, or taken the bus. She's not stupid.' I can't allow my thoughts to veer off the way they've been going recently, not when it comes to my family.

I press my phone to my ear. 'Hi,' I say, when the woman answers. 'It's Grace's mum calling. I was wondering if you saw her when you picked up Charlotte from the sports centre earlier?' I listen keenly, but she apologises, telling me that Charlotte went home with Alice.

I call Alice's mum, but she doesn't remember seeing Grace, and certainly didn't give her a lift. Alice doesn't know either. I phone three other contacts and get the same answer each time. Grace was on the coach back to Birmingham but no one remembers what happened to her after that.

I call Adam, even though I know he's in meetings. Predictably, there's no reply.

'Now what?' I say, thumping the steering wheel. I should probably just drive home. Grace will no doubt be back by now, poking about in the fridge for something to eat.

Instead, I reach into the glove compartment for my Maglite and get out of the car. I swear I just saw something move in the trees.

It's probably just an animal, I tell myself, aiming the torch across the car park, or a stray dog. As I walk closer to the trees, away from the glow of the single orange light, it feels as though I'm being swallowed up by the darkness.

'Hello?' I call out. 'Who's there?'

I stop several yards from the perimeter of the wooded area. I'm sure I heard a noise, a twig being snapped, someone moving. I flash the torch through the trees, squinting to get a glimpse.

It's nothing except my overwrought imagination, I think, annoyed with the way my heart is tripping over itself. But the detective inside me can't let go. I'm sure something caught my eye.

'If there's anyone there,' I call out, 'I'm a police officer and this is private property. Make yourself known.'

Slowly, I drag the thin beam of light across the thicket, striking the mossy trunks of larger trees as well as the younger saplings pushing up in between. All my torch picks out are an assortment of crushed cans, crisp packets and sweet wrappers, plus a dustbin sack of fly-tipped rubbish. I hate it that I actually feel scared, even though the chances of anyone being in there are remote.

It's as I'm about to head back to the car that I see it lying on the scrubby ground. A glove. Unmistakable.

For a few seconds, all I can do is leave the torch light shining on it, hoping it will magically disappear as if it was never there. But the purple and yellow stripes, the wonky finger holes and the loose knit of the cuff are enough to remind me of the agonising weeks it took Stella to knit the fingerless gloves as a present for her big sister.

I reach down and pick it up. It's slightly damp, having been sheltered from the worst of the rain by the canopy of trees. Instinct screams at me that I shouldn't even be touching it, that I should be wearing my own glove, a latex one, photographing where the item lay, bagging it and handing it over to forensics.

Oh God, Grace!

'Get a grip, woman,' I say immediately, trying to convince myself that it means absolutely nothing, apart from a moment's carelessness on Grace's part.

5

We've been in the air for two hours. Owen is peering through the small porthole with a plastic tumbler of gin and tonic twirling between his fingers. He exudes an air of calm, as if he's never had a problem in his life.

Me, I'm clutching my tray table with both hands, not because I'm a fearful flyer, but because in this case I'm a fearful arriver. Owen senses that I'm reluctant to talk and has largely left me alone, apart from asking a few simple things that would have seemed strange not to find out.

'Drink up. It'll help you relax,' he says, stretching back in his seat. He glances at my tumbler, then at me.

I shrug, give a little smile, wanting to tell him that I could down an entire bottle of gin and still not relax. But to appease him, I lift the glass to my lips and sip.

'Owen . . .'

'If it's another gushing thank you, you don't need to say it.' He laughs, shaking his head gently.

'Sorry,' I say. 'But I couldn't have done this without

you. There was no one else in India I could have asked for help.'

Then it strikes me. There isn't anyone else *anywhere*.

'It's a shame we didn't meet under better circumstances,' Owen says quietly.

I almost expect him to reach out, rest his hand on top of mine, but he doesn't, and the moment passes. The passenger to my left struggles up from his seat and walks off down the cabin. I take the opportunity to stretch out.

'Agreed,' I say, pensively. 'Anyway, I really do appreciate your help, so thank you. And I promise that's the last time I'll say it.'

Owen pours the remainder of gin from the little bottle into his glass. 'I somehow feel responsible. It was me who delivered the bad news, after all.'

'It was hardly your fault,' I say, gripping the armrest as a jolt of turbulence makes the plane shudder. 'How long will your business partner be staying on in India?'

While we were waiting at the check-in queue before the flight, Owen outlined the reason for his trip to Delhi, told me he was there for work.

'Business associate rather than partner,' Owen corrects. 'We're both freelance architects, but work independently. I've known Paul since my university days.' He pauses and gives me one of those broad infectious smiles, somehow making me feel better. 'Back then, we were the bad boys, if you can believe that. Heaven only knows how we ever qualified.'

It is indeed hard to believe. When I look at Owen, and

then when I think of Felix, they seem like opposite poles of a planet, the universe. Even if Owen told me he'd just killed someone in the aircraft toilet, he would still not be bad by comparison.

'My university days seem a lifetime ago,' I say, far more pensively than I intended.

Of course, it sets Owen off on a new line of questioning. He wants to know everything about me.

'What did you study?' he asks, skilfully swirling the tumbler around on the tray table, the ice cubes clinking.

'Not hotel work, in case you were wondering.' I laugh evasively.

I don't want to talk about myself. It reminds me too much of *him*, too much of who I became – a long way from the hopeful young woman who set off to university to forge a promising career. Shedding my skin is what I went to India to do, but this necessary trip back to England makes me feel as if I'm putting it back on. Stepping back into the unknown.

'If you're an architect, how come you were in India on business?' I say, changing the subject.

'Paul recently took on a client, one of those *mega-*clients,' he says with a devious glint in his eye. 'The type of brief that you wait most of your career for. The truth is, it's more than he can handle alone, so he asked me to partner up. The job is to build our super-rich Russian client a country residence in the style of the old Raj slap bang in the middle of Shropshire. Hence the trip to India.'

I think about this. I think about how unlikely the world

is. I think about all the rich people in it, and the crazy things they do with their money. I think about Owen and his smile, and I think about him coming to India to study old buildings from the colonial days, taking photographs, sketching rough ideas, him and Paul chatting about their ideas on the veranda of Hotel Bestluck late into the humid night.

And then, of course, *he's* on my mind again, leaving a greasy, unpleasant trail as he passes through.

'People certainly want odd things in life,' I remark, and Owen laughs.

I knock back my gin and tonic, unbuckle my seatbelt and excuse myself before my neighbour returns to his seat.

The toilet smells faintly of urine, and after I've washed my hands, I stare into the mirror. I grab the wall handle as the plane suddenly lurches, as if we've dropped a hundred feet. A few more bumps and it stabilises. I breathe again, noticing how pale my face is. There are tiny rosy crests of worry on my cheekbones, sitting beneath the angled frown of my sad eyes. My once-vibrant red hair hangs lank, and my neck looks scrawny. I don't look well.

I make my way back to my seat.

'Time for some fine dining,' Owen says, holding up the tray of food that's arrived in my absence so I can settle down again.

We each peel back the foil, exposing various lumps of food covered with a slick of grey sauce, and burst out laughing. But it doesn't feel right; it hurts in my heart.

'There's nothing else for it,' Owen says, pressing the call button. 'More gin, wine, whatever it takes.'

And it's not very long before I'm fast asleep.

Birmingham Airport is a far cry from the heat and colours of Chandni Chowk. Its grey, clinical interior suits me well as I try to blend into my surroundings, become an unnoticeable shadow. I've already told Owen several times that he doesn't need to wait with me, that if he wants to go off ahead, beat the long queues at passport control, then he should do so. I feel exhausted from the bad news and the long journey.

'Of course I'm not going to leave you,' he says with his arm outstretched behind him, pulling along his flight bag.

A surge of passengers overtake us, eddying around us as if we're rocks in a stream.

'Thanks,' I say gratefully, aware of just how many times I've said that in the last twenty-four hours. 'But you'll have to leave me soon anyway.' I glance sideways at him, fumbling in my leather bag for my passport.

'At least let me make sure you get a taxi safely.'

I nod in agreement and mumble another thank you. We shuffle through passport control, me feeling terrified, half expecting armed immigration officers to flank me and lead me away, their fists shoved under my armpits, my feet skimming the floor as I'm intercepted, taken away and locked up again.

But a few minutes later I'm light-headed from relief in

baggage reclaim, heading towards carousel four, hoping the conveyor belt will soon start moving.

'You've travelled light,' Owen comments, lifting my backpack from within the jumble of suitcases.

'I prefer it that way,' I say, remembering my hurried escape from England. I didn't even check in a bag on the way to Delhi. All I had was my handbag and the clothes I was wearing. I just needed to get away.

We proceed through customs and out into the public area, the ramps each way lined with faces hopeful that we are their missed loved ones. I am not anyone's loved one, I think, not any more. Then I tense up because he's there in my mind again, and I can't help a furtive glance at all the people waiting, just in case.

'So,' Owen says with a note of finality, 'the taxis are this way.'

I nod and follow him.

'Where are you heading?'

Then it hits me. It's not as if I haven't thought about this since deciding to come back and sort out my parents' affairs, I just hadn't anticipated the moment actually arriving.

I say the first thing that comes to mind: 'Home.'

Owen holds open the cab door for me. 'You take this one then,' he says. 'I'll get the next.'

'No, really, after you,' I say. My voice sounds thin and unconvincing. I don't know what to tell the driver.

Owen frowns, looking at the queue behind us. He gently takes my arm and leads me aside, gesturing to the old couple waiting behind that they should take this taxi.

'You do have somewhere to go, don't you?'

'Of course.'

The truth is, I could go to my parents' house, it's just that I don't want to. The memories would be too painful and, even though he's in a coma, he knows where Mum and Dad lived. What if he suddenly wakes up?

'To be honest, I'm not entirely sure where my keys are,' I say unconvincingly. 'I mean, don't worry, I can get in, it's just I'll have to . . . well, you know.'

I'm making it worse. I just wish he'd leave, let me figure out what I'm going to do.

Owen sighs and folds his arms. His hold-all is slung across one shoulder and his flight bag is propped between his feet. He seems authoritative, as if he wants to be in control, but is also sensing I'm going to put up a fight. I like him, but he's not a part of my life. He needs to go now.

'You mean you'll have to break in?' Owen frowns. 'Look, it's none of my business, but having come this far with you I somehow feel responsible. How about if I drop you at a hotel? It's late,' he says, glancing at his watch. 'Nearly midnight. You'll be able to get a good night's sleep.'

Even as he's talking I'm shaking my head. However tempting his suggestion seems, I can't possibly go to a hotel. I wouldn't even have enough money to pay for one night. I feel the warm wash of tears in my eyes. I have been so stupid. I should never have come back.

'No, it's fine. You've done enough. Thank you, Owen.' I can't help the laugh. 'And I really promise that's the last time I'll say it.'

I hold out my hand to say goodbye. We both stare at it, watching the increasing tremor, until he puts his hands over it in an attempt to immobilise it. The shakes just transfer up his arms. He sighs, scuffs his feet, and glances around awkwardly.

'No. I will not leave you like this. I'm not asking why, Isabel, but for some reason I think you are vulnerable.'

We're both silent for a moment amid the airport noise. What I really want to do is drop to my knees, cover my face with my hands, sob, and beg him to take me somewhere warm, somewhere safe, somewhere away from all the mess I've got myself into.

'I can't afford a hotel,' I tell him truthfully. 'So cat burglar it is, I'm afraid.' I grin and pick up my backpack, turning back to the taxi rank. 'Bye,' I add, being careful not to thank him for the thousandth time.

'I have a room,' he says suddenly, causing me to stop with one foot in the taxi. 'I don't mean like that, of course,' he continues, noticing my blush. 'And it's actually more than a room. It's an entire flat, in the basement of my house.'

The people in the queue behind us groan as I hesitate again.

I turn back to Owen hopefully.

He shrugs. 'It's empty at the moment. My last tenant left just before I went to India and I didn't have time to find another. It's going to be a while before the agent can get someone else in. It's yours for tonight at least if you want it.'

'That's kind, but—'

'Then accept. You'll have your own front door with your own key. It's clean, it's warm, and it gets you out of a tight spot right now.'

'Why are you doing this?' My eyes narrow suspiciously, and I hear how ungrateful I sound. Even though something inside me is saying take the flat, something louder screams not to. Mistrust is my middle name.

'Because you've had a terrible twenty-four hours. And it's good to help people.' He smiles. 'And besides, I like you.'

My blush blooms fully then. I give a little nod, staring at the ground.

Owen ushers me into the taxi and gets in after me. As we drive off, I can't help one last glance round to check *he's* not there, climbing into the cab behind.

The orange soda-coloured spray of streetlights along the deserted A45 catches in my eyes, making me feel dizzy, nauseous.

I am in a taxi with a man I met yesterday. I am going to spend the night at his house.

My fingers curl around the strap of my handbag, and my nails dig into my palms at the madness of my situation. How can a week that started with such feelings of hope, with the first seeds of what I thought could be happiness, have transformed into what can only be described as a living nightmare a few days later?

'Are you OK?' Owen asks. He reaches across and taps my knuckles. When I look down, they are white. My shoulders are drawn up to my ears. 'Everything's going to be OK,' he says reassuringly.

I realise I owe him some kind of explanation. It's not fair to take advantage of his hospitality and kindness without him knowing anything about me.

Ironically, at that moment we turn on to a road I know well – a route I used to take to work. Although saturated by darkness, the familiar scene sparks a memory. I clutch my handbag strap even tighter, although in my head it's the steering wheel I am gripping.

It was the morning after our first date that I went into work feeling as if the sun was shining from behind my face. Everyone noticed. Jan commented, saying it must be love already. I was coy about it, didn't tell them what he'd done. I wanted it to be my little secret – his and mine for ever – and I even went back at lunchtime to take photographs.

Every tree along the central reservation of Highgate Middleway had a pink ribbon tied around the trunk. To this day, I don't know how he figured out when I'd be at that exact spot, sitting in traffic, drumming my fingers on the steering wheel, looking at my watch, praying I wouldn't be late. But the text came in at exactly the right time.

Pink ribbons for you, my love.

I suppose he thought it was necessary, given what had

happened the night before at the end of our date. It was such a romantic way of making it up to me.

'It was a bad relationship,' I blurt out to Owen, but it doesn't come out right. 'Really bad,' I add, as if that explains everything.

'The man in hospital?' he replies instinctively.

I nod, biting my lip, staring out of the window.

'I'm sorry to hear that,' he says.

Tears pool in my eyes, although I don't actually cry.

Fifteen minutes later, we pull up outside a tall terraced house with stone steps leading up to the front door. Owen pays the driver while I get out of the car, pack slung on my shoulder. I glance up and down the street, having no idea where we are. Harborne, Selly Oak, Moseley . . . I wasn't paying attention when he told the driver where to go.

'One forty-three Claremont Road, Harborne, just so you know,' Owen tells me, as if he's read my mind and senses my anxiety. 'Come on, let's get inside. It's cold.'

There are streetlights around, but it still feels shadowy – the kind of place where someone could easily lurk unnoticed, watching, waiting for the right moment. The sort of place *he* would like.

I follow Owen up the steps, reminding myself that Felix is in hospital, paralysed and in a coma. It makes me feel a tiny bit better.

'It's nice,' I say, admiring the house.

'I've lived here ten years now,' Owen says, struggling with the lock for a moment.

From the top of the stone steps I can see a semi-subterranean level with another set of steps leading down to a second front door. That must be the flat, I think, so why is he taking me up here?

'I'm sorry,' I say, suddenly fearful, 'but I thought you said I would be staying in a separate flat?' The undertones of anger are unmistakable.

Owen opens the front door and goes inside quickly. An alarm system beeps loudly, and a few seconds later it silences.

'Relax,' he says, coming out again and pointing to the basement. 'That's where you'll be, but I had to turn off the alarm first. It was set for the whole building while I was away.' He grins warmly, leading me down to the lower level.

The basement flat door opens more easily and we go inside. 'It's one bedroom and the kitchen is tiny, I'm afraid, but I think you'll find everything in order.' He flicks on the lights as we go round.

'I'm sorry to sound so ungrateful. This is lovely. Perfect,' I tell him, looking around.

I drop my backpack on to the sofa, feeling slightly ashamed. I follow him into the bedroom, where he pokes around in a small cupboard.

'Look, here are some sheets, pillowcases and stuff.' He pulls them out and leaves them on the bed.

'That's great,' I say. Then I manage a little laugh. 'And thank you. *Again*.'

Owen removes a small pad and pen from his inside

jacket pocket. 'Here's my number if you need anything. Don't hesitate to call. It's a bit chilly, so I'll turn up the heating on the way out.'

He raises a hand in a friendly half salute, pausing briefly in the hallway to adjust the thermostat before leaving. The door clicks locked behind him. I didn't bother telling him I don't own a phone.

For a moment, I stand frozen, lost and alone in the middle of the small sitting room, but I force myself to move because there is work to be done.

First I begin by checking the front window that faces the street slightly below ground level. It is modern and double-glazed and, after I've made certain it's locked, I remove the key and go to the tiny kitchen just off the living room. The whole place smells slightly damp. I make sure the kitchen window is locked, too, and also remove the key. I do the same in the bedroom and check the front door three times, pocketing all the keys. I am grateful the tiny bathroom doesn't have a window.

'No one can get in,' I tell myself rationally. I learned in the group sessions that if you say things out loud, if you voice your thoughts confidently, realistically, you're more likely to believe them.

Don't let the anxiety own you, they said. I never told them that mine had me by the throat.

After I've made up the bed, I slip out of my clothes and put on a long white T-shirt. I clean my face and brush my teeth and, shivering, get into bed. The sheets are crisp and cool, and smell musty from the cupboard. The ceiling light is off, but there's a faint orange glow filtering through from the streetlights above the living-room window. I lie on my back and close my eyes, knowing it'll be a while before I sleep.

Sleep must have come eventually, though, because suddenly I sit bolt upright.

I heard a noise.

I listen, hardly daring to breathe. I grab my watch. It's two-fourteen a.m.

Then the noise again – a rattling, clicking sound, coming from the narrow hallway. Someone is at the front door.

A little whimper escapes my throat as I get out of bed and shove on my jeans. In the kitchen, I open the only drawer. There are two sharp knives and I remove the bigger one. Back in the hallway, I stare through the peep hole in the front door, just in time to see a man's figure retreating up the steps.

6

I knew she was the one for me from the moment I saw her – a siren of vibrant hair and brilliant blue eyes scream-ing out to me. Such a rarity. My very own four-leaf clover.

I orchestrated a chance encounter in the packet food aisle of a supermarket to bring us together. She thought it was chance, anyway. I'd actually been watching her on and off for the previous two months, and that day I'd been tracking her between the chemist, several clothes boutiques, and the bank. And once I'd caught her interest, as I was mulling over the pros and cons of an instant noodle meal, she wasted no time chastising me. I liked that about her, that she was forthright and opinionated.

'You do realise that's full of crap, right?' she said, grinning to make sure I knew she was being pleasant rather than pious.

I noticed how she moved her trolley to the side so it wasn't wedged between us. I'd grabbed a basket when I'd walked into the supermarket, stalking her at a safe distance up and down the aisles. Then she'd caught me red-handed with the plastic pot of food, which just happened to be next to the more wholesome foods she was studying.

I've since gone over this scene many times in my mind, and the only thing I regret is laughing so loudly, so gawkily, before I'd even said a word. She looked puzzled, probably thinking I was an idiot. I remember the look on her face so well, how her soft cheeks pinked up like a baby's, her lips parting, until I finally shut up. I kick myself often when I think about it. I shouldn't have been so zealous.

'I had no idea,' I said. I turned the plastic pot round, pretended to read the ingredients list. I immediately frowned, looked straight at her and announced dramatically, 'Guilty as charged.'

Then I took my eyes off her and looked in her trolley. Predictably, I saw a load of organic fruit and vegetables alongside a few cuts of lean meat and fish.

'What would you recommend for a single chap wanting a quick meal?' I asked. It was important she knew I was available.

She made a show of thinking and pondering my question, accompanied by a long drawn-out *hmmm*. Then she acted coyly, half turning away from me, tipping back her head to expose the full length of her pretty neck, flashing a wide, toothy smile. She tucked back her wayward red hair and said, 'I think I'd go to a restaurant.' Then she laughed.

And that was that. Easy.

I agreed with her that eating out was by the far the

most preferable option for a single man, but only on the condition that she came with me, to make it even more pleasurable.

Of course, she accepted my invitation, but with her own condition: that we went to a little place she knew where they served organic, locally sourced food.

Quite frankly, I wouldn't have cared if we'd gone to a motorway service station, or if our dinner had come directly from the moon. I simply wanted to get to know her better. She was beautiful. More than beautiful. Exquisite and rare, exactly the kind of woman I'd been looking for my entire life.

And we'd met in a supermarket.

So she thought.

She arrived on time. I'd got there early, of course, making sure we were given the best table. Right from the start I wanted her to know how much I cared, how much she meant to me. I sat sipping a badly made Bloody Mary, relieved when the door to the little bistro swung inwards and she came in, fixing her eyes on me almost immediately.

'Hi,' she said, smiling beautifully. 'Look, it's crazy,' she continued in an equally crazy voice, 'but I don't even know your name.'

She approached me like a gusty breeze, smelling of sandalwood and ginger, as well as being tainted by the scent of the sweet summer air.

'I'm Isabel. Isabel Moore.'

She held out her hand and I took it, rising from my chair. I didn't bother telling her I already knew her name, and a thousand other things besides. I'd done my homework.

'You realise that if you hadn't shown up, I'd have had to spend the rest of my life hunting you down.'

For a second there was a flash of something in her eyes, but then she relaxed and laughed at my joke.

Five minutes later and we were chatting as if we were old friends. We ordered a bottle of wine – I insisted on the most expensive on the menu – and the funny little eclectic bistro she'd chosen gradually filled up with diners.

'In case you were going to ask if I come here often,' she said with a smile and in a slightly silly voice, 'the answer is yes. I know the owner and we have our book group meetings here. Mum loves the afternoon teas they do, and anything from the fish menu is unbearably good.' She pointed to the appropriate page.

She was completely normal. Well balanced. Perfect. A ten out of ten.

'Locally sourced from a Birmingham canal, perhaps?' I chipped back with a wry smile through a long sip of wine.

'Touché,' she said good-naturedly, and we were off, without a moment's silence for the rest of the evening.

'I think that's so exciting,' she said later, while plucking a huge green-lipped mussel from its shell. 'Did you always want to be a pilot?'

'Honestly, no. I learned to fly in my late twenties and went on to get my commercial licence soon after. Nowadays I take private hire jobs, picking and choosing when I work.'

'That's so glamorous. It makes my job seem rather dull.'

Her mouth was full as she said this. I remember because she had to dab her chin with a napkin. She was clearly in awe of me, and I admit, this made me love her all the more. It was just the way things should be. I wanted her to be oh-so-proud of her future husband.

'I'm not at all artistic,' I said truthfully in response to her telling me about her job. 'But that doesn't mean to say I can't enjoy collecting beautiful paintings.' I thought she'd like that, and I was right. I made a mental note to go out and buy some.

'Oh my goodness, I would love to have enough money to invest in some decent artwork. The best I ever come across is the work of my A Level students. Some of it is quite stunning. Artists of the future,' she told me, tapping the side of her little freckly nose, as if she was tipping me off. Our main courses arrived – she'd gone for the sea bass and I had ordered the whole lobster. It was the most expensive dish, of course, and when Isabel told me that she'd never actually tried it before, I made her take some from my fork.

'Close your eyes,' I told her, easing the chunk of fleshy white meat between her lips.

She gave a little moan, chewed, and then her face

virtually melted in delight. I gave her some more because, actually, it wasn't the best lobster I'd ever had.

Then we had coffee, but not dessert, and finally I ordered two of their best Cognacs.

After I'd paid the bill, we left the restaurant and went for a walk. It wasn't too chilly given the time of year, but when I offered my jacket to drape around her shoulders, she accepted gratefully.

'It's lovely,' she said, fingering the expensive fabric.

'I like nice things,' I told her, giving her a glance up and down, to which she responded by blushing.

Within the frame of her fiery red hair – it was as if her DNA had somehow invented an entirely new colour just for me – her flushed cheeks completed the look of innocence, of desire, of needing to be taken care of. My arm slipped lightly around her waist, and I was relieved that she didn't protest.

As we walked, Isabel told me that she was an only child, that she'd always loved to paint, and that no one knew where her artistic talents had come from because her parents weren't creative at all. Her background was average and middle-class, pleasant and contented, and she had undemanding expectations of life. I already knew she was perfect, so she didn't need to explain. She was mine for the taking.

'Would you like me to drive you home?' I asked, as she handed back my jacket. She'd confessed to missing the last bus. Then, when I told her that I'd never been on a bus in my entire life, she'd bent double from laughter, the little nubs of her spine standing out beneath her thin top as she leaned forward. I was overcome with an urge to run my finger down them, but didn't.

'A lift would be wonderful, thank you.'

I gave her back my jacket, and she drew it close around her, uncomplaining about my even tighter grip around her waist as we set off for my car.

'But only if you let me take you around the city on a bus one day,' she said. 'You'll be surprised at what you see.'

'The promise of a second date already,' I said, knowing in reality I would never go on a bus. Still, it confirmed that she wanted to see me again.

We took a short cut back to my car where I'd left it parallel-parked outside a row of shops. Isabel let out a little whinny of what I assumed was delight when she saw it – a top-of-the-range Mercedes – and opened the passenger door with appreciation in her eyes.

'A little gift to myself last month,' I told her, watching as she got in.

But she suddenly stopped, pulling out of the car again with a shocked expression.

'Felix,' she said, 'there's mud all over the seats.'

She pointed inside and, when I looked, sure enough there was a large pile of wet greeny-black muck dumped on the leather upholstery.

'Oh Christ,' I said, pushing my fingers through my hair.

I frowned, glancing up and down the street as if that would provide answers – although what had happened was patently clear. Someone had dumped mud in my car. It looked like sludge from the bottom of a river.

'Who would do such a horrid thing?' Isabel said in a sweet but worried voice. 'It doesn't look as if anyone broke in.'

And she was right. I examined both doors of my coupé and nowhere could I see scratches or evidence of the locks being tampered with. Then we both spun round towards the sound of a voice coming from a narrow alley nearby.

'That's because I had a key,' the woman said, striding towards us.

She wobbled in ridiculously high heels, her black Mac billowing as she approached. She'd not bothered with make-up, but she didn't need to. Her face was striking enough, just like her sister's, but it was also bright red and sweating, matching the colour of her boyish cropped hair. She was filled with a rage so powerful I could almost taste it.

'Who's that?' Isabel whispered. She clung to my sleeve nervously as the enraged woman came right up to us, dangling the car key like bait. I knew if I grabbed it, she'd be quicker.

'Who the hell are you and what have you done?' I demanded, pretending not to know her.

In truth, I'd had my eye on her sister for a while, and had been involved with her for a few months now. But I hadn't exactly got round to ending things before asking Isabel out. Finishing things off was so hard, and besides, I wasn't sure I wanted to yet. I was hedging my bets.

Generously, or perhaps recklessly, I'd also lent her a key to drive my new car. The stupid woman had obviously found out about my new infatuation and told her sister, who was now going for revenge by proxy. I felt disappointment welling inside me.

The irate sister glared at Isabel, then back at me. 'You're a disgusting creep and a liar,' she said, spitting at my feet. 'Alex is better off without you.'

She stalked around me in her stupid shoes, no doubt trying to intimidate me on her sister's behalf. 'You want to watch out, love,' she said to Isabel. 'Don't trust him with the shit on your shoe.'

'You're mad,' I told her, feeling Isabel recoil against me. I drew her tighter within my arms for safety. 'Completely and utterly *mad*. I have no idea who you are, but I'll be calling the police unless you hand over my car key and leave us alone immediately.'

Her chest was heaving from erratic gulps of air, and she was growing more hysterical by the second. 'I *hate* you. You've made Alex's life a fucking *misery*, you bastard.'

She drew back her arm and threw the key down a nearby drain with great force, kicking the side of my car several times. Then she hobbled off, looking back, flailing her arms and calling out obscenities.

I raised my mobile phone at her like a weapon, glaring menacingly, even though she knew that after everything, I wouldn't risk calling the police.

'It's OK, she's gone now.' I pulled Isabel towards me, and she rested her head against my chest. I felt her warm breath through my shirt. As if by magic, she slowed my racing heart.

'Who was that, and what was she so upset about?'

'I have absolutely no idea,' I said, glancing around to make sure she wasn't going to come back. 'But she bloody well wants locking up.'

I didn't say anything else. Instead, I put on a cheerful voice and told her I'd call us a taxi. 'It'll only be a few minutes,' I said, hanging up. Isabel seemed appeased.

A quarter of an hour later we pulled up outside her flat and she thanked me for a pleasant evening. Then we made a couple of jokes about its unusual ending while the taxi driver waited patiently.

'Watch out for something nice on your way to work tomorrow,' I told her as she stepped out of the cab.

Isabel grinned quizzically and walked up to her building's door, giving me a wave when she looked back.

'Carry on,' I told the driver, imagining Isabel lying in bed later, wondering what on earth I'd meant.

7

'I'm sorry you got so upset, love,' Adam says, and I wish
he hadn't because all I want now is to plunge into his
arms and get swallowed up. 'You seem so anxious.'

'I don't know what to think,' I say flatly, even though
I know he's right. I was probably imagining it all.

He's referring to last night when I came back from
the sports centre in a mess, having forgotten Grace. I'd
dashed inside calling out her name, barrelling into the
kitchen as if I was on an organised raid. I was greeted
by Stella demolishing a packet of Doritos, and Adam
leaning against the worktop chopping vegetables. I stared
at them for a few seconds before all my fears bubbled
to the surface. Then I broke down in a mess of guilt and
panic.

'Where *is* she?' I'd said, rather pathetically in hindsight.
She's my daughter. I bloody well should have known.

'Who?' Adam had asked, giving me a smile.

'And what are *you* doing home?' I'd continued, feeling
confused.

'My last couple of meetings were cancelled,' Adam explained. 'And where is *who*?'

'*Grace*, for heaven's sake. I was meant to fetch her and she wasn't there. I . . . I was running late.' And then another wave of guilt for not being able to afford a second-hand car for her – she passed her driving test over a year ago now.

'Yeah, Grace said you'd forgotten her,' Stella chimed in. 'She was really mad, but it's OK because the coach driver had to come back to his station this way and said he'd drop her off at the end of our road, although she said it took for *ever* because he had to stop somewhere else first.' Stella scrunched up the packet and dropped it in the pedal bin.

'You mean she's home?' I'd asked as casually as I could. They didn't need to know that my insides were on fire from guilt and . . . and something else. That same something else I'd tried, and failed, to describe to Dr Lewis.

'Yes, I'm home, no thanks to you,' came a voice from the doorway, as my eldest daughter sauntered into the kitchen.

She was cool with me for the rest of the evening, but normal again by morning when she needed a loan to go out shopping with friends. I didn't care. As long as she was safe, that was all that mattered.

'Tell you what, Stell,' Adam says now. 'Why don't you take all those books into the dining room? You'll get more peace in there and your mum and I need to talk shop.'

Stella glares at each of us in turn. Her eyes narrow into suspicious slits. The doubting look she gives us would have, only a short time ago, been a good-natured grin.

'We do?' I say when Stella has vacated the kitchen.

'We do.'

Adam, who's preparing the evening meal again, sounds serious. He washes his hands, wipes them on a tea towel, then rests his elbow on the mantelpiece above the old range fireplace. We decided to keep it when we revamped the kitchen of our old terraced house years ago. It could do with a bit of an update again, to be honest.

Adam looks uncomfortable. 'I'm worried about you, Ray.'

I burst out laughing. 'What are you on about? I thought it was something important.' I pray he doesn't notice the tremor in my voice. 'Why don't you finish peeling the potatoes? I'll do some carrots.'

Adam sighs. 'You're so on edge. I'm concerned for you.'

'Well you needn't be. I'm absolutely fine.' I hate lying to him, but there's no point in him worrying too. I don't want him to think I can't cope. My arms clamp across my body and my feet press together, as if I'm standing to some kind of guilty attention. 'The only thing wrong with me presently is not enough sleep.' I force a yawn to illustrate this.

'Bob had a word with me yesterday,' Adam continues. I see immediately where this is going. 'I understand that you're tired, love, and you need to do something about that, but it's leading to mistakes at work. Those reports for the CPS—'

'There is no way that was my fault. I was busy with—'

'Then you need to explain to Bob what happened.'

'Jesus Christ, it's like being at bloody school. How dare you go behind my back, Adam. That's really not on.'

Sometimes I wish we weren't in this job together. Sometimes I wish I was a lawyer or a teacher, or I worked in a supermarket. Anything not to feel as if I'm constantly in my husband's shadow.

Adam holds up his hands in defence. 'You know I'd never do that, Ray. Bob came to me, if you must know. He's worried too. He didn't think you seemed . . . yourself. And I agree.'

I go up to the mirror hanging on the wall by the door and make a point of staring into it, tapping the glass. It's childish, I know, but it's that or lose it again.

'I'm definitely still me,' I say with a silly grin, before swinging round and pulling a load of unrelated food from the fridge.

Adam comes up to me and hooks his hands around my hips from behind. I'm trying to get the carrots out of their bag but the plastic is impossible to puncture. I slam them down, knowing it's me I'm frustrated with, not the carrots. My shoulders relax as I allow myself to sink back into Adam's embrace. It feels good.

'I'll sort the reports first thing tomorrow. It's not too late.'

'Bob will appreciate that,' Adam replies.

He presses his face into my hair and nuzzles down to

my neck. It's what I need, and it takes half an ounce of the worry away. If only he knew that it wasn't just these couple of reports I had to catch up with.

'Bob also asked if I knew how the interviews went with the Gresham brothers today,' Adam continues, dealing another blow. 'I told him you'd let him know.'

For a second, I freeze, then I can't help slipping out of his grip. I turn to face him.

'You were discussing that with Bob too?' I shake my head, feeling quite upset now. 'Does he think I'm incapable?'

'Of course not, Ray. He just wanted to—'

'It was my interview, Adam, and I'll take care of it. Frankly, Bob should come and see me himself if he has issues with the way I work. It's not fair to put you in the middle.'

I want to draw a line under it, though the truth is, I didn't get a chance to do the interviews today.

'You're just so on edge these days, Ray,' he says in such a sympathetic way it brings tears to my eyes.

I hack up the carrots into irregular chunks, having finally got them out of the bag.

When the tears subside, I face him again, unsure what to say. If I tried to explain, would he understand? Probably, I think, even though it's me who sees her every night as she wakes me at three a.m., stroking the sweaty strands of hair plastered across my forehead with her skeletal fingers, her decaying skull-face leering close, the remaining flesh blue from hypoxia. He doesn't have to look into her eyes, see her sunken cheeks and her cracked and violet lips. Adam doesn't hear her voice as she whispers in my ear night after night, begging me to help her, to find her killer, to let her be a mother to her little daughter again.

'I should have taken her seriously, Adam,' I say, shaking my head, leaning back against the worktop.

By the look he gives me, he knows immediately where this is going. He pulls me close again.

'It was as if she knew she was going to die, but I ignored her.'

'She had other issues, Ray.' He puts a hand on my shoulder. 'It wasn't your fault.'

Thank God for Adam. He holds me tight, bringing me back down, making me remember the sensible, practical, rational side of all this.

'And it wasn't just you, remember?' he continues. 'Others were involved as well. Everyone did what they could.' He trails off here, picking up again after a moment. 'You know as well as I do that she was taken seriously, but she couldn't provide any proof. Surveillance uncovered nothing but a slightly unhinged woman going about her rather unstable life. We don't even know that her death was related to the allegations.'

I take a breath. Adam is right. In fact, it turned out the man Alexandra Stanford claimed was hounding her day and night, Jimmy Hardwick, didn't even exist. We had a description, of course, from Alexandra and her sister, but after her death the photo-fit didn't produce the results we'd hoped for. A hundred calls came in about the image, some names overlapping, and we followed them all up. Every single person was eliminated, leading me to believe that Jimmy Hardwick didn't have a single friend. Or even a real life.

'Thanks,' I say, sniffing and fighting back the tears. 'For a dead woman, she's a bloody nuisance.'

I pull off a piece of kitchen paper and blow my nose.

'It's the onions,' I say, and Adam has the good sense not to point out that I'm actually chopping carrots.

Stella and Grace polish off their unnameable supper with lightning speed. Adam eats more sedately, chatting to his daughters about the things we catch up on when we're all seated around the kitchen table. Unusually, I remain quiet.

'I have more studying to do now,' Stella says with a heavy sigh, although I don't fail to notice the stifled grin. I sometimes wonder if half the time she's chatting to her mates on Facebook.

'Good for you,' Adam says, oblivious to any late-night mischief cooking up in Stella's mind. Or perhaps it's just me being paranoid and uptight, like I am about most things lately.

Stella gets up and clears a couple of plates and some glasses, leaving them by the sink before going back upstairs. Showing her age, Grace rises serenely and clears the rest of the table, before unloading the dishwasher that hasn't been touched since last night.

'It's OK, love, leave it,' I tell her, flapping my hand at

her. 'I'll sort it.'

Grace nods and leaves the room, while I pour myself another glass of wine. I offer some to Adam, but he shakes his head.

'You didn't eat much,' he says.

I stare at my plate, shrugging. 'I wasn't very hungry. I'll put it in the fridge.'

I get up, but Adam presses me gently down again with a hand on my shoulder.

'Ray, it's clear you've lost a load of weight in the last couple of weeks. You have dark circles under your eyes, I sometimes see your hands shake, and you talk in your sleep.'

'What sleep?'

'Exactly, and sometimes you're not even in bed.'

It's true. I'll probably be down here, warming up some milk or watching rubbish on the television. 'My mind races, that's all.'

'Mum,' Stella says, appearing in the doorway. Her hands grab on to the frame and she lolls forward in a stretch. 'Why can't I stay overnight at Ben's party next week? Everyone else is.'

'Not this again.' I sigh. 'I thought we'd agreed that Dad would pick you up at midnight.'

Stella immediately looks at her father, her eyes large and pleading.

'I don't remember that,' Adam says, stretching an arm round our daughter when she plonks herself on his knee. She looks both ridiculous and cute. 'Surely there's no harm in her sleeping over?' he says.

'Thanks for the support, Adam.' I knew this would happen. 'Ben's parents aren't going to be there, and there's going to be alcohol. I told you about this, don't you remember?'

There's a pause while Adam thinks. Then he shakes his head. 'I'm not sure you did, love. Perhaps you didn't get round to it.'

It feels as if hot lava is pushing up inside me. I'm sure I told him about the party – certain as I can be, anyway. I definitely remember speaking to Ben's mum about it. She told me the teenagers would have the run of the house, and although I didn't say anything to her, I thought it was a crazy plan, how a couple of our officers would no doubt be called out there at two in the morning.

'I'm sure I told you,' I find myself saying, though rather vaguely now. I touch my forehead and sip more wine. Maybe I *am* mistaken.

As Stella is about to protest, Adam sends her away with a promise that we'll think about it. Once she's out of earshot, he turns to me, leaning forward on his elbows with his hands outstretched in readiness to take mine.

'I think you should consider seeing the GP,' he says matter-of-factly. 'What do you reckon?'

I stare at him, knotting my fingers together. My teeth are clamped so tightly I think they might crack.

'I just get so overwhelmed with it all, Adam,' I say, ignoring his question. I need to confide how I feel. 'Dealing with the kids' issues, ferrying them around everywhere, making sure there's food in the fridge, petrol in the car, clothes on our backs, organising the cleaner – assuming she even bothers to turn up – paying the bills, going to school parents' meetings—'

'Lorraine, please, don't do this to yourself.' Adam has grabbed my hands. I stare down at them, noticing my knuckles are blanched white. 'What I said, about going to the doctor. I think you need to.'

I look him in the eye. 'Don't be so ridiculous. That's the last thing I'm going to do,' I reply, yanking my hands free before walking calmly out of the kitchen.

8

I wake with a start. Sitting up, I clutch the duvet to my chest, staring around the unfamiliar room, wondering where I am. For a moment I'm convinced I'm back there, that they caught me and locked me up again.

It's for the best, Isabel, I hear him say through the darkness of my mind.

But no, I see that I'm not there, otherwise there wouldn't be glass covering the watercolour painting hanging on the opposite wall, or a dangerous leather belt left threaded through the top of my jeans. Let alone laces in my trainers.

I get out of bed and put on my clothes, catching sight of myself in the mirror – the fleeting glimpse of a ghost. It's then that I remember climbing between the chilly sheets last night, finally succumbing to sleep, only to be woken, sweating and frightened, a couple of hours later by someone at the door.

I go into the hall, taking the door key from my back pocket, fumbling with the lock. There's no one outside, of course, although something on the ground catches my eye. It's a large black plastic sack tied in a knot at the top. For a second, my heart hammers, but then I see the note stuck to it.

Sorry if I woke you. Thought these would be useful.

The handwriting is straight and careful, easily legible, I notice, as I unpick the knot. Inside, I find a couple of towels smelling of sweet fabric conditioner, a man's bathrobe, and three tea towels for the kitchen.

My tight heart relaxes. It was only Owen being kind.

I grip the door and take a deep breath before closing it and carefully locking it again.

The low morning sun angles its way into the basement flat, making everything seem not quite so awful. When I arrived last night I was exhausted and scared, fearful of what would happen to me now I was back in England, who would find out. But now, in the light of day, even travelling with a man I barely know seems slightly less distressing – though no amount of sun can take away the sick feeling when I think about my parents, how I'll never see them again. I'd always dreamed of coming home one day in the future, after things had died down, been long forgotten. Letting Mum and Dad know I was OK.

I fill the kettle in the tiny kitchen, peering out of the semi-subterranean window to get a glimpse of the garden, but all I can see is paving slabs, a few terracotta clay pots with twiggy and straggly herbs folding over the top, and a small patch of lawn.

I open some cupboards, hoping there'll be a packet of tea or jar of coffee, but I'm out of luck. The little refrigerator hums, but is also empty. I will need to go food shopping later. In the meantime, I decide a shower and fresh clothes will make me feel better for what I must face today. Namely, dealing with the death of my parents and whatever that may entail, given it's been over a month since the accident. My grief comes out as the scalding water flows over my body.

The cold air stings my nostrils as I venture outside and up the steps to ground level, carefully locking the flat door behind me. I shiver, staring at Owen's blue front door. I'll need to buy a coat later as well as food.

Then my heart bangs with worry again. When I left for Delhi, there was nothing in my bank account. Not that I dare use my debit card or a cash machine anyway. No one must know that I'm back. I'll just have to survive on my meagre earnings from Bestluck, which didn't convert to very much at the airport. If absolutely necessary I'll sell a few things from Mum and Dad's house. The thought fills me with sadness as I knock on Owen's door.

'Good morning,' he says cheerfully a moment later. 'How did you sleep? Have you had breakfast? Please, come in.'

I hesitate, swiping back a loose tendril of damp hair. 'I don't want to disturb you. I just came to ask if there's a shop nearby. I need some groceries.'

I offer him my best smile, trying to convince him that this is all perfectly normal behaviour for me, that my pulse isn't galloping at a thousand miles an hour, and I don't have an urge to glance behind me every twenty seconds, that I always fly halfway round the world with strangers.

'Don't be silly,' he says. 'I've got coffee brewing, the toast is on, and I'm wicked with a frying pan and a couple of eggs.' He couldn't hold the door open any wider if he tried.

My mouth waters at the thought of food. I haven't eaten anything since my half-touched aeroplane meal. I glance past Owen into the depths of his house. It looks homely and inviting. A long hallway with a staircase leads down to what must be the kitchen. I hear the radio on in the background.

Owen ushers me inside with a hand on my back. 'I won't hear of you eating breakfast alone,' he says. 'Not after everything you've been through.'

I fight back the tears and do as I'm told, inhaling the nutty smell of fresh coffee. Fifteen minutes later, Owen slides a plate of fried eggs on toast in front of me, and I have my fingers wrapped around a hot drink.

'Do you have to go to work today?' I ask, not knowing what else to say. He doesn't look dressed for the office.

'I've given myself the day off,' he replies. 'No doubt the jet-lag will catch up with me later. Anyway, I have some work I can do here at home.'

I nod, tucking into my eggs, eating way too fast. It brings about a cascade of unstoppable anxiety as I chew through unwelcome memories. My eyes fill with tears.

Slow down, he used to say to me when we ate at restaurants. Then the prolonged stare, followed by his foot tap-tapping against my shin. We'd sit with our fingers linked across the table, him reluctant to let go, even when I tried to pull away.

'You're showing me up, Belle,' he whispered, casting his eyes around to see who was watching. 'Please don't eat like that, my love. You know I enjoy taking you to fine restaurants.'

When we got back to his place, he cooked me another plate of food, showed me how to eat it properly. He forced me to finish it, even though I was full and felt sick. A month after that, I left him for the first time.

'I'm sorry?' I say to Owen, freezing with my fork halfway to my mouth. 'What did you just call me?' My hands are shaking.

Owen looks perplexed as he wipes his mouth with a serviette. His knife and fork are together, his plate pushed aside as we sit opposite each other on stools at the breakfast bar.

'I didn't call you anything,' he says affably. 'I just asked if you wanted more coffee.'

I shake my head, offering a little smile at the same time. 'No, I'm fine, thanks,' I say quietly, although I'd swear on my life he just called me Belle.

'I'm not sure I can face it yet,' I tell Owen, flapping the dog-eared letter from the High Commission in front of him half an hour later. It also shows a UK number that I'm meant to call for assistance. 'Though I know I'll have to eventually.'

Owen takes the letter from me. 'It's the coroner's number,' he says. 'Feel free to use my phone.'

He takes a handset from its base and passes it to me.

I breathe in deeply and close my eyes. 'Thanks,' I say, knowing he's right. The sooner I get this over with the better.

I dial the number, and it's answered after three rings. A young woman about my age cheerily announces that I've reached HM Coroner for the City of Birmingham and asks how she can direct my call. A moment later I'm through to a similar-sounding woman called Angie, who kindly listens to my story. She tells me how sorry she is to hear about my mum and dad, and then asks for the reference number on my letter. A couple more questions for security and she offers to send me a copy of the coroner's report for each of my parents. She asks for my address.

I turn to Owen, hand clamped over the mouthpiece. 'She wants my address,' I say uselessly. He must wonder why I don't use my parents' house, but the less time I have to spend there the better.

'Feel free to use mine,' Owen says, jotting it down. 'Give them my email address and phone number too, if you like,' he adds helpfully, and I do exactly that.

Angie promises she will send a PDF file as well as a copy in the post.

'One other thing,' I say to her, hoping she can help. 'Do you know where the accident happened? I'd like to pay a visit.'

She hesitates, and the line goes silent for a moment. It's as if she's not certain what to say. But then she recites the location and details without drama or emotion, though in a reassuring tone, as if it never even happened. I write it all down, thinking that she must do this every day, perhaps several times.

'And the last question, I promise,' I say with a dry mouth, unable to help myself. 'Would you know which hospital the driver of the car was taken to?' I need to know, to check he's still there.

'The Queen Elizabeth Hospital,' Angie reveals after rustling some paper. She doesn't realise she's driven a bolt through my heart. 'It says he was taken there on the twenty-eighth of September. Again, I'm so sorry about your losses, Miss Moore. If there's anything else I can do, just let me know.' Then she says goodbye and hangs up.

Ten minutes later, after I've accepted a second coffee, Owen checks his phone and tells me the coroner's email has arrived in his inbox. I can't stand to read the reports yet, and he understands entirely. Everyone is being so kind.

'Are you sure you don't mind?' I ask for the thousandth time, careful not to thank him again, fuelling the standing joke between us.

'It was a choice between sleeping, working, or helping you out. While I admit that sleep is pretty high up on my list of priorities right now, I figured you could do with some support.' Owen indicates to go left at a junction. 'And a lift.'

'I'm sorry to be such a nuisance.'

I stare out of the car window. I'm on the brink of telling him that visiting the accident spot is something I really *need* to do, that once I've seen where it happened it may help me move on a little, come to terms with what's happened. But I don't. It sounds hackneyed, as if we'll fall for each other or something afterwards, just like in the movies. I know that's never going to happen. The thought of getting close to someone, confiding in them, allowing them to get to know the real me, is unthinkable.

'I understand completely,' he says. 'Besides, you've actually saved me from an appointment I'd forgotten about.' Owen glances across at me. 'Client from hell,' he continues. 'It's times like this I need an assistant to bluff for me.'

He laughs, and says something else, but I don't really hear him. I'm thinking about the last time I saw Mum and Dad, what I said, hoping I'd been kind and loving to them.

We were having a picnic, I think, and they'd picked me up from *that place*, to take me out for the day. Felix wasn't there, much to my parents' disappointment. Mum was in her slim-fitting jeans – she still wore them, even in her sixties – and Dad was in his sailing sweatshirt, navy blue with a white stitched-on logo.

Tetch their terrier was zigzagging between us as we sat on the old woollen blanket that they'd used for picnics for as long as I can remember. Mum's famous chicken sandwiches were spread between us, stuffed with everything from avocado and mayonnaise to rocket and roasted red peppers.

'Tetch!' I say suddenly, as Owen brakes. 'What on earth happened to their dog?'

I cover my face with my hands. It hadn't occurred to me before now. I imagine myself unlocking the door to their house, being confronted by rotting dog flesh, finding his fly-ridden body jack-knifed by the back door as he'd tried to escape, starving, dehydrated.

'Won't the police have taken care of him, or a neighbour?' Owen says.

He's right. Poor Tetch will be with strangers now, pining for Mum and Dad.

'He was an angry little bugger,' I explain with a tentative chuckle. 'The first day they got him, Dad kept calling him tetchy. It stuck.'

Then I see a petrol station ahead and ask Owen to stop. A few minutes later, I get back in the car with a bunch of wilting chrysanthemums.

'Dad would have hated these.' This time the laugh comes properly, stays fixed on my face until it turns into sobs. 'He grew orchids,' I add, blowing my nose.

Owen's hand leaves the steering wheel, sweeps down on to mine.

'Let's just get this over with,' I say, and Owen drives on.

We pull over in a narrow lay-by, the hazard lights flashing as we get out.

'By my reckoning, it happened somewhere along here,' he tells me, gesturing left and right, glancing at the map on his phone again.

Cars speed past us as the road changes from a dual carriageway to a single lane about a hundred yards behind us, whipping up a fierce wind. I shield my eyes, squinting, staring around. The narrowing of the road from two lanes to one causes the cars to merge, but they don't seem to slow down. It's easy to see how an accident happened, but not fair it was my parents. They always lived life so carefully, the least reckless people I knew. But the bend is sharp, the camber wrong. Probably the council have it marked down as an accident black-spot.

I remember how *he* liked to drive fast, terrifying me, until I begged him to stop.

'Look,' I say, running off along the narrow verge – a blend of scrubby grass, crumbled tarmac and litter.

Owen calls out above the noise, telling me to be careful. A hundred feet or so along the crash railings, the metal is buckled and distorted. Panting, I stop and stare at it, my hands resting on my knees as I bend forward, catching my breath. Owen draws up beside me.

'Do you think this is the spot?' he says.

Cars continue to speed past, ballooning out the back of the anorak I borrowed.

'I think so,' I say, unable to take my eyes off it. According to Angie at the coroner's office, the car landed on its roof down the embankment the other side of the barrier. 'I hope it was over quickly.'

I feel cold and desolate inside. I can't stand to think of what killed them – head injuries, broken necks, abdominal trauma. I want to believe that they were driving along and everything suddenly went black and peaceful.

What I hate more than anything is that the last person to see them alive was *him*.

'Look,' I say, suddenly spotting it. 'There's a bit of paint on the barrier.'

I lean forward and drag my finger over some thin dark green streaks. He was in the Jaguar then. I recognise the colour.

'You know what the driver of this car once said?' I say, unable to help myself. I turn to face Owen, finding myself close to him, feeling his warmth as we are pressed together for safety against the speeding traffic. 'He told me that he'd been searching for me all his life. He told me that I'd never be able to leave him. Not alive, anyway.'

I crouch down and lay the flowers beneath the crumpled metal, wondering if killing my parents was the next best thing to killing me.

9

'Back in March, getting on for eight months ago now,' I say to the assembled team, swallowing down the guilt from all the wasted time, 'Melanie Carter's body was found floating in the canal. White female, early twenties, and, as you all know, a student here in the city.'

I take a deep breath as the image of Melanie's body percolates my mind, overlapping the etching of Alexandra that's already in there. Bob's got me recapping this case until we all believe it happened yesterday. We're no further forward than we were when she was discovered.

'A chap who works a tour boat caught her leg with his hook. She was face down in the Gas Street basin. The stupid bugger dragged her over and tried to haul her out.'

I pause, taking a sip of my coffee, looking at the shift team. For some reason, my hand is shaking, and I pray none of the officers in the incident room notices. I feel as if I've been awake for a month solid. It's as if my body is staging an uprising.

'By the time the first uniforms got down there, she'd

been pulled from the water, dragged over the side and dumped in the hull of his boat. He thought he could save her, but instead caused cervical lacerations and head trauma. But she was pretty messed up anyway. You've all read the path reports a hundred times, I hope.'

Preservation of life is the first building block in the five principles of dealing with a murder scene, so the old man was correct in thinking he should try to save her. But when I got down to the basin, I was more concerned with the second priority, preserving the scene itself, than anything else.

Truth is, I was shit scared I was going to blow it. Bob had put me in charge.

I swig more coffee, remembering the woman I'd peered down at in the rocking hull. I'd felt sick within seconds, though couldn't be sure if it was because of the comings and goings on and off the boat that kept up the nauseating sideways rolling motion, or because of her sad, waterlogged face.

I always look at their eyes first. I can't help it. They're sometimes closed, other times not. This young woman's were open, her irises a light grey – the colour of a moody sea or an overcast day. Staring somewhere I couldn't see.

She reminded me so much of Alexandra, but that was probably because of her hair – the colour of autumn on a sunny day. I was still trying to get behind the glassy sockets of her eyes, delve into her last thoughts, when the police surgeon officially pronounced her dead.

DC Ed Rowlands nudges me, bringing me back to the room. He hands me a pile of notes, giving me an encouraging smile. I thank him, feeling grateful I have a good team behind me.

'The scene proved extremely tricky, of course,' I tell them. 'It was so . . . well, so fluid.' There's a snigger from someone at the back. 'But the entire basin and immediate area was sealed off in reasonable time. No boats or people were allowed in or out for a day and a half.'

I shudder as I recall the near fight that broke out between a couple of uniforms and several boat owners as they protested against my decision to clear the vicinity. One of the lads nearly ended up in the water.

I was staring at the sodden body lying at my feet, one arm draped across her concave belly covering the gap where her rucked-up top didn't meet her jeans, the other arm levered behind her head from when she'd been landed like some kind of urban mermaid.

That's when I spotted the wound on the inside of her wrist. A patch of skin had been roughly cut away, leaving a red-raw area about the size of a slice of tomato.

And this gets me thinking about Alexandra. About her ankle. About how I owe it to her to keep her case alive, make sure it gets the focus it deserves.

I remember the rest of Melanie's skin had taken on an otherworldly greeny-grey hue, and her fiery hair was tangled up with slimy weed that had come out of the canal with her. The old man who had found her was sitting in the stern of the boat, shivering and wrapped in a blanket, telling everyone he had a granddaughter about the same age.

'The dive team arrived at the scene quickly,' I say to the room, stifling a yawn with the back of my hand. About three others follow suit, sitting there with gaping mouths. It feels hot and airless in here. 'Big priority was given to getting witness statements, gathering material, interviews and a scene sweep as fast as possible. We'd closed down a very public area. There were businesses involved.'

With the Alexandra Stanford murder the previous month, I didn't want a panic. We needed to be in and out as fast as possible without compromising the investigation.

'I'm meeting with DS Bob Canon shortly to revisit crossovers and relevance with the Stanford case,' I say, winding things up. 'Meantime, you've all got the reports and statements, as well as assigned tasks based on the case review. We will continue on this as a standalone, but keeping very open minds. I don't want any prejudices or assumptions. Not yet, anyway,' I add.

What I'm saying goes against everything I believe. I don't want to treat this as an isolated case at all. Even though he thinks the same, Bob is playing by the rules for now.

Then my heart bangs inside my chest, a surge of something hot and molten upsetting its rhythm as I remember the outstanding reports and interviews I owe him from other cases – the backlog of work that makes me constantly feel as if I'm drowning.

'Ma'am?' says an impatient voice. 'Want me to go back

to the businesses around the area? Brent and I could cover them this morning.'

After the reconstruction on *Crimewatch* last week, we're still following leads from the public.

The keen young DC eyes me hopefully. He's worked well for me in the past so I give him the go-ahead to assemble a small crew.

'Those who are able, let's reconvene at five p.m.,' I say, after allocating more tasks. 'Meantime, fresh CCTV resulting from the airtime is being rechecked as I speak.'

I glance at my watch. This is the worst part of any investigation – the ongoing strategic management, knowing where to go when you've hit dead end after dead end. Even with several decades of experience I still feel as if I'm fumbling around in the dark. It's the nature of what we're dealing with.

'Thanks, everyone,' I call out as the officers filter away, grabbing pastries from the tray as they leave.

It's not even the procedure, I think, watching the rumblings of movement in the room. Strip out the paperwork and that's the easy bit. It's more the whys and the hows, the unquantifiable questions that often never get answered. *Think Murder* the manuals plainly tell us; work down from the worst.

It's just that everyone else's worst is different to mine.

I slide off the edge of the desk I've been perched on for the last twenty minutes. My left leg thrums with pins and needles – the same feeling as inside my head. Adam walks past the door, glancing in before turning away quickly.

'Get on with it then,' I say to the remaining three officers. 'Any time today is fine by me.'

They nod, leaving the room in a flurry of crumbs, empty coffee cups and jacket-donning. I yawn again just as Adam appears at the doorway to the stuffy room.

'Not surprised you're tired,' he says, hands on hips, as I shove a few things into my black bag and reach for my coat. 'You were up half the night.'

'That still left a whole half for sleeping.'

Truth is, I didn't sleep through that part either.

'Did you want something?' We rarely see each other at work unless we're on a case together.

'I came to say I'm sorry,' Adam says, pulling an apple from the pocket of his black windcheater and leaning against the door frame.

'For what?'

'For being late, of course.'

'Late for what?' I put on my mac and slip the strap of my heavy bag over my shoulder.

'This meeting.' Adam casts an eye around the incident room. His sandy hair is glistening wet.

'What meeting?' I try not to show my brewing concern.

'This one, of course. Are you going to fill me in or not?'

He takes an impossibly large bite out of the apple. His eyes narrow, like they do when he can't help a grin, making a spread of lines that reach from his lashes to his temples. The fingers of his free hand swipe across his newly cultivated stubble.

'Oh no, Adam,' I say slowly. 'Oh no you bloody well don't. This one's mine.'

He sees the shock in my eyes, holds his hands up in defence, the apple included. 'Didn't you see the email Bob sent out?'

I shake my head. I've not had a chance to check.

'He should have made certain you knew the score first.' Adam sighs, giving me a look, hoping I'll forgive him even though it's not his fault. 'I'm sorry, Ray. He probably assumed I'd tell you.'

My whole body tenses. I take a deep breath, just like the anxiety website suggested. At three a.m. there isn't much else to do that won't wake the entire house apart from search for medical diagnoses and advice.

'Look, I know it's your case, but I'll be helping you on this now, so you'd best tell me where we're at. Besides, Bob thinks we'll work well together.'

'Since when?' I glance at my watch. I haven't checked my messages since first thing, which is unforgiveable.

'Since about two hours ago.'

'Fine.' My teeth butt together in a painful clench, the strange shape of my face no doubt signalling to my husband that I'm less than happy about it. 'You can begin by trawling the PNC for—'

'Want to know something?' Adam asks, taking another bite of the apple.

He's bloody grinning behind the core.

'Two days before she was killed, Melanie Carter told

a friend at university that a man had been hassling her. She believed she was being stalked.'

'*What?*' I grab the nylon sleeve of Adam's windcheater and pull him into the room, kicking the door shut behind him. 'You knew this before *me?*' My cheeks are on fire.

For the second time, Adam raises his hands to halt my anger. 'I thought you'd be pleased. I picked up the news while you were busy in here.'

'Bob could have told me personally,' I say. 'Yet again.'

I pace around the room, waving my arms about, my coat flapping, my bag slipping off my shoulder and dropping to the floor. It spills its contents just as Bob comes into the room. I don't know if he heard.

'Everything OK?' he asks, glancing between us. 'I take it you're on your way back to check out this new development, Lorraine? Uniform have been trying to reach you. There's some fresh material they want to run past you. I can send Adam if you'd rather.'

I'm down on the floor unable to move, my hands trying to conceal the contents of my bag – a hairbrush, a tampon, a packet of Kalms, a box of codeine pills.

'Essential kit for a DI, sir,' I say to Bob with a forced smile.

I reach for my phone and see five missed calls. The ringer must have flicked off in my bag.

'I just need a word with Lorraine before she goes,' Adam says, pulling me up off the floor.

Bob leaves, muttering about being on time for our two o'clock meeting.

'Take a look at this before you go, Ray.' Adam hands me a printout.

I shrug my coat back on properly and tuck up the hair that came loose from my clip. I suddenly feel exhausted. Adam is standing close. I glance up at him, taking the paper.

'Sorry,' I say. 'I'm just tired.'

'I know,' he says, giving me a kiss on the cheek. It makes me want to fall against him, have him take me home and put me to bed. We rarely show each other affection at work.

I scan the words. It's not much to go on. I drop the paper down by my side.

'The university friend passed on the information following the reconstruction,' Adam says.

'Anything else?' I ask. This is potentially huge.

'Apparently Melanie had felt very scared and harassed. She confided in the friend just before she died, saying that she felt ashamed that she'd got herself into a bad relationship. She hadn't been able to talk about it before because of that, apparently.'

Again, it reminds me of Alexandra Stanford, how we weren't able to help her. Now it's too late.

'Bob isn't dismissing links between the two cases,' Adam says. 'Far from it. But he needs to be certain. There are no forensics to prove it. But at least we can go in forearmed.'

'What, you mean when we compare this to the description of a man who doesn't exist?' I flap the paper about. 'And what's with the *we*?'

'*We* as in I'm coming with you.'

Reluctantly, I let Adam drive while I catch up with some calls. Then I re-read the description Melanie's friend gave in her brief statement. It could be the same man, I think, but then again, it could be a coincidence.

'Thanks, Adam,' I say, suddenly relieved that he is right beside me.

10

Isabel fell in love with me just after the bell sounded for break. It was only the second time she'd ever seen me. Her brilliant blue eyes flashed disbelief as she swiped a strand of her vibrant hair off her cheek. Even her face seemed to transform into a heart-shape as I told her the reason for my visit.

'You shouldn't be here,' was, disappointingly, one of the first things she said, in a high-pitched whisper fuelled by excitement. Her throat was closing up at the thought of my offer.

'You've got, erm . . .' I touched my own nose to indicate that there was paint on hers. Pink paint, as it happened, and I wondered if even her nose was expressing its love for me by sporting such a romantic colour.

'Oh,' and she dashed to a little mirror above the art-room sink, dabbing at it with a wetted paper towel.

That was when the bell rang, causing all the kids to drop what they were doing and slope off.

'You can't actually be serious,' she said on her return from the sink, making out I was crazy.

I forced my hands into the front pockets of my jeans and tilted my head to the side. I gave her a big smile, making sure it peaked when her attention was fully on me.

Her eyes kept darting around the messy studio, and her mouth twitched, clearly desperate to yell something at the departing kids. The room smelled disgusting – a combination of pheromone-drenched teen sweat, clay, and white school glue. I wouldn't have survived in it many more minutes. I just wanted to take her away from it all.

'Deadly serious,' I told her as she virtually popped. Seeing her joy plumped up my heart. I imagined grabbing her waist right there and then, dragging her into the store room I'd spotted on the way in, and making love among the clutter.

I withdrew my hands from my pockets.

'It's an incredible, amazing and utterly ridiculous proposition, and I'd love to,' she said, as excited as if she had a sparkler going off inside her mouth. 'But I can't,' she added solemnly. 'And you shouldn't be in here. I'll get it in the neck if you haven't officially signed in.'

I thought about her getting it in the neck. Then I thought about how easy it had been to get in here in the first place without being challenged. I'd heard that schools were like prisons these days – a far cry from the grandiosity of the place I was sent. Not so this one, it seemed.

The idea of being surrounded by a thousand rude and

slumping teenagers had virtually killed me, but needs must. She worked in a school, I wanted to spend time with her, so what choice did I have? My plan was, if challenged, to pretend to be a supply teacher. Albeit one on a decent salary. It was clear my clothes were superior to those worn by the shabby-looking staff I'd spotted. Leaping fences isn't my style, and a confident stride on to school premises had resulted in my being approached only once, by a middle-aged man in a dark blazer with a frosting of dandruff on his shoulders. I told him I was new, and he sent me towards reception, from which I instantly veered away once he was out of sight.

The art block was easy to find – a painted cinder block hut that the school had let the kids run riot on with spray cans, daubing it in railway-style graffiti. I entered the building, catching hold of the pass-coded door as a pretty young student was coming out.

Isabel hadn't been hard to locate either. There were three separate art rooms leading off a narrow corridor painted a shade of yellow that added to my feeling of being in a place that was already sucking the soul from me. Imagine working or studying here for years and years, I thought, harking back to my schooldays, grateful now that my father had hated me enough to pack me off to boarding school at the age of eight. It was better than staying home with him.

It was her happy voice which finally drew me to her studio. I'd positioned myself in the doorway, easing it open with my foot, not my fingers.

And there she was. Isabel – my pre-Raphaelite beauty painted with colours that didn't seem to exist in real life.

She'd done a classic double-take when she saw me.

'Felix!' she said.

All the kids in her class suddenly turned, staring, wondering who naughty Felix was.

'Indeed,' I said smoothly, ignoring the students.

She glanced at her watch.

'I want you to come out with me tonight,' I announced. 'Will you?'

Some kids sniggered.

'Where?' she asked, stunned. I could tell by the sugar frosting blooming on her cheeks that she was pleased to see me yet also embarrassed by the class witnessing her courtship.

'Paris,' I said. 'I know a place.'

More sniggers, but they were immediately drowned out by Isabel's incredulous laugh. Then she yelled at two boys arguing over paint brushes.

'You shouldn't be here,' she said.

It was then that I told her about the paint on her nose, and the bell rang, and she told me I couldn't be serious and I promised oh, but I was. I really, really was.

'How will we get there?'

'In a Cessna Citation.'

She didn't know what that was of course, just as she didn't think to ask how I knew where she worked.

'But my passport . . .' Isabel's face revealed the first

crumples of worry. She touched her temple. 'And I've got work tomorrow.'

'Your passport is all sorted,' I said. 'Your mother couldn't have been more helpful. She found it and gave it to me.'

'She did?'

I nodded. 'And you'll be in bed by two at the latest – just about OK to tackle school tomorrow.' I had to be careful; I didn't want to overdo it. It could seem scary, stalkerish even, and that was so very far from the truth.

'I don't know what to say.'

She was almost laughing, shaking her head so that her sweet orange hair quivered at her cheeks. Her tongue sat between her top and bottom teeth in indecision. I felt myself growing hard.

'Then say yes,' I told her. 'You don't need to do anything except be ready by six. We'll be dining by eight, back in Birmingham by one.'

And that's when she fell in love with me, when the crazy azure of her widened irises spun on the colour wheel and ended up a sickly heart-pink.

It turned out that Isabel had never been to Paris before. She'd made it as far as Majorca one year, she told me as she soaked up the glittering lights of the city as we sped from Charles de Gaulle in a limo.

'Another year we went to mainland Spain.'

'Nice,' I said, remembering how her nose had stayed pressed to the porthole window of the small jet for most of the flight. I'd opened the champagne as soon as we'd broken the circuit and handed her a brimming glass.

'One of the perks of taking an empty leg at the last minute,' I'd said, raising my glass to hers.

'Is this the type of plane you fly?' she'd asked, relaxing back into the cream leather seat once we were well and truly airborne.

'Very often,' I'd told her. 'Mike up front is doing us a favour by allowing us to hitch a ride. He's a good mate. There will be some other passengers on the return journey, but it's not a problem. By not flying, it means I don't have to bother with all the paperwork at the airport.'

I undid my seatbelt then and put my feet up on the seat across the tiny aisle. My left hand rested on the glossy walnut table, keeping a grip on my glass. The aircraft bumped and lurched briefly, causing me to instinctively grab on to my seat with my left hand.

'I'm a terrible back-seat passenger,' I'd told her, laughing, looking away.

After dinner we headed for the Seine.

'That was an incredible meal,' she said, making my heart swell as she described the four courses ingredient by ingredient, even though she was no gourmet.

The walk wasn't without ulterior motive of course, and I steered her in a certain direction as she blindly went on about wild rabbit pâté quenelles, and langoustines drenched in daisy crème. I wanted to make the evening special, one that she'd remember for ever, even if as things stood so far she was unlikely to forget.

The night air was still, but not so the city. It was even more vibrant than London, as if every single one of its inhabitants, whether sleeping or awake, was intensely aware of their own style as it crackled out of them, the effect rubbing off on us just by being there.

I admit, I got off on that – the sophistication, the glamour, the way it made Isabel look at me as we'd broken open our langoustines, dribbled Dom Perignon, sucked our fingers clean of garlicky sauce.

'Are you in love with Paris?' I asked, really meaning me.

It was easy to locate her hand, take hold of it, swallow it up in mine as we sauntered along the river bank. There was no resistance from her.

'Totally,' she laughed.

We were halfway across Pont Alexandre III, the Tour Eiffel a glowing beacon in the background, when I turned and kissed her roughly, biting down on her lips, forcing my way inside her mouth.

When she pulled away, shocked, gasping, I asked her, 'Are you drunk?'

I'd already made sure she was.

She nodded wildly, grinning inanely, her inhibitions fluttering above us like butterflies. There was a bead of blood on her lip, so I leaned forward and kissed it off.

'Good,' I said. 'Then follow me. There is a surprise.'

She didn't protest when we entered the tattoo parlour, the cleanest-looking one I could find online before our visit, and she didn't say much either when I helped her slip out of her top. She clung on to me unsteadily. Her breasts, sitting unaware in her shell-pink, too-small bra, smelled of salty popcorn.

I eased her on to the bed, helping her to lie down on her front. I laughed with her when she nearly fell off because of her boozy limbs, and watched as Henri etched the dark ink into the back of her neck, accompanied by the music of her moans as it dawned on her what was happening. She didn't even care.

'Now you'll never forget,' I told her, admiring the perfect symmetry of the infinity symbol inked just below the surface of her skin.

11

Compared to how I've been living these last few months, Owen's house feels like a favourite sweater, a comfy pair of slippers, or a feel-good movie. It's well furnished, yet comfortable and lived-in; the kind of place that makes you feel safe and warms your heart.

Even so, while he's out getting pizza and wine, I take the opportunity to look around, just to make sure there are no nasty surprises. I've learned it pays to be careful. I laugh bitterly at that thought as I test out my hard-learned mantra in this new environment.

'You can never be too careful,' I say several times over while stalking from room to room.

The words sound insulated and smothered, the depth of their true meaning dulled by the thick-pile rugs, the giant floor cushions and the intricate tapestries hanging on brightly painted walls.

My idea of caution is somewhat ironic, I realise, as I prepare to indulge in an evening of food and wine with a virtual stranger. In fact, I'm shocked at how I have moved from extreme caution to recklessness in just a couple of days.

I close my eyes and drop down backwards on to the sofa, like that game of dares where you fall into someone's arms, trusting them to catch you. I doubt Owen's sofa is going to let me down at the last moment. Not like *he* did, I think, remembering the party he insisted we go to at short notice.

'Come on Fee, you twat,' one of his old boarding school friends had jeered, beer bottle waving around in one hand, a joint dangling limply between careless fingers on the other. 'It's your turn. Let's see if she's just in it for your money and your ugly face.'

A whole group of them exploded in rank laughter.

We'd been there several hours and were out by the pool. It was a humid night and they'd been taking coke, maybe something else too. Some were swimming naked, others were sprawled on loungers off their faces, while several couples had disappeared into the bottle-green depths of the night-time garden to have high-pitched, squealing sex that they made sure we all knew about.

'You trust me, don't you, Belle?' Felix whispered to me privately.

He put down his drink, threw his cigarette on to the grass and came up close to me. His breath smelled smoky, beery, and amber – a missed warning that things were about to change. He gave me a hug and kissed my neck, showing the others just how close we were. I felt so proud.

'Of course,' I said quietly, looking around the dozen or so playing the game.

I didn't know anyone at the party, and Felix hadn't seen them since his schooldays. It was a last-minute online reunion, and they were impressed he was a pilot. Most of them seemed to brag about living off family money. They were all drunk with swollen, red-rimmed eyes, calling each other by their public-school nicknames. Felix was his middle name, he told me coyly, when I questioned why a couple of them had called him George. He confided that he'd always hated his first, that it reminded him too much of his father, so when he went away to school he'd decided to change it.

It had soon become clear that I didn't fit in with his old friends. I'd hinted we should leave, but didn't want to spoil Felix's fun. He was enjoying catching up, remembering old times. But after a couple of hours, the only thing on my mind was the late hour. I had to get up early for school the next day, and should never have come. As ever, he was persuasive, insistent, so I agreed to play the game. Besides, I didn't want to show him up.

Felix played to the crowd, pretending to roll up the sleeves of the pink cotton shirt he was wearing, even though they were already turned up casually to reveal his tanned forearms, the cuffs flapping. He took a stance with his feet wide apart and his arms outstretched as if he was about to catch a baby from a burning building. His beige knee-length shorts and black Crocs looked mildly comical against the backdrop of exposed flesh around us.

It was some small mercy we hadn't joined in the skinny dipping. It wasn't like any party I'd been to before.

Everyone started clapping and cheering.

Fe-*lix*, Fe-*lix*, Fe-*lix* . . .

I knew I'd have to do this in order to go home, so decided to get it over with, positioning myself a few feet from him. I would fall backwards, he would catch me, then we could leave. I'd had enough of his childlike friends, and just wanted to be alone with him, enjoy his company for the last part of the evening. I forced a grin.

'You ready, Belle?' he growled playfully, while winking affectionately.

Then he let out a silly laugh like a pirate. It reminded me of why I adored him, found him so exciting. He was like no one I'd met before – so silly at times, yet always loving, while still being serious and deep, as if there were a thousand layers of him to peel away.

And it thrilled me that he'd chosen me to do that. I couldn't wait to show everyone the special bond we had, the trust that had built between us already, how we'd do anything for each other, even after only a few weeks. And we still hadn't slept together. I respected him for not rushing things, even though the thought of it made my insides melt.

'Ready, Cap'n,' I replied with a silly salute, turning my back, getting ready to be caught. I didn't look round again, just listened to the crescendo of jeers and cries and allowed myself to fall backwards into his arms when the noise reached its peak. I trusted Felix completely.

I don't recall much else. Just the headache that lasted for days, the mocking laughs above me, someone muttering *stupid bitch*.

I freeze, clutching a cushion to my chest.

A noise. Is Owen back already?

I haven't finished looking around his house. I need to convince myself he's not hiding anything from me. Mistrust is a scar buried deep inside. I hold my breath, but don't hear anything else.

The front living room smells faintly damp and unlived-in, but I assume that's because Owen's been away. There are several bookshelves filled with paperbacks, and in one corner of the room there's a small but tidy desk. Not his main work desk, I assume, but rather a quiet place at home to write letters or check emails. I imagine his professional workspace filled with natural light, a large architect's drawing board in a minimalist and modern office.

There's a drawer in the low wooden coffee table, so I slide it open. Inside there are a few batteries rolling around, a couple of remote controls, a *Radio Times* three months out of date, some folded wrapping paper and a bag of mint humbugs. I close it again, smiling at the normality of Owen's life.

In the kitchen, I poke around in the cupboards and drawers, not knowing what it is I'm looking for, but that I'll know it when I find it. All I come across are cooking utensils, crockery, pans, glassware and some mugs – exactly what I'd expect to find in a kitchen. The larder cupboard isn't very well stocked, just a few cans of soup, a packet of porridge oats and a nearly-empty box of cornflakes, along with various tins of vegetables. There's a half-eaten tube of pink and yellow iced biscuits, the sort you'd find at a kids' birthday party. I check the use-by date – still edible.

It makes me wonder if he's got a child, or perhaps more than one, and they come to stay. But nothing else about the house downstairs suggests that children visit. I daren't risk checking the bedrooms in case Owen catches me up there.

One kitchen drawer is stuffed full of restaurant menus and bills, as well as other bits and pieces including a few pens, a stapler, some rubber bands and a tape measure.

I lift out the bills. Nothing is in any particular order and I don't suppose he'd notice if I put things back differently, but I'm careful just the same. There's a council tax bill with Mr Owen J. Brandrick and this address printed at the top. It's current, though perhaps a duplicate he's taken. There's also a water services bill and an invoice from a local garage for £273.65 to fix the exhaust on his car.

I put everything back in the drawer as I found it. No mention of a Mrs Brandrick anywhere, or any sign of female possessions for that matter. I've already checked out the coat cupboard and the neat rack of shoes in the hall. It all belongs to a man – a man who shops for himself, judging by the top-end yet safely unimaginative brands.

Just as I'm about to give up, as certain as I can be that I don't have to worry about an irate wife coming home from a tiring week away on business, or returning from a trip with a group of girlfriends, I catch sight of a red light blinking above me.

On, then off again.

I wave my arm then freeze dead still, waiting a second or two. It goes off. I let out a breath.

'Oh thank God,' I say, relaxing at the sight of the motion sensor.

I remember Owen switching off the alarm when he unlocked the place. I track my eyes around the plaster cornice, looking for more, and, sure enough, there's another one in the opposite corner covering the back door of the house.

I go around the whole of downstairs locating them all – there are plenty, more than I'd have imagined – and then I dare to poke my head upstairs to spot others on the landing, along with a smoke detector. The bedrooms will no doubt have them too.

When we arrived from the airport it was late. I was too tired to notice if the flat was also covered, so I dash down to check. As I suspected, each room has several sensors positioned to pick up all angles. I lean back against the cool wall.

'Nothing bad is going to happen,' I tell myself. 'You are safe. Owen is a normal man living in a normal house with a normal job. He's gone to get normal pizza and normal wine and—'

My thoughts are interrupted as I hear footfall on the concrete steps outside the flat.

'Isabel?' he calls out, waiting outside the slightly open flat door. 'Are you down here?'

'I'll be up in a moment,' I call back.

Five minutes later, I find Owen has left the front door ajar for me.

Inside, he's busy laying kindling in the cast-iron grate, setting it atop knots of rolled-up newspaper. His back is to me, the long length of his spine showing through his shirt, which has risen up above the waist of his jeans. His skin is smooth and pale, his waist tight and lean, while his forearms, exposed by rolled-up sleeves, are muscled and strong.

For a moment, I watch as he blows into the base of the grate, waiting until the flames creep up through the carefully arranged cone of wood. But then I see he has his phone in his hands, that he's texting, sending a picture message. For a moment, I think it's a picture of me.

'Hi,' I say, causing him to turn round suddenly.

'Oh, hi,' he says, quickly switching off the screen. 'I didn't hear you come in.'

12

'God, I'd forgotten how good pepperoni is,' I say through a mouthful of pizza.

We're sitting on floor cushions beside the low table in the living room. I feel something warm inside, a welcome respite from the constant pain of losing my parents, although I can't help feeling wary of it. I know it's only temporary, not my real life.

Owen smiles, his mouth also full.

'You have a good security system here,' I continue, trying to sound casual.

He passes me a piece of kitchen paper as my pizza droops back into the box. I glance up at the motion sensor, hoping he doesn't think I'm odd for mentioning it.

'That was Helen's doing,' he says after a moment's thought.

He eats like a man. Nothing affected or repressed about the way he gets the food into his mouth, hooking up a trail of mozzarella with his finger, scooping half the slice between his lips at once.

I think of Felix, the way he tentatively forked minuscule pieces of the finest restaurant food, usually leaving at least half on his plate. I was taken by it at first, not thinking it strange. Everything Felix did was a delicious mystery to me, something to be exposed and enjoyed.

Then, stupidly, incomprehensibly, I am struck by a feeling of sadness at the thought of him lying in a hospital bed, connected to a feeding tube pumping soulless nutrients directly into him. He may never taste real food again.

But the thought is fleeting, an inescapable lapse of judgement – inevitable after believing you loved someone. Believing they truly loved you too.

'Is Helen your wife?' I say after too much time has passed.

Owen has put on Fleetwood Mac's 'Little Lies' softly in the background.

'My ex,' he informs me with a resigned shrug and nod, picking up his wineglass and taking a slug. 'After the burglary, she went mad for security.'

I silently thank Helen. 'Do you put the alarm on at night? Is it possible to activate the flat's system independently?'

Owen laughs as he peels another slice of pizza from the box. He gives me a sideways glance. 'You survived the madness of Delhi. A safe corner of Birmingham shouldn't worry you.' He bites into the pizza with a broad mouth. 'Then again, Bestluck was a funny little sanctuary, wasn't it?'

'I'm just conscious of crime,' I say, hoping it will

convince him. I can hardly tell him the truth – that if I'm found, my life will be over for certain this time.

'I don't tend to use the alarm unless I leave the house empty for long periods. There is a way to separate the two systems, but I'd have to ask Helen how to do that. And I can assure you, that's not a task I—'

'Really, you don't have to explain.' I wish I'd not brought it up. I don't want to raise suspicion, and I'll be gone soon anyway. 'You've done so much for me already.'

'You're actually doing me a favour by being downstairs. The place feels cold and damp if it's not lived in, and it'll be another couple of weeks before I can get a tenant signed up.'

In two weeks' time I intend to be back at Bestluck, getting on with my job, camouflaged in the bustling market, or safe in the tiny top-floor room Raksha said she'd save for me.

Knowing Felix as I do, he'll come out of this coma tomorrow, and when he does, his first thought is going to be me. I don't even know for sure he's still unconscious and already I've wasted a day. Apart from visiting the accident site, which wasn't particularly helpful, all I've done is buy a coat from a local discount store, pick up a few provisions for my fridge, and drink coffee and eat pizza with Owen. Tomorrow will be more productive.

'I won't be here that long, I'm afraid,' I tell him. 'If it's OK with you, another night or two in the flat would be great. Then I must think about my return flight.'

Owen pulls a face. 'Will you have everything dealt with

by then? Won't you need time to sell your parents' house, move out their belongings? Aren't you going to arrange a memorial service for them? Contact relatives?'

All his questions floor me. He doesn't understand; *can't* understand. I like Owen, but I'm not prepared to tell him about my past, what happened, how I escaped, from *where* I escaped. That's when people judge, form their own opinions. I can't have anyone building a picture of me.

'Mum and Dad wouldn't want a fuss,' I say, hoping that will satisfy him.

No, they wouldn't want any of this, I think, remembering how Mum had already begun planning my wedding to Felix. I'll just have to arrange to have the house cleared and sell it from Delhi. It's the best I can do.

We eat in silence for a few minutes, the soft hiss of the glowing coals reminding me of the crickets in India.

'Is there anyone who can help you, Isabel?'

'Not really,' I say truthfully.

My parents were only children and I am their only daughter. Christmases and birthdays were low-key, with occasional cards from more distant relatives in Dad's home city of Vancouver. His parents came to England when he was seven. Mum was from Holland, born just outside Amsterdam. She was a science lab technician and never spoke of her family, as if they were something to be ashamed of.

I grew up assuming they'd all died over the years.

'I come from a really small family,' I say, hugging my knees to my chest. The red wine has made a channel of warmth inside me, and after just half a glass I can feel the gentle loosening of my thoughts. It's been a long while since I touched alcohol. 'But I'll manage,' I add.

Owen becomes thoughtful. 'Would it help if you knew more about the accident?'

I skimmed through the report sent from the coroner earlier, but it was clinical and didn't tell me much.

'Maybe.'

'We could look online. See what that throws up.'

I shrug. 'If you like,' I say, mildly curious. It's not going to bring them back. Rather, it will probably just set off another wave of grief. Every morning I go through it – a few blissful moments of not remembering, and then it hits me.

But as Owen goes to fetch his laptop, I realise it's not my parents I want to find out about, it's Felix.

Owen puts the laptop beside the pizza box. He types in *fatal car accident Birmingham September 2014* before asking my parents' names and adding *John and Ingrid Moore*. The screen is suddenly filled with reports of accidents and black-spots and fatalities on motorways across the West Midlands, details of various news websites, government statistics, and legal firms offering no win, no fee compensation claims.

Towards the bottom of the page there's a link that relates to my parents. Owen clicks on it and reads out loud. I can hardly bear to listen.

'Husband and wife, John and Ingrid Moore, suffered fatal injuries when the car in which they were passengers overturned on the twenty-eighth of September 2014. Traffic officers, an ambulance and fire crew arrived promptly at the scene, and the road was closed for several hours. The Birmingham couple, seventy and sixty-two, were taken to Queen Elizabeth Hospital, but later died from their injuries. They are believed to have one daughter.

'The driver of the car, Felix Darwin, a thirty-nine-year-old pilot, survived the accident and was also taken to Queen Elizabeth Hospital for treatment. He remains unconscious. It is believed Mr Darwin was taking the couple to the airport when the accident happened.

'Investigating officer PC Brian Campbell commented, "This notorious stretch of road has claimed five lives in as many years. Not only was there more tragic loss of life, but the road was closed, causing major delays in the city. The government needs to allocate funds for addressing such accident black-spots."

'A friend of the family who wished to remain unnamed said, "John and Ingrid were a lovely couple, real pillars of the community. They will be sadly missed by all their church friends."'

I bow my head, tears filling my eyes. Then I steal a brief glimpse of a zoomed-in picture of the scene, the same spot where we stood earlier, next to the metal barrier, although the actual section of road is out of shot. The car's tyres are in the air, trails of smoke winding up from the engine, and the emergency services are standing around.

Owen quickly hits the back button on the browser. 'Are you OK?'

I shrug, feeling numb, and swig down more wine. I reach for the fingerpad and click on another related link. It's a similar piece from the blog of a local newspaper. This time the photograph is from a slightly different angle and, from a casual reader's point of view, it could be anyone's accident, anyone's parents. I can't see the registration number of Felix's Jaguar like I could on the first website. Somehow that anonymises the crash for me.

'I've seen enough,' I say quietly.

Owen scoops several more nuggets of coal on to the fire.

'Do you think he's still in a coma?' I ask. I can't bring myself to say his name. 'What if the High Commission's information was out of date and he's got better and been released?' The fear in my voice is evident, but I mustn't reveal my panic. 'Can you recover from a coma in a month?'

'Let's hope so,' Owen says, pouring a second glass of wine for each of us.

'*Hope* so?' I blurt out. 'No, no, you don't understand.' Then that feeling inside comes again, pressing against my ribs.

'We could phone the hospital if it's worrying you.' Owen looks taken aback, probably having found my comment distasteful.

'Perhaps,' I whisper, looking out of the window.

It's dark, and Owen hasn't drawn the curtains yet. Felix could be outside the house right now, peering in at our cosy little tryst, planning his next move. A wheelchair wouldn't stop him getting what he wanted.

'It might make you feel better to know for sure.'

'Yes,' I say thoughtfully. 'I think you're right.' I don't say that I'm secretly hoping they'll tell me he has died.

Owen passes me his phone and reads the hospital number from the internet. I get transferred through several departments before finally being put through to the head injuries unit.

'Are you a relative?' the nurse asks. She sounds tired but friendly; about my age.

'Kind of,' I say, knowing that won't be good enough. 'Partner, actually.' It nearly kills me to say it. Out of the corner of my eye, I see Owen shift on his cushion. 'I've been away and I only just found out about the accident.'

'I'm so sorry, love, but Mr Darwin left this ward four days ago.'

'He *left*?' My heart thumps. Oh God, I knew it. He's out! I hardly hear what she says next.

'I'm afraid he wasn't improving at all. He's been moved to a longer-term facility with more specialist care.'

My heart slows again, and I let out some kind of noise halfway between a grunt and a laugh.

'So he's still in a coma?'

A pause. 'Yes, he is,' the nurse replies with caution.

'I see.' My mouth is dry. 'A facility, you said. What does that mean? A hospital?'

'A care home for longer-term patients.' Her voice is conciliatory, as if she's just shattered my world. 'You can be assured Mr Darwin is receiving the best care.'

The nurse reels off the name and address of the care

home. I indicate to Owen that I need a pen and paper, and jot down the details. Then I hang up.

'You sure you're OK?' Owen asks. He must have spotted the tears pooling in my eyes.

I give a little nod, then laugh, unsure why. 'Yes, yes, I'm fine.'

I think of Felix, supine, covered from feet to neck in a crisp white sheet, machines all around him registering what life is left in him, a clipboard at the end of his bed, a nurse checking on him every half hour, seeking out bed sores.

I listen for my emotions: the tug of guilt, a thread of remorse, a flicker of regret at what has happened. I sense none of these things, although I will admit to a thin chink of sadness somewhere deep inside my broken heart. It didn't have to be this way.

'He's still in a coma,' I say. 'Not responding.'

I loved him once.

Owen looks at the details I've written down and taps out another internet search. He turns the screen round to face me, and I see a picture of Woodford Grange Nursing Home behind the heading of their website, with the subtitle Long-Term Care Facility beneath. My eyes skim the medical services they offer, finally settling on 'With ten state-of-the-art private rooms, Woodford Grange offers patients and their families the best in medical care. NHS patients accepted by arrangement.'

I squint at the small location map in the bottom corner.

'Owen,' I say, peering at the screen. I click on it to

enlarge it, but the link doesn't work. 'Is this . . .' My mouth goes dry. 'Is this anywhere near here?'

He takes a look. 'It's about five minutes' walk away,' he confirms. 'You go up to the main road, turn left, take a right after the big set of lights, and Woodford Avenue is a bit further up. It's a nice area.'

He stands up and gathers the pizza boxes.

'Handy for visiting,' he adds with a smile, leaving me sitting on the floor as if I've been crushed.

Later, I can't sleep, so I get dressed again, pulling on my new coat like a protective layer. I lock the flat door behind me and go quietly up the outside steps, careful not to make a sound. I venture out into the night, fearful, knowing I shouldn't be doing this.

The air smells still and dangerous, freezing my lips as I walk briskly towards the main road, puffing out shots of icy breath. It's two-forty a.m.

Soon I'm at the large intersection, turning right where Owen said. Woodford Avenue is easy to find – a wide, tree-lined street that, if it had been daytime, would have made for a pleasant stroll. But as things stand, I tread tentatively down the avenue, past a mix of large detached homes, buildings carved up into smart flats, a doctors' surgery and a dentists' practice, and finally, midway along on the right, the imposing façade of Woodford Grange Nursing Home.

A breath snags in my chest, making me cough. I stand opposite the looming red-brick building, reading the navy blue and gold sign attached to the front wall of the in-and-out driveway. It bears the same logo as the website.

'He's in there,' I whisper, hardly daring to open my frozen mouth in case someone hears.

I shudder inside the warmth of my coat. Suddenly aware of the streetlight above me, I move beneath the cover of a tree.

Lights are on inside the care home, and all but one of the windows has curtains or blinds drawn across. I hold my breath as a nurse walks past a ground-floor window. She stops and stares out, almost looking directly at me, before raising her arms and swishing the curtains closed.

As I stand in the shadows, I can't help wondering if Felix is in that room; can't help wondering if I'm any better than he was as I lurk outside in the dark, watching, waiting, wondering.

13

There's a terrible noise around me – blaring horns, something urgent going on, a din dragging me out of my sleep. I wake up with a lungful of gasped breath, my eyes drawn wide with fright even though I'm so tired I could sleep for a month.

I turn to my right. Someone is banging on the car window.

'Wake up, you stupid cow,' he says, his scowling face pressed to the glass. 'You've missed the lights twice!'

I'm about to wind down the window but decide against it.

Horrified, I crunch the car into first gear and just make it across the lights before they turn red again, cutting off the car behind as the man leaps back into his seat.

'Fuck,' I whisper to myself, heading home slowly. I repeat this for most of the journey. It's dark, it's raining, and I've just bloody well dozed off at the lights. I can see the headlines: *Sleeping Detective Causes Traffic Pile-up . . . Drugged-up Cop to Blame for Serious RTA . . .*

By the time I pull up outside our house, the rain has turned from a nasty late October drizzle into a torrential winter storm. My usual parking spot has been taken by a green car that started pulling up outside our house a week ago when new neighbours moved in, so I end up squeezing into a tight spot round the corner in the next street.

I dash from the car to my house. No one has thought to put on the outside light so I fumble the key into the lock, clutching my bag, a stack of files and some shopping I picked up, as well as Adam's grey suit from the dry cleaners.

I stumble into the hallway, dropping everything on to the floor before kicking off my soaking shoes and removing my dripping coat. It's freezing in the house, making me wonder if the boiler's packed up again. It should have come on several hours ago.

'Grace, Stella – anyone home?' I call up the stairs.

I know my daughters are here from the sliver of warm yellow light seeping from beneath Stella's door. I hear the soft hum of their voices as they chat to each other, plotting sisterly mischief, even though Grace is too old for all that.

'Grace, shouldn't you be at work?' I yell.

After her A Levels, she decided to take a year out, saving up with a couple of part-time jobs, as well as getting some voluntary experience working with special needs children. She intends on spending a few weeks next summer travelling before studying Physiotherapy at university. We're so proud of her, and she deserved a break.

'I called in sick,' she yells back down the stairs, adding an overstated cough at the end.

In the kitchen, I stare at the abyss that is my fridge.

Several potatoes roll about when I open the vegetable drawer, and I find the pot of hummus has developed its own ecosystem. I chuck it away, unpacking the stuff I bought from Spar down the road – chicken quarters and some frozen chips and veg will have to do for tonight.

I flick on the oven and slide a baking tray out of the cupboard, thumping the pale pieces of meat on to it. After my session with Bob earlier, I can't avoid these reports any longer. I have to get them done tonight. If I'm not able to concentrate fully on the Melanie Carter murder case, he'll pull me off it completely.

I glance at my watch again – a habit I can't break – and remember that Adam said he'd be back by eight – ten minutes ago.

The doorbell rings so I call out for someone to answer it as my hands are covered in raw meat, wondering if Adam has forgotten his keys. It rings again, so I rinse my fingers quickly, wiping them on the tea towel as I head for the hall, kicking my shoes out of the way and unlatching the door.

It takes me a moment to register who they are. Remembering why four of our oldest friends are here, on my doorstep, huddling under two tiny umbrellas and holding bottles of wine, a bunch of supermarket flowers and a slab of beer, grinning as if they haven't seen me in ages (they haven't), takes even longer to figure out.

'Lorraine, *hi*,' Maggie sings in her usual cheerful way.

She steps forward for the obligatory peck on each cheek, which quickly turns into one of her unstoppable hugs. It gets her out of the wet and inside, something that's not going to happen with me blocking the doorway, my mouth gaping open. She takes off her coat, and I notice she smells fresh and showered, and is wearing a wool wrap dress, one I doubt she wore to work. Her dark curly hair gleams, and she has lipstick on.

'I can't tell you how much I've been looking forward to seeing you,' she says. 'I've been thinking about tonight all week.'

She drapes her coat over the banister rail, while the other three follow her inside, each administering warm hugs and kisses and bestowing their wares on me until my arms are too full to close the door.

Then Adam runs up the path behind them. As he comes inside, I make a pained, wide-eyed face that only he can see.

'Did you forget?' he whispers while giving me a hug, banging the door shut behind him with his foot. Then he's greeting the others as they shake off the rain.

'Yes, I damn well forgot, Adam,' I say to everyone, feeling so angry at myself. It's pointless hiding my mistake, so I shrug apologetically, handing Adam the wine, flowers and beer. 'Work has taken over a bit at the moment,' I say, hoping they'll understand.

All I can think about are Bob's reports.

'So I'm afraid we'll have to share a few meagre bits

of chicken between eight of us with some frozen veg and chips, and afterwards you can all help me with some urgent reports that need to be filed first thing in the morning.' I cover my face, sliding my hands down to my neck. 'I bet you're all really glad you came, aren't you?'

Maggie, Chris, Damon and Ellie know me well enough to tell me, one by one in their own humorous way, that I am indeed an idiot for forgetting that I'd invited them for dinner. I bumped into Maggie in Tesco only a week ago and, as we hadn't seen each other literally in months, we decided a night together was essential.

They follow me through to the kitchen.

'I wasn't joking, see?' I tell Maggie, pointing at the raw chicken as she turns the screw cap on a bottle of wine. She knows where I keep the glasses, and in a few seconds she's gently pushing a large glass of red into my hand.

'I know you weren't, love,' she says, enveloping me in another hug. Her full and warm body – the body that no doubt dishes out a hundred hugs a day at the primary school where she teaches – helps me relax a little. I even manage a little laugh, opening the kitchen drawer to remove several takeaway menus. I decide that a few hours not thinking about work, chatting with friends, will do me the world of good.

'Indian or Chinese?' I ask.

As penance for forgetting, I offer to fetch the food. It's only a short walk and, to be honest, I need the time to clear my head, to think about how I'm going to fit in the work I need to do.

I've known Maggie and Chris since Grace began primary school, and I also know that their idea of a Friday night get-together often ends some time early on a Saturday morning. Thoughts of spiking their drinks so they pass out on the sofa cross my mind, but I doubt their babysitter would thank me.

No, I'll just have to pull an all-nighter to get the reports done, as well as the extra catching up on the Melanie Carter case so I can run some thoughts by Adam tomorrow. Technically I have the night off from that job, but as any DI knows, leaving work behind when there's a murder investigation is impossible. I doubt I'll sleep anyway, although at least I managed to get the Gresham brothers interviewed today.

The rain has turned into a misty drizzle. I hug my coat around me, trudging through the puddles. We phoned through the orders half an hour ago and by the time I'd had a few sips of wine I began to feel extremely grateful for the extra company tonight. The way the day had unfolded, I was in need of a couple of drinks and some friendly banter.

I walk on, taking a short cut down a narrow street that quickly funnels into a dark pedestrian alley. Trees overhang the high brick walls on each side and the light from the road behind soon fades to nothing. I think back to my meeting with Bob.

'I know you don't want to jump to conclusions about

the two cases, sir,' I said to him, 'but I've now interviewed Melanie Carter's university halls roommate. It was interesting.'

Bob's office seemed stark and characterless due to a shift-about in the department a couple of weeks before. No one had had time for arranging pot plants and pictures, and all his stuff still sat in boxes behind the door.

'Sit down, Lorraine,' he said, pouring out tea. Bob is traditional and always insists on a teapot.

Until now he'd officially remained on the fence about the Alexandra Stanford and Melanie Carter cases being linked, but he was beginning to change. Over the months, we all had.

From the frustratingly small amount of evidence procured, both forensic and witness-based, our original thinking was that Alexandra Stanford had been opportunistically mugged and robbed on her way back from a night out. She'd put up more of a fight than the attacker had banked on, and it had gone horribly wrong. Someone intent on snatching her bag had ended up committing murder. That she'd previously reported being harassed was perhaps a cruel coincidence, although during the month prior to her death, she'd made no complaints. However, it was also a complication, and something I couldn't forget.

But Melanie's roommate changed all this.

Bob and I went over the witness statements again. We only had two that were worthwhile, and to my mind they were unconvincing – a taxi driver who reckoned he'd possibly taken a fare from her during the evening, or seen someone resembling her, and a nightclub doorman who hadn't even correctly picked out Alexandra's face from a selection of photographs. He thought she'd been inside the club for only ten minutes, and remembered someone with red hair leaving looking upset. And of course, as is often the way when it's needed, their CCTV system had been down for a few days.

'Her clothes were pretty suggestive,' Bob had remarked earlier. 'Suggestive of a night out,' he'd added quickly yet sheepishly when he saw my incredulous look. He was right though: Alexandra's short sequinned skirt, her gossamer-thin halter top with no bra beneath it, silver high heels and an empty clutch bag dumped nearby all implied she'd been out on the town. It's just that no one could definitively confirm this. The last known sighting of her was pulled from the CCTV of a bus heading towards the city. She got off after fifteen minutes in Digbeth, and after that we lost her.

'She left the club very upset, if the doorman's statement is reliable – assuming it was even her,' I said, going over the scene photographs for the thousandth time, sliding them around on the desk. 'But just because she's dressed up like the dog's dinner doesn't necessarily mean she was going for a night out. Especially as the doorman isn't a hundred per cent certain it was her. Alexandra may have been meeting someone. She may not have been anywhere near a club.'

Bob shrugged rather dismissively. 'So let's get to your

relevant *stuff* between the two cases,' he said drily, annoyed that I was challenging the official line. It was more a case of him not wanting the cases to be linked after all this time, and facing the ramifications of that. Truth be known, we all felt the same.

I pointed to the pictures again, tapping my pen on the desk, though he didn't seem to know what to say. My theory: he was worried that he'd got it wrong, that changing his mind would undermine his authority. Bob liked to mull things over, but too much time had already passed for my liking. At this rate, it wouldn't be long before both files sank to the bottom of a very big pile of other, more pressing issues and left to fester. Meantime, if we were dealing with a serial killer, what we didn't want was another woman dead.

'The medical examiner's photographs show that Alexandra's ankle had been abraded, almost stripped of a layer of skin. There was a dark greeny-blue shadow remaining in the area of raw flesh. Look.' I show him the picture again. 'It wasn't as deep as the similar patch on Melanie's wrist.' I pass over Melanie's pictures for comparison.

'So Alexandra grazed her ankle while fighting her attacker,' Bob said. I hoped he was just playing devil's advocate. 'We're certain she put up a good fight from the path report. You'd expect to see injuries like this. You know that as well as I do, Lorraine.'

'I'm sure it's more than a graze, Bob, and you know it.'

I stare at the pictures again, wondering if I'm wrong.

Then I read out a section of the report where the pathologist had speculated that a non-surgical instrument had possibly been used, after she'd died, to remove the area of skin – some kind of scraper or file was suggested. It stated there was also evidence of a tattoo on the ankle.

'Melanie had a very similar injury on the inside of her wrist, although the pathologist confirmed the injury occurred before she died in this case. Which would figure, because she died in the canal from drowning.'

Bob was nodding, pushing up his glasses as he scoured the report and photos again.

'Melanie's wound was deeper, more definitive, as if someone had targeted that area on purpose. Perhaps got the hang of what they were doing second time round,' I suggested, sliding another statement in front of him. 'In this statement from February, Alexandra's mother confirmed that her daughter did indeed have a tattoo on her ankle, having got it about a year before her murder. She didn't know what it was of, but described it as a figure of eight. We tried to trace the exact type of ink and tattoo parlours in the area that used it, but the sample was too poor to get a match. Officers interviewed dozens of local tattooists, but none remembered doing a figure of eight on an ankle.'

Bob took off his glasses. He stared at me, allowing me to go on.

'And here's the good bit. Even though Melanie's parents said their daughter had no tattoos, that she'd never do anything so stupid, when Adam and I interviewed her roommate from university earlier today, the girl confirmed that Melanie *had* got one. She'd kept it a secret from her parents, apparently, saying they'd go mad. And guess what? The university friend said it was some kind of symbol.'

I showed him the sketch the friend had drawn for us, watched as his eyebrows raised high above the rim of his glasses.

'The infinity symbol,' I said, folding my arms. 'A figure of eight, near as dammit.'

Bob said nothing.

'Sir?' I said after a few seconds.

He looked up and sighed, clasping his hands under his chin. I had no idea what he was thinking.

'Well,' he said, dead-pan. 'It's food for thought, I'll give you that.' He pulled a wistful face. 'But then again, they've each got hair and legs in common, too.' He pushed back in his chair. 'Do you know how many people have tattoos these days? My Lilian has been talking about getting one. She's thirteen years old, Lorraine. Thirteen.'

I shrugged a reply, pinching my mouth into silence.

'Kids, eh?' I eventually managed. 'Grace went through a phase too,' I told him, which was true. I still can't be sure she doesn't have some kind of tribal symbol inked across her back.

'You know as well as I do that even if we have the makings of a serial killer here, the likelihood of him leaving a signature is about as likely as you getting a tattoo.'

I raised my eyebrows, trying not to react. 'Alexandra's mother didn't believe her daughter would go out dressed like that in a million years. Melanie's mother said her daughter would never contemplate a tattoo. Who were these women trying to impress, Bob?'

Bob looked thoughtful. His face suddenly seemed wise, etched with years of experience. I didn't understand why he was being so resistant. Maybe it was to test me, to see how far I would go. *Push your team hard, Lorraine*, he'd once said to me. *Wring them out.*

'And who was impressed *by* them?' I went on. 'Whoever it was had a certain type, don't you think?' I slid the pictures back in front of him. 'They look similar.' No one was denying it, but of course, it could again be coincidence.

'Alexandra had a young daughter, but Melanie Carter didn't have kids,' I continued as Bob studied the pictures yet again – one bruised, bloodied and strangled, her skin pale against the dark ground; the other waterlogged, tinged blue, her eyes staring out at us. I couldn't give up on them, not now. I wanted him to know everything about them. 'Alexandra was an air stewardess and lived near the airport, Melanie a student. Alexandra was eight years older, and apparently in a relationship, although didn't live with her partner. Melanie was single. Alexandra came to us, hysterical about being stalked, although couldn't provide proof. Melanie never complained of being harassed, though she'd confided in her friend—'

'Let's definitely keep an open mind,' Bob interrupted,

glancing at his watch. 'I know where you're coming from, Lorraine, and of course I can see the similarities. But bear in mind, it could still just be a case of buses.' He suddenly looked pleased with himself.

'Buses?'

'None for ages then two come at once,' he replied, looking solemn.

I stop dead still, nearing the end of the dark street.

'Hello?'

I'm almost at the road that will take me up to the well-lit high street, but I feel the presence of someone – someone so close, I expect a hand to come down on my shoulder.

I swing round, muscles tense and ready, but there's no one there. I take a moment to scan the dark spaces between the trees where the wall is crumbling, certain I'll see a shadow slip away.

But then I'm reminded of my paranoia when I went to fetch Grace, how as I'd left the sports centre I'd called for a couple of uniforms to give the spinney the once-over, convinced there'd been someone lurking there. Twenty minutes later they confirmed the site was clean, not even evidence of any animals.

My mouth is dry from the lingering red wine. I swallow down my fear, telling myself that there are only so many nights I can go without a decent night's sleep before even a phone ringing nearby or the squeal of a happy child is guaranteed to trip me into a panic attack.

'Anyone there?' I call out nervously, wanting to make sure. Then I walk on, hands shoved in pockets, my breath sitting high up in my throat.

Ten minutes later and I'm inside Wing Yum's. It's packed with people waiting for their food. I can barely get to the narrow counter, and when I give them my ticket number I'm told it'll be a while yet.

I take the time to gather my thoughts, to figure out how I can condense three ten-page reports into a couple each after everyone's left, and what my next actions regarding Melanie and Alexandra will be.

Then I see a man across the street.

The plate-glass window of the takeaway is dripping with condensation and spattered with crudely painted-on back-to-front lettering advertising their opening hours, but I'm still able to watch him, standing inside the bus shelter on the pavement opposite. I can't see his face, but he's very thin. Was he staring at me?

He's smoking a cigarette and is dressed in a long dark coat with a black knitted hat, the peak of which is tipped forward, obscuring all but his pointy chin. His hand comes up to his mouth every few seconds, a bead of orange glowing at his mouth. When he sees me looking, he turns away.

Adam locks the front door and comes back into the living room. I gather up half a dozen empty silver foil trays, stacking them precariously in one hand while carrying several glasses with my other. I head for the kitchen. Adam is close behind me with empty cans and a couple of wine bottles.

'I still can't believe I forgot they were coming,' I say, squashing down the rubbish in the bin.

'I can,' Adam replies. 'I'm surprised you remember your own name at the moment. You're overworked, Ray, and . . .'

I go back into the living room with a wet cloth before I can hear what he says. He's right, but I don't know what to do about it. Maggie offered to help clear up, but I refused, preferring everyone to leave so I could get on. Even though it's gone midnight, there's still time left to make progress with the reports.

I wipe down the coffee table, scooping rice and spilled food into my hand. Adam is suddenly behind me, his palms coming down on my shoulders. As I stand up, his lips press down on my neck.

'No, Adam,' I tell him, as gently as I can. 'I really can't tonight.' I point to my laptop on the side table. 'I have loads to get done.'

'Lorraine . . .' But he stops, sighing, knowing he's on a hiding to nothing.

'A strange thing happened earlier,' I tell him back in the kitchen as I'm rinsing out the cloth. I instantly regret bringing it up. He's going to think I'm really losing it. 'It's probably nothing, but I thought I heard someone following me down the street to the takeaway. And there was a man waiting outside while I picked up the order.'

'You should have called me to fetch you, love.'

'You couldn't have left the others alone, especially after I'd forgotten they were coming. Anyway, it was probably nothing.'

I have no idea where the lie comes from. I can still feel the fear burning inside me as I walked briskly home, almost running by the time I got back.

'Ray, I'm so sorry you were scared,' Adam says, settling his hands down on my arms again.

'I shouldn't have mentioned it,' I say, feeling silly. I don't think he believes me, and he's probably right.

'Maybe it really is time to see the doctor, love. Get yourself checked out.'

When I don't reply, unable to tell him I already have, he gives me a kiss before heading off to bed.

By ten to two the overdue reports are finished and emailed to Bob. Although rather more brief than I'd have liked, it's a weight off my mind. I make another coffee before reading through DC Rowlands' earlier interviews, making a long list of action notes, the main one being a request for the details of every single stalking or harassment case in the last year within a five-mile radius of the city.

Alexandra Stanford may have been ignored, and Melanie's fears heard too late, but that doesn't mean we shouldn't take similar reports seriously. The chink of acknowledgement I saw in Bob's face earlier mustn't be wasted. I need him onside if I'm to pull in the resources to get a team together to cover this. It could be a lengthy process and may come to nothing, but I don't see myself ever sleeping again if I don't cover all the bases.

Yawning, I jot down some more notes to mention to Adam tomorrow, suggesting that some of our top officers reprioritise their load. Then I re-read the statement made by Melanie's university friend, Amy. She hadn't come forward before, having quit her course early for health reasons, because she'd felt vulnerable and scared. She admitted she'd tried to pretend Melanie's death hadn't even happened, and only got in touch now because she felt guilty after seeing the reconstruction on television. Her mum convinced her to call the number.

The girls had known each other for two years, and were both studying Sociology. Amy had noticed a change in Melanie about a year ago, as if she was becoming depressed. At first Amy thought she was struggling with her work, but it later became apparent it was a man. An older man who wouldn't leave her alone.

'He was cunning though,' Amy told us. 'He always seemed to know when she was alone. I never saw him. Not properly, anyway.'

A man who likes redheads with tattoos, I think to myself, doodling over and over a figure of eight on a scrap of paper.

Just after three, I decide there's still enough time to sleep before the alarm goes off at six. I go into the spare room so I don't wake Adam. By quarter to four I'm getting out of bed again – not because of work or insomnia this time, but because I thought I heard a noise.

I creep downstairs and head for the kitchen. I flick on the light, slip quietly into the rear porch leading off the utility room, and find that the back door is unlocked.

I open it, staring out into our small patch of garden. The side gate is banging in the wind, even though it's always kept closed. I go outside, grab it and shut it, my bare feet stinging on the gravelled area where we and several neighbours store our dustbins. There's no one there – just the distant sound of a dog barking. Taking a last look out into the night, I go back inside and upstairs to bed.

14

I stifle a yawn, but thirty seconds later it's back. I sit in front of Bob, trying to stay alert, trying to stop my mouth opening and my eyes screwing up, but it's hard. Besides, the look he gives me makes me wonder just how supportive he's going to be. I've always been able to rely on him to give me leeway, to give me the benefit of the doubt, to let me follow my instincts. But now, I'm not so sure. I need to play his game, especially if I want to keep Adam onside. If only I could explain how I feel, how I'm finding it hard to cope; but I can barely admit this to myself, let alone anyone else.

'Late night, Detective?' Bob says. His purple tie is loose around his short neck, the colour clashing with his sandy beard. He has hair to match, cropped and neat, and his alert grey eyes sing out to me that he had a great night's sleep, despite the early hour he arrived at the office.

'Not really,' I say, remembering the ridiculous time I sent the email to him.

'I'm afraid the reports will need more detail than you

gave,' he tells me, as an aside to the main reason for our meeting. He spreads his hands out on his desk. 'I'm sorry to do this to you, Lorraine, but they'll get rejected in their current state. I realise it's—'

I'm already holding up my hands. 'It's fine.'

I'd been expecting it. Part of me doesn't even care any more. I have a headache to split a rock in two, and I didn't have time for breakfast. My stomach gurgles with the remains of last night's Chinese food.

'I'll get on it later.'

This prompts Bob to glance at his watch just as a young constable stops by his office.

'Ma'am,' he says to me hopefully. He nods at Bob briefly. 'I was just wondering if you'd had a chance to sort out those references. My exams are next week.'

He is fresh-faced and keen, reminding me of myself a decade or two ago. I know his work and he's good at what he does. He'll have no problems with his exams. His only stumbling block is my tardiness.

'Of course . . .' I say, staring at him, hoping he doesn't mention it's the third time he's had to remind me. 'I'll get on to it later this morning.'

'If you could, ma'am, I'd really appreciate it.'

'Yes, that's fine,' I say calmly, giving him a tight smile, wishing he'd just go.

After a second's hesitation, the constable gives Bob a quick glance and leaves, heading off down the corridor, no doubt going to bad-mouth me to his colleagues.

Bob stares at me, eyebrows slightly raised, waiting a

moment before continuing. When he does, his voice has changed. It's slow and deliberate, as if he's trying to get the measure of this stranger sitting in front of him.

'I genuinely forgot,' I explain. 'I'll catch up with him later.'

Bob nods, accepting what I say, but when I leave his office it feels as if there's something uncomfortable hanging between us, something that wasn't there half an hour ago. Whatever's been fogging up my mind, clamping itself around my entire being as if I'm slowly separating from the rest of the world, is now wedged firmly between me and my boss. Things have got to change before it gets between Adam and me.

In the incident room, several officers stare at me, looking concerned. I wonder if I'm imagining it, when Rowlands slides a list of names across the desk to me.

'They are all within a five-mile radius of the city centre and each complaint occurred within the last twelve months. Some are more serious than others.'

He watches as I read the list. Twenty-four names in all.

'You'll see I've separated some out, as you asked. With these, there was absolutely no evidence of these women being stalked, even though they were insistent. The top three out of the eight are the most notable.'

I nod and bite my lip. It's almost as if Alexandra Stanford has joined us in the room, pacing angrily around me, her fists balled into tight knots by her side, as they were when I first met her.

It was only coincidence that brought us together in the

first place. Early in the year she'd been pestering and begging the desk sergeant for several days in a row, lurking around the station inside and out, approaching any officer who would stop and listen to her. I suppose by being in the vicinity of the building she somehow felt safe, as if he wouldn't get to her there. Whoever *he* was.

'He fucking stole my log,' the woman said to me outside the main entrance the first time I encountered her. She looked as if she hadn't slept in weeks.

I'd actually been looking for Adam. It was raining and we were supposed to be travelling home together because my car was at the garage.

The water had turned her hair almost blood-coloured – long, rusty-red strands plastered to her cheeks. I assumed she was crying, though her face was soaking anyway. Her words were choked and barely intelligible.

'Calm down,' I said, hardly able to leave her in such a state. She'd fallen on the steps and was rubbing at her knee, muttering over and over about some notebook she'd lost. 'Is there someone I can call for you?'

She was shaking her head frantically, the ends of her hair spraying water droplets.

'He fucking took it,' she spat, as if she hadn't heard me. 'I knew he would. Now they don't believe me. No one will *ever* believe me.'

She was hysterical so I took her inside to calm her down. I put her in a quiet interview room, and got someone to make her a cup of tea. I texted Adam to let him know I'd take a taxi back later.

'If you tell me what's been going on, I'll get someone to talk to you.'

She told me that her name was Alexandra Stanford and that she had a stalker – a man she'd dated for a short while, but after she'd ended it, he wouldn't let her go.

I was as reassuring as I could be. I'd already heard about her case, knew how her sister had previously come to vouch for her and corroborate her story, and I also knew that everything had been done to help her. These types of complaints are notoriously tricky to prove, and even if we think it's worth pursuing, evidence-gathering is a lengthy and often unrewarding process. Many times, the case will never make it past the Crown Prosecution Service, let alone result in a prosecution.

I tried to calm the poor woman, but she wouldn't stop crying. If I'd known then what I now know about Melanie, it would have been different.

'He won't leave me alone,' she said, hiccuping with sobs. She went on to tell me that he often broke into her house, that he cut off her hair once while she was asleep, rearranged things in her home, or just sat in her bedroom at night, watching her, so that when she woke up, he was there, staring at her. 'And the gifts just won't stop coming. Expensive things – jewellery, porcelain ornaments. All kinds of stuff I don't want from him.' She told me she'd had to take time off work as an air stewardess because of the stress.

I had a word with the officer who had previously dealt with her. 'Can't you see she's vulnerable?' I said. 'Something needs to be done.' It wasn't my responsibility, but I couldn't just send her away.

'She's always here these days, ma'am,' he said, tapping the side of his head and giving me a look.

'We've followed procedure, but there's simply no evidence. She's a bit of a nuisance now, to be honest,' another officer added, while trying to remain sympathetic.

I went back to talk to Alexandra. She explained how her carefully kept log of events that would help secure some sort of action against him had strangely disappeared from her house.

'You are aware, love, that despite lengthy investigations and much time spent by our officers on this case, they can't actually locate the person you claim is harassing you. In fact . . .' I paused and swallowed. I could see the pain in her bloodshot eyes, making the whites appear cracked. 'We haven't been able to identify anyone called Jimmy Hardwick at the address you gave. Your stalker, as you know him, doesn't seem to exist.'

I double-checked the address with her, but she confessed that she'd never actually been to his house during the short time they'd officially been seeing each other. She admitted it could be fake, that she'd been taken in by him. She said he was very persuasive, charming.

The property belonged to a family who had never heard of Jimmy Hardwick, and their background checked out. I also went over the description Alexandra had given in her statement, showing her file pictures in case it threw something up. But we weren't able to identify him, and even his mobile phone number proved unhelpful. It wasn't in use.

'He was always so secretive,' Alexandra confided. 'But he won me over because he was so fascinating and alluring when we were dating. But then he began to get more and more intense, wanting me to do weird things. Stuff I wasn't into.' She bowed her head.

I had to go shortly after that, but I left her in the care of a couple of other officers, talking about protection and strategies to help her cope. I didn't think any more about Alexandra Stanford until her body turned up in an alleyway a few weeks later.

'Thanks, Ed,' I say, staring blankly at the names DC Rowlands has given me.

None is familiar. I wish Alexandra's name was on there, meaning she was still alive, meaning that I could go and interview her properly, like I'm about to do with the first woman on the list.

Bethany Adams doesn't hear me knocking on the door of her flat, although I hear her – singing at the top of her voice. If I wasn't on police business, I wouldn't mind stopping and listening. She's good, trilling out a song I recognise yet can't quite place.

I knock again, louder this time. The singing stops, and moments later a woman answers the door.

'Bethany Adams?' I ask, and she nods cautiously. 'I'm Detective Inspector Lorraine Fisher. I was wondering if I could come in and have a word.'

She nods again, stepping aside and allowing me in.

'I can't believe you're actually here,' she says with a soft yet suspicious smile. She shows me into her small living room, looking me up and down. 'Talk about shutting the stable door,' she remarks incredulously.

Bethany looks to be in her early twenties with waves of blonde hair – not the type of person I imagined to be belting out such a powerful song. She's beautiful and sweet, and it's hard to believe anyone would want to harass her.

'*Sweeney Todd*, isn't it?' I ask, hoping I've got it right.

'I'm Mrs Lovett,' she says, nodding proudly. 'It's dress rehearsal tonight.' Bethany lets out a laugh that reminds me a little of Grace.

'Have you always lived in Birmingham?'

'Mostly, yes. I was at university here and kind of got stuck here after I graduated. I'm an actress really, you see, but making a living is hard. London's far too expensive. Until my big break comes, I'm doing shifts at a call centre.' She rolls her eyes in an overstated way, as I imagine she might do on stage.

'And earlier in the year, you became involved with someone,' I say, seguing into the reason for my visit.

Bethany rolls her eyes again and I notice her pale cheeks spread with the beginnings of a raspberry blush. 'No,' she snaps, frowning.

'It's why I'm here. To ask you about . . .' I glance at my file. 'About Joe Douglas.'

I'm playing devil's advocate, but very often women will lodge a complaint about a long-term partner. Many times it turns out to be a domestic dispute rather than a classic harassment case as initially reported. And it obviously makes a difference to how we proceed.

Bethany flinches. 'There was no way I was involved with him, just so you know. He just became a bit obsessed with me.'

'You made a harassment complaint against him.'

'Why the sudden interest? When I reported him, I was made out to be a nuisance.'

'Such complaints are tough to prove,' I tell her, doubting she was treated as a nuisance. 'We pretty much either have to catch them in the act, or we need a lot more than your say-so. Did you keep a log of the alleged incidents?'

It's a sad fact that the majority of victims don't make a record, let alone in the detail required for it to be viable in court. Mostly, they cling to the hope it will all just go away, believing each violation will be the last.

'No,' she says. 'I didn't know I had to.' Her eyes flick nervously between me and her fingers.

I explain how a real-time diary, logging not only the act of harassment itself but things such as what the per- petrator was wearing at the time, car registration numbers, even the weather conditions, is what's needed even to begin a case against him.

'Can you recall if any of our officers paid Mr Douglas a visit, or gave him an unofficial warning?' Our records don't indicate this, but I want to double-check.

'No,' Bethany laughs indignantly. 'They just took down a few details from me then sent me packing.'

'It's just that I ran a few searches on the name and the address you gave, and I can't find any record. Did he move perhaps?'

Bethany shrugs. 'Quite likely,' she says evasively, almost as if it never happened.

'Is he still harassing you?' I ask, concerned she could be in danger.

She shakes her head vehemently. 'No. He eventually lost interest and it all stopped.'

'In your statement from January, you said that he would phone you incessantly, make threats to your personal safety, stand outside your door, or sit in his car across the street watching you, following you when you came out. You even thought he'd been in your flat, but couldn't prove it.' I skim-read the rest when Bethany's eyes fill with tears. I don't want to traumatise her.

'What if I said I believed you about everything that's happened?' I watch her reaction. 'What if I was willing to help find this man, make sure he's not going to do it again?'

'Fuck, no,' Bethany says, wide-eyed.

She's on her feet, pacing the small living room, wrapping her arms around her waist.

'Just leave it, will you? I don't want it stirred up again. It's fine, I've dropped the case now.'

She goes to the window and stares out, suddenly turning to face me, silhouetted by the bright day outside.

'Promise me you won't do anything. *Please*? Luke wouldn't be happy.' She covers her face.

'Who's Luke, love?'

'Luke Manning,' Bethany says, as if I should know. 'My boyfriend.'

'Ah,' I say pensively, although I can't help feeling that she's putting on some kind of act.

I leave the 1970s block of flats to the sound of Bethany warming up her voice in a series of frantic scales. On the way back to the station I drive past a row of shops and, on a whim, I pull into a parking spot.

Inside the pharmacy, I get the usual grilling about what other medication I'm taking, why I'm buying a large box of codeine pills, if they're for me, and do I know I mustn't take them for more than three days in a row. *How about three bloody weeks?* I growl in my head, knowing they're the only thing that will keep me going. On impulse, before the pharmacist rings them up, I grab a box of Pro-Plus from the shelves.

'For my daughter,' I say pointlessly, shaking the box before placing it on the counter. 'She has a late-night job. And exams.'

But the pharmacist isn't interested in my excuses. I hand over the money and make my way back to the car. I swig some water from a bottle and wash down a couple of pills. By the time I get back to the station, having stashed the boxes in the glove compartment, I'm feeling a hell of a lot better.

15

I don't understand why Owen would do this, why anyone would be so kind to someone they barely know. In turn, it makes me wonder what he's after, what his intentions are. I can virtually hear Mum's disappointed voice: Oh Isabel, think about it, will you? He's only after one thing. I thought Felix was the only man for you? You're so good together.

The truth is, Mum never saw the dark side of Felix – the side that sent shivers of pleasure through me one moment, yet slayed me with a look or a single word the next. In their company he was always charming, caring, the perfect husband for the daughter they so desperately wanted to see happily married. Mum and Dad were traditionalists. Since my teenage years I'd always felt as if I was a slight disappointment to them, not quite living up to their expectations. Even after all the bad stuff kicked off, they refused to believe it outweighed all the good things.

Now I can hardly bear how much I miss them. It makes

me feel sick to think that I'll never see either of them again. I fight back the tears, block out the guilt, suddenly feeling completely alone in the world. Though I can't help wondering that if they were alive, they'd be utterly ashamed of what I've become.

I turn to Owen, holding the new mobile phone gratefully. I can't believe he's done this for me.

'I'll get some cash and pay you back,' I tell him.

The phone is basic, but will allow me to make the calls I need. And, being pay-as-you-go, no one will know I'm using it. Even if Owen had to give a name to activate the SIM, it doesn't matter to me. It'll be at the bottom of someone's wheelie bin in a few days' time.

'Nonsense,' he says. 'It was cheap as chips at the super-market. I couldn't resist.' He grins.

'Why are you being so kind to me?'

Owen breaks off from unpacking groceries into the fridge. He straightens up, rubbing his lower back. 'Honestly?' Something in his eyes twinkles. 'Because I like you.'

I can't help the smile. 'I'm really grateful. Thanks.'

And I truly am, but there's something else bothering me, something so foreign-feeling and abnormal that it takes me a while to figure it out. It's only when he asks me to stay for coffee that I realise what it is.

I like him too.

I'm drawn to his kind face, his sharp blue eyes, and the way his stubbly bottom jaw juts out when he's thinking. I like the way one thumb hooks into his belt loop as he's talking to me, as if he doesn't quite know what to do with his hands, and I find his gentle manner endearing and safe.

What's bothering me most is that in a few days' time I won't ever see him again.

There's a moment's awkward silence as he makes the coffee, and all I can think about is how he doesn't really know me; can't possibly understand what I've been through and how damaged I've become. He certainly doesn't need someone like me in his life. I resolve to be more cautious, watch my back like never before.

'I hope it proves useful anyway,' he says, giving me a quick look as he bends down into the fridge. But then he stops thoughtfully, hand on the door. 'Do you think knowing more about your parents will bring you some peace? I can sense you're really struggling.'

He makes a sympathetic face before retrieving a packet of chocolate cookies from one of the shopping bags. He puts them on the counter as if they'll fix everything, telling me to help myself.

'When I lost my dad to cancer,' he continues, 'I found talking to the doctors who'd treated him incredibly comforting. They gave me a deeper understanding of what Dad had gone through. It helped me come to terms with my loss.' He leans on the worktop counter, facing me. 'Don't bottle it up, Isabel.' He smiles warmly.

I don't want to admit it, but Owen is right. The phone call to the hospital gave me no closure whatsoever about Mum and Dad; all I found out about was *him*. I do need to know more about how they died, if their lives ended peacefully.

'Does that make sense?' he asks.

'Perfect sense,' I say with a sigh. No one's ever understood how I feel quite so well.

I glance at my new phone, noticing that it's barely charged.

'I'll have to wait until this is ready to use, though.'

Truth is, I want to know now, but the thought of speaking to anyone myself seems far too painful to contemplate. As ever, Owen senses my trepidation.

'Would you like me to call for you?' he offers.

I barely need to give a nod before he has his laptop open on the hospital website again, getting the correct number.

A moment later, he's talking to a secretary, explaining who I am, and requesting the relevant doctor calls me back as soon as he can. Owen recites my new mobile phone number before hanging up.

'The consultant is in surgery right now, but she promised he will call you. His name is Mr Thomas.'

Later, back downstairs in the flat, I discover the only signal to be had is by the kitchen window. I leave the phone on the sill charging while I make a list of things to do, but I've barely sat down before I hear its shrill ring tone.

I stare at the screen, panic-stricken by the 'No Caller ID'.

'Hello?' I say nervously, but breathe out when the caller

introduces himself as Mr Thomas, consultant neurologist at the Queen Elizabeth Hospital. He sounds slightly breathless, as if he's walking – perhaps down a long hospital corridor, dashing between wards or theatres.

I instantly warm to his soft tones as he launches into an apology as well as condolences for the loss of my parents. He tells me he remembers them well.

'I appreciate everything you did for Mum and Dad. I regret not being there for them.'

Thankfully, Mr Thomas doesn't ask where I was.

'Did you . . . did you treat both of them?' I ask, hoping the details will ease my guilt.

'Indeed I did. And I'm afraid their injuries were severe. I did everything I possibly could.'

Mr Thomas sounds as if he's told thousands of grieving families bad news. His voice is deep and reassuring, yet strangely upbeat too, suggesting the whole process, from trauma to death, is entirely natural to him.

'Thank you,' I say, not wanting to sound ungrateful, but I need to know more. 'So, did they . . . do you know if they—'

'Suffered?'

It's as if he can read my mind. If he can, he'll be seeing Mum and Dad lying in adjacent hospital beds, covered in crisp white sheets with peaceful smiles on their faces, their interlinking fingers bridging the small gap between the beds, holding on to each other even as death is imminent. Mum and Dad had been in love since the moment they met.

'It's hard to tell,' he says.

My heart bangs out a single almighty thud. I let out a sob.

'Their injuries were very serious indeed. I can provide medical details if you wish, but you may find it upsetting.'

For a moment, I don't say anything. I *can't* say anything.

'Sorry, no . . . I don't . . .'

My hand goes to my forehead. I thought this would help, but it's not helping at all. I just want Mum and Dad back. I fight against the tears, feel my ribs tighten around the ache in my heart.

The consultant must have misheard me, because he continues, thinking I do want the details.

'I first encountered them in A&E with head, facial, neck and upper body lacerations. They'd each suffered massive blood loss . . .'

His voice fades into a stream of painful jargon. I simply can't believe he's talking about my parents.

Femoral compound fractures to both legs . . . the paramedics stopped the bleeding . . . the main problem was her neck . . . massive nerve damage . . . cranial fractures . . .

'Please,' I whisper, but the consultant doesn't hear me. I take the phone away from my ear, but I can still hear him.

Your father's spinal injuries were severe . . . the contents of his skull . . . I opened him up on the operating table . . .

'No! Stop!'

I think I'm going to throw up. I slide down to the floor, leaning against the kitchen unit. I can't feel anything – not

160

the cold tiles, not the cupboard door as I bang my head backwards against it, nor the splinters of floorboard as I gouge my nails into the wood.

I wish I hadn't heard those things. I'll never be able to erase them.

'Mr Thomas,' I say as bravely as I can. The bitter tang of bile is in my mouth. 'I think you must have the wrong patients.'

Convincing myself of this is the only way I can make sense of it.

'No, I remember them well. It was their personal story that stuck with me. Before she died, your mother mentioned that someone dear was missing. A daughter, I believe. I'm so sorry if you've lost a sister too.'

I'm breathless, unable to speak.

'Your mother managed to tell me that they were going to start a new life in Spain. She mentioned someone called Felix, how good he'd been to them, how he'd been like a son to them. I am so very sorry for your terrible losses, Miss Moore.'

I don't bother saying goodbye. I just press the end-call button with a shaking finger.

I sit perfectly still for what seems like ages.

It was my fault they were leaving England; my fault Felix was driving them to the airport.

My fault Mum and Dad are dead.

Finally, when I'm able, I run out of the flat, scrambling up the stone steps to Owen's front door. Tears blur my vision as I bang on the knocker, pressing the bell over and over. I just want to be with someone, anyone, until this terrible feeling inside me subsides.

'Hey,' says a voice behind me. A pair of steadying hands are placed on my shoulders. Owen has also just come up the steps from the street. 'What's wrong? I've just been to the library to return some overdue books.'

I turn round and fall against his chest. I sob into the strong valley of his shoulder, not caring that my arms are wrapped tightly around his waist. I hear the key go into the lock above me and Owen shuffles inside with me still attached to him. I know I'm talking gibberish through my hysteria, but I just can't stop crying.

'I . . . I just wish I'd never called him.'

He lowers me on to the sofa and covers me with a blanket. Then he makes me sweet tea and gets me to tell him everything the doctor said, even though it hurts like hell.

'I'm so sorry,' Owen says calmly. He's sitting right next to me, our thighs wedged together on the sofa.

I nod, grateful that he is there.

We spend the next hour talking – or rather I talk and Owen listens, and gradually, slowly, the shock of what I have just learned sinks in. While it doesn't hurt any less, I somehow feel more detached.

Exhausted, I rest my head back against the cushions. Owen's palm slides over my forehead and down my neck. The backs of his fingers brush along my jaw.

'Try not to think about it. I'll stay with you.'

'Thanks,' I say. He's a good listener. But I haven't told him about Mum's last words, how she said that Felix had been kind to her and Dad. The thought makes me feel sick. Mum wouldn't lie.

'Perhaps you should visit their graves,' Owen suggests in a soft voice.

I look up slowly, opening my raw eyes. I give a little nod. 'You're right,' I say, feeling a pang of sadness that I don't even know where they are.

With Owen's help, it only takes a couple of phone calls to establish that my parents' ashes were interred at Bluebell Meadow, a natural burial ground near Kings Norton. Somehow they don't seem so irretrievably lost any more. Before we leave, I wash my face and freshen up. I must at least try to stay strong, even though I can't imagine the hurt ever going.

'It's just like Mum and Dad,' I tell him on the drive there, trying to be brave, 'buying up a pair of plots in an eco-cemetery.'

I had no idea they'd done it.

I imagine them coming to look together, wandering around the meadow, picking out the exact spot where they wanted to be laid to rest among the wild flowers, maybe choosing a commemorative tree to be planted on top. I envisage them looking at cardboard coffins for their remains, and requesting no pretentious plaques or faded plastic flowers. They'd have asked for a simple service with only one short hymn.

When we get there, I force myself to imagine that it's someone else's grave we're visiting, not the premature resting places of my mum and dad. It's the only way I'll get through this. When I left England, it didn't cross my mind that I'd never see them again. I hoped one day it would be safe to come back, that life would somehow go back to normal after I'd explained my mysterious disappearance, after everything had died down.

I shiver and pull my coat around me as we get out of the car and head for the cemetery office. The door is locked.

'Damn,' Owen says, glancing at his watch. 'They said they'd be open. It's only half three.'

'Maybe they'll be back in a minute,' I suggest, stamping my feet. It's freezing, with a bitter wind whipping between the regiments of graves. The bright sprays of flowers decorating some of the headstones seem incongruous in this weather.

Owen glances around. 'Bluebell Meadow is up that way, look.' He points to a sign. 'The man I spoke to on the phone gave me the plot numbers, so we could walk up there if you like.' Owen rattles the door again.

'Let's do it,' I say, feeling relieved. I don't want to pore over records, or discuss with a stranger why I wasn't at my parents' funeral.

We walk off up the gentle incline, heading away from the acres of graves with their fancy marble headstones. Some have brilliant gold writing, while others are neglected and crumbling, surrounded by knee-length grass and dotted with empty glass jars that were once filled with flowers.

'I want to be chucked into a river when the time comes,' I say, slightly breathless as we reach the entrance to Bluebell Meadow. A list of do's and don'ts for the cemetery is displayed on a board. Some smart-arse has written 'Don't die' in marker beneath it.

'A little premature to be thinking like that,' Owen says, giving me a look.

For a second, I think he's going to slip his arm around my waist as we enter through the narrow gate, but he doesn't. We trudge on.

The meadow is a large triangle bounded on two sides by woodland and on the third, in the distance, by a dual carriageway. Young trees are dotted about the huge field, presumably to mark the graves of loved ones. As we walk along the tarmac path we can see the mown pathways cut through wilder areas where the interments take place. Here and there we pass by mounds of freshly dug soil, or some that have much shorter, newer grass growing on them. Benches made from rustic poles are placed in pleasant spots, some with plaques to commemorate the dead.

We walk on in silence for another five minutes until we are at the furthest reach of the meadow, right over by the woods.

'Down here, I think,' Owen says, pointing to a discreet sign. He leads me towards the wooded area and on into a sheltered dip.

'This is typical of Mum and Dad,' I say, feeling close to them already. 'Wanting to be off the beaten track and away from everyone else.'

They always liked their privacy.

Owen pulls a scrap of paper from his pocket and looks at the numbers he scribbled down. He glances around, then back at the paper again.

'This way,' he says, linking his arm through the crook of mine.

Something warm winds through me, something comforting, making me feel momentarily grateful and safe, as if I'm not about to visit my dead parents at all.

Eventually, towards the end of the sodden mown path, we stop.

'Here,' he says, pointing down. 'Plots 274a and b. This is where their ashes are buried.' He stuffs the paper back in his pocket and gives my arm a squeeze. 'You OK?'

'I think so,' I say quietly, staring at the comparatively fresh mounds.

I'm shocked by how small they are – no more than a foot or two square each. How could my vibrant and alive parents be reduced to lumps of earth as insignificant as these?

I lay down the flowers we stopped off to buy, letting out a little sob. 'They don't even have name plaques.' I rein in the tears, thinking about what's at stake if I lose control.

'No one has,' Owen replies, pointing to others.

He's right. I study a few of the other nearby graves,

marked only by a change in the ground level or the smallest of wooden number markers hidden in the grass.

'It's not the ethos of the meadow, although I believe they have to be able to locate the plots in case of exhum—' He stops. 'One of my relatives is buried here. The meadow is meant to be more like a nature reserve. It's a beautiful place to sit in summer. There are wildflowers everywhere.'

I smile gratefully, looking up at him. Our arms have come apart so I ease my hand back through the nook of his elbow.

'It's my fault they're dead,' I say, wondering which is Mum and which is Dad. I desperately want to tell him everything, get it off my chest, but I can't.

'You're too hard on yourself,' he says kindly. 'You weren't even in the country when it happened.'

'Exactly,' I say, wishing I could tell him why. 'The fact is, Felix shouldn't have been anywhere near my parents,' I continue, revealing as much as I dare. 'I think he was trying to get at me somehow.'

Owen pulls a surprised face. 'And risk his life in the process?'

'You don't know him,' I say, although he has a point. 'He probably didn't bank on ending up in a coma.'

I shudder at the thought of him waking up; shudder, too, at the thought of Owen finding out the truth about Felix. He'd think less of me for putting up with him, for tolerating what he did to me. Even though I sometimes long to get things off my chest, I know I can't. The truth will go with me to my grave.

After a few moments' silence, I kiss my fingers, bend down and touch each of the soft mounds that contain my parents' ashes. Then I touch Owen's arm. It's time to go.

It's as I turn to leave that I see the shape of a man disappearing into a clump of trees across the meadow, his long camera lens glinting in the sun that has momentarily broken through the dark clouds. If I didn't know better, I'd swear it was *him*.

'Let's get out of here,' I say urgently, walking briskly back the way we came.

It's time to see for myself that Felix is in a coma.

16

'He's utterly charming,' I overheard the mother tell the daughter as I stood outside the kitchen door, listening, biding my time.

Stealing a look at the pair of them, it made me wonder if John and Ingrid Moore's reproductive organs were as sterile as their plain looks and their boringly neat house, if their daughter was, in fact, adopted. Any resemblance to Isabel was purely through their last names.

I heard Isabel mutter a coy comment back to her mother about how it was early days, that we'd only been dating a couple of months and it wasn't yet serious, but how she thought it could be given time.

I went back into the kitchen after my trip to the bathroom, thinking about what I'd overheard. I'd been deadly serious from the moment I set eyes on her.

'*Ansellia africana,*' I said loudly, interrupting whatever other tittle-tattle mother and daughter were exchanging. 'And that beef looks delicious, Mrs Moore. Just how I like it. Nice and rare.'

Ingrid Moore, with her cropped boyish hair and powdery pale skin, was balancing the roasting pan on the lower door of the oven. There was nothing out of place or haphazard about the woman, despite her slightly precarious predicament. She glanced helplessly down at her juice-spattered lemon-coloured trousers, then back at me before looking imploringly down at her daughter, who was wiping a tea towel down her mother's legs.

She gave me a precisely measured grin. It was then I knew she adored me, just like Isabel.

At lunch, seated at their polished rosewood dining table, John told me about the pitfalls of growing rare orchids, particularly *Ansellia africana*, the Leopard Orchid, which I'd found balanced on the cistern in the guest lavatory.

I didn't tell him about the pitfalls of orchids falling off cisterns and being shoved, slightly snapped, back into their pots.

'Isabel tells me you fly,' Ingrid said, aware of how boring her husband sounded. She dabbed at her narrow mouth with a paper napkin. Her lips were the same colour as her skin, her hands sinewy and strong.

'Indeed,' I said, enjoying the moment. 'I work for a private charter company, so I pick and choose my hours and destinations. I prefer the quick Euro-hops. There and back in a day. Especially now,' I added, turning my attention to Isabel.

She was struggling to cut her piece of beef so I pulled her plate towards me and cut it for her. The beef had clearly been grabbed from a supermarket, but I stifled the urge to say anything.

'As a lad, I dreamt of becoming a pilot,' John said. He was wearing a neat navy blue V-neck sweater, probably bought from Marks & Spencer, with a blue and white check shirt beneath. For his age, he seemed lean and fit, although somewhat short for a man. 'That or an astronaut,' he added. Then he laughed, and I had no idea why.

'May I serve myself some extra gravy?' I asked Ingrid.

She was also wearing clothes no doubt purchased from a mid-range store – those fat-spattered pale yellow trousers with a black cardigan, and some kind of nondescript top beneath. A tight string of fake pearls glinted under her surprisingly firm jaw.

'It's quite delicious, Mrs Moore.'

'Of course, Felix. Help yourself. Isabel, help Felix with the gravy, will you?'

The mother was keen to please, grateful that I wanted more of her reconstituted gravy – also bought from the same supermarket, I speculated.

Pleased that I wanted her daughter, too.

'Belle tells me you also used to work at a school, Mrs Moore.'

The mother stole a look at Isabel, a swelling expression hijacking her face, probably because I was referring to her daughter in such fond terms.

'Yes, I was a chemistry lab technician.'

'Mum worked there for nearly thirty years, didn't you Mum?' Isabel added.

Before I had time to digest the various stories that percolated around the table in the small but pleasant dining room for the next hour, it was time for coffee in the living room.

And then it was time to leave.

With Belle, of course.

She was coming back to mine so I could work out when best to fuck her, what to do with her. We'd not done it yet and it was beginning to kill me, especially as I already knew she was *it*.

The One.

But I was nervous. It was a hard thing to get my head around. Not that I'd ever admit it. Besides, all that would be eclipsed by the surprise I had waiting for her at home.

'It was a pleasure to meet you,' I told John and Ingrid at the door. 'And Mrs Moore, have a think where you'd like to go . . . Copenhagen, Venice, home to see family in Amsterdam. I can arrange it.'

I gave her hand an extra squeeze and drove Isabel back to my canal-side penthouse in the city. We climbed the white tiled staircase to my apartment, which occupied the entire top floor of the newly built block. I never took the lift, I'd explained to Isabel the first time she came here. She'd done the maths, worked out how much benefit our loved-up and extra-healthy hearts would get from the extra beats.

I unlocked the door. We went inside. Isabel screamed.

I folded my arms, watching her.

'What's going on?' she said, looking confused.

She laughed incredulously, but then just kept repeating 'What's going on . . . what's going on?' as she walked about the flat fingering her stuff, almost as if she'd never seen it before.

'Why have you done this?' She pressed herself close, looking up at me.

I felt myself growing hard inside my trousers, but had to time it right. They're all angry at first, and I hadn't expected Isabel to be any different.

'Please, Felix, answer me,' she said with a shake in her voice.

'Oh, Belle,' I said sadly, taking her shoulders and guiding her towards her pale pink velour sofa, which frankly looked ridiculous next to my black leather corner set-up. That would be resolved once she'd grown used to phase one. 'I have done you the biggest favour of your life, that's what. Now, let's have a cup of tea.'

I tried to press her down on to the sofa, but she wouldn't budge.

'I just don't get why you've . . .'

Her incessant voice rattled about my flat, so I pulled her close, holding her against me.

'Why are you growling?' Isabel asked.

I hadn't realised I was. She eased herself away from me and my dick sprang forward as far as my trousers would allow. She glanced down. Then she burst out laughing, while I stared at her neck – pale and slim. Vulnerable. I wanted to make her stop.

'Tea makes everything seem better,' I said, shoving my thumbs in my belt loops and hitching up my trousers.

I turned for the kitchen, and by the time I got there my erection had disappeared.

She came up behind me.

'You're completely crazy, and that's why I love you so much,' she sang. 'But we're going to have to take this stuff back tonight. I'm so busy at school all next week. We have an inspection.'

She wrapped her arms around my waist from behind, her head melding with my spine.

I froze. Three things there. She said I was crazy. Second, she just told me that she loved me.

I'd won there then, although I'd always hoped the admission would be more romantic – at least during a candlelit dinner.

Third, there was no way I was taking her stuff back. Ever.

'Belle,' I said, turning within her arms. 'I am not crazy. Crazy in love with you, perhaps.' I wiped a tear from her eye. 'But your stuff is here to stay, my love. And so are you.'

'What are you talking about?'

Isabel's cheeks pinked up. I liked it when they did that. It aroused me.

'You've moved in with me, of course. That's what you wanted, isn't it?' My voice was evenly measured and earnest.

'Not really,' she said. 'When did we decide that? I don't

remember.' She was shaking her head, chewing a nail, but also trying to remain calm. 'I never said I was moving in with you, Felix.'

I'd wanted things to stay calm, but she was beginning to ruin everything.

So I slapped those pink cheeks, ever so lightly, and made them a touch pinker.

She fell quiet immediately.

'You told me you wanted to move in, Belle, don't you remember?' My voice was flat and smooth. 'How can you be so forgetful? So *ungrateful*?'

I turned back to making the tea, shaking my head. She'd stayed in my flat the last two nights anyway, sleeping in the spare room of course, but making use of my company nonetheless. Our marital bliss-style evenings snuggled together watching her crap on television weren't particularly enjoyable, but had to be done. That's when the removals company had gone into her place, using the key she'd given me, and worked their magic on her meagre belongings with boxes and tape, bringing her stuff here while we were eating tough roast beef.

'I'm sorry, I don't remember,' she said, sounding calmer now but still shaking a little as she touched her cheeks. She blinked and picked up a pile of Delft-style print tea towels sitting on my shiny work surface. 'These are mine,' she said. 'Mum brought them back from Amsterdam for me.'

'They look grand in here.' I swallowed and smiled.

'My stuff looks out of place in your flat, Felix,' she

said, frowning, looking unsure of herself. 'I swear I didn't agree to you moving it.' Isabel's voice was barely a whisper, wobbling like a child's. 'I'm going to call Dad. He has a trailer. He will help me take it back. I'm really sorry, Felix, but I think this has all happened too soon.'

'Isabel. *Belle*, my love. You asked – no, you *told* me that you wanted to live with me. You said you adored me, that you didn't want to be with anyone else, and what fun it would be to share this flat together. I did what you wanted. I thought you would be pleased.'

She walked the length of the kitchen and back.

'I just don't remember saying those things, Felix.'

Her face was anguished, pained, trying hard to dig up the memory. She knew that uncovering a recollection about us living together would now be the easier option, even if it wasn't true.

'Oh lovely Belle, you are overworked and tired from those relentless brats at school. Soon there won't be any of you left for me.'

I looked at her breasts tucked coyly beneath her white blouse, probably stuffed into one of her too-small bras, eager to get out.

'You were sitting on the edge of my bed, remember? It was only two nights ago, when you told me you were staying over and I made up the spare room. You told me how much it would mean to you to move in here. You looked me in the eye, Belle. You said it, didn't you?' I cupped her jaw tightly. 'You wanted this. Tell me you did.'

She sighed, her expression sad and sunken. I knew she

wanted to say yes, but instead she pulled her phone from her pocket, pressing some buttons, waiting for it to connect. Her neck was angled back, her face tilted within my palms.

When she took a breath to speak, I swiftly took the handset. She let it go, her mouth dropping open in shock.

'Mr Moore?' I said when he answered. 'It's Felix here. Isabel wanted to tell you some good news earlier at lunch, but wasn't sure how you'd take it.'

I spoke slowly and calmly, adding an extra flourish of confidence as I dodged Isabel's protestations. I already knew John and Ingrid Moore adored me. I stared at Isabel, who made a weak grab for the phone again. I frowned, indicating she should be quiet. She knew it was for the best and finally fell silent, knowing I was only trying to help.

'Sorry, John, yes, Isabel's fine. She's just sneezing. Anyway, the exciting news is that Isabel has moved in with me. Yes, it's marvellous, isn't it? We're serious about each other. Really in love.'

Isabel stared at her feet.

John was ecstatic for us, mumbling something about it being about time, that his daughter would die an old maid if it was left up to her, and how absolutely delighted Ingrid would be at the news. He went on and on, peppering his tiresome conversation with chuckles and congratulations. By the end of his proud-father speech, I'd almost grown quite fond of him. Even if he was the dullest person I'd ever met.

I ended the conversation and hung up. I smiled inwardly. There was no chance John Moore's daughter would die an old maid, but I didn't tell him that of course; didn't tell him anything of the sort.

For a time, Isabel tried to adapt to my ways, and seemed accepting when I told her how I liked things done. But she still kept getting things wrong.

For instance, I explained the direction our shoes must face when placed on the rack in the hallway, how the cutlery should be arranged a certain way in the drawer, and that the mugs must be placed with their handles facing to the right in the cupboard.

There were hundreds of things, if I'm honest, and I didn't think it was unreasonable to ask her to learn. But it ended up with me having to tell her to try harder.

Then one day she said, 'Felix, I just don't see how this is going to work. I love being with you, you know I do, but maybe our ways of doing things are just too different.'

I stared at her, then at various points around the kitchen – her trail of disorder. She'd put the teaspoon down on the work surface *and* placed the bread in the toaster the wrong way up. All in the space of thirty seconds. I'd told her a thousand times, if not more.

'It's not a lot to ask, Belle,' I said from over the top of the newspaper. 'It's actually really easy. What's so wrong with a little order here and there?'

She fell silent then, staring at her feet as she always did when she knew she was in the wrong. Then she became emotional, hiccuping out a couple of sobs, spit collecting at the corner of her mouth until I paid her some attention. Her orange satin robe, the one I'd suggested she shouldn't wear as it made her complexion appear puce, fell open at the waist, revealing large cotton pants and a band of flesh above. I'd never thought of Isabel as plump, but then I'd never seen her properly naked. I wasn't ready for that yet.

'Look,' I said, coaxing her to me. 'All I want is for things to be good, for us to be happy, and for me to take care of you.'

She leaned back against the wall, her hair covering her teary face. Women did this kind of thing, I'd heard.

'You know, you're losing your hair, Isabel,' I told her, concerned because orange nests had been sticking to my feet.

'That's not true,' she replied, looking up at me. She touched her head, feeling around.

'Alopecia is caused by stress.' I went to her and took her in my arms, and for a moment she succumbed. 'You need to calm down.'

'I'm not stressed,' she said stiffly. 'I'm just tired. And I think we . . . I think we need a break.'

'You've only been here a few days. Let things settle. Let us become used to one another.'

'No, Felix. I need some space.'

Her shoulders shook, making her appear fragile, and I noticed the way her lower lip quivered – a beacon of vulnerability.

'But where will you go, Belle?' I asked, genuinely concerned.

'Home to my flat, of course,' she bleated, stomping off to her bedroom, presumably to pack.

'I don't think so,' I said from the doorway.

Isabel whipped round, her moon face shining pure shock.

'I gave up your lease when you moved out. I hope that's OK.'

17

Bob is sitting across the desk from me – the second morning I've ended up in his office before work begins.

His face is stretched taut across his skull, as if whatever he's about to tell me is causing him great concern. But I also sense weariness in his demeanour, a general sagginess in the way he's sitting. I wish he'd hurry up. I need to get on. I glance at my watch in the hope he'll get the hint.

'There's been a complaint, Lorraine.'

He steeples his fingers beneath his chin, but only for a second or two. They end up on the desk, fiddling with a pen.

'A complaint?' My mouth is dry. 'About what?'

'About you, I'm afraid.'

There. It's out. He can relax now, get on with his morning's duties while I absorb the shock.

'Not an official one, you understand, but enough to make me very concerned about how things are going for you. In fact . . .'

Bob falters, and it's here I raise my hands. I stand up, then sit down again.

'A *complaint*?' I don't believe it.

It feels as if he's talking about someone else, not me; not Detective Inspector Lorraine Fisher who's spent two decades in the force, battled against sexism, held on to her position despite taking maternity leave twice, been run ragged trying to give her daughters the best while always being professional at work, given everything to everyone from the bottom of every cell in her body.

I shake my head, narrowing my eyes. I open my mouth to speak, but nothing comes out.

'Two complaints, actually.'

Bob's face pinks up, showing me he isn't enjoying this any more than I am. We've worked on cases together for five years. He knows I'm good.

'Who?' It comes out quietly.

He's already shaking his head slowly, pinching his lips together to indicate that it's not important, that we don't need to go there. I feel my heart skipping a few beats, trying out a new rhythm as it absorbs the news.

'At this stage, that's not the issue, Lorraine. I'm more concerned about you. You're making mistakes, and that's really not like you.' He pauses to draw breath; to take his verbal sword from its sheath. 'Why not take a week or two off, get your head together. I think that's what you need, then we can take it from there.'

There's a barely perceptible tremor to Bob's lower lip

that he thinks I won't notice. I find myself feeling sorry for him having to tell me.

'A week or two off?' I say like an echo. 'What about the Carter review? I can't just walk out on it.'

I stand up and sit down for the second time. I grip on to the chair to prevent it happening again. Something is slipping inside me – the first stones of a landslide if I don't take back control.

'I realise that, Lorraine, and that's what I'm worried about. Your workload has been heavy, not to mention the weekend shifts you've been pulling. I shouldn't have put you on this one, not with everything else. When did you last take a holiday?'

'Jesus, Bob.' I shake my head, unable to understand. 'I'm reviewing two possibly linked murders and you want me to book a fortnight in Benidorm?'

My mind rattles back through the months, which turn into a year and then some, searching for when I last took time off. All I come up with is two days in May when I had a stomach upset. The previous summer I'd taken a week off for what was meant to be a relaxing break at my sister's place in the country. It turned into a nightmare when her son went missing.

'I don't think a holiday is the answer,' I tell him, frowning, realising there must be a mistake. 'And please don't be concerned about me. I'm absolutely fine. I'll work harder, sort myself out. I know I've been a bit preoccupied, but trust me, things will change.' I sigh, hating that I sound so desperate. 'Maybe if you tell whoever made the complaints to come and see me, I can sort it out with them. I'll do whatever it takes.'

When Bob doesn't reply immediately, my heart beats frantically, nervous of what he's thinking.

'I can hardly sort things out if I don't know what's wrong, can I?'

'I understand,' Bob replies matter-of-factly. 'But I'm trying to keep this simple for you, Lorraine. You're one of my best detectives, and I certainly don't want the situation to escalate into anything formal at this stage. But I sense there's something going on, something you need to deal with. So, like I said' – his hands come down gently on the desk again, accompanied by a big sigh – 'take some time off, and come back refreshed. I'll get Adam to hold the fort while you're gone. Call it a holiday.'

It's at this point I'm convinced my heart actually stops for a few seconds. Then I've got Melanie Carter in my head again, her waterlogged body being hauled from the canal, dribbling green and brown froth from her mouth and nose. Predictably, the image of Alexandra Stanford appears too, her neck mangled and bruised, standing on the canal towpath, watching, hands on hips, shaking her head at my incompetence. Wondering why I can't see what's obvious to her.

I cover my face. I can't believe this is happening.

The door clicks open behind me just as my body involuntarily draws in a huge breath. I swing round to be confronted by Adam.

I turn back to my DS. 'Leave it with me, Bob,' I say

desperately. 'Let me prove to you that I'm fine. It's nothing a good night's sleep won't fix. You know as well as I do that it's just a misunderstanding. Let me handle it.' I glance at my watch again. 'Please.'

'Love,' Adam says, his hands coming down on my shoulders.

I shrug them off. Then I stand up again, and this time stay standing up. Bob remains behind his desk. The slippage inside me gathers pace as I look between them both.

'I'm sorry, Bob, but there's nothing in the rule book that says I can be forced to take holiday at a moment's notice.'

'You don't have to take *official* holiday,' Adam says, moving round beside me. I feel his pitying stare. 'Just grab a few days to yourself. It'll do you no end of good.'

'No, Adam, she's right,' Bob says, surprisingly, changing tack. He sighs and turns to his computer for a second, entering a password, preparing to get on with his work. He looks at me briefly. 'I can't force you, Lorraine, but I'm strongly suggesting you consider what I said.' He stops and swallows. 'It's in your best interests. Let me know your decision in the next hour or so.'

Part of me wonders if he's right that I need some time off. I've probably already overstepped the mark, and should just capitulate and go home. If I don't, he could escalate things, even though I know he doesn't want to.

I try to speak but nothing comes out. Instead, I nod, defeated, and grab my bag and coat. I leave Bob's office and rush to mine, but stupidly turn the wrong way down the corridor.

When I double back, I catch a few words of a conversation between Bob and Adam. I hear 'fragile' and 'stressed' in the mix, causing the rest of the landslide to fall as the tears collect in my eyes. I want to tell them that this isn't me, it's not who I am, but I can't risk making a scene so I walk swiftly past.

I know I shouldn't be doing this, not after I went back to see Bob to agree to take time off, but it's just finishing off one or two loose ends. It can't hurt.

'You'll thank me for this,' Bob had said, grateful that I'd finally seen sense and complied. I'd forced a smile, and gone to collect some things from my office before leaving.

It was easy enough to find out where Bethany's boyfriend, Luke Manning, lives – he's had two driving offences in the last couple of months. No one will know what I'm up to. It's important for my own sanity that I ease myself out of work. That's what I tell myself anyway, desperately worried that the team, when they go over things, may perceive my latest ideas about the Carter case as non-priority, or worse, fuelled by incompetence.

I know Bob is only concerned about me, but acquiescing to his wishes, accepting his sympathy, did not come naturally. Perhaps I can prove, somehow, that I've not entirely lost it. Besides, I owe it to Alexandra and Melanie at least to try.

So here I am, on Drayton Avenue, peering up at a 1950s

semi, wondering if anyone actually lives here, because the place looks dilapidated and almost abandoned. Dirty and ripped sheets hang at the windows and the weeds in the front garden are waist height.

'He's away, love.'

I swing round. A man working on his car in the street is leaning out from the shelter of his bonnet, flicking an oily hand at Manning's house.

'Away working,' he explains.

Giving up on the doorbell, I approach the neighbour.

'Do you know when he'll be back?'

I have a feeling it's going to be futile speaking to Luke Manning anyway, but I want to check if he knows anything about the elusive Joe Douglas. My gut says it's worth a shot.

Then in my mind I see Bob's grim expression, hear him suspending me officially when he finds out I've gone behind his back.

I give my head a little shake, unable to take in the day's events. For the first time in my life, I've been dropped from a case.

The man shrugs. 'Maybe today, maybe three weeks' time,' he says unhelpfully.

'Do you know where he works?'

'Several places. I know he's a delivery driver for one of them office supplies companies. Taking stuff here, there and everywhere. He told me he went to Budapest once.'

The man straightens up, his grimy vest riding up over his belly. He passes a spanner from one hand to the other.

'It's not very regular work though. Reckon he takes what he can when he can. He's a nice chap.'

The man comes closer to the wall at the front of Luke Manning's overgrown garden.

'One of them actor types, apparently,' he says with a sly wink. 'Told me he's holding out for the big time.'

Like his girlfriend then, I think, wondering if they met through the theatre. Part of me wonders too if I'm keeping the conversation alive to delay going home, forestalling the inevitable when I'll be forced to listen to the sound of my own sad and slow heartbeat, pondering what comes next.

'How long has he lived here?'

'About a year. When old Mrs Clegg died I warned the council that squatters would move in, and to begin with I thought I was right. Before I'd even put the phone down, Luke Manning and his rusty white van had taken up residence.' He shakes his head, turning up his nose at the house attached to his neat abode. 'But turns out he's renting the place from Mrs Clegg's son. As I said, Luke seems a good sort.'

For some reason, I suddenly come over nauseous. The man's voice merges with the sound of a refuse truck emptying bins, a chattering stream of uniformed school kids walking with their teachers, and the distant wail of a siren. I take hold of the gate post until the feeling passes, telling myself to go home, do as Bob insisted. Why can't I just forget about the Melanie Carter case, leave it to the rest of the team?

'Anyway, I see him coming and going sometimes, and we exchange nods and a few words about this and that, you know. My missus says it's good to keep in with the neighbours and all cos you never know when you might need them.'

'Quite,' I say, heading for my car. I stop and half turn back. 'I don't suppose you know the name of the company he works for, do you?' It's a long shot.

'I do indeed,' he says proudly, waving the spanner at me. 'He came back one day with "Cain's Office Supplies" stuck on the side of his van. I said to Margaret, I said, will you look at that. He's got "Cain" written on his van. Our grandson's name,' he adds for my benefit.

I thank him and leave, feeling the first buzzings of a migraine as I get in my car. Instinctively, my hand goes into my bag for my box of pills as flashing lights begin to zigzag across my eyes.

I wasn't intending on stopping at the trading estate, but a quick search on my phone told me Cain's Office Supplies was virtually on the way home. What harm could it possibly do? Besides, the thought of explaining to Stella why I'm back early isn't appealing.

Their premises is a drab building, the last in a row of single-storey warehouses on a small estate made up mainly of plumbing and electrical wholesalers. The chilly reception area is furnished with some stained chairs and a low table strewn with tatty brochures. The drinks machine in the corner makes gurgling noises, emitting a smell of burnt coffee.

The woman behind the reception counter, mid-fifties, looks up from her work, sticking her finger between two pages. 'Can I help you?' she says, followed by a smoker's cough. She's wearing a sleeveless vest that barely covers her pudding-waist rolling over her too-tight jeans.

'I'm looking for an employee of yours, Luke Manning. I don't suppose he's around, is he?' I don't bother telling her I'm a detective. Probably because I'm not sure I am any more.

'Luke?' she says incredulously. 'You'll be lucky.'

I glance behind her, into the warehouse. To one side, large metal shelving units hold cardboard boxes of all sizes, electric forklifts zipping between them. The other side is stacked with pallets of unidentifiable shrink-wrapped goods that look as if they've recently been unloaded through the gaping roller door to the side.

A couple of men in yellow jackets walk past with clipboards, and then, from behind them, another man emerges and walks into the reception area. He's good-looking, wearing jeans and a grey T-shirt with an open check shirt over the top.

'He's hardly here these days,' the woman continues, followed by another cough. She turns round and sees the man. 'Yeah, that Luke Manning, bloody part-timer seems to waltz in and out when the fancy takes him,' she says loudly and with a wry grin. 'Talk of the bleedin' devil,' she adds good-naturedly, nudging the man in the ribs.

'You gossiping about me again, Sylvia?' he says smoothly. He gives me a quick look.

'This lady wants to see you,' Sylvia tells him.

In my current state of mind, being described as a lady doesn't seem like much of a fit.

'How can I help?' Luke says in a deep, velvety voice. It fits with what his neighbour said about his acting ambitions, even if his slightly scruffy appearance doesn't. 'You're lucky to catch me. I'm technically off work at the moment, just stopped by to pick something up.'

'Shall we sit over here for a moment?' I say, moving across to the chairs for privacy.

When we are seated, I show him my warrant card and explain why I'm here, telling him about Beth and how early in the year she reported a man called Joe Douglas for harassment.

Luke Manning remains silent, but blows out in shock when I've finished. 'I had no idea,' he says. 'Poor Beth.' He shakes his head, pushing his fingers through his dark hair. 'I probably shouldn't tell you this, but . . .' He trails off, looking uncertain.

'You probably *should* tell me,' I say, the subtext of which reminds him I'm a police officer.

'Well, Beth can be a bit . . . emotional,' he explains, looking pained. 'Almost a bit histrionic at times. She likes the attention, I suppose.' He gives a fond smile. 'I've never heard of anyone called Joe Douglas, I'm afraid, and I wouldn't mind betting Beth was blowing things out of proportion a bit. You know, for the sympathy.'

'So you've never seen anyone lurking outside her flat, phoning her, following her?'

Luke shakes his head vehemently. 'No. I'd have done something if I'd thought she was in trouble. It was probably just some chap she met.'

'OK, thanks for your help,' I say, not sure what to think. He seems genuine enough.

I stand and shake his hand, sensing he's watching me as I leave the building.

By the time I get to my car, my head is pounding out the rhythm of a full-blown migraine. I glance at my watch. Too soon for more codeine, I think, squinting through the pain, wondering if it really matters. Surely they just put those instructions on the box to stop idiots overdosing?

18

'You've got the job!' Owen jokes, trying to cheer me up.

His good mood is the antithesis of mine. He swings round at his drafting desk, pulling off his reading glasses. His workspace is just as I imagined – bright and minimalist, nothing like his home. I imagine he finds the contrast refreshing, somehow comforting.

I know he's not serious, so I stand there, smiling instead of answering. On the way back from the cemetery a couple of days ago he told me that he'd put out an advert for an assistant. 'Secretary-slash-receptionist-slash-general-dogsbody,' he said. 'Do you think I'll find anyone who'll put up with me?'

That night we drank wine again. After visiting my parents' graves I was too upset and afraid to be alone, and anyway, Owen insisted I help him taste some new bottles he'd bought. He was selecting some for a drinks reception he's going to be hosting for potential clients. It was just what I needed.

'I'm sure you'll get lots of applicants,' I said, feeling tipsy, secretly jealous of whoever got the job.

All I ever wanted was to settle down, do my work, have a family. There's no chance of that now. Owen has done so much for me since we met in Chandni Chowk, and I am very grateful. I won't deny that my feelings for him have grown too, although I'm not stupid.

Added up, it equals nothing more than neediness and infatuation.

'Very funny,' I say, at last responding to his comment about the job. I stand with my arms dangling limply by my sides. After what I've been through this morning, I feel utterly deflated and empty. Seeing my parents' house, picking through their things, was more than I could stand.

When I went inside, I was shocked by the smell of the place. I was expecting it to be musty and airless, but I was wrong. I swear Mum's perfume was hanging in the air as if she'd just breezed through the living room; the doughy smell of her baking seemed to linger in the kitchen. Dad's study still had the rubbery hessian odour of new carpet – he'd had it fitted just before I . . . just before I was sent away. The bathroom was as fresh as if the cleaner had recently visited.

I wandered round in a daze, not knowing what to tackle first. I sat at Dad's desk and pulled open the filing cabinet. I drew out a file marked 'Will' and another which contained details of their mortgage and various property brochures from when they'd been looking to buy overseas. I also took details of the bank accounts and investments they owned. I could tell they'd been sensible with their money.

Then I saw it, and my heart finally cracked open.

They'd left me a gift.

Wrapped in pretty tissue paper and tied up with a ribbon, the box was stashed at the back of Dad's desk cupboard.

For Isabel, the attached card read.

They always left me a little present before they went away, even when I was an adult and came over to water Dad's beloved plants.

If you find this, please contact us. We're heartbroken and miss you so much. We pray every day that you're alive and well. And then came a Spanish phone number in Dad's handwriting. Except they never made it to Spain.

My stomach knotted and twisted. Even if they were alive, how could I call them after everything that's happened? They'd be even more heartbroken if they knew the truth about my life.

I held the gift – a little piece of guilt, I always used to think as I opened the chocolates or perfume they'd buy me because they weren't taking me with them. They often went holidaying or caravanning alone.

Now the guilt is all mine, I thought, as the tears came.

I couldn't face opening it – it felt like chocolates, and they could well be past their best by now anyway – so I put it back in the cupboard again and closed the door. After that, I couldn't bear to be there any longer. I yanked the curtains closed before locking up and leaving.

Thankfully, there'd been no sign of Tetch, no desiccated body to greet me. It didn't look as if the neighbours, who were friends with Mum and Dad, were home to ask what happened to him, but I wasn't about to draw attention to myself by asking. That would have to wait for another day. I just wanted to get out and get back to Owen. I felt safe with him.

'Really, Isabel, I'm not kidding about the job,' Owen says, seriously this time.

He gets off the stool at his desk and heads towards me. For a fleeting moment I imagine him pulling me into an embrace, feel his mouth dropping down on to my neck, working his way round to my lips. My skin erupts into a thousand tiny goose-bumps. Thank God I'm still bundled up in my new coat so he can't see. There's no way I'll be able to get close to anyone ever again.

'Yes, boss,' I say in a silly voice, partly fuelled by my erroneous thoughts, partly by nervousness.

I clap my cold hands together, wondering if I can spare some money to buy gloves. Having seen what I need to sort at Mum and Dad's place, I realise it was far too ambitious to think I could go back to Bestluck in just a few days, even though I'm terrified of being in England a moment longer than I need to be. Felix saw to that. I'm still looking over my shoulder, despite him being in hospital. It's instinct now. There's no getting away from the fact that liaising with solicitors and estate agents, sorting out the will, chasing funds, selling the house and dealing with their possessions is going to

196

take weeks, maybe months. I've been naive.

'I'm serious,' Owen says, making a move towards the kettle, filling it with water and placing it on its stand. There's a small kitchenette in one corner of the open-plan space consisting of three glossy white units, a cream Smeg fridge, a two-ring hob and a sink. He flicks the switch and takes a couple of mugs from the cupboard.

'Coffee?' he asks. 'Of course, you should be making the drinks really.'

I feel my cheeks pink up. 'Oh, I'm so sorry. Here, let me help.'

His hand comes down on mine as I go to open the fridge. 'I was *joking*,' he says. 'But keeping me in a constant supply of coffee is an essential part of the job, you know.' He winks.

'It is?'

'You'd be responsible for pretty much every aspect of my life, apart from the actual plans and designs, of course. I wouldn't expect you to do that.'

That grin again, set beneath his honest eyes, as blue as any I've ever seen, framed by hair that falls easily into a messy yet endearing style. It makes my heart bang out of time, makes me look away in case I reveal an ounce of what I'm feeling; what I've been through.

'I'm sure you could find someone way better than me.' It's true. He wouldn't want me if he knew how damaged I am.

Self-preservation drives me over to his desk. I take a peek at his work, pretending to be interested. Anything to escape his gravitational pull. Mathematical and unintelligible plans are taking shape on a vast expanse of architect's paper.

'Yeah, I could do that no problem,' I say, forcing a laugh and willing my hot cheeks to lose their colour. 'Anyway, I'm an art—' I stop, not wanting to talk about my life back then, when I had a purpose, a job, my own flat. It seems a million years ago.

'Look, Owen, I only went out to post a letter for you. It hardly qualifies me as your assistant.'

'Ah, but that's where you're wrong. I've been vetting you.' He leaves the kitchenette, concentrating on carrying two very full mugs.

'You have?'

Thankfully, I heard the humour in his voice. The thought of anyone vetting me, checking up on me or watching me is otherwise chilling.

We sit on the brown leather sofa set against the back wall.

'But seriously, Isabel, I think having a job, even a temporary one, would do you good. Take your mind off things. And it would really help me.'

My cheeks turn scarlet again. 'Oh goodness, I'm such an idiot.' I roll my eyes. 'You need a paying tenant in the flat. Here's me, unemployed and useless, squatting in your basement. This is so embarrassing. Look, I'll be coming into some money soon, so if you let me know what I owe you for these last few days I'll—'

Owen's finger comes down on my mouth.

'Shh.'

He releases it, slowly trailing it down my chin.

'Indeed you are an idiot,' he tells me, but in a nice way. 'You're welcome to stay in the flat as long as you need. I like having you there. You're good company.'

I pray the disappointment doesn't show on my face at simply being 'good company', even though my feelings are still too raw for anything more than friendship. I stare at my lap. Owen takes my mug and places it on the low table. He turns sideways to face me.

'Isabel, let's be clear about this. I *want* to help you.'

I feel the soft breeze from his words brush over my face. He's close, and clasps my hands. I try to look him in the eye for a few seconds, but it's too much.

'I really like you,' he says genuinely.

I raise my eyes to his again. Maybe I misheard him.

'The flat is yours for as long as you need. I'm in no rush to let it. And I am serious about you giving me a hand with the business. I'm pretty desperate now I have this new contract. It could be part-time and temporary to start with, give you a chance to sort out your parents' affairs. I'll pay you a good rate, and there'll be no pressure to stay on.'

'Owen . . .' He doesn't understand. 'Look, that's very kind of you, but I intend to return to India as soon as I can. Maybe even as early as next week.'

I know that's an impossible timescale as far as dealing with things goes, but I say it anyway. As much as the offer is tempting, I can't accept. It's too risky to become so settled, not to mention leaving a financial paper trail if he doesn't pay me cash, even if it is what I crave. I will have to move into my parents' house, even though *he* knows exactly where it is. I imagine him waking up, leaving hospital and heading there, zombie-like, to find me.

Owen shifts closer. The leather creaks beneath him.

'You're a puzzle, Mees Eezee,' he says, mimicking Javesh.

I'm suddenly hit with a pang of homesickness for Bestluck.

'I don't understand why a young woman like you would want to go back there. Let's face it, it was a bit of a dump, and you seemed very alone. You don't even speak the language.' He shakes his head.

'Bestluck is *not* a dump,' I say, even though that's exactly what I thought of it when I first walked in after seeing the 'Help Wanted' sign in the window. 'And thanks for the "young", but flattery won't get you anywhere.' I grin, and play-punch his leg to break the tension.

A tingle shoots up my arm, and I stop, thinking. Perhaps taking a part-time job with him and staying in the flat is the answer. No one knows where I am that way, so maybe it is safer than my parents' place. My money will run out in a few days and applying for benefits is a risky option. Perhaps he'll agree to pay me in cash for now. After that, it doesn't matter. I'll be gone.

Owen stands up. 'Look, I understand,' he says, sounding slightly disappointed. 'I won't pressure you any more. I'd better get on. This client's breathing down my neck.'

He stretches before taking up his position at his drafting desk again.

I sit there, staring at him, watching as he slides his glasses on to his nose. His face tenses up with concentration.

'OK, I'll do it,' I say, instantly regretting it.

Owen looks up from his work.

'I've had some experience of administrative work.'

It's a lie, of course. Owen doesn't know that I was Head of Art at a secondary school, that I have no clue how to run an office.

Suddenly, I see the smug expression on Felix's face when I accused him. I wanted to scream at him, hit him and bite him I was so frustrated. The pure calm he exuded made me look utterly mad.

'Why would you think I'd do anything to damage your career, you silly girl?' he'd said, locking down my flailing hands in one swift move. 'I'm on your side, darling. But you told me you wanted to leave anyway, said that you couldn't stand to be there a moment longer after what had happened. Surely it's a blessing in disguise.'

'How can it be? I've lost my job.' I tried to break free. 'I might as well have admitted my guilt. I was going to fight them. I just don't understand why you needed to be involved.'

He pulled me close then, allowed me to hear the soothing beat of his steady heart. 'Darling, I came to the school because I was worried about you, not to interfere. You were in such a state, I had to find out if you were OK. I wanted to help.'

I looked up at him from the crook of his shoulder, studying his expression. Something flashed in his eye, but I wasn't sure what. Perhaps it was a reflection of my madness, the first sign of me letting go – letting go of myself. It was true, I was certainly upset, in a terrible state, knowing I was most likely going to lose my job and, worse, never be able to teach again.

A complaint of a sexual nature had been made against me by a fifteen-year-old boy. I was dealing with it – Dad had recommended a solicitor who was working on the case, and I was in touch with the union. But Felix was always there, as if he was somehow a part of it, although he insisted he was just trying to help and support me.

When the complaint magically vanished three weeks after I'd been suspended, the Head wrote and told me that he appreciated me handing in my notice, that it was for the best under the circumstances. My career was finished.

'But I *didn't* hand in my resignation,' I explained pitifully to Felix for the tenth time.

He'd put me to bed, made me a cup of tea. He sat next to me, stroked my head.

'The stress has made you forget,' he said. 'You've become muddled, you poor thing.' He leaned forward and kissed my forehead. 'It's a good thing you've got me, isn't it?'

I gave a tiny nod, and watched as Felix left the room, clicking off the light.

It was just before I fell asleep that I realised how much

I did in fact need him, especially now I didn't have a job. He'd been right all along – moving in with him had been the best thing.

In the days that followed, even though Mum and Dad had been all for me fighting the accusation, which was of course untrue, they had to accept that Felix had been a rock for me, something of a hero, stating how lucky I was to have him by my side. Within the space of a month I'd lost my flat and my job. It wasn't long afterwards that I found myself asking his permission even to go out.

'When do I start?' I say to Owen as cheerfully as I can manage.

'How about tomorrow?' he suggests.

A warm, satisfied look spreads across his face. He's genuinely pleased. If I wasn't so nervous about staying in England, so fearful of the consequences, this could be just what I need. As it stands, it's a means to an end.

'Monday to Friday, ten until two, if that suits. I'll pay eight fifty an hour, cash if you prefer.'

'That sounds perfect,' I say, unable to sound too enthusiastic until I've done what I need to do. It's the only way I will find peace as long as I'm here.

Half an hour later, with Owen's offer to join him for dinner still ringing in my ears, I know I can't put it off any more. If I'm to stay in England a minute longer I need to know for sure. I need to convince myself that Felix can't hurt me. Unless I see him in the flesh, lying in his hospital bed, helpless, unconscious, at death's door, I won't believe that he's not out there looking for me, waiting to strike and do his worst.

During the short bus journey from the office, I remember the last time I saw him. Felix didn't know it was the last time we'd be together, of course, and I forced myself to be normal – as normal as someone in a place like that is meant to be, anyway.

I could tell he still adored me, even after everything, and he wanted me to come back home. He made a pact with me. 'If you get better and return to me, my love, I promise I'll never mention the past or what's happened.' I'd just stared at him, not feeling like me any more. 'Deal?'

I'd agreed, playing along, even though part of me still wondered if I did want to go back to him. Perhaps I should knuckle down, continue the therapy and work on myself and my shortcomings. Felix had stuck by me, after all, and perhaps he just wanted the same as me – a loving, happy relationship. We'd even talked about having children once. Then he left the hospital, and that's when I knew I had to get away. I'd be forever in his control otherwise. Besides, it wouldn't be the first time I'd escaped.

After the short journey, I'm facing Woodford Grange Nursing Home again, suddenly feeling as if I can't go through with it. What if he senses I'm there or, worse, wakes up? Visiting him goes against the urgings of every sensible cell in my body, and my damaged mind screams out at me to flee while I can.

'You have to do this,' I whisper to myself, staring at the building from across the street.

The chilly autumn air cuts across my cheeks like a sharp slap, and my smile falls away. Felix would approve of the building's grandeur, I think – it would once have been filled with well-to-do Victorian gentlemen going about their business. I often wondered if he'd been born into the wrong era. I'm sure he would have preferred the misogyny of the late nineteenth century.

I think of Owen's words of comfort – *I think it's right for you to visit.* But now I'm not so sure, and Owen can't possibly know why.

Taking a deep breath, and shoving my hands inside the warm pockets of my coat, I decide to go through with it. The tree-lined street is quiet, with only one or two cars cruising slowly past. I cross the road and stand within the cover of some bushes directly outside the large building, catching my breath. The sign on the front wall is modern and freshly painted, and the garden and parking area are neat and well looked after.

A young nurse hurries up the front steps. She's wearing a short padded jacket over a white and blue uniform, and she looks over her shoulder before going inside as if she's worried she's late.

I draw in a deep breath, leave the cover of the bushes and walk tentatively up to the entrance. I try the big brass handle but it's locked. I press the button on the entry system and wait. When I explain to the receptionist who I am, that I've come to visit a patient, the door buzzes, allowing me to push it open. Cautiously, I go in.

Once inside the large tiled reception hallway, I am

struck by the tang of disinfectant and despair. The smells usually associated with the soulless wards of a modern hospital somehow seem out of place in this old converted building. My heart thumps madly.

A large staircase sweeps up behind a glossy white desk, which has on it a slim computer monitor, a leather-bound diary and a tall vase of white lilies. The expensive grandeur can't hide the fact there are sick people behind the closed doors. There is a little brass bell on the corner of the desk and I'm just about to ring it when a middle-aged woman comes out of what looks to be an office off to one side. I hear the voices of several other people in there, discussing Christmas and shopping.

'Hello,' she says kindly. 'How can I help you?'

'I believe you have a patient called Felix Darwin,' I say. 'He was in a car accident. My parents were killed.' I drop my eyes down. I didn't think to check on visiting times.

'I'm so sorry to hear that,' she says in a quiet voice. 'Yes, we do have a Mr Darwin here. May I ask if you are a relative?'

I stare at her for what seems like an age, not knowing what to say. She has unremarkable brown hair with a few strands of grey woven throughout. Her gold-rimmed glasses are out-of-date and make her look older than she probably is. Dull grey eyes stare back at me pitifully.

'I'm his wife,' I say, swallowing down the lie, hoping it will get me in.

From that moment, I get swept along. There's no backing

out, and by the time I'm in there, staring at him, disbelieving my own unfocused eyes, I feel dizzy and sick, as if I'm going to pass out any second. The sight of him after all this time takes my breath away.

Thin and pale between the sheets, and brittle as a rice cracker, Felix seems so much smaller than when I last saw him. My hand goes over my mouth.

I stand and stare, unable to speak.

Just moments ago, the receptionist introduced me to Megan, Felix's nurse for today. Before we went in she explained to me in the corridor that his appearance might shock me, that he wouldn't be the man I remembered. It was the same nurse I'd seen scuttle up the steps shortly before I arrived.

In turn, I told her that we were officially separated, that I'd been away for a while. She gave a slow nod, probably disapproving.

'It's not uncommon for relatives to think their loved ones are actually dead when they see them in this state,' she told me.

Dead, I thought as we stood outside room number nine. I wondered if I was the only relative actually to wish that were true.

'In here,' she said, letting me go in first.

Now, in his room, keeping a distance of at least six feet or so, I can almost imagine that I was mistaken all along, that this helpless, pathetic man couldn't possibly have done anything evil at all.

I'm transfixed by the way his eyebrows curve softly

over the sunken sockets of his closed eyes; how his once-deep chest is now almost concave; the way his arms, weak and limp, lie like sticks at his sides. And I can't help wondering what has happened to his powerful, muscular legs when I see the thin traces of limbs beneath the sheets. The skin on his face is grey and powdery.

'Are you OK, Mrs Darwin?' the nurse says.

I manage a small nod, desperate to tell her my real name.

There's a tube coming from Felix's mouth leading to a machine at the head of his bed. I follow the electrode wires attached to his chest back to the machine and the steady trace on the screen above his head. Several other bits of equipment monitor the little bit of life that is left in him, informing the doctors that it's still worth hanging on.

Then I follow the power leads from the machines to a central bank. There's a red master switch to turn everything off. My fingers curl within my pockets.

Suddenly, I'm laughing hysterically.

'Are you sure you're OK?' the nurse asks.

I feel the spread of her warm palm on my back. She pulls a chair across for me to sit on, but I can't. I need to get out; I need to escape finally, once and for all, now that I've seen him like this.

'I'm fine,' I tell her, my voice quivering. 'But I have to go now.'

Something like a sob, though not for the reasons she thinks, leaves my mouth as I make a dash for the door.

I run back down the corridor and through reception. Thankfully, the woman in the gold glasses is nowhere to be seen, and I lunge for the heavy front door, launching myself into the car park and then the street. I run down the road until I'm breathless and my throat burns from the cold.

It's only when I'm halfway back to Owen's place that I allow myself, for the first time in ages, to believe that maybe, just maybe, everything could turn out all right.

19

I'm stuck rigid. As good as dead.

Practice makes perfect, I tell myself.

How I'd love to twitch my nose, blink my eyes, or even take a big sigh – but I can't. My finger begs to scratch an itch, but no. It sits there at the end of my arm, quite stiff. It doesn't feel like part of me.

It's all a waiting game. Lying here, biding my time. What choice do I have? I've nothing else to do after all.

I let go of the sigh I've been holding, even though no one hears it, even though it doesn't actually come out. It's a metaphorical sigh; the sigh of my life. An expiration. The culmination of everything I've been working towards. It never had to be this way, I think.

It feels as if I've been in this place a lifetime already. How I wish *she* would hurry and come, breeze through the door in her carefree way, her beautiful hair shooting shards of fiery light, her slightly crooked tooth exposed when she grimaces at the sight of me.

The sound of her voice would be enough – enough

medicine to hang on, reason to keep going, remind me how things were.

It was never meant to end like this, even though she refused to believe that. She made it bad; she made it wrong. All I ever wanted was to love her, to have her love me back. It was the same for all of them, although she was the special one with that crazy mix of red hair and blue eyes. In the end, they were all the masters of their own fate.

The nurse flits around my room like a pale moth. I can't see her, of course, and I have no idea what she's doing, clattering around me while I'm like this. I imagine her lithe body, all dressed in white, her skin almost see-through, her hair angelic as she dotes on me. My mouth waters at the thought of her bending and stretching over me, gently wiping my skin with a warm cloth, adjusting my position with the help of another nurse as they count *one-two-three-shift* and haul my useless withered frame over on the bed.

Nurse! I want to call out. *Nurse, hold me tight!*

But then, in the darkest corners of my mind, she turns into Mother, morphing from agile and healthy into dragging and sick, the dead weight of her lying on top of me.

Mother is to blame. She started it; made me different – an outsider, unlovable.

I still miss her dreadfully.

After nearly four decades of denial, I accept that no one will ever want me. Nearly no one. By default, she's the only one for me.

I was eight years old when I wriggled out from under her dead body. She'd had a massive heart attack while reading me a bedtime story. She melted down on me, convulsing, staring at me through her huge azure eyes, her scarlet hair matted with spit and the puke that bubbled up.

When she finally stopped moving, my useless skinny-little-boy legs carried me far, far away from her. I ran screaming, terrified, calling out for my father. He was nowhere to be found.

I later discovered he was fucking a pretty young employee from one of his burger bars in the back of his estate car. Dad was fat and greasy with wispy long hair that stuck in black and grey strands over the domed bald part of his head.

Growing up, looking back, I never understood how he'd bagged a hot young girlfriend like Linda – not when he had cheesy stuff oozing from his skin, and a nasty thing growing on his nose.

In my early teens, I developed a crush on Linda after she ruffled my hair and gave me free chips and Coke. She did more than that for Dad. But she always saw me as just a kid, never the good-looking young man I was turning into.

When I was fifteen, Dad took me aside. A funny noise funnelled up his throat as he spoke.

'Son,' he said, laughing at me, 'it's time I gave you these. You can't be too careful. Make sure you use 'em. Every single time.'

Then he shoved me, and I don't know why. A sharp jab to my shoulder before handing me a packet of twelve condoms. I still have every single one of them.

'I think there's probably time for me to grab a quick cuppa then, Mr Darwin,' the nurse says.

Is she expecting a nod of my head, a twitch of my finger? I'd like to shove it right up her nose. The lazy girl has only just come into work, panting and blustering about, telling no one in particular how busy she was, that she'd not long received the urgent call to come in.

She closes the curtains before leaving.

Bitch, I think, but don't say it. Who does she think is paying her?

And then I'm salivating again at the thought of what I could do to her given the chance, but it's not long before the door opens again. A breeze washes over me, as well as the sound of two women's voices.

My heart stops, as if I'm dead already.

I listen again as best my useless ears and brain can manage. I would hold my breath if I could, but with this ventilator tube in my mouth, it's tricky.

I can hardly believe it.

Her perfect voice rings around me, its soft tones a drug of the best quality. Surely this must be an auditory hallucination of the highest level, some kind of medical enigma over which I have no control. I wasn't expecting this so soon.

Belle has come back to me!

How I want to tell her that I can hear her, that I'm in

here. Oh Belle, you should never have left me. You know we are meant to be together, and you coming back to me is further proof of that. Think of the wonderful life we will have together, darling, just as soon as I'm better. For I will get better, you know.

What's this? A sob . . . you're leaving?

No, please don't go!

But it's too late. As quickly as she came, my Belle is gone, her voice fading into the distance. I am helpless. Stuck and paralysed by my own inadequacies.

20

I leave Cain's Office Supplies disappointed that Luke Manning couldn't tell me anything about the elusive Joe Douglas. My head throbs, but I decide that it doesn't really seem worth pursuing it further. Especially given what's happened today.

Several white delivery vans follow me out of the premises as I drive without much purpose back towards Moseley. In fifteen minutes I'm parked up and standing in the travel agent's shop on Alcester Road requesting the key to the park. I'm hoping the peace and sanctuary will help my headache, as I can't stand the thought of taking to bed. I'd never sleep anyway. I pay my deposit and leave, clutching the black fob in my hand, walking further down the busy road to the narrow park entrance.

Adam thinks I'm mad when I come here. 'A key to a park defeats the whole point of a public space,' he once told me. 'What do you want to go and stare at water for anyway?'

Then he'd suggested that a ten-mile run with him would

do my mind far more good than sitting and contemplating, that running was the best medicine for everything from self-doubt and anxiety to low mood.

'But I like to sit and think,' I'd told him in defence, though didn't bother justifying my more recent visits to the park and lake. There's something appealing, secretive almost, about fetching the key, unlocking the gate, knowing that not many people are aware of the hidden oasis.

I turn left, ducking down the walkway between the two walls of the estate agents' offices, but stop before reaching the locked gate at the end of the dark passage. I look over my shoulder, convinced I heard someone. There's no one there.

But when I turn back to the gate again, there's a man blocking my way. His hands are on his hips and he's staring at me intently.

'Are you going in?' he says, tilting his head to the side.

His face, serene and clean-shaven, doesn't fit with the torn and dirty clothes he's wearing, or his slightly aggressive pose. He's not a big man, but I immediately feel threatened, by his eyes more than anything. In his early forties, I'd say he was some kind of builder's labourer, but I quickly change my mind. His face isn't weathered enough. For some reason he's holding out his hands, and I see they are smooth and clean.

'Yes, yes I was,' I say nervously, using the past tense because it suddenly doesn't seem such a good idea.

'Then allow me,' he says, reaching out and taking the fob from my hand.

A deafening voice in my head screams out to me to say something to him, to stop him, to tell him I'm a police officer. But I just stand there dumbly, unable to do anything except walk cautiously through the heavy iron gate when he beckons me on.

'Ladies first,' he says with a waft of his hand and a smile that seems pleasant enough.

I go in through the gate, mumble a quick thank you, and walk briskly down the slope, past the ice house and deserted tennis courts, hardly daring to look behind me in case he's following. It's only when I'm down by the water, breathless and shaking and feeling ashamed of myself, that I realise I forgot to take back the key.

I stare back up the tree-lined hill. There's no sign of him.

'Just great,' I say under my breath. 'That's my deposit lost then.'

I drop down on to a bench overlooking the lake, forcing myself to relax and unwind for just a few minutes in the hope it will ease my head. I pull my coat around me as the cold air chills my skin, breathing in deeply. There's a tight pressure in my chest now, making it hurt.

I look around me, my foot tapping impatiently, trying to get back the feeling of calm I used to have when I came here. It amazes me how so many trees, paths and walkways, plus three acres of water, can fit into the centre of Moseley. It's a beautiful sanctuary, although suddenly it seems more threatening with that strange man lurking.

Out of habit, I check my phone for messages. There are usually loads but my screen is blank.

My throat tightens, so I tilt back my head for a few seconds, fighting the tears. The sky is a dreary milky-grey with swirls of black looming in the west. I look down again as two ducks waddle past my feet, but the way I'm jittering and fidgeting scares them off.

I get up and walk to the bank. The murky water of the lake instantly reminds me of the canal, makes me think of Melanie. Her mother is naturally still in pieces, according to the family liaison officer who updates her from time to time. The poor woman lost her husband last year to cancer, and then her daughter, too. I can't imagine how she'll ever have a normal life again.

Then my errant mind fixes on Grace, how next year she'll be packing up her stuff and heading off to Leicester University. A surge of adrenalin takes my breath away at the thought of her out late at night, being followed, alone, terrified as footsteps draw closer and closer as she makes her way back to halls.

I stagger back to the bench and sit down.

'Stop it!' I say, letting out a sob.

I'd do anything to get rid of these thoughts and crazy worries. Since Alexandra Stanford begged me for help, since we found her body, they haunt me day and night. It must be some kind of punishment.

My head drops down into my hands, and I lean forward, elbows on knees. A big sigh escapes my lungs.

Oh, Alexandra . . .

I'm beginning to think that Bob is right, that my work isn't up to par and I need this break. I'm glad he doesn't know that I wasted my time visiting Beth and then her boyfriend, but I was hoping Luke would be able to throw some light on Joe Douglas, whoever he is. But it seems that Beth's claim of harassment is random or, according to Luke, possibly even attention-seeking. I can't see how it can have anything to do with either of the two murder cases. I'm relieved I didn't do it on police time.

I stare up at the trees, black and veiny against the sky. My guilt has led me down a dead end. I let my emotions get in the way.

Buses, I think, hearing Bob's wise voice in my head. *Two just came at once.*

My shoulders hunch up to my ears and a shiver works its way down my spine.

There's a noise behind me so I swing round, but I see nothing except the ducks wandering off and a woman coming down the hill with a buggy.

I get up, deciding to head home. I'll no doubt have to field questions from the girls about why I'm back, but my head is still hurting and I need to lie down.

Another noise comes from the undergrowth as I start to walk back up the hill towards the gate. I've only taken a few paces when I kick into a jog. I daren't look back, but I'm convinced someone's there, following me. I can almost hear their breath – a crackling rasp as they try to keep up.

I run faster, panting as I struggle up the hill. When did I become so unfit?

I can see the gate in the distance now, and just as it dawns on me that I'll need the fob to open it, I trip and fall, my arms splaying wide, my hands skidding along the rough ground. My chin hits a stone and there's a shooting pain in my right ankle and up my leg.

'Owww,' I cry, curling up and rolling over.

I try to get up but the pain in my ankle is too bad.

Then there's the shadow of a man looming over me. I scream at the sight of him, causing a groundsman to come rushing out of a nearby maintenance hut. The man above me is dangling the key, holding out his hands and backing away.

'Sorry, didn't mean to scare you,' he says, his eyes wide and terrified.

The groundsman comes up to me. 'What's going on? Are you OK?'

'I was just trying to give her back her key, but she freaked out and fell over,' the man says, chucking the fob on the ground beside me. He strides off. 'Hysterical cow,' he calls out.

The park-keeper helps me to my feet. I brush myself down, trying to regain some dignity, but the pain makes it hard. I pull up the leg of my trousers and see that my ankle is already blooming purple.

'You want to get that looked at,' the park-keeper tells me as I attempt to hobble off up the remainder of the hill to the gate. I thank him, telling him I will, although I have no intention of doing so. It's nothing a top-up of codeine and some ice won't cure.

It takes me half an hour to make it to the car, by which time I can't feel my toes from the swelling. I have to take off my shoe. Driving proves impossible so, grudgingly, I phone for a taxi to take me to A&E. Three hours later I arrive home with crutches and a plastic Aircast boot on my leg.

Stella is doing her homework at the kitchen table, and Adam is poring over some documents. He looks up, staring at me in disbelief. He comes over to me with a shocked expression.

'I think this is fate, Ray,' he says, reaching out to give me a hug.

I raise a crutch to whack him on the shoulder, before thinking better of it. Instead, I hobble off.

21

Owen gives me a lift to the office on my first day. He was up early running errands, and came back just before ten.

I apologise for my outfit. 'I'll go shopping soon,' I tell him as we park round the back of the studio. I feel self-conscious in my old sweatshirt and tatty jeans.

'It's dress-down Friday every day at Brandrick's,' he says with a grin, unlocking the unit – a small brick building with a large front window, which drenches the space in natural light. It's in a mainly residential street but flanked on each side by a couple of other professional suites – a firm of solicitors and an employment agency.

I pick up the post from the mat and, taking Owen at his word, make us both a strong coffee.

'There's actually a pile of mail that needs opening, some from when I was away,' he says. 'And my email inbox is a nightmare. I've set you up with your own account and sent you a document detailing how to respond to the general enquiries that come in. I'll forward stuff on for you to deal with. The landline phone's yours to answer, although it doesn't ring much. We often get wrong numbers, just so you know. I mainly use my mobile for business. And I like lunch at one prompt. There's a deli round the corner. They have a website where you can order online. The log-in details are also in your inbox, and you'll find all my favourites stored. Mix it up a bit, eh?'

Owen smiles, not seeming like my friendly neighbour any more but definitely like my efficient boss.

'OK,' I reply, feeling overwhelmed.

'This will be your desk,' he says. It's in the window and has a silver laptop on it.

There isn't much furniture in the studio, almost as if he's not quite finished moving in, but I decide that Owen prefers the minimalist look which seems to be so trendy these days. I laugh inwardly. What do I, a recluse, know about trends?

'The drinks reception is in three weeks and needs finalising. Again, all the information is in your inbox. You'll need to chase replies, liaise with the venue, caterers et cetera. It's important for it to be a success. The contacts came off the back of an exhibition and are all hot leads. I'll be taking on new staff if it goes well, perhaps opening a new branch, so, you know . . .'

'We need to get it right,' I add, hoping he'll appreciate the 'we'.

I don't remind him I won't be here in three weeks' time.

Owen nods, satisfied, before taking up his position at the drafting desk. He pushes in earphones and gives me a quick smile before getting on with his work.

This is it then, I think, sitting down at my desk.

I am a real person again with a job and a flat, even though I have no intention of keeping either one for very long. It's too dangerous, though Owen doesn't know this. Sitting at my desk in the window makes me feel like a shop display. It fills me with fear. Even though I've seen Felix in hospital and I know he's unconscious, and that he can't walk, the scars are deep. I half expect to see him standing under the tree opposite, watching, biding his time. It's a far cry from when I was hiding in Raksha's tiny attic room.

By late morning I've cleared Owen's inbox, replied to all the important emails, opened and filed the mail, and ordered him a tuna salad. Before getting started on the event details, I make us another hot drink.

'Let me guess,' Owen says with a sly look as we take five minutes to sit on the sofa. 'Before your stellar career as a chambermaid, you were . . .' He makes a thoughtful noise.

I tense up. Once he starts digging, finds out what I did, there's a chance he'll remember the piece in the local paper. Even though the allegations were dropped, people form their own opinions. Prejudice is impossible to escape, especially because of where they put me.

'Were you a nurse?' he suggests. 'You seem the caring type. Or perhaps you looked after children, or . . . you were a chef? Something creative.' He's enjoying the game, batting my life around as if it was fun.

'Actually, I was an art teacher.'

I didn't mean to tell him, but now it's out, it doesn't seem so bad. There was once a time when I was proud of my job, although it seems a lifetime ago now.

'You're a dark horse,' Owen says, reaching for his coffee. 'I'll give you some creative jobs in that case.'

I almost sigh with relief. He's helping me chip away my fears one tiny piece at a time. I want to hug him, even though he has no idea what he's done or why I feel so grateful. I go back to my desk to distract myself. It's that or I'll start crying.

'Thanks,' I say, far too late for it to sound genuine. Owen is engrossed in his work again. I turn round and try to catch his eye. 'I'd like that.' And it's true, I would. I grin, even though he has no idea why.

I stare down at my grubby sneakers, my bitten-down nails, catch sight of my reflection in the large window. My hair is a mess and my skin pale and sallow. I haven't seen a hairdresser for nearly a year. I want to change all this.

But by lunchtime, I've checked my thoughts again. I'm being reckless. An isolated existence is the best I can hope for now. Once I've sorted out Mum and Dad's finances, I'll have enough money to supplement my life in India.

But I can't get *him* from my mind – lying in the nursing home, barely alive, his wizened heart clenching and unclenching erratically inside his puny chest.

Even after I fetch Owen's lunch from the deli round the corner, contact the drinks reception venue to check the booking, and reply to a new client email, I can't shift the image of him from my mind.

Is he growing stronger each day, every heartbeat struggled out especially for me? What would he think if he knew I'd visited? He'd think I'd come to see him, of course, not believing for one minute I was checking that he couldn't hurt me. But that was Felix through and through – convinced the world was spun around him.

I can't help hating him for haunting me, even from the depths of a coma. Yet I still can't help sensing a pang of regret somewhere deep inside. It could have been so good.

'Hello, Brandrick's Architects, how may I help you?' I say, answering the phone. I catch Owen's eye and he smiles. I listen to the caller, unsure what they're talking about at first. 'Oh, no, sorry. I think you've got the wrong number. OK, bye.'

'I've been on to BT about it,' Owen says, shaking his head.

He glances up at me several times more during the next few minutes, not speaking, just looking.

I feel uncomfortable, but it's not his stare that is unsettling me. No, it's the visit to Woodford Grange – bringing back memories I thought I'd put to rest, reminding me of times lost, of hopes and dreams shared. I don't think I ever loved Felix more than the day he hung one of my paintings – a poor attempt at a portrait of him as a birthday gift – on his living-room wall. 'Picasso meets Francis Bacon,' he'd said with a laugh, admiring the twisted face. It was my style, and I knew he was just being kind, but I also saw the true love in his eyes.

I loved him once, too.

The feeling is fleeting. He killed my parents, stripping me, finally, of everything.

I try to concentrate on the remainder of my work, but at two o'clock, when I leave the office in a daze, barely hearing Owen's thanks for my good work, I don't immediately notice that the direction I'm heading in doesn't lead back to the flat.

'Hello again, love,' the receptionist says as I tentatively go through the front door.

Today she is wearing a pink blouse with a large bow at her neck. She's hunched over some paperwork and seems to be glad of the distraction.

'I don't think there's been any change overnight, but Megan will fill you in on your husband's condition. Just take a seat and she won't be long.' She gives me a long look.

'Thank you,' I say, sitting down in one of four chairs lined up against the wall opposite the glossy white desk.

The word *husband* makes my guts knot. Being a small nursing home, she must know most of the patients and their families personally. What must she think of me, the scruffy timid creature sitting opposite her?

I cross my legs then uncross them again, noticing that the lilies have dropped some petals on the floor since yesterday. Coming from the room behind the desk, I hear the same hushed voices discussing something. To my surprise, it appears to be about Christmas and shopping again. People get worked up about it so early, I think, promising myself I'll be safely ensconced at Bestluck by then.

Megan appears. 'You can come through now,' she says.

I didn't hear her padding down the corridor in her white, soft-soled shoes. She's pale and sweet with eyes that could never mean anyone harm.

'How is he?' I ask as we head towards Felix's room. What if he's woken up? My pulse quickens.

'No change, I'm afraid. The doctor saw him earlier.'

'Can he hear people talking to him?' I ask. We're right outside his door.

The nurse looks unsure. 'Some people say that patients in a vegetative state can hear their surroundings, yes. And certainly it's possible that given time he will slip in and out of consciousness, though never be fully aware. We do have patients like this who go home to be cared for long-term, but it's a full-time job, usually undertaken by a relative.'

My cheeks burn scarlet as I imagine myself bed-bathing Felix, cradling his lolling head, wiping dribble from his chin. I shudder at the thought, though I can't help wondering if things would be different if he had to rely on me.

'I'd like to think he can hear us,' I say, surprising myself as we go into his room.

Megan drags over a chair for me.

'Then just pretend he can,' she says with a kind glance before checking Felix's temperature, pulse and blood pressure. She makes notes in a file, then pulls the curtains closed across the window. 'The afternoon sun gets in his eyes,' she says thoughtfully. 'I'll leave you two alone for a while.'

I'm about to beg her to stay, to tell her that being left alone in a darkened room with Felix is the stuff of my nightmares, but it's too late. She's gone.

I stare at him for a full ten minutes, hardly daring to move. The tube down his throat looks uncomfortable, but the soft wheeze of his breathing is hypnotic.

'Felix?' I dare to whisper.

I watch for a response, but of course there's nothing. He's been this way for weeks now, although I can't help thinking that if he's going to wake up for anyone, it'll be for me.

I pull my chair closer. It can't hurt. His hands lie by his sides, on top of the thin white sheet. The skin on them is dry and papery, while the skin on his face is pale and slightly stubbly, as if he's not been shaved in a couple of days. He was always so meticulous about his appearance.

I have an overwhelming urge to reach out and touch him, to see if he feels the same as I remember from the early days – warm, alive, caring. We had some tender moments together, and I know I'm partly to blame for when things went wrong.

'It didn't have to be this way,' I whisper, although I'm probably convincing myself. What if things had been different, and I'd been more reasonable, less suspicious, more understanding?

'You're imagining things, Belle,' he'd said when I found the earring. It was in his car, in the passenger footwell, and it wasn't mine. 'I bought you those just after we got back from Paris, don't you remember? I thought the green would look beautiful against your hair.'

Green, I thought, shaking my head, staring at it. The colour of jealousy. I'd never seen it in my life before. But two days later, when I couldn't let it drop, Felix produced the other earring from a drawer, saying he'd found that lying around too, proving I was indeed mistaken. I didn't say anything else, even when both earrings then disappeared entirely. It was true I wanted him for myself, but I should have listened to my gut.

I glance at the door, making sure it's closed tightly. I don't want anyone to hear me.

'If you loved me, why did you always hurt me so much?'

I turn away, catching sight of a newspaper, folded open and left on a side table. I imagine a nurse reading it while observing Felix. The headline makes me catch my breath: *Canal-Girl Killer Linked to Alley Strangler*.

A team of detectives from West Midlands Police believe the death of student Melanie Carter in March could still be linked to the murder of airline employee Alexandra Stanford. The body of the 28-year-old cabin crew member was discovered dumped in an alley in

February. Both cases remain open, and are under review.

On Monday, investigating officer DI Lorraine Fisher refused to comment, but did state that even though no arrests had been made, the cases would continue to receive the same level of attention. There were also rumours that the 45-year-old detective had been suspended, although this has not been officially confirmed.

In a press conference, DI Adam Scott said, 'Following our recent televised reconstruction, we have new evidence to assist us working forward at speed. We urge any witnesses with information to contact us, as well as asking the public to remain vigilant.'

I chuck the newspaper on the table, barely able to finish reading, shuddering from the chill that sweeps through me, even though the room is warm. For a moment, I can hardly breathe. It sounds as if the police are beginning to make progress. What does this mean? I stare at Felix, thinking of what he's done, of everything that's happened. I need to be more careful than ever, I think, fixing my stare on his helpless body, the slow but steady rise and fall of his chest. My hand goes to the back of my neck where the infinity symbol is buried beneath my hair.

'Your first power-play,' I say, thinking back to how Felix wrong-footed me on our second date. By the time we got to the tattooist, it was too late. I was lost – drunk on wine, but intoxicated by him. He'd extracted me from a life I hadn't even realised was mundane.

Staring up at me from the upturned newspaper are two small photographs of Melanie Carter and Alexandra Stanford. Melanie's face looks distorted and ugly from where the paper is creased, and Alexandra appears sad and anxious, as if she knew what was about to befall her. It's almost as if they're speaking to me, calling out from within the newspaper to help them. I turn it over, unable to look a second longer.

'I had to get away,' I tell Felix. I want to reach out for his hand, dig my nails into his veiny skin. 'From you, that place you put me in. From everything.' If he could hear me, he'd never understand.

My fingers knit together in my lap like they used to in the group sessions at the hospital. I remember the agony of sitting in a circle of strangers, waiting nervously for my turn to speak. My face would fall parallel to my legs in shame as I searched for something to say, something that would make them believe there was nothing wrong with me, that I was innocent in all of this, even though I wasn't.

'Just tell us about yourself, Isabel. Not what happened to you. We don't want to upset the others,' Justin, the group counsellor, said at my first meeting.

It was Felix who convinced my GP to have me admitted. I have no idea how he was so convincing, but for a while I begged them, told my doctor there was nothing wrong with me, that it was *Felix* who needed help, but all that achieved was to show them that I was hysterical and out of control. In hindsight, hospital was the safest place for me. I was hidden away, out of sight.

'Take *back* control,' Justin had told us during that first session. I liked him. He wore a rainbow striped shirt, as if it would somehow cheer us all up, make us pull ourselves together. 'Manage your thoughts, grab them and ring-fence them. Then you have the power to change.' His face shone like a full moon above that ridiculous shirt, reflecting colours across his plump and sweaty face. He was so full of zest, of hope.

At the end of each session he had us setting tasks. 'A partner and a promise,' he sang out. 'Look them in the eye and make your pledge. This time next week we'll report back.'

I didn't tell my chosen partner, a sunken-eyed waif of a lad as long and skinny as a string bean, that my promise was not to be here this time next week. I knew, ultimately, that I had to escape. I wouldn't be safe here for ever. Meantime, I made up some promise about eating healthily, getting more exercise. In return, my dead-eyed partner stared directly at me and, with a blank expression, told me his pledge was to kill me. It was almost as if he'd been reading my mind.

By the end of the first week, alone in my room at night, awash with diazepam and haloperidol, the television chattering in the background, I almost understood what Justin had said about taking control of my thoughts. But it was a bleak realisation.

To feel hopeful ever again must have meant that I was, by then, hope*less*.

Mad, Felix had insisted as he'd kissed me goodbye. I was beginning to believe him.

There's no sign of Owen when I get back. I'm relieved, because I don't feel like being sociable. I go down the steps to the basement front door. The descent is treacherous and slippery, so I steady myself on the wall. It's not icy, but moss and lichen cover the old steps and the drizzle has slickened the surface. It's dark already, even though it's only late afternoon.

Once inside, I flick on the hall light.

It doesn't come on.

For a second, my heart jumps, until I convince myself that it's just a blown bulb or, at worst, a fuse has gone. I feel my way to the living room, not yet familiar with navigating my way around in the dark. The whole place feels cold and unwelcoming, but I tell myself that as soon as it's all lit up, when I have the television blaring out some mindless reality show for comfort, when I put the heating on and warm up the fish pie I bought from the corner shop, everything will seem OK again.

'Thank God,' I say, breathing out as the lights in the living room work just fine.

I unzip my coat and go through to the bedroom at the back. All I want is my food, my pyjamas, a cup of tea and an early night. Working at the office has taken it out of me, not to mention the effect of seeing Felix again.

Face your fears . . . Forgive your enemies . . . Justin's words rushed through my mind all the way home, and I felt the familiar giddiness of something inside me unravelling. I knew it was fear.

I put the bedroom light on and scream. I can't help it. Even before I work out what it is or what it means, I know it's going to be bad.

I ram myself back against the wall, trying to get away from the photographs spread out on the bed. My eyes scan the rest of the room.

Someone's been in here . . . *he's* been in here. But how is that possible?

I don't know which is faster, my thoughts or my heart, but after I've grabbed a knife from the kitchen drawer, stalked through the entire flat twice, terrified and shaking, looking nervously behind every door, in the wardrobe, under the bed and behind the sofa, I go back into the bedroom and pick up one of the pictures.

It's of me, looking dejected and too thin. My skin is grey and loose, and I'm sitting alone on a bench in the hospital grounds at Sandy Acres. I'm holding a cigarette and scowling, looking slightly away from the camera, oblivious to the zoom lens that has found me, intruded upon my solitary moment of misery.

Who took this?

I pick up another picture, and as if the intrusion of the first image wasn't enough, this one has captured me with Owen just a few days ago when we visited my parents' graves. I am a sorry and sad sight, hands shoved in pockets, head down, with Owen standing beside me.

The final two photographs are of me again, though this time I don't immediately recognise where I am – somewhere in the city, on my own, striding purposefully. One captures me looking back over my shoulder, my mouth slightly open, my face a picture of fear, while the other shows the back of me, my hair flowing behind. It looks as if I'm running away.

I feel sick. Fighting it down, I drop the pictures back on to the bed. Someone has been watching me, following me, has broken into this flat. I know I should call the police, but what good would that do? They'd look at my past, and they'd never believe me. I can't take the risk. I need to get out of here, but I can't leave yet. My mind races, trying to work out what it all means, but then the vomit comes into my mouth and I have to run for the bathroom.

22

I can't recall the last time I lied to Adam, if I ever did. I feel small and deceitful standing in front of him in our kitchen, but all it takes is a whisper from Alexandra Stanford, a tug deep inside my conscience, and my resolve rushes back.

'The cinema?' he says, looking puzzled. 'Since when do you ever go to the cinema?'

'Exactly,' I tell him before limping out of the house, unable to look him in the eye.

He calls after me, asking how I'm going to get there with my leg like this, but I pretend not to hear.

Once in the car, I unstrap my boot, shoving my bad foot into a shoe. It hurts like hell, but allows me to drive.

Adam has the night off, and Stella and Grace are occupied with friends. The itch I've had since Rowlands gave me the list of names is so big there's no way I'm going to last the evening without knowing more about the women on it.

The office isn't completely deserted when I arrive in

the department, although it's thankfully quiet. A handful of officers populate the dimly lit space, hunched over their desks, stuffing down quick snacks and gulping coffee.

'I've just come to collect some stuff,' I say to a couple of the detectives as they track my path to my desk. They glance at my leg. Word is bound to have spread about my 'suspension' – it was printed in the newspaper, for God's sake – even though it couldn't be further from the truth. I want to shout it out, plaster a poster on the wall: *I'm just taking a holiday!* But Adam says I should let it go, that he'll put anyone who asks straight on the matter, tell them I'm working from home until my ankle heals. But it still cuts deep, and of course if he finds out I've been in here tonight, he'll be less inclined to cover for me.

I hobble over to my area, and I'm grateful to see that no one is using my desk, as so often happens as soon as anyone is off sick or on holiday. It doesn't take me long to get stuck into what's been bugging me, although I'm bound to be lagging behind. If Ed Rowlands made it known I'd requested this list, Bob will either have written it off as a waste of resources, or have a couple of DCs cracking on with interviewing the women too.

'Thought you were off, ma'am,' a young detective says cautiously as she walks past.

I look up, unable to recall her name, though I know she's been working here a few months now. My mind once took notice of these things, filed away useful snippets, helpful fillers that would one day come in useful. Now it seems as if I'm more concerned with survival, with getting through each day without making too many errors. A frown sweeps across my face, although I quickly replace it with a smile.

'I am until this heals,' I say, tapping the plastic boot, making sure she sees it. 'But I just needed to fetch a few things.' I make a show of gathering up some books.

'Sorry to see that, ma'am. Hope it's not too painful. You make sure you rest up,' she says, walking away.

Any gossip clearly hasn't percolated too widely, and I'm grateful for that.

Soon, I'm poring over the next case file from the list. It concerns a woman called Isabel Moore, who also complained of being stalked and harassed by her partner. The trouble began when she tried to end their relationship.

I shake my head and stretch. There's nothing much to go on in this file apart from Isabel's regular complaints. It makes for repetitive reading. No action could be taken because she failed to supply clear evidence to prove that he was harassing her. She stated the man was making her life unbearable, yet even though she was instructed to keep records by our officers, no logs were forthcoming.

I read on, angling the desk lamp over the pages. There are some handwritten statements, and some printed from the computer. I imagine the officer in Miss Moore's home, clipboard balanced on his knee, taking down everything she told him, instinctively knowing that the woman was in trouble but, frustratingly, not being able to do a damn thing about it.

I also discover how the investigating officers went to

interview the man in question, gave him verbal warnings to keep away from Miss Moore, and informed him what would happen if he continued to harass her. The attending officer noted that he was cold, unapproachable, almost as if he were untouchable. According to the records, there was even a brief period of surveillance of his activities, but no evidence was gathered.

'Goodnight, ma'am. Don't let the bedbugs bite,' the young officer says, heading for the door. She's layered up in motorcycle gear, a helmet tucked under her arm, leaving a leathery smell in her wake as she strides past.

I smile vaguely in her direction and raise a hand, before returning to the reports. I hope she doesn't tell anyone I was here.

If the complaints hadn't stopped abruptly earlier in the year, leaving the file looking a lot like a movie without an ending, I probably wouldn't have felt inclined to sling on my coat, grab my bag and crutches, and seek out Miss Isabel Moore. But it's too similar to what Bethany told me about Joe Douglas – in that it all just ceased. In my experience, it generally doesn't happen like that. Either the harassment continues indefinitely, action is eventually taken, or the woman gets hurt.

Not wanting to draw any more attention to myself, I quickly photocopy relevant pages from the files, put them away, flick off my desk lamp, and leave the building. Thankfully, no one sees me limping through the car park, wrenching off my Aircast and stuffing my foot into my shoe. In the car, I wince against the pain as I press the pedals, breathing through it, reaching into my bag for a couple of pills.

The indicator switch clicks a depressing beat at the lights, especially now that the rain has begun again. Red and orange streaks sweep across the smeary windscreen like horizontal fireworks as I wait.

It's probably futile, but I want to pay a visit to the last address on file for Isabel Moore. It was given in her statement at the end of January and noted as being that of her parents. It's not far out of my way – wherever my way actually is, I think, driving away from the junction.

'*Have* I lost it?' I wonder out loud, barely realising it was me speaking until the words sink in. Everything in my life feels lost right now, slipping inexorably through my fingers.

I turn on the radio. Loud music blares out when I was expecting the news on Radio 4.

'Thanks, Stella,' I mumble, jabbing at buttons to try to get my preferred station back.

In the end I give up and turn it off. My thoughts are as blurry as the windscreen.

The front garden is overgrown. It stands out among the other cared-for patches that line the suburban street. Even before I knock, I can see no one's home: most of the other houses have their lights on, but this one is dark and unlit.

When no one comes to the door, I go to the adjoining neighbour's house and ring the bell, telling the woman who answers my name and showing her my warrant card.

241

She gives it a cursory glance, staring at the one crutch I'm leaning on.

'Terrible, wasn't it?' she says, as if I know what she's talking about. 'Poor Ingrid just wanted to start again, you know. Pick up the pieces.'

'I'm sorry, I don't know,' I say, confused, though grateful she seems chatty. Most neighbours are usually helpful and willing to talk about local goings-on. True to form, this woman is one of them.

'What a way to go,' she continues. 'When their daughter disappeared, John and Ingrid were inconsolable. They called the police for help, of course, but they weren't much use. Just put her on a missing persons register. In the end, they decided to start a new life in Spain, but were killed in a car crash before they even made it to the airport.'

The woman shakes her head in sympathy.

'As for their daughter, Isabel, all Ingrid ever wanted was for her to be happy, to marry her off.' Then she points at the house next door. 'But . . .' She crosses her arms tightly, leaning in towards me and whispering. 'Well, between you and me, it was almost a blessing that she vanished.'

'Why is that?'

'Poor John and Ingrid did everything for that girl. If you ask me, she was nothing but ungrateful, didn't do herself any favours.'

She raises her voice again, allowing her arms to drop by her sides.

'As for the state of the garden, I've said to Bill a hundred times, really, Bill, we should go in and lend a hand. You know, sort out the weeds and lawn. Someone's going to want to sell the place and—'

'So, just to clarify, Mrs . . .' I say.

'Mrs Welland.'

'To clarify, Mrs Welland. You say that the owners—'

'John and Ingrid Moore.'

'They were killed in a car crash and their daughter, Isabel Moore, is missing?' I try to hide my incredulity.

'Correct,' she replies.

I wait a few seconds – a useful tactic. Thankfully Mrs Welland hasn't yet burned herself out.

'A while ago, Ingrid told me that Isabel had met a nice man. A *pilot*, don't you know. She hoped they'd marry.' Mrs Welland suddenly looks pained, her face crumpling. 'But then Isabel went a bit off the rails. Up here.' She taps the side of her head.

'I'm sorry?'

'You know, not right up here.' She taps her head again, harder this time, as if I should know what she means.

I nod slowly, hoping she'll go on.

'She was in hospital for a couple of months in the spring. After a while, Ingrid told me she was getting better, that she'd be coming home soon. No one liked to talk about it much, being a mental place and all. But then one day, I heard that Isabel had vanished.'

The woman leans closer again.

'Some say she escaped. No one's seen her since. Ingrid and John blamed themselves, of course. That poor man, her boyfriend, was driving the car when the crash happened. Ingrid said he adored Isabel, you know. He'd mentioned marriage to John, asking for her hand and all that.'

'What a terrible story. Do you know what happened to the driver?' I can't help wondering if he's the same person Isabel made the complaints about, the one she said she'd broken up from.

'I do,' Mrs Welland replies, looking pleased with herself. 'A man came calling not long ago, looking for Isabel. He had some things to return that he'd borrowed. He was handsome and tall with a big shock of curly dark hair. He asked me to pass on the news to Isabel about the crash if I saw her before she was found. I'm afraid it's both good and bad.'

I raise my eyebrows at the unstoppable woman.

'Turns out Isabel's boyfriend is in a *coma*.' Her face creeps into a shocked expression, as if she's finding out all over again. 'They're not sure if he'll ever wake up.' She shakes her head, dislodging a scarf that was tied round her hair. She holds it between her hands. 'He's a vegetable,' she mouths almost inaudibly.

'How terrible,' I say, disappointed I won't be able to interview him. 'Do you know the driver's name?'

'Felix Darwin,' she says, confirming what I thought – the same name as in the file. 'Apparently they moved him to one of those long-term care places. I said, Bill, I said, you know they've moved him in there to die, don't you?' She folds her arms, leaning against the door frame.

'I'm sure it's not *quite* like that,' I say. 'Do you know the name of the nursing home?'

'As it happens, I do. That nice man gave me their card in case Isabel came back. He told me to give it to her. He was quite insistent.'

Mrs Welland leans inside her hallway and opens the drawer of a small, old-fashioned telephone unit. She retrieves a card and hands it to me. 'Keep it,' she says. 'No use to us.'

'Thanks,' I say, popping it in my bag.

'And this is Isabel, look,' she says, leaning inside again and producing a small photograph in a wooden frame. 'We had a street party for the Queen's jubilee. We all brought out tables and bunting, see, and everyone shared the food. Isabel's the one at the back in the red and blue dress. A pretty lass, don't you think?'

I stare at the picture she's holding. Isabel is half hidden in the group of people, but I get a look at her face. 'She is indeed,' I reply, but as soon as I look up again, Mrs Welland clicks the door shut and I hear the key turn inside.

Woodford Grange Nursing Home is on a familiar route, located halfway down a street I know quite well. For some reason, I almost recognise the smart red-brick building. Most of the properties down here have been given over to consulting rooms, practices, flats or solicitors' premises, only a few remaining as actual homes. I can't imagine what such a place would cost to buy – well over a million, I think as I approach the door.

'I'm a detective from West Midlands Police,' I say into the intercom. 'I'd like to speak to someone about a patient.'

The door buzzes and I limp inside.

The woman at the reception desk is slightly frosty and flustered, as if I've caught her off-guard, but then so are the harangued receptionists at my GP's practice. I ignore her brusque manner in the hope I can get a favour or two.

'Are you the relative of a patient?' she asks.

'No. As I said, I'm a police detective.'

I show her my warrant card, but she doesn't give it much of a glance. Her face is pale and tight, reflecting the clinical surroundings, and she seems nervous, as if she's not used to dealing with matters outside of the ordinary. I soften my approach.

'I'm really sorry to call in unannounced, but I just wanted a few details about a Mr Felix Darwin.'

At the mention of his name, I can see I'm in the right place. A flash of recognition sweeps over her. I don't suppose there are too many patients here at any one time.

'I'm not at liberty to discuss patients' details,' she tells me, quite rightly. 'But it puts me in an awkward position, what with you being the police and all.' She gives a bitter little smile. 'I can see if Mr Darwin's doctor is free to chat with you.'

'Thank you,' I tell her, and take a seat as she instructs, thankful to take the weight off my ankle.

She walks off down a corridor behind her desk and veers off into a room at the end.

Woodford Grange is clearly a private establishment,

probably with an arrangement to take NHS patients if required. Half of me is inclined to agree with Mrs Welland – that they sent Felix Darwin here to die.

A few minutes later the woman returns.

'Unfortunately, Dr Lambeth is busy with a patient right now. Can you tell me the nature of your enquiry?' she says.

'I really just want to know if it will be possible to interview Mr Darwin any time soon.'

'He's in a coma,' she replies flatly. The pitiful look on her face confirms my thoughtless question.

'I'm sorry to hear that,' I say. 'There are some issues from a while ago that need clearing up.'

The woman's eyes narrow, as if she knows more than she's letting on.

'And there are one or two things about the accident that need clarifying. Does Mr Darwin have any relatives I could contact?'

The woman sighs and drops down into the chair behind her desk, shaking her head as if she's suddenly found some sympathy for me. She looks into a computer and taps away at the keyboard, before giving a quick glance down the corridor.

'His wife Isabel visited him recently, but I don't have any more information.' She suddenly looks horrified, as if she's said too much. Her hand goes over her mouth. 'My boss would sack me for even telling you that much.'

I mull over this. As far as I'm aware, Isabel and Felix didn't marry.

'Well perhaps you could give her my card when she next comes. Ask her to call me. It's really important.'

The receptionist nods, saying she will.

'And the prognosis for Mr Darwin?'

She opens her mouth to speak but shakes her head instead, not knowing what to say. Then the telephone rings and she answers it, dismissing me with the aversion of her eyes.

23

Owen turns the music up full blast. 'It'll do you good.' He pulls a silly face, his curls flopping over his eyes like a teenager's unruly hair. 'Get your moves ooon,' he croons.

He shimmies across the wooden floor in full view of the bay window, hands in the air. His hips perform a seductive figure of eight. His eyes are closed and the expression on his face pulses out the beat. I can't help bursting into fits of laughter.

'You look like . . .' I bend forward, hands on knees, doubled up. 'Like a cross between Adam Ant and Michael Jackson.'

Then his arm is around my wrist, so tightly, so suddenly, it sends shockwaves to my heart. I can't help tensing and letting out a little scream. He stops dancing and raises his hands apologetically.

'God, I'm so sorry, Isabel. I just wanted to cheer you up. You seem so serious today.'

Rick Astley's 'Never Gonna Give You Up' continues to blare around us. It brings the smile back to my face.

'No, no, I'm sorry. It's me, not you.'

I shake it all from my head, letting the upbeat music drag me out of my dark place. I tell myself over and over that right now, here in this room with Owen, I am safe. Nothing bad is going to happen. I throw my arms above my head, pulling some crazy dance moves to match Owen's.

'You're not the only one who can get it *ooon*!'

I strut provocatively in time to the music. Our eyes lock together, far too long for it to be coincidence. It's me who looks away first, and then my heart sends one almighty pulse up my throat.

'Time for some more wine,' Owen says, topping up each of our glasses.

'Did you decide on the New Zealand Sauvignon Blanc for the event?' I say, trying to sound normal, aiming the remote control at Owen's iPod dock and turning down the music.

'I did indeed. And did you manage to sort things with the venue?'

We spend the next ten minutes awkwardly discussing work until Owen apologises. 'Let's not talk shop.'

He comes up to me, taking hold of me much more gently this time. He prises the glass from my tense fist and places it on the worktop, gently encircling my wrists with his large hands. I feel myself being drawn close to him. This time, I don't protest.

We stand pressed together at the waist, the tops of our thighs warm against each other. His arms are steady and strong, wrapping around me, while mine are shaking and dangling.

'How about that meal out then? There's a great Thai place round the corner.'

I smell the wine on his breath, the waft of his words on my skin.

'I'd like that.' I don't know where to look. Any moment, I expect to feel the warmth of his mouth on mine. But it doesn't come.

'Great,' he says, backing away. 'Grab your coat from downstairs and I'll meet you outside in five minutes.'

I knock back the last inch of my wine. I'm wary of going into the flat after what happened. I haven't mentioned it to Owen. He'd kick me out in a flash if he thought I'd lured an intruder into his property – especially an intruder who won't give up, who will hound me wherever I go. Once again I can feel the weight of my life slowly, steadily, closing in on me as I'm backed into a corner. I sense it's only a matter of time.

It turns out a meal with Owen is just what I need. The restaurant is full, but thankfully we are given a small table for two at the back. Owen pulls out my chair for me, and I sit down cautiously.

Felix used to do the same, usually at the start of an intense evening during which criticisms were rife. He once passed me a perfume spray under the table, saying I should put it on, that it used to belong to his mother. I stared at the old-fashioned bottle, tried a little on my wrist. It wasn't my type of scent, but I doused it on my neck anyway. Felix smiled appreciatively, took a tight hold of my hand across the table.

'Mother would buy herself a new bottle every Christmas,' he explained, breathing in deeply. He'd already told me she'd died when he was a boy.

'What's up?' Owen says, breaking my thoughts. 'You look pensive.'

I shrug out of the memory, unfold my napkin. 'Oh, nothing.' I smile, looking at the menu.

'Thanks for everything you did today,' he says.

'It's what you're paying me for.'

It's true, I worked hard at the office, and then, after visiting Felix, I spent a couple of hours at my parents' place, picking through the desolate landscape of their lost lives. Each left me exhausted, the latter utterly morose.

Owen sighs, watching me.

'Tell me to butt out, Isabel,' he says, leaning forward on his forearms. 'I know you have a lot on your mind, but recently you've seemed particularly upset about something.' He takes the wine list from the waiter and thanks him. 'Can I help at all?'

I fiddle with my napkin, eventually dropping it on the floor. Our hands meet as we both lunge to pick it up. Owen laughs, handing it back to me.

I don't know where to begin. A huge part of me wants to spill everything, tell him that someone has been following me – him too – and that they broke into the flat and left pictures on my bed. But I don't trust myself not to pour everything out, and it's not fair to involve him in my mess. If I do, he'll only go to the police, believing he's helping, and I just can't face how I felt earlier in the day – completely torn, but also as if I should tell someone official what I knew.

After I left my parents' house, I actually began the long walk to the police headquarters, thinking it was for the best. Everything in Mum and Dad's place had upset me, and I didn't think I could carry on. With what I know about Felix, with that write-up in the newspaper, Melanie and Alexandra's faces staring back at me, I wasn't sure how much longer I could hold it inside. With tears streaming down my face, I kept my head down and marched on. I was literally scared for my life.

But halfway to the police station I felt as if Felix was talking to me, begging me to turn back. He might be in a coma, but he still has a hold over me. I stopped, thought of the consequences, and did what the inner voice implored.

'Thanks, but there's nothing you can do,' I reply to Owen, biting on my bottom lip like a squirming kid.

I open my menu and scan the list of dishes, not feeling hungry.

'Really? I might be able to help.'

'I'm just a bit confused.' I attempt a smile but it doesn't work. 'Still grieving.'

The waiter pours water for us.

'I'll be going back to India soon, although certain things are tempting me to stay.'

Of all the things I could have picked to change the subject, that was not the right one.

'Such as?' Owen asks, giving me the same mysterious look as when we were dancing. But then he's shaking his head. 'God, I'm so sorry. That was really insensitive. With everything that's happened, it's obvious why you need to be in England.'

'But you're wrong,' I say, and again it's as if my mouth has disconnected from my brain.

Owen looks at me over the rim of his glass. His eyes are reflected in the water.

'It's not the dead who are keeping me here,' I tell him, digging my nails into my palms under the table.

As a distraction, Owen orders some wine. I still feel giddy from the glass or two we had at his house.

'What I'm trying to say,' I continue, 'is that even though I'm back in England because of terrible circumstances, if it wasn't for that, I'd feel quite settled.' It's a lie, of course, because of those pictures on my bed, but I want to stop Owen from prying. I've never felt so unsafe, even though I thought I'd proved that Felix can't hurt me. 'It's weird. I feel . . .' I hesitate. The right words won't come, so I stare into Owen's eyes instead.

'I feel the same way,' he says.

He takes hold of my fidgeting hands across the table.

'You do?' If things were different, I'd be pleased to hear this. Owen is very attractive.

He's nodding. 'From the first time I saw you at Bestluck,

if you want the truth. For a few coins, Javesh told me everything I needed to know.'

He grins and says *Mees Eezee* in a silly voice.

'I was disappointed when he told me you lived there, that you wouldn't be heading back to England any time soon. Had I known what bad news that letter contained, I wouldn't have been quite so keen to hand-deliver it to you. It was my clumsy way of getting to meet you.'

As he speaks, there's a whooshing sound in my head, as if I'm standing under a waterfall.

'*Really?*'

'Really.'

'I think this is where it gets complicated,' I say. No one deserves someone like me.

'It doesn't seem very complicated from where I'm standing.'

Owen's thumbs rub over the backs of my hands.

'Take it from me, it is.' My eyes flick down the menu in panic. 'I'll have the steamed dumplings, followed by the king prawns. How about you?'

'Isabel . . .'

He looks at me in a way that makes my stomach roll.

'You don't understand, Owen.'

My eyes hang heavy between us.

'You've been through hell with what happened to your parents, but there's something else. I know there is.'

I barely have the energy for the level of deceit required right now. All I want is to curl up alone in my bed, sleep for days, and hope everything bad will be gone when I wake up.

'Will you let it go if I tell you that you're right?'

The waiter pours the wine and takes our order. I barely hear myself reciting things from the menu. Nothing seems real as the guilt grows – as well as the guilt I feel for having dinner with another man. It's as if Felix is here, watching us. Even though I know he isn't.

'OK,' he says, 'no more questions, although I'm sorry to hear you have other problems.' He takes a long sip of wine, all the while staring at me. 'You know I'll help you if I can.'

I look away grimly. It's the first time in ages that things could almost be going right for me, yet I have no choice but to walk away. If I tell Owen the truth, I'll be putting him in danger.

'It's all very cryptic, but I understand,' he says finally, checking his phone discreetly. He places it face down on the table. 'If there's someone else, please tell me.'

I want to laugh loudly. How can there *ever* be anyone else so long as Felix is alive? But it's not what I need to hear from Owen. I want him to grab me by the hands, pull me close across the table, force a kiss from me with his palm flat around the back of my head. Tell me a million times that everything is OK, that he'll protect me and keep me safe from all the bad things that are creeping up on me.

Instead, we chat about why he became an architect, how it was never really his idea and he was just pleasing his father. He tells me that he didn't do well at school, scraped into university. Fond memories cause him to smile, making little creases form around his eyes. When he moves, I smell his cologne, the soft fresh scent of his shirt.

'Do you think you'll ever go back to teaching?' he asks, followed by a string of other questions.

The inquisition reminds me of the grilling I got at my parents' house earlier. Their neighbour, Mrs Welland, was out of her front door as soon as I walked up the path, almost as if she'd been waiting for me.

'Isabel! Isabel!' she called out, her arms flapping wildly, from the other side of the low fence that separated my parents' shamefully overgrown front garden from her neat lawn and beds.

I flinched at the sound of her voice, hurrying to get the key into the lock. I wanted her to go away. When I didn't acknowledge her, she hurried out on to the pavement and flopped up the front path in her slippers. I stood cowering in the porch.

'Where have you *been*? People have been looking for you,' she said urgently. Her mouth was puckered, her manner accusing as she went on and on about me disappearing, hurting my parents, causing so much trouble.

'Hello,' I responded timidly, turning back to the stiff lock.

'There was a man here a week or two ago, wanting to return stuff. And the police came again, too.' She was breathless from her ranting. She wasn't making sense.

'The police?' Surely the accident had been dealt with weeks ago. And I had no idea who the man might be.

'A detective. She wanted to talk to you.' Mrs Welland pulled a smart phone from her pocket, incongruous-looking in her old hand, and tapped at the screen.

'She wanted to talk to *me*?' I said, trying to hide the shudder and shock that coursed through me.

She nodded. 'I make a note of everything these days. My memory isn't what it used to be.' She gave a slightly girlish giggle, which made me feel sad. She was about the same age as my mum. 'Detective Inspector Lorraine Fisher was her name,' she said, waving the phone at me. 'She seemed kind.'

I nodded, barely listening to her now, and said the name a few times over in my mind, fixing it in place. After Felix found out I'd been logging everything, he destroyed my notebook. I had to learn to keep track of things without writing them down. I became used to holding on to details.

'Aren't you hungry, Isabel?' Owen asks. Then there's a warmth on the back of my hand, as if an external heart is pulsing life into me. 'Your food's here.'

I jump, pulling myself back into the moment. 'Sorry,' I say. 'I was miles away.' I give him an awkward smile.

Owen tucks into his starter, crunching and dipping and biting, offering morsels my way held precariously between chopsticks. I take a dainty bite from a fish skewer and make an agreeable sound, smiling appreciatively. I only manage to eat half of my dumplings, sliding the plate away.

'You were going to tell me about your job as an art teacher,' he says, making me feel sick all over again.

'I won't teach again,' I say truthfully, even though there's no reason why I shouldn't. Allegations were dropped, no charges brought against me. 'There are other things in life to try.'

When he asks me what, I shrug a coy non-reply, picking at a prawn cracker to distract myself.

'You're a mystery, Mees Eezee,' he says fondly.

He leans forward, his forearms exposed on the table, and I wonder if he's going to take my hand. He doesn't.

After our main course, after we finish the remainder of the wine, we leave the boozy, spicy atmosphere of the Orchid Garden and amble back towards Owen's house. The night is still and cold, the kind of night when, as a child, I would lie on my back in the freezing garden, enthralled, staring up at the cloudless sky.

Owen stops suddenly. 'Look! Did you see it?' His face is close to mine as his gloved hand points skyward. His other arm is around my waist, pulling me towards him. 'A shooting star.' His finger draws out the trajectory.

'I missed it,' I say, screwing up my eyes. 'But I'll make a wish anyway.'

A second later, I breathe out, laughing and giggling like that little kid on her back again.

'Let me guess what you wished for,' Owen says, turning me round to face him.

I shake my head. 'You never will.'

And then his mouth comes down on mine, kissing me deeply.

'That?' he says afterwards.

My head swims as the heat spreads through me. I don't have the heart to tell him that he was wrong.

Early the next morning when I ring the entry bell at Woodford Grange, the receptionist clearly hasn't long arrived. She's only just pinning on her name badge – I notice she's called Penny – and she seems very flustered when I ask to see Felix.

'Visiting doesn't begin until midday.' She glances at her watch, then down the corridor. The place seems rather deserted, with no sign of any staff. 'I suppose it would be OK for you to visit, but I'll have to check first.'

'I'm sorry,' I say sheepishly. 'But I'll be at work later.'

Penny disappears for a short while, then returns, telling me I can go down to his room.

Felix is wearing a different-coloured gown today. The crisp lemon yellow cotton reflects on his face, making him look jaundiced, sicker than ever. Someone has shaved him. The drip stand hovering over the head of his bed has two bags attached to it – one containing a white, milky-looking liquid, the other filled with what I assume is saline. Thin tubes wind their way down to his body – one disappearing into the back of his hand, where the cannula is stuck on with white tape, the other going beneath his gown, presumably to a deeper line. His breathing is slow and steady, and his eyes are closed. Dead still.

'Hello Felix,' I find myself saying softly. It feels as if someone is watching me, judging me. 'I've come to see you again.' Even if he was awake, he'd struggle to hear me.

I unzip my coat and put down my bag. The room is warm and airless.

'I'm only here out of guilt, you know.' I want him to be clear on this.

Then, accidentally, I make the sound he hated – somewhere between a laugh and a snort. In the end, I grew used to feeling ashamed of everything I did wrong.

'I did love you once.'

The words float between us. He doesn't move.

'But that wasn't enough for you, was it?'

Felix had an irreparable hole in his heart that neither I nor all his other women combined could fill.

Numbness followed my discovery of them, of course, instigating my escape from his captivity. Ironic, seeing as I was just growing accustomed to his possessive ways – almost enjoying the sanctuary he and his clinical flat provided. After the scandal with the boy at school, it actually became a respite – from the shame, from my family, even from myself. I didn't have to think about anything while in Felix's safekeeping. I felt loved and cocooned.

All part of his plan, I now realise, but cage an animal and either it dies or finds a way out.

'I don't want you going in there,' he'd told me from the start.

It was his flat, after all. I'd assumed keeping out of the

smallest bedroom was just another of his obsessive foibles. There were so many of them.

Don't make the bed like that . . . don't put your shoes there . . . make sure your toothbrush is facing the wall . . . don't put different types of plate in the dishwasher together . . . don't run the hot and cold tap at the same time . . . don't wear red on a Sunday . . .

'Mother would have had words with you about that,' he told me once after I'd opened the curtains in the wrong order. He explained that I had to learn to do things her way, that she'd be cross if I didn't comply. I didn't know it then, but she was an impossible act to follow, although one that Felix would never cease trying to teach me.

Then, one day, the room wasn't locked.

I was bored, pacing up and down, waiting for the sound of his key in the front door. Absent-mindedly, I tried the handle of the forbidden room – a small box room he used as a study.

It opened.

At first, I was disappointed. There was barely anything in there – just a desk, a chair and a bookshelf.

The thick album was the only thing in the desk drawer. I lifted it out carefully, mesmerised by the picture of a woman stuck on the front, a beautiful redhead with faraway eyes. I immediately knew she was his mother – he'd handwritten the dates of her birth and death beneath.

Her eyes unnerved me, making me feel as if I was looking into a mirror. I knew she was called Ellen and that she'd died when Felix was young, but that was all. He was secretive about her, protective, as if he didn't want to share her.

I opened the book, expecting old photographs and memorabilia about her, but I couldn't have been more wrong. There were photographs in there, yes, but not of his mother.

I stopped, listening out for his return. I knew he'd kill me if he found me in there.

I turned the pages, transfixed by the beautiful women contained within the leaves. Each one was unmistakably a poor replica of his mother – some with hair to match, others with the same cheekbones or staring eyes.

I read his annotations, scribbled above or below each picture. There were hundreds of them.

Annie – too unpredictable. Breasts small. Smelled wrong. Teeth crooked.

Pamela – accommodating, but overtly sexual. Nails stubby. Hair too short and unwashed. Overweight. Generally unpleasant.

Natasha – perfect in character. Laugh good. Too timid, but can be changed. Willing to try. Possible, especially as eyes right colour.

Alexandra – A rare one! Physically perfect. Waist narrow, legs shapely, hair and eyes 10/10. Keep on list!

Later, he'd written that he told her he loved her, had been on many dates with her, and even paid for a tattoo. He'd added a doodle that made my skin crawl.

The infinity symbol.

The dog-eared pages went on and on, cataloguing dozens of women he'd tried to match to his mother.

Julie K – refused exclusivity. Career-minded and little free time, although hair good and build right. Keep open mind. Bit of a cow on phone.

Kat – nothing more than a prostitute. Mother would have hated.

Angie – headstrong and rude. Avoid! (Shame, promising.)

Melanie – A strong contender. And so deliciously young! I love her, but need her to love me back. (Got her the tattoo, but things became weird. Parents trying to contact me. Lying low, though finding that impossible.)

Isabel –

Nothing was written about me. Just blank space next to the thirty or forty photographs he'd pasted on my pages. I barely recognised myself. Photographs taken covertly. Naked. Sleeping. Driving. Some taken before we'd even met that day in the supermarket.

My skin went cold. Sweat broke out the length of my spine. The list went on and on, over a hundred pages stuffed full of similar-looking women. It must have taken him years to create, if not decades, judging by some of the fashions.

The album was his dossier.

His catalogue of women.

His human resource.

All entries were dated, some overlapping, and several of them with me, including Alexandra. Each woman's address and phone number, date of birth, schools attended, and a brief, one-sentence summary were included.

For my summary he'd simply written: The One.

So why was he treating me like this?

I cried for an hour, and then I called my mum.

When she arrived, I couldn't bear to show her the album. I was too ashamed, and she'd only have gone to the police. I'd already marked my card with them, made them believe I was a nuisance. I just didn't want any more trouble.

Mum listened as I confessed some of Felix's weird habits, the things he made me do, and for an hour she comforted me, telling me everything would be OK.

'Dad can have a word with him, if you like,' she said, trying to help.

I didn't tell her it wouldn't do any good.

'You know that Felix adores you, don't you darling?' she crooned into my hair, rocking me. 'Don't forget, if he's never lived with anyone before, he's probably finding it just as hard as you are. And his job must be very stressful. Give him time, sweetheart. You're so perfect together.'

It was then I knew that Mum would never understand what he was like. It was impossible to explain Felix's behaviour without making myself sound crazy. I soaked up Mum's comfort, allowed her to look after me for the afternoon, and then she left, making me promise I'd call her if I became upset again.

Then, an hour before Felix was due back, I ran away.

'I hope you see the irony,' I say to him as he lies in his hospital bed. 'You lying there. Me free to go.'

I didn't tell Owen I was coming here today, not after what happened between us last night. It's because of that I'm visiting. I need to keep checking that Felix hasn't woken up.

'It's odd,' I tell him honestly. 'Part of me still wants to love you, have things back the way they were.'

And it's true, even though I know it's impossible. After I found the book, I realised how much I loved him, how much I wanted him for myself. Mum had been right: beneath all of Felix's funny ways, his controlling behaviour, he really loved me back. But it was my desire to be the one, the *only* one, which drove us apart in the end. Even now, I sometimes wonder how I'll get through the rest of my life without him.

I half expect his eyes to flash open. Instead, mine clamp shut, shocked by my admission. I pray he can't hear me. And then I do the unthinkable: I slip my hand beneath his flat palm as it lies face down by his side. His skin is cool and dry.

'I thought you were the one, too,' I tell him.

It feels like an ending.

Suddenly I leap up, retracting my hand as if I've been electrocuted. I scrape back my chair, gasping for breath.

For a second, I can't move, but then I grab my bag and dash for the door, running down the corridor, not looking back. I try to conceal my panicked breathing as I run past

Penny at reception. She looks up to speak, but I don't hear her.

The sting of Felix's grip is still burning my hand as I charge down the street.

24

I've never piloted an aircraft in my life. The thought of it fills me with fear and dread. I'll travel in them if absolutely necessary, but otherwise I like to keep my feet firmly on the ground.

Of course, the women like it that I'm a pilot – all uniform, dark glasses and glamorous destinations – but I'm careful how I play it. Sleight of hand, smoke and mirrors, a dash of charm, and they believe what they want to believe.

I am, in fact, the one and only Mr Beefy, proud owner of forty-two burger bars situated up and down the country, many found at motorway service stations. Thanks, Dad, for my magnificent inheritance.

It was when I arrived back from Rome that I discovered Isabel missing. Well, not really Rome of course, but that was what I was primed to tell her. I'd even changed my suit to rid myself of the greasy burger smell from the branches I'd visited that day, and used one of my stash of airport duty-free bags, popping in a box of her favourite perfume to give her.

She can't have been missing long because the spicy scent of her still lingered in my flat, and there seemed to be an orange hue hanging in the air, like some kind of vapour trail, such was the glow of her hair.

I dashed around, flinging open all the doors in my flat, even cupboards and wardrobes, just in case she was playing some kind of game.

And then I found the spare bedroom door unlocked. My book was not in its exact place.

For a second, the world went black as I thought of the consequences.

I strode back into the living room, standing barefoot (shoes and socks always off at the door), with my tie half undone, my underarms damp with sweat, as something began to boil deep inside.

Isabel couldn't be gone. It simply wasn't possible, and I wasn't going to let it happen. I would find her and bring her home. Back where she belonged.

We were way beyond love. She was *mine*.

After all the trouble I'd gone to streamlining her life, it made me angry that she could cast me aside so easily. How ungrateful she was! I'd saved her a fortune on rent, and fixed it so she need never work again, and this was the thanks I got.

In the kitchen, I took a glass from the cupboard. I filled it with water, drank greedily, then hurled it across the room, watching as thousands of tiny jewels scattered across the polished floor.

Without a thought, I walked through the mess, my bare feet crunching in the glass. I imagined pressing the same number of diamonds into Isabel's skin until beads of her blood burst out around them.

It was the pure ingratitude that made me angry.

When I'd calmed down a little, I called her parents. I just needed to get her back. As I spoke, I picked shards of glass from my heels. Ingrid was saccharine, asked me where I'd been in my jet today. She was flirting. Trying to win me over.

I didn't tell her I'd been to the services near junction twenty-eight of the M6 to fire my manager at that particular Mr Beefy for pilfering eighteen hundred pounds from the till over the last three months. Instead I told her that I'd just returned from Rome, that I was exhausted, and I was wondering if she'd seen Isabel because she wasn't at home. I told her I had a surprise for her.

'Actually, I haven't heard from her in a while,' Ingrid replied – cautiously, it seemed to me.

I had to play it carefully. I didn't want her hiding things from me.

'Not since you both came for Sunday lunch, in fact,' she added.

I sensed she was lying. Then she whined on some more about Isabel being headstrong sometimes, about how she needed her space, about how much she adored me nonetheless.

It pissed me off. She didn't need space. She needed me.

I hung up none the wiser, although I believed Ingrid didn't know where her daughter was. I spent the evening driving around various places I thought Isabel may have gone.

She used to love the cinema, was always on at me to go and watch films with her, so I headed out to the retail park multiplex. I bought tickets to every show and went into each screen in turn, stalking up and down the aisles with the torch on my phone lighting my way. People moaned and jeered, grumbling as I interrupted their viewing and knocked into them as they stuffed popcorn into their mouths. But Isabel wasn't there.

I visited the council gym where she sometimes jogged on the treadmill, or used that ridiculous machine that made her look like an incompetent skier. But there was no Isabel there either, just muscled people staring at my crumpled suit and bloody bare feet shoved tightly into Isabel's pink flip-flops.

I drove around some more, weaving between lanes on the dual carriageway, bumping over speed humps down quiet suburban avenues, speeding recklessly through the city centre, not caring about the cameras.

Once or twice I saw a red-headed woman walking along, so I slowed down to take a lingering look, knowing full well it wasn't Isabel by the stoop of the shoulders, the length of the gait, or the clothes she was wearing. But that didn't matter – in my mind, I pretended I'd found her, that I'd taken her back home to keep safe.

I couldn't understand why she'd done this to me, why she would reject all the love I'd given her. Something began to stir inside me, something I'd not felt before.

Then I remembered her friend.

'I've known her since for ever,' Isabel had said not long after we met. She'd laughed and gesticulated, telling me all about Bethany. I'd already made it clear I wasn't interested in meeting any of her friends, but then she asked me about mine. My cheeks flushed, ruddy and ashamed. How could I tell her that the last proper friend I'd had was when I was eight years old?

After my mother dropped dead on me, none of the boys at school would come near me. They said I had a disease. Stories spread, telling how I'd killed her. Poisoned her, strangled her, stabbed her with a bread knife.

They said I was a murderer.

When they pushed my head into a urinal, I saw my mother's glassy eyes filled with agony as her heart twisted and knotted inside her fragile chest. I remembered how she used to amuse me by drawing squiggles over the odd-shaped strawberry birthmark she had on her arm, each time creating a different shape or animal around the pink blemish.

'This one's called infinity, darling,' she told me just before she died while inking what looked like a figure eight on her skin. 'It means I'll be here for ever.'

Then she drew a couple of eyes on it, making me giggle.

I've often wondered if she knew of her fate, had had some kind of premonition.

The *Secret Seven* book was still in her hand as she gasped out her last words. She didn't finish. Her eyes got closer to mine as she fell forward, staring coldly as if she didn't know me.

She'd lied about being there for ever.

Bethany Adams had no idea who I was. We'd never actually met. Isabel had talked about her incessantly, of course – Bethany this, Bethany that – even pointed out her flat window to me once as we'd driven past. And if things went to plan, she would never find out who I was. I just wanted to make certain she wasn't harbouring my Belle. That she hadn't taken her from me.

Of course, I could have just knocked on her door, asked her if Isabel was inside, and indeed as I sat outside her building in my car that evening, I considered doing just that. But when I was least expecting it, she came out, making me catch my breath as I blew across the surface of a piping hot coffee.

I immediately knew it was her thanks to Isabel's description. She was much more beautiful than I'd imagined, all graceful movements and lithe limbs as she danced down the front steps of the flats, heading right towards my car. Her eyes were alert and keen, her blonde hair bright and glossy. Had she been red-haired, she would have been near perfect, and definitely on my list.

Bethany veered away at the last moment, almost skipping as she went. She wore tatty denim shorts with thick tights beneath, and canvas trainers on her feet, her slim legs making for tantalising territory between the two. A brightly coloured cloth bag swung at her side.

Without taking my eyes off her, I got out of the car, locked it, chucked my drink into the gutter and walked briskly after her.

She was easy to follow, and had no idea that I was ten paces behind her. I'd have followed her to the ends of the earth if it helped find Belle, yet I had no idea what it was about her that lured me. Perhaps I'd caught a whiff of Isabel on her.

A short while later she arrived at a dreary-looking building that I discovered was an insurance call centre. She pulled a plastic card from her bag, swiped it through the security lock, and glanced back over her shoulder.

She hesitated then, spotting me. Her pupils widened, and she swished back her hair, giving me a coy smile. Then she went inside. To work the evening shift, I presumed.

There was a pub on the opposite corner, a grim-looking place called The Railway Carriage. I went in and sat on a velour banquette, sipped red wine and watched Bethany's workplace out of the window.

Three and a half hours later, she emerged into the night amid a stream of similarly aged young employees. A couple of them yawned, checked their phones, and headed off in different directions.

I quickly downed the remainder of my fourth glass of wine, and appeared on the street just as Bethany waved goodbye to a couple of co-workers.

Again, she was easy to follow. At one point I was only

three or four paces behind. I heard her talking on her phone, saying something about an audition, that she would find out if she'd got the part tomorrow.

I drew closer, unable to resist.

'Excuse me,' I said politely.

She spun round, literally leaving the ground a few inches. She gasped.

'Don't be afraid. Do you have a cigarette?'

Bethany looked me up and down. Her face was the colour of butter, and melted into an expression I couldn't read.

'No, I don't,' she said nervously.

Then she walked off, kicking up her pace.

I went after her. I was drunk, and my feet hurt.

'I just want a smoke,' I said. 'Nothing else. Nothing funny.'

'Leave me alone or I'll call the police,' she said, walking faster. She didn't scream.

'Please, I'm not some weirdo.' I hated the desperation in my voice. I was twelve again. 'Sorry to have bothered you.' Then I stopped and turned, ready to veer away.

'Wait,' I heard a second later.

With my back facing her, she couldn't see my smile. I made sure it was gone by the time I swung round on my heels.

'I've got a couple. They were a friend's. Just take them.'

There was something in her voice that said she was only doing it to get rid of me, but then there was kindness too.

Bethany rummaged in her bag, her pretty hair falling over her face. I had to fight the urge to tuck it back behind her ear for her, even though it wasn't right; even though *she* wasn't right.

'Here,' she said, thrusting a crumpled pack of Marlboro Lights at me. 'Have them.' Her hand was shaking.

'Thank you, Bethany,' I said, delighting in the way her face screwed up from fear because I knew her name.

She turned and ran off down the street.

Later, sitting in my car again outside her flat, I watched as she closed her curtains and went round putting on all the lights. I stayed until morning, barely dozing, and surprised her at seven a.m. with a bag of fresh bagels. When I asked if Isabel was with her, if I could see her, when I said I knew she was hiding her, she slammed the door in my face.

I'd never felt so angry. Never felt so determined to get inside and see the truth for myself. Whatever it took.

25

I can't face going back to the flat, but I can't face going to work early either. My feet slam against the pavement as I charge down the street, narrowly missing shoppers, pedestrians and mothers with pushchairs. I have no idea where I'm going. My chest burns as I suck in the cold air, and my hand burns even more from what Felix just did to it.

Eventually I stop, panting, outside a McDonald's. Hair is stuck to my face with tears and snot. I can't run any more, so I go inside, heading straight to the toilets. I turn on the tap to its hottest setting and plunge my hand underneath the stream, dousing it in soap, scrubbing him off.

I lean back against the wall, sliding down so my knees are bent, my head hanging forward.

He squeezed my hand.

'No. He didn't. You're imagining it, just like everything else. Stay real. Stay in control. It did not happen.'

I say this over and over until I believe it. Then I leave the toilet, go back outside, and start walking. Anywhere.

It's only when I'm a mile further on that I realise instinct has drawn me to her. A sweat breaks out on my face, partly from exhaustion but partly from relief. I should have thought of this sooner, but fear has made me avoid people I once knew. I'm desperate now, though, and, as I head for her street, I pray she's home.

I slip into her building just as someone's coming out. Tentatively, I go up to Bethany's door, noticing the number four plaque has slipped a little. I draw a deep breath as I knock, remembering all the good times we used to have together. Visiting her will do me good, and perhaps she'll be able to help, even though she knows nothing of the horror I've been through. But she is vibrant, cheerful, carefree, my oldest friend. If nothing else, the company will do me good. I hate it that I had to desert her. I hope she's not angry with me.

'Oh. My. God. I don't bloody believe it,' Bethany says, holding the door wide. Her face is ashen.

For a second, it looks as though she's not pleased to see me. I open my mouth. Close it again, nervously tucking my hair behind my ear. I should never have come.

'Hello, Beth,' I say eventually, staring at her.

She is wearing a pale pink cardigan, round-necked, and buttoned up to the top. She has on white skinny jeans and her feet are bare. Her almost see-through blonde hair tumbles around her shoulders. A slick of rose lip gloss makes her look so pretty and fresh.

'It's been ages, hasn't it?' I add, hating the way it makes me sound.

'*Ages*. Totally bloody *ages*,' she says cautiously, as if she's thinking how she should act with me. I know I hurt her, and can't expect her to be normal with me right away.

I raise my eyebrows, nervously opening my arms a little. Then, to my sheer relief, as if she's decided to forgive me, Bethany smiles. A smile blooms on my tight face in return. It's just what I need.

'Come in then,' she says, still staring at me as if I'm a ghost.

I thank God that she's decided not to hold a grudge.

She takes me inside, where I immediately notice some new stuff – a huge TV, a leather sofa, smart curtains. Bethany never used to have money for things like that.

'Nice rug,' I say, noticing that's new too. I pull off my coat and chuck it on the back of a dining chair.

'Forget the rug,' she says, flashing a guilty look. 'I've been so worried. You just vanished. Everyone's been trying to find you.'

I wonder if that was anger in her voice.

'I've been finding my*self*,' I say, thankful for the genius response. 'A bit of travelling, getting over some stuff, dealing with things. You know. I'd have gone mad if I'd stayed in teaching for the rest of my life.' My laugh sounds slightly demented, summing up my erratic behaviour.

When we were together, Bethany never met Felix. He made it clear he wasn't interested in my friends – not that I had many anyway. It was just the two of us against the world, he said. I was upset at first, but realised it was only

279

because he was so besotted with me. He didn't want to dilute or share me. I banked on changing him gradually, thinking that our wedding would be a good place to start. But it never happened and, in the end, I was relieved no one had ever met Felix, that I'd never really discussed him with anyone.

It was actually Bethany I called when I arrived in India, although only for a few seconds. I hadn't planned on calling anyone, but it was out of guilt that I did. I didn't tell her where I was, of course, or why I'd run away as she didn't know the full story – no one did. But I wanted her to hear my voice, let her know I was OK, in the hope that it would somehow filter back to my parents. I wanted them to know that I was alive, but the thought of calling them directly was too painful. They'd never have forgiven me.

But when we spoke, the line was bad, and Javesh was jumping around in the background, trying to grab the phone and hooting out the song he'd made up about Bestluck, how it was the best hotel in Delhi. I felt bad for ages after I hung up, not knowing if the message would ever get through to Mum and Dad.

'I can sympathise with the going mad bit,' Bethany says, bringing me back to what I was saying. She rolls her eyes long and slow.

She's always been dramatic, but it makes me wonder what she knows. Suddenly I'm concerned she read my story in the paper, about the pupil reporting me. I'd lost touch with most people by the time the complaint was made, but it made the local news for a day or so. Did she find out I was in *that* kind of hospital?

'So what's new with you?' I ask, changing the subject – anything to help me forget that Felix just squeezed my hand. 'Do you have much work on? Are there any nice men in your life?' Bethany has always been flighty with boyfriends.

She lets out a dubious laugh, narrowing her eyes at me as if she suspects I know something. 'God, if it was later in the day, I'd crack the wine. There's so much to talk about, you wouldn't believe.'

She continues to look pensive, and I sense there's definitely something big on her mind, something she'd love to tell me about and get off her chest. Instead she moves off into the kitchen to put the kettle on, so I don't press her. Having been gone for so long, I'm in no position to grill her about her private life.

'I am seeing someone,' she admits modestly when I join her in the kitchen. 'But it's low-key for now. He's an actor, too. In fact, he got me a new job.' Bethany swallows nervously, as if there's more but she can't tell me.

'How exciting,' I say, feeling a pang of regret. If things were able to develop between Owen and me, if my life was ever to be normal again, I would suggest that Beth and her new man come out with us for a drink one evening. I'd love Owen to meet her.

'Beth?' I say, when I notice she suddenly looks upset. There are tears in her eyes.

'Truth be known, I'm not really enjoying the work. It's

a bit of a . . .' She stares at me, searching for the right words. 'Well, I thought it was a job I could do, but it's a bit of an odd one, to be honest.' She tucks her hair back. 'I'm kind of regretting it. But at least it pays well.'

She puts coffee mugs and a pile of cakes on the table, and for the next hour we don't stop talking about old times. The conversation stays firmly on track, occasionally touching on the new man in her life, with me being careful to sidestep my missing time. But then Beth floors me.

'Anyway, the police were useless,' she says, eyeing me carefully.

It feels as if she's watching for a reaction.

'The police?' I don't move.

'As if I was going to keep a log,' she goes on. 'Like, "Excuse me, sir, would you mind stalking me *after* I've written down the weather and what clothes you're wearing."' She shakes her head and bites into a cake. Crumbs stick to her cardigan. 'Bad times,' she adds. 'Bad people.'

'I had no idea. I'm so sorry,' I say, not sure if I can bear to hear any more.

Back then, my own problems were taking over and I'd been ignoring my friends. Her problems with this man must have happened after I'd run away from Felix, and gone into hiding. It wasn't long after that that he found me and put me in hospital. No one wanted to know me then, and I lost contact with the outside world.

Bethany shrugs and sips her coffee. 'It was weird. I thought it was all done with, but another cop came to see me the other day. She said she'd reopen my case if I wanted.' Her mouth is full of cake, her eyes watching me.

I clasp my fingers around the hot mug until they burn.

When I don't say anything, she continues. 'I told her no way, that she should leave well alone. It's all stopped now anyway.' She gives me a tight smile.

'Best let sleeping dogs lie,' I say quietly, wondering what prompted the police to reopen the case.

I try to concentrate as she confides more about her new job.

'They pay me a lot,' she says, as if that makes up for her dislike of it. 'Although, had I known exactly what the work entailed before I committed . . .' She trails off, shaking her head.

'Is it acting work?' I ask.

'Kind of,' she replies, bowing her head. 'I get five hundred quid every time I take a phone call.'

'Oh, *Beth*,' I say, realising she's trying to confess something to me. I feel so sorry for her. It's not just me who's had a hard time. 'You promised me you'd never do anything like that.'

'God, no!' she says indignantly. 'It's not *that*.' She shakes her head, sighing, as if she wants to tell me but can't. 'Just put it this way, I thought I was doing the right thing by taking the job. It was a chance to make some decent cash for a change, but the people involved have turned out to be . . .' She looks away briefly. 'Less than scrupulous. I wish I'd not got involved, but it's too late. If I leave now, they'll . . .'

'What kind of phone calls?' I ask, wondering if it's something I could do for some extra cash. But judging by Beth's discomfort, I'm not sure I want to.

'A bit like the call centre,' she says evasively, flapping her hand. I can tell she's lying. 'I have to do other stuff too, but honestly, I only took it for the money.'

'Well, Luke sounds like a good chap to know,' I say, not wanting to embarrass her any more. 'I'm pleased things are going well for you.' She'll no doubt tell me more in her own time. I'd intended on asking her advice about my situation, maybe hint at what has happened, but I can hardly offload on her knowing she's got her own troubles.

I'm about to ask to see a photograph of Luke when my phone rings.

Bethany stares at my cheap handset, then looks away sadly.

'It's me,' Owen says down the line. There's a pause. 'Are you coming into work today, or did last night make you run a mile?'

He gives a tentative laugh, and my heart skips a beat at the thought of it.

'Oh God, I'm so sorry!' I look at my watch. 'I'll be there as soon as I can.'

He blows me a kiss down the line.

I say goodbye to Bethany, promising I'll come back soon. After a brisk dash back to the office, I'm sitting at my desk with Owen working nearby. The warmth of his stare on my back makes it impossible to concentrate.

*

'A strange thing happened today,' I say to him later. We're eating a late lunch – a couscous salad – and sitting on the office sofa. Technically I should be finishing in ten minutes, but as I was late and there's so much to do, I told Owen I would stay on. Besides, it'll take my mind off things.

'Is everything OK?' he asks. Some couscous falls off his fork and on to his trousers.

His eyelashes are long and dark, his nose slightly crooked. Beneath his white shirt I know that his shoulders are lean yet muscular. I try not to think about last night, how we lay, exhausted, in his bed, the moonlight beaming in through the window across our bodies, the duvet kicked down to our ankles. I barely slept.

'I went to see Felix earlier.'

I pull a pained face, hoping that will be enough to explain why. I don't want him to think I have feelings for him, yet I can't tell him the real reason why I went. As long as he's out of action, we're both safe.

I put my salad on the low table in front of us, suddenly not hungry.

'I understand,' he says kindly. 'Someone you love is very sick.'

'I don't love him,' I say quickly. 'I did once, but not now.'

Something shifts inside me; something I don't understand.

'Oh God, Owen, he moved his hand. I swear he did.'

There. I've said it. I cover my face.

'The doctors must be pleased with his progress,' he replies.

I swallow. 'That's the thing,' I say. 'They don't know. I didn't tell anyone.'

'Ah.' Owen's eyes grow wide. 'Then I think you should. It might impact the way they manage his case. Besides, you'll feel terrible if you don't.' He takes hold of my hand. 'I can drive you there, if you like.'

'No, really. It's fine.'

But Owen won't take no for an answer. When he's finished his lunch – I can't face eating mine – he leads me out to the car. Ten minutes later, we're at Woodford Grange.

'I suppose another visit so soon will be OK,' Penny says, scowling first at me then at Owen.

'I'll wait out here,' Owen says, sensing Penny's annoyance. He gives her a withering look when she turns, and winks at me as I look back from down the tiled corridor.

As ever, the place is deserted, with all its virtually lifeless patients secreted behind the other doors.

In his room, Felix is lying perfectly still. Megan is tending to him, gently washing around the hollow of his chest. She looks up.

'Hi,' she says with a smile, while rinsing out the flannel in a bowl of soapy water.

I smile back, unable to manage much more. My bag slides off my shoulder as I tentatively sit down. I stare at his hand, watching closely for the slightest twitch. But there's nothing.

'Is Dr Lambeth available?' My voice seems lost and pathetic, but I need to get this over with.

'I think it's his day off,' Megan says. She adjusts her pale blue tunic. 'There are several other doctors on duty, though. Would you like to speak to one?'

'Maybe you could just pass a message on for me.'

'Of course,' Megan says. She gives me a kind look. 'First, though, come here.'

Curious, I go round to her side of the bed and, before I know it, she's pressed the washcloth into my hand.

'We've had good responses from patients when loved ones care for them. Don't be afraid. Why don't you wash his face?'

'Me?'

Megan nods, taking my hand. She guides it to his face, dabbing it around his nose and mouth. There are crusts either side of his lips. They've removed the ventilator since I was last here – another sign that he's improving.

'I'll be back in a moment,' she says, leaving the room before I can stop her.

I stare at my hand, the whiteness of the cloth blending with the pallor of Felix's skin. My whole arm is shaking as I wipe his face. I can feel the warmth of his skin, the gentle shudder of his tentative breaths. A pang of regret creeps up my fingers, my arm, into my mind as I think of everything that we had, as well as everything we lost. It is both terrifying yet oddly sad. I glance back over my shoulder, hoping Megan will return, but she doesn't.

Then, unable to help myself, I drape the flannel over

Felix's entire face, shroud-like. His nose protrudes, and his nostrils gently suck in air, making two indentations. The slope of his forehead gives way to hair that looks surprisingly clean.

In case Megan returns, I whip the washcloth away.

Felix's eyes are wide open. He's staring directly at me. I scream.

Then I recoil, stumbling and knocking into a drip stand, backing away from the bed, not taking my eyes off him. For the second time today I grab my bag and run for the door.

In the distance, I swear I hear him call out 'Sorry' in a voice I barely recognise.

26

'Grace is really worried about you,' Adam tells me. 'And Stella is concerned too. They've noticed that you're on edge, and it's making them jumpy.'

I've only just got home when I'm faced with Adam telling me this.

'They're even talking about security themselves. I noticed Stella checking that the doors are locked several times, and she refused to open it to pay the milkman earlier.'

'I had no idea,' I say, hobbling to a chair. I put my ankle up on the one opposite. Driving always makes it hurt.

'I know you didn't, love, but they pick up on things.' He has a rare glass of wine in his hand. 'Have you gone to the doctor yet?'

'I'll have a chat with them later,' I say, avoiding his question.

Adam sighs. 'And Ray,' he says, sitting down beside me, 'I know what you're up to. Bob asked me if you're still working on the case. I had to lie for you.'

'What are you talking about?' My cheeks burn red, and I'm not sure if it's from the first glug of the red wine Adam just handed me, or because he's right. 'Anyway, why isn't Bob following up on that list? Why don't you organise a team? They all complained of stalking, Adam, just like Alexandra and Melanie and—'

'Love, it's in hand. Don't you think we're working through every possible angle? We've had two extra teams going round the clock since the reconstruction.' He sighs. 'Look, if you're not careful, we're going to bump into you while you're out sneaking about.'

'That's not fair. I've been home resting,' I say, even though I can tell by his expression that he doesn't believe me. 'I even went to the doctor as you suggested.'

I grab my bag from the floor and rummage through the muddle inside. I pull out the pale green prescription form, smoothing it out. I flash it in front of Adam's face, hoping he won't notice the earlier date.

'See?'

Adam looks sheepish. 'I'm just really worried about you, Ray.' He puts down his wine and approaches me, arms outstretched.

'Well you needn't be.' I turn away.

I'm about to tell him why when Grace comes into the kitchen. I rein in my thoughts, taking a breath.

'Hello, love. Are you just off to work?'

She stares at me, almost as if she pities me.

'I'm not going.'

She clatters the assortment of dirty crockery she's brought down from her room into the dishwasher.

'How come?' I say, noticing the look Adam gives me.

'I don't really feel like it.'

I glance at Adam, then back to Grace again.

'Why, love?'

'No reason.' Tears begin to well in her eyes as she closes the dishwasher door and turns round, shoulders hunched. 'Since you thought someone had followed you, and since you found the back door unlocked, I'm just a bit scared, that's all.' She gives me a look. 'Stella is, too.'

'Oh, love,' I say, feeling terrible. 'How about I drive you to work and pick you up afterwards?'

'Don't worry.' She glances at my wine, then at my booted-up leg. 'I've already called in sick.'

I rest my elbows on the table, leaning my forehead in my hands. Because of me, my daughter is becoming a recluse. When I found the back door unlocked a few nights ago, I asked Stella and Grace about it the next day. Each denied having left it open, but they looked scared. Adam swore he'd locked it before bed. Perhaps I left it open – I can't truthfully remember. But then I do many things these days without realising. Add to that all my other fears, and it's no wonder they're twitchy.

'You're just not . . . *Mum* any more,' Grace continues, cutting straight through to my heart.

I slide my hands down my face, sighing heavily. 'I'm sorry to hear that, Grace, but I'm really tired and in a lot of pain. Can we talk about it tomorrow?'

'But you'll be at work,' Grace says. 'Every time you say we'll talk about something, we never do.'

'That's not true, Grace,' Adam says in my defence. 'Mum's been off work the last couple of days so you've had ample time to talk to her.'

My face goes back into my palms.

'No she hasn't,' Grace replies, looking confused and shaking her head as she leaves the room.

'Thanks,' I say to Adam.

'Thanks?' he replies, sitting down opposite me. 'Do you really think I don't know what you're up to?' Adam lays his hands down on the table. 'It's for your own good, Ray. I can only cover for so long before it gets out and Bob takes things further. I don't feel comfortable telling him half truths.'

I stand up, but sit down again in agony, sloshing wine on the table. I feel shaky and upset. 'I'm only trying to salvage my career, Adam. What's left of it. You have no idea how hard it is to be taken off a case. I know you'll do a good job of handling it, but it's almost *worse* that you've been put in charge. I'm faced with it every day, whether I like it or not.'

'Oh, Ray.' Adam shakes his head.

'I virtually had to creep into the office, making up excuses for being there.'

Adam rolls his eyes. 'I thought you hadn't been to the office.'

'I was going to tell you,' I say, even though I probably wouldn't have done.

'That's it,' Adam says, raising his voice slightly. 'I want to help, but I can't cover for you any longer. Not when you're . . .'

I frown as he trails off, glancing towards the door. I don't want Stella and Grace to hear.

Adam offers me a pitying look. 'Not when you're like *this*,' he finishes quietly. 'Not yourself. A bit . . .' He pulls a pained face.

'A bit *what*, Adam?'

'A bit mad, if I'm honest.'

27

I don't care. I pour another glass, filling it so full it over-
flows. Owen takes the bottle from my hand.

'I think you've had enough.'

'I'd agree with that,' I say, not meaning the drink.

Owen fetched a takeaway Indian meal tonight, though
after what's happened, I'm just not hungry. He seems to
be enjoying his, though, and even lit a candle, setting it
on the low wooden table in his living room.

I fall back against the sofa, uncrossing my legs which
are stiff and uncomfortable from sitting on the floor. I
plump the big cushion.

Owen breaks off a hunk of naan bread.

'It really got to you earlier, didn't it?'

'He woke *up*,' I say yet again.

Owen can't possibly understand the enormity of
this.

I stare at the ceiling before snapping off a tiny piece of
poppadom. I dunk it in some chutney, forcing it down. I
have to eat something.His eyes were so bright, as if nothing

had even happened to him. At first I thought he was dead, that some bizarre post-mortem muscle spasm had opened his eyelids. That would have been typical of Felix: freaking me out even after he'd gone.

But then he spoke.

'And he just said "Sorry"?' Owen reiterates. 'Nothing else?'

'Just that one word.'

To me, it sounded like a thousand.

Even as I ran away, I sensed his pain. The heartfelt message he was conveying. I imagined him frustrated and locked inside his body, stiff from lying in the same position for weeks. I almost stopped; almost went back, begged for things to be how they once were. But the sensible part of me got me out fast, dashing past Owen, calling for him to hurry. Penny had just looked on in shock.

'They told me the prognosis was bad.'

But then they don't know Felix.

'I wish you'd eat properly,' Owen says. He shifts closer, rubbing my shoulders. 'And I wish you'd let me call the nursing home, find out how he's doing. You might even be able to speak to him.'

'It's not that easy for me,' I say, shrugging, trying to find the courage to tell him how I feel about Felix, about what he did to me, about everything that happened. Even a tenth of it would explain my behaviour to him. 'We didn't get on so well in the end.'

It's as much as I can manage for now, although Owen is right – finding out more would perhaps help. I need to know if he's still conscious, still confined to bed. My irrational side is wondering if he's discharged himself, searching for me right now, perhaps about to knock at the door, even though I know that's impossible.

Before I can stop him, Owen is on the phone. He holds out the handset. 'Want to speak?'

I shake my head, feeling suddenly terrified, shifting further away. Today was such a shock.

'Thanks for your help,' he says, hanging up after a short conversation. 'Apparently,' he tells me thoughtfully, watching my reaction, 'Felix is still conscious and doing well.'

Suddenly there's a loud whooshing sound, making me flinch and feel woozy. I realise it's inside my head.

'He's still disorientated though. They'll be doing extensive tests on him tomorrow. It may mean a move back to the Queen Elizabeth. We'll know more in the next few days.'

'Is that it?' I say, as if I was expecting some kind of cryptic message.

I'm coming to get you . . .

Owen leans forward, clasping my hands. He stares into my eyes. 'They said he's looking forward to having visitors. It's probably not what you want to hear, Isabel, but they said he's looking forward to seeing *you*.'

'He killed my parents,' I whisper. I can't help wondering if it's payback.

'I doubt he feels good about that.'

I bury my face in my hands. He doesn't know Felix,

although if the doctors have told him the news, he's probably feeling bad, working out his next move. He always claimed to like Mum and Dad – or at least he made out he did – but the worst thing was, they were very fond of him.

We talk some more – me working out what I should do, Owen listening intently, trying to help – and before long I'm curled up on the sofa, nestling against him. Not long after that, I'm asleep. When I wake, light is streaming in through the gap in the curtains. I'm still lying on the sofa, covered in a woollen throw, and Owen is nowhere to be seen.

'What if he's changed?'

Owen doesn't realise it, but I'm worried it could be a change for the better.

'Sorry,' I add. 'I didn't mean to interrupt your work.'

I stare over his shoulder. It looks ridiculously complicated. One wrong measurement could topple an entire building.

He removes his glasses and looks up at me.

'Your hair,' he says. 'It's incredible in that light. May I take a photograph?' The sun is bright and low, forcing its way in through the front window of the office, showing up the dirt on the glass and every dust mote in the air.

I don't get a chance to answer, because Owen's phone is suddenly in his hand, aiming at me. I try to smile, but don't quite manage it.

'What if who's changed, anyway?' he continues.

'Felix. I read that people's personalities can change when they wake up from a coma – for better or worse.'

When Owen went out to meet with a client earlier, I quickly looked online. Some patients have been able to speak a different language; there were even reports of a toddler coming round from a coma with a serious nicotine and alcohol addiction. If those things are possible, then surely a milder-mannered Felix is possible.

I can't get what he said out of my mind.

Sorry.

In the past, it was all I ever wanted him to say, but he never once did. Perhaps things could have turned out differently if he'd shown some remorse, made me believe us being together hadn't all been in vain. But, playing that single word over and over again in my head since he said it, listening out for subtle intonations, hidden meanings, I'm beginning to doubt it contained any contrition at all.

Owen laughs, stretching back on his work stool. 'Don't be silly,' he says good-naturedly. 'How would you know if he's changed after one word?'

It's impossible to explain.

Sorry chased me down the corridor and out of the building; *sorry* was a glimpse of the past, the future. And *sorry* was something Felix never, ever said.

'You've worked so hard this morning, you should finish on time today,' Owen says on the dot of two. 'And it's none of my business, but Woodford Grange isn't far.' He winks, taking a slurp of the coffee I've just made him.

'You should visit, even if it's just to lay a few ghosts to rest.'

I give him a hug before I leave, whispering thank you, telling him that he's right, although not for the reasons he thinks.

I need to know how long I've got before I must leave the country again.

'Don't worry, love,' Penny says when I apologise to her for running out yesterday. 'Many relatives get emotional when loved ones wake up.'

I nod, thinking she's about to say more or give me something, but she stops because Megan is suddenly there with us to take me down to Felix's room. We're in the corridor when a doctor strides past, nodding pleasantly. I imagine they've all been discussing the miracle of Felix. I make some banal joke about Megan always being here, about her never having a day off and working too hard. She smiles awkwardly.

'What you must remember,' she says, 'is that he's lost a big chunk of time. It's natural for him to want to fill that in. While we've been going about our usual business, his body and mind have been shut down. He'll need to relearn some basic skills.' She tucks her hair behind her ear, looking slightly nervous. 'Muscle coordination and fine motor movements are tricky for him. His speech is slow and considered, too.'

'I understand,' I reply, following her into Felix's room.

Immediately, I see things are different. The curtains are

pulled wide and the lower part of the sash pane is up, allowing the late-autumn sun and cool air to stream in. Felix always insisted on good ventilation. There's a vase of roses on a table in the corner.

And there he is. In bed, semi-reclined, with cables and a plastic tube winding down from the machines. He looks a lot more like the Felix I once knew.

I inch closer.

His eyes are closed, his face calm. Everything in front of me goes floaty and swims, as if I'm not really here. I grip the back of a chair for support.

'Felix? Felix?' Megan sings, gently rubbing the back of his hand where the cannula once was. 'You have a visitor.' She turns to me and smiles. 'Nothing to worry about. He still sleeps a lot, but it's different to before.'

I open my mouth to speak but nothing comes out. Having seen he's still bed-bound, I'm tempted to leave – I know as soon as he hears my voice, he will wake up.

'Aren't you going to say hello, Felix?' Megan continues, as if he's five years old. He would hate that. 'Your wife is here, look.'

I open my mouth in horror, but a terrible noise comes out – the sort of noise produced by knots of fear stuck in a throat. After all this time, after everything that's happened, I am here, in front of him, waiting to face everything – a place I never thought I'd be again. It's the stuff of my nightmares, reminding me of the sweat-soaked nights I suffered in the early days at Bestluck.

Megan frowns and gives me a funny look. And, of course, Felix opens his eyes.

'Ah, there you are,' she says. 'Come on, let's sit you up a bit more.'

She presses a button on the side of the bed and raises it a few more degrees. Felix doesn't take his eyes off me. His expression is flat, as if he doesn't recognise me. He looks empty inside – none of the anger, the sadness, the bitterness or the hatred is there. Just . . . *stillness*.

'I'll leave you two alone. I'm sure you must have lots to talk about. Here, sit down, love.'

Megan does a quick check of Felix's monitors, adjusts his pillows and sheets, and then, before I can protest, she leaves the room in her soft-soled shoes.

Felix tracks me as I slide down into the plastic stacking chair.

I can't look back at him.

The air is sharp and cold. I shiver.

Slowly, through the silence, my gaze rises across the bed, over his wasted body, up to his chin. I stop at his mouth because I can't stand to be drawn inside his eyes. His lips are dry and thin from where the ventilator was taped in place. Once, I would have rubbed coconut balm into them, then kissed it right back off.

'Are . . . you . . . cold?' he says, very slowly.

The crackle in his voice makes me tense. I haven't heard him speak in so long. He sounds hoarse and weak, each word laboured and unformed.

'A little.' I still can't look at him.

'Win . . . dow.'

Does he want me to shut it? If I ever interfered with how he liked things, did things wrong, I got into trouble. God knows, I did my best to please him.

'Window,' he says again.

I get up and close it, tripping on the end of the bed. I hold my breath, then sit down again, barely able to swallow because my mouth is dry. My heart is beating so fast it feels as if it might give up altogether.

'Sorry.'

That word again. Slurred, as if he's drunk. As if he doesn't mean it.

I stare at my lap, picking my nails.

'So . . . sorry.'

There's a rustling sound as his fingers crawl haphazardly across the bedding towards me, as if he wants me to take hold of them. They look clean and unused, baby hands on a man, as if he's been reborn. My own fingers tingle.

'Felix . . .' I don't know what else to say.

His eyes are filled with tears. One drips out as his head lolls to the side, bringing him closer to me.

Instinctively, I reach out to straighten his pillow, to get him upright again. His neck looks uncomfortable, as if he has no control over it. For a moment, as I'm plumping the pillow, I hold it just above his face.

How easy would it be? I think. I could call for help, tell them he just stopped breathing.

As if he's read my mind, his hand suddenly comes up and takes my wrist – not harshly, but gently, as if he wants to remind himself what it's like to feel another person's skin.

I stay still, allowing him this, even though my instinct is to pull away. It's nearly killing me, having him touch me. He smiles, although it's lopsided, not at all like the pointed grimace I remember.

I put the pillow back behind his head. 'Better?' I sit down again.

He nods, giving a slow blink. 'You . . . came back to me,' he says croakily.

'You've caused quite a stir by waking up,' I tell him nervously.

He would like that – defying the odds, being the centre of attention.

'Feel . . . bad,' he says after a moment's thought, as if he's lining up words in his brain. 'Caused so much pain.'

'You shouldn't think like that,' I say, realising I'm only humouring him.

I look away for a moment, trying not to provoke him. I have no idea what he knows, how much he's figured out himself, what he remembers.

'They told me . . .' His eyes turn grey and cloudy. His head teeters back and a strange noise bubbles up from inside. 'What happened.'

I put myself in his position, how it feels to kill two people. I remember my parents, clenching my teeth, fixing on his eyes, determined not to let him get the upper hand.

'I was trying to . . . to help them,' he says, a touch more fluently now, as if explaining will make it OK.

I'll never forgive him for what he did.

'You always drove too fast, Felix. You were always so *angry*.' I take a deep breath. There was so much more than that.

'I missed you,' he whispers, taking me by surprise.

His head drops back again, and a wheeze escapes his chest.

'Missed me?' I repeat incredulously.

'You shouldn't have left me.' A slice of a smile pulls his lips even thinner. 'No, no, no . . .'

My heart claps out an uncertain beat as his eyes slowly fall shut.

When I get back to my flat, there's a package on the basement doorstep. Old fears are rekindled at the sight of a delivery – emotions I thought I'd left behind. With Felix conscious again, it feels doubly dangerous.

Back then, I was always advised never to open the gifts, to store everything in a safe place, complete with the packaging. They told me to log how they were delivered, the date, and any other relevant details. It was routine advice for stalking and harassment cases – the advice they gave to all victims, I learned. Without proof, the police were sympathetic but powerless. I was trying to regain some of that power, until Felix stole it away, that is; drove me to take control in other ways.

But this packet is so tempting, and of course it's not going to be from him. A corner of the outer brown paper is torn, revealing a pretty and expensive-looking box beneath – tiny violet flowers scattered in a delicate print over a dark grey background. It's exciting and alluring.

'Owen,' I whisper with a smile, going inside the flat. He knows how upset I've been. It would be just like him to send me something to take my mind off things. Opening it will give me an excuse to go upstairs later, to thank him personally.

Grinning, I ignore my inner caution and rip off the outer layer of paper. The box inside is indeed beautiful, tied up with a magenta ribbon. I pull it undone, noticing the handwritten tag attached.

For my love, stated simply in careful handwriting.

I lift the lid slowly, revealing cerise tissue paper.

Perhaps some exquisite bath oil, or a delicate lace camisole, I think – the perfect antidote to a bad day.

Then a nasty stench makes me recoil. I drop the box on the table and back away, pinching my nose.

Mustering courage, holding my breath, I lean forward and pull back the tissue paper with the tips of my fingers.

The rat's face is serene, but its eyes are open and staring. A heavy black tail winds up its body, getting trapped by the lid when I slam it back on.

28

When I discovered her little hidey-hole above a kebab shop, my shrivelled heart felt as if it had been basted in warm syrup.

Belle was not lost at all.

She didn't know I'd found her, of course. Her cat-and-mouse game would have kicked off again. Me, the cat, wanted to keep her right where she was, play with her a little longer. How things panned out after that was up to her.

I discovered she'd rented the nasty little place in Sparkhill after making a list of 'Let Agreed' properties in the area I reckoned she might be in from a website, all within the correct timeframe. My fourteenth attempt had me sitting outside this dreary-looking flat, wondering if I should move on, then bingo! Belle emerged from the shabby door a short while later in jeans and trainers, her hair tangled, and with a shopping bag over her arm. People are so predictable.

A kebab shop, I thought, staring at the building after

she'd walked off. She lives above a kebab shop. She was now my very own Mrs Beefy, watching her trashy TV as the stink of greasy meat wound its way upstairs.

What had each of us become?

The first thing I did was send her a sign. Something to show her all was not lost, that I wasn't irretrievably angry with her, and that there was still hope for us. We were destined to be together, after all, but I understood that she wanted to take things slow, that I'd rushed her by moving her into my flat, by helping her leave her job.

My feisty Belle!

I knew she'd be short of money, being unemployed and also now unemployable as a teacher, so the very next day I sent her a thousand pounds in cash via Fed-Ex. I sat outside her flat in my car, arriving half an hour before I'd arranged the delivery.

The courier arrived exactly on time. He approached the door of number 14b, just to the left of Kenny's Kebabs, and rang the bell. A moment later, Isabel opened the smeary glass door. She was wearing a spotty towelling robe with the hood up, and pink bath slippers on her feet. She looked snuggly. And a bit dirty. She also looked puzzled. But she signed for the packet anyway, and shut the door.

From here on, it was left up to luxurious fantasy. The two windows above Kenny's were obscured by grimy net curtains, so I had to imagine her padding back upstairs into a dingy living room, turning my packet over and over in her hands.

Then I envisaged her tugging on the perforated strip, releasing the flap, and shoving her hand inside. I closed my eyes and pictured her face – an eclipse of joy and puzzlement.

Who had sent her these crisp twenty-pound notes? How much, exactly, was she holding?

I saw in my mind's eye her fingers riffling through the money, counting it up, counting it again, her heart twittering in her chest, her eyes blinking rapidly.

It was me, Belle. Me, your adoring Felix.

It gave me great pleasure to be her secret admirer. So much joy that I reached inside my trousers. No harm done.

The next thing I did was send her a dress. I went into the department store and was assisted by a nice young lady about the same size and shape as Isabel. Nowhere near as perfect, of course, so when she came out of the fitting room wearing the garment I had selected for Belle, I raised my hand to block out the view of her mousy head.

'Turn around,' I instructed.

Her behind looked like a bucket of jelly, but I knew Isabel's wouldn't look quite so bad.

'I'll take it,' I said, and had it gift-wrapped in perfumed tissue paper.

The bored young lad loitering at the end of Isabel's street was more than happy to knock on her door and hand-deliver the box for a tenner. 'Tell her that she'll know who it's from,' I told him, making sure he understood. 'That I'll never give up, not for a single day.' The boy looked perplexed for a moment, but promised to do as instructed.

This time imagination was not entirely needed as I spotted the silhouette of Isabel wriggling and squeezing into her new dress. Had she put on weight? I wondered as I watched her force and tug the fabric over her thighs.

No matter, because the next morning at ten she emerged from 14b wearing it. I tailed her slowly on foot, mesmerised by her high heels and new dress beneath the cream coat she'd paired with it.

Nice for a sunny winter morning, I thought, pulling my cap lower over my face.

She disappeared inside an employment agency, but emerged ten minutes later with a grim expression on her face. She tried another, then another, no doubt registering her details at each. After this she headed back to her hidey-hole, and so did I. I bought a sandwich and ate it in my car. I bought tea and drank that too. All the while watching.

Later, Isabel emerged into the street with a bag of rubbish. She went down an alley at the side of her building, returning empty-handed a moment later and going back inside.

Quick as a fox, I was out of my car and down the alley. There was only one big dumpster, overflowing, with Isabel's yellow-tie bag balanced on top. I lifted it off the heap carefully, not wanting it to split open.

I stashed it in the boot of my car and drove home to savour it. I didn't want to miss a thing. It was the remains of Isabel's daily life – a life from which I had been excluded. For now, it was a way back in.

I gently undid the bag, inhaling deeply. I wanted to absorb each item. First out was a half-crushed egg box containing cracked shells. I breathed in the scent of her omelette or whatever it was she'd made. I dreamt up her day, her week, the missing time, from the contents of this rubbish sack. Isabel had finished her value brand teabags that day, as well as drained a tiny milk carton. She'd eaten lots of breakfast cereal, had been peeling vegetables galore – perhaps she made a soup – and, as I worked further into the bag, setting out her things in a grid on the wooden floor of my special room, I discovered it was that time of the month. My poor, poor baby.

And then I found it. The plastic carrier bag containing the dress.

At first I thought the soft contents would be another gem of a surprise. Imagine my shock when I recognised the jade floral fabric.

I shook it out, held it up, and my discovery only got worse. Isabel had taken to the garment with scissors, hacking and slashing it with abandon.

No matter, I told myself, remembering how ungrateful she could be. I would send her another dress. A more expensive one this time. This one was clearly not to her liking.

But a day after it arrived, a red one this time, the same thing happened. I sent another, then another, and not only dresses. I sent silk scarves, leather bags, size five shoes, and a state-of-the-art television. Everything went in the bin, except for the latter, which she took to a charity shop.

Enough was enough.

To show her my displeasure, I sent her an unidentifiable dead creature I'd found on the road – suitably chastising, I hoped, for a pious ex-school teacher who'd chosen to live above a kebab shop rather than with me.

I was outside, watching as I'd taken to doing for eight or nine hours a day, when the police pulled up outside Isabel's flat for the first time. Two uniformed officers got out of the car that they'd parked on double yellow lines. I was doing the same, but on the opposite side of the street. When they glanced my way, I drove off. No point arousing suspicion.

I cruised around for a while, and when I returned, they'd gone. It had been nearly three weeks since I'd discovered where Isabel was hiding out, and it was time to make myself known. Especially now she'd involved the police.

I kept on sending the gifts of course, but now she didn't throw them away. Had the police made her see sense, I wondered, and told her to keep them, enjoy them? Either way, she never once thanked me, never once made contact with me. Her rejection of me was utterly disappointing. I would have to get through to her another way.

'Didn't know no boyfriend was living up there.'

He was the son of Kenny Kebab, about seventeen, and carving off ribbons of dry-looking meat from a rotating pole. He glanced up at me in between dealing with customers and squirting runny white stuff on to their packets of food.

'Well there is a boyfriend,' I told him politely, 'and I'm him. The thing is, I've lost my keys. It's embarrassing, I admit, but my girlfriend told me there was a spare available.' I was taking a punt, but chances were it was true. I held out a twenty-pound note. 'She said I had to ask nicely.'

'Shouldn't really,' the skinny boy said, but the shop was filling up with lunchtime trade and he was alone behind the counter. He snatched the money and rummaged in a drawer beneath the till, eventually pulling out a piece of string with a couple of keys dangling from it. 'Bring 'em back before closing,' he said, and went back to work.

Oh I will! I thought, heading straight for Key Express just down the road. I got three copies made, just to be on the safe side. I returned the key to Kenny Kebab junior without him even looking up from carving.

Isabel's door – grimy, with a rotting, flaking frame – looked as inviting as a five-star hotel. I knew she was out, having watched her leave earlier, and I couldn't wait to get inside.

Once I'd slipped into the dark and narrow hall, I went up the stairs, savouring every tread with its dirty worn carpet. At the top there was another locked door, which I entered with glee.

But my joy soon turned to disappointment. Isabel had

been living like a slob – a woman who had lost her way; lost her mind.

The flat consisted of three tiny rooms – a bedroom, a bathroom, and another room overlooking the street that served as somewhere to cook and sit. Everywhere was strewn with rubbish and clothes; it appeared as if it had never been cleaned. It was a far cry from my sparkling canal-side penthouse with views of Centenary Square beyond.

In this main room there was a boxy portable television in the corner, with a stained velour sofa not fit for a dog angled towards it. The kitchenette at one end was piled with dirty plates and empty food containers, and the whole place smelled not only of kebabs but also of misery, despair. The bedroom was the most disturbing – vile carpet, an unmade bed with filthy-looking sheets, and worst of all, a dozen or so gifts I had lovingly chosen and sent to her piled up in a dingy cupboard.

I dropped down on to her bed, staring at the hoard. Thousands of pounds' worth of beautiful clothes, jewellery, handbags and accessories, gone to waste. Most hadn't even been opened. Then I saw the notebook on her bedside table. Initially, when I flipped through it, I was filled with joy – Isabel had made a log of every gift I'd sent her, as well as noting each time I'd called or written to her, or had someone deliver cash or flowers to her. Happiness coursed through me as I read that she'd spotted me on the street in my car, and had detailed all those times too, as well as noting down what I was wearing, where exactly

I'd parked, even what the weather was like. But when I saw two police officers' names in the front of the book plus their phone numbers, I realised it hadn't been written out of love. Isabel was going to use it against me.

No matter, I thought, popping the little notebook in my jacket pocket. If she didn't have it, she couldn't prove anything.

While I was there, I decided to give the place a good clean and tidy. No woman of mine should be living this way, so, pulling on gloves, I set to work, polishing and scrubbing as best I could. I even dashed out to buy fresh flowers, placing them in a chipped vase on the table.

Then I got back inside my car and waited.

Three minutes after Isabel arrived home, she emerged on to the street wide-eyed and frothy-mouthed, her face spattered with fear as she tore up and down the pavement either side of her gaping door, searching for something, *someone*.

I tooted the horn. She stared across the street.

I'll never forget that look. It was cast across her face with the potential to remain fixed for ever. Pure hate crossed with something that looked a lot like terror. Either way, it wasn't pleasant.

I waved cheerily as I drove off. There's no pleasing some people. But, to be on the safe side, I returned home via the GP that I knew she still used and trusted. Only the previous week I'd followed her there to an appointment.

The receptionist provided me with a pen and paper, and I composed a caring and thoughtful letter to Isabel's doctor, alerting him to her fragile mental state. Her mood was very unstable, I told him, as well as expressing my concern that the poor girl was on the brink of something cataclysmic.

29

Staking out Woodford Grange Nursing Home helps fill some of the void in my days. Absolutely nothing has happened in the two hours I've been sitting here today, apart from a couple of staff turning up for work. At least I assume they're staff and not visitors, because even though they weren't wearing uniforms, they haven't come back out again. Besides, visiting time doesn't start for a couple of hours yet, according to the sign. I just hope no one from the unit shows up.

A delivery truck rumbles down the road. It slows, and for a moment I think it's going to stop at the nursing home, but it carries on past, halting to make a drop-off a few buildings down.

I have a log book on my knee and I've already taken a few photographs, but I could be sitting here all day, of course, with nothing to show for my trouble.

His wife Isabel visited him recently, the receptionist told me, and that's why I'm here. I have an idea what Isabel looks like from the photograph the neighbour showed me, so I'm hoping I'll recognise her if she comes. Apart from marching in and asking the receptionist if she gave her my card, which isn't an option if I don't want to risk Bob finding out what I've been doing, I don't see how I'm going to get in touch with her otherwise.

I pour another cup of coffee from my flask. I stayed in bed until after Adam left for work, promising I'd take it easy today, rest my throbbing ankle. Now, my Aircast lies discarded in the passenger footwell of my car, allowing me to drive, even though it still hurts like hell with every gear change.

Knowing Adam, it's quite possible he's got someone watching me, making sure I do as I'm told, trying to protect me and save me from myself.

I pop a couple of pills in my mouth and swig them down with the last inch of water in my bottle. The bitter taste makes me shudder, and the numbing of my pain helps the next couple of hours go fast.

And then I see a woman walking along the street in my wing mirror, early to mid-thirties with a shock of wavy red hair escaping from a hood. She's approaching the nursing home. She stops, hesitating just outside, looking nervous and uncertain, as if she wants to go in but can't decide. For a moment, I'm filled with the same feeling I get in the middle of the night – panic, guilt, a sense of failure.

But then I realise it's because of this woman's appearance: there's no doubt she looks uncannily like the photograph Mrs Welland showed me. And there's more than a passing resemblance to Alexandra Stanford – and, truth be told, to Melanie Carter as well.

Three young women with red hair. All living in the same city, and all complaining of being harassed or stalked.

Slowly and discreetly, hardly breathing so I don't steam up the car, I raise my phone, aiming the screen at her. The woman pulls her black padded coat around her tightly, stamping her feet against the cold. Some more of her vibrant red hair springs out from beneath the hood as she takes a phone out of her pocket, making a quick call.

She seems more at ease after she hangs up, prompting her to take a deep breath and go up to the door. She rings the bell, which tells me she probably doesn't work there.

The photos I take aren't great, but they show her face well enough when zoomed in.

Once she's inside, I start the engine and slowly drive down the street. I turn the car round and head back up to a different vantage point. She came on foot, so I'll be following her on foot when she leaves, ankle allowing.

I don't have to wait very long.

'Good afternoon, Brandrick's,' she says crisply, although slightly breathlessly.

The red-haired woman stayed only half an hour at the nursing home. I kept a good distance, following her back to the building she's just gone inside. Thankfully, she took the twenty-minute walk, or painful hobble in my case, slowly, and ended up in what appears to be a firm of architects according to the plaque beside the door. I took a picture of the details once she'd gone inside, dialling the number on it from round the corner.

'Hello,' I say pleasantly. 'Is that Isabel?'

'Yes, it is,' she says in a cheery voice. 'How can I help you? You only just caught me. I'm not supposed to be in the office at this time but—'

I hang up.

I don't have to wait long to see where she goes next. Shortly afterwards, she emerges from the small office and heads off down the street at a brisker pace. My ankle kills without my boot, but there's no way I could keep up otherwise.

A couple of times she looks back over her shoulder, but doesn't give me a second glance as I pretend to chat and laugh on my phone.

Ten minutes later, she heads down a pleasant residential street lined with tall Victorian townhouses. She stops at one and checks around her before dropping down some steps to what seems to be a basement flat.

It must be where she lives because she takes a key from her bag and unlocks the door. Now I just need to work out how to approach her without it getting back to Bob that I'm still on the case.

It happens in the corner shop near the frozen vegetables. After I'd limped back to Woodford Grange to fetch my car, I decided to drive past Isabel's flat again, perhaps wait for half an hour to see what happened. There was still time before Adam got home.

It was as I was finding somewhere to park that I saw her come up the steps from her flat and stride purposefully along the pavement. I quickly reversed into a space and lagged behind her to the convenience store up the road.

'I always go for the petit pois,' I tell her when I see her looking at bags of peas. 'They're much sweeter.'

Isabel flashes a look at me as if I'm mad. I give her a friendly smile. She sidles further along the freezer.

'It's Isabel, isn't it?' I say, moving closer.

She virtually jumps back against the wall, her face full of fear.

'Who are you?'

She glances around. Her eyes are narrow and suspicious. A deep frown digs in at the top of her nose, making her look ten years older. I have rarely seen anyone look so terrified.

'My name is Lorraine Fisher,' I say, holding back as long as possible on the detective part. 'I saw you at Woodford Grange earlier. Were you visiting someone?'

'What the hell?' she says, scowling. She throws a packet of peas into her basket, along with a frozen macaroni cheese microwave meal, and heads for the till. 'Have you been following me?'

'Please, I'd like to talk to you about Felix Darwin.'

She doesn't reply, even though I'm standing right behind her. I can see her shoulders are hunched and shaking. There are three people ahead of her in the queue. The cashier rings a buzzer to get help with the growing line of customers.

'I just want to talk to you. It won't take long. Please?'

Of course, if I learn anything helpful, I'll have to find a way of telling Adam without letting on about what I've done.

I'm tempted to get out my warrant card, but if it gets back to Bob that I was interfering, he'll escalate the complaints before I can clear out my desk. The irony of my predicament shoots a pain through my stomach. That, or it's the painkillers messing with me.

Isabel turns to face me. 'Go away,' she says. Then she turns her head away again, her hair a firewall of red between us.

'I might be able to help you. I know you had problems with Mr Darwin that were never fully resolved.' I keep going, knowing she's listening. 'It's just a chat, that's all. Nothing sinister, I promise, and—'

'Who the fuck do you think you are?' she spits out, having swung round sharply, knocking my leg with her basket. 'The sodding police?'

'Yes,' I say, and, once she's paid for her groceries, we leave together.

Isabel Moore's flat is freezing and smells musty. My warrant card got me inside her home, yet virtually reduced her to tears as she led me down the steps.

She tells me she's not been living here long, that she feels vulnerable and wasn't expecting visitors today. After I convince her that I'm just here for a chat, she scuttles around trying to make the radiators work, but says that she'll have to ask the man upstairs for help. The landlord, I assume.

'I left my contact card at Woodford Grange in the hope that you'd phone me,' I say as the kettle boils. 'The receptionist told me that you'd been visiting Felix Darwin.' I'm hoping she'll tell me why she's been going there, after all the complaints she made against him.

'There's no sugar,' she says, ignoring me.

She puts two mugs of tea down on the table, then sits on a plastic-padded dining chair while I take the sofa. We're both still wearing our coats.

'People have been looking for you,' I tell her, remembering what Mrs Welland said.

She stares at the floor and shrugs. 'I was trying to get away from *him*.' Her bottom lip rolls into her mouth and she bites down on it. She still looks terrified.

'Felix?' I've heard how abused women are often unable to keep away from their partners, feeling somehow that they don't deserve happiness or freedom. The hold the abuser creates is often too strong to break.

She nods. 'You'd have made yourself scarce too,' she says, eyeing me.

'I had a look at the statements and complaints you made about Mr Darwin.'

At the mention of his name, she tenses again. She hugs herself, rocking backwards and forwards. Her distress is palpable.

'He gave you a pretty hard time, by the sounds of it.'

Isabel blows out loudly and shakes her head. 'Is that what you think?'

'You tell me.'

Silence.

'The thing is, love, there was no evidence. Nothing we could act on. It was his word against yours.' I want to tell her that most cases of this nature never make it to court, but I don't. It's a depressing statistic for someone like her.

Isabel swallows as if a dry crust is lodged in her throat. 'Don't you understand? That's what he does.' She shakes her head hopelessly. 'He made me out to be crazy, even violent towards him, when it was *him* doing it to *me*.'

'It's a shame I can't talk to him too,' I say, doubting he'll ever be well enough to interview.

'If that's what you want,' she says, sounding annoyed, 'go right ahead. But be prepared for the lies.' Isabel swallows. 'He's so slick, so believable, so bloody convincing, he literally drove me mad.' She lets out a frustrated sob, as if she's already said too much and regrets it. 'I'm so scared of him, I just don't know what to do.'

She looks exhausted, worn down, and I feel desperately sorry for her. Her skin, apart from a few freckles and a tan on her nose and cheeks, is grey and sallow. I can only imagine the power he must have over her if he's even lured her back while unconscious. I wonder if this will turn out to be the worst case of co-dependency I've ever seen in a domestic case. If he wasn't on life support, I'd be concerned for Isabel's safety.

'It's a bit tricky to talk to him while he's in a coma,' I say.

'But that's the terrible thing,' she says, dragging her eyes, filled with tears, up to meet mine. 'He woke up.'

'So why have you been visiting him?' I say softly.

Isabel gives a pitiful little shrug. 'So I know he's still in hospital, that he can't hurt me.'

She stands up, goes to the front window and rattles it, trying to pull up the sash pane. She checks the lock, tightening it with her fingers.

'Want to know how many times I do this at night?'

I don't answer, hoping she'll tell me, but she doesn't. Instead, she just lets out a slightly demented laugh.

'He had me put away, you know. Had them all convinced. He said I was mentally ill, that I imagined everything, that I lived in a fantasy world.'

'I'm sorry to hear that.'

'They believed him, too. Everyone. My parents, the doctors, the stupid counsellor they forced me to see week after week.'

Isabel spins round, thrusting her head forward and glaring at me.

'They said Felix was a good man, that he loved me and was trying to help. They told me I was the one causing all the trouble, that I was jealous and ungrateful, that I had anger issues.'

She sits down again, leaning forward and cradling her head in her hands. Her arms are shaking.

'They said I was *mad*.' She beats out the words in a

staccato voice. Her chest cramps up as she gasps for air.

I want to help her, really I do, but I keep any useful wisdom locked up, hidden away, almost fearful of treading the same path myself.

'I ran away from him once, but he found me. He watched me constantly, and sent me stuff every single day. Clothes, shoes, expensive electrical goods, dead birds.'

She pulls a tissue from her pocket and blows her nose.

'Everywhere I went, he was there, following me, hounding me.' She laughs. 'The first thing he sent me was a green dress. I didn't realise it was the start of that particular nightmare.'

'Go on,' I say, trying not to focus on how her story is making me feel. While I want to trust her, part of me can't help wondering if she was admitted to a psychiatric unit for a good reason. But then Alexandra is on my mind again, screaming at me to help her, not to let history repeat itself.

'The fabric was all slashed up and ripped, as if he'd taken to it with a knife. I threw it away, but he must have gone through my rubbish. It came back a couple of weeks later with a dead bird wrapped inside it.'

'That's a terrible thing to happen, Isabel.'

She stares at me, then she starts nodding vigorously. She's on her feet again, pacing about, looking so frightened. 'But now he's *awake*!' She blows her nose. 'As long as I know he's still bedridden, then I'm safe,' she says. 'But as soon as he's discharged, I'll have to hide again. No one helped me before. Why would they now?'

I try to make sense of what she's saying, feeling the guilt as she stares at me, her eyes begging me for answers. I need to speak to Felix Darwin myself, if I can wangle it without being flagged by Bob or Adam.

'It's so weird seeing him like that,' she says, almost wistfully. 'A man with such power over women, now bedridden.'

My ears prick up. 'Go on.'

'Let's just say he liked lots of women. And he knew what he liked, too. Heaven help them if they didn't live up to his expectations.' Isabel sits down again, seeming calmer now. 'The thing is, I didn't mind doing things his way. I wanted to please him. Despite everything, we were good together and I loved him, believe it or not.' She lets out a remorseful laugh.

'Relationships can go bad,' I tell her. 'It's not your fault.'

'But do you want to know the *very* strangest thing?' she says, as if she hasn't heard me. She briefly covers her face, looking, when she reappears, as if she's in another place.

'Go on.'

'The strangest thing is that I always think I still love him, no matter what he does to me. I always believe that there's still hope for us.'

I dare to reach out and touch her hand, wanting to tell her that's quite common in situations like this. I can't help noticing that her skin is the same alabaster colour as Alexandra's.

30

I close the door, trying to stay strong. I tell myself that the cop's visit isn't a bad thing, that she only wanted to help, even though she knows nothing about me, my life, my situation. It's not been a good day all round, especially since someone phoned the office, saying my name and then hanging up. Who could possibly know I work for Owen?

I peer up through the front window, watching the detective limp up the steps and on to the street above, making sure she's really gone. I hope she doesn't come back. To take my mind off things, I heat up a microwave meal. But I just stare at it on the plate, not feeling at all hungry.

I can't help wondering if Owen is upstairs, thinking about me like I'm thinking about him. I thought I heard him come back earlier – the sound of his feet on the steps, the click of his key in the stiff lock – but then I was distracted by the detective and her prying, feeling relieved that she didn't seem too bothered about pursuing things.

Opening it all up again, delving into things that are best left dead, isn't going to do me any good at all. But someone like her would never understand that.

I scrape the meal into the bin. It's a far cry from the healthy food I was once so passionate about. Briefly, I'm reminded of Raksha's delicious meals – her cinnamon-coloured potatoes that tasted like heaven, her lentil dhal fragranced with cardamom and bay, and the doughy bite of her handmade naan breads. I suddenly feel desperately homesick for Bestluck, for escape, and can't face spending the evening alone.

Outside, I double-check that the front door to the flat is locked and head up to see if Owen would like some company. Besides, being with someone will make me feel safer. I knock on his door, hoping he's home, but there's no reply. I knock again, trying to remember if he said he was going out.

Still no answer.

Tentatively, I try the handle. He's told me several times to make myself at home. Oddly, the door pushes open easily, as if the lock has been left off the latch. I go in, listening out for the sound of the kitchen television blaring out the news, or the classical music he likes to have playing on the radio.

But everything is silent.

'Owen, it's me. Are you home?'

Nothing, so I walk down the long hallway with its old patterned tiled floor, taking a moment to trail my hand over his coat draped over the banister rail. I press my face into the lining, inhaling his scent.

'Hello?'

He could be in the shower, I think, wondering whether to go up and surprise him, but something draws me on towards the kitchen. It's where he spends most of his time.

I push open the door, hoping he'll be standing at the counter, chopping vegetables, offering me a glass of wine, asking me if I'd like to stay for dinner.

But the kitchen is in darkness, the gentle hum of the refrigerator the only sound.

I flick on the light.

The scream burns my throat as it roars up from deep inside, my lips stretched wide. My fingers tear down my face, ripping at my skin, covering my eyes.

'Oh my God . . . *Owen*!'

I run across the kitchen and drop to my knees beside him. He's lying on his side, curled up in a pool of plum-coloured blood, his fingers scratching through the mess, trying to reach out to me.

'Owen . . . *Owen*! Oh fuck, what happened? Who did this to you?'

His face is bruised and battered and he has one hand clamped across his chest, from where the blood is oozing. He doesn't reply, though he tries. Red froth bubbles at his mouth as he stares up at me.

Then I see the phone, the landline handset, lying on the floor beside him. A tinny voice rattles from the earpiece.

'Hello . . . hello, caller, can you still hear me?'

I pick it up. 'Hello?'

'This is the emergency services. Please confirm that you are assisting the caller.'

'Yes, yes I am,' I say weakly. I feel dizzy, faint, hardly able to believe this is happening.

'Help is on the way, but for now I want you to tell me if the injured man is breathing,' the female operator says. She is calm and in control – the complete opposite of me.

'Yes, yes, OK, hang on.'

I hold my shaking finger beneath his nose, not knowing how to check properly, while staring at his wounded chest.

'Oh God, I don't know,' I tell her. 'He was moving when I found him, and he groaned a bit. Stuff is coming out of his mouth.' I hiccup out a sob.

Whoever did this was silent and swift. If only that detective hadn't come, I might have heard something or been able to prevent this.

'OK. Tell me how he is lying. Is he losing much blood?'

'He's curled up on his side. There's a lot of blood around him. All over the floor.'

Owen makes a gasping sound – a laboured breath – and his hand twitches, pressing against his chest. More blood flows from him.

'He's still bleeding,' I tell the operator. 'Please, send help quickly.'

'They're on their way, love. Stay calm. Get a towel or something similar to press against his wound. Be quick.'

'OK, OK,' I say, scrambling to my feet.

There's a neatly folded tea towel draped over the

cooker rail. I grab it, scrunch it up and try to move Owen's hand away from his wound, but it's stuck rigid against his chest area. His muscles have gone into some kind of strange spasm, perhaps from the blood loss. I do my best to stem the flow, pressing on his ribs, making him wail, although his protests are weak. Then I hear a hammering on the door, followed by footsteps in the hallway.

'Paramedics here . . . hello?'

'In here!' I call back.

Seconds later, a man and a woman wearing green uniforms rush into the kitchen, carrying black bags of lifesaving equipment.

'Please, oh please help him! He's been stabbed, or . . . God, I don't know!'

I stand up, cupping my mouth with my hands, backing away to give them space. I think of calling Lorraine Fisher, but I know the police will be on their way anyway. I can't believe this is happening. I should have listened to my gut; should have got out while I could.

'OK, Cath, let's find where this blood's coming from and get a line in,' the male paramedic says calmly. 'Get his BP monitored, please, and I'll get an ECG set up. Check his airways, and let's find a pulse now.'

The pair are steady but swift, crouching beside Owen, unpacking some kind of portable monitor, snapping on gloves and unwrapping packets of needles and tubes and God knows what else.

The scene goes blurry in front of me as I move back,

leaning against a worktop. Who would have done something like this? Shards of light flick across my eyes, making it hard to focus.

'Do you know how long he's been like this?' the man says, twisting round.

'I . . . I don't know. I just found him . . . I've been here only a few minutes.' My voice barely works. 'Is he going to be—'

'Dan, quick,' the female paramedic calls out. 'Defib now. He's gone into arrest.'

They work fast, unpacking a machine, setting it up in seconds, and pushing two paddles beneath Owen's shirt so they are pressed against his skin. I turn away. I can't stand to watch.

'Clear,' I hear Dan call out.

Owen makes a sound that doesn't even sound human.

'Check for a pulse.'

'Nope, go again,' the woman commands, and they repeat the process.

I bury my head in the nest of my arms, still leaning on the worktop where Owen prepared a meal for us just the other night. How can this be happening?

'Cath, any pulse?'

And then I hear the machine shock him for a third time.

After the sixth, maybe the seventh attempt, after my palms are gouged and raw from my nails digging in, a hand comes down on my shoulder.

'I'm so sorry,' Dan says. 'We did everything we could,

but his blood loss was too great. He went into cardiac arrest and we couldn't save him.'

My body goes cold. I can't move, certain I'm going to wake up soon.

'Time of death, nine minutes past six,' the woman says quietly, taking a blanket from her bag and laying it over Owen's top half. 'I'm so sorry, love,' she says to me. 'Are you next of kin? We'll need to know.'

I have no idea if I answer, or shake my head, or even speak. Dan takes hold of me and guides me to a chair. They get a blanket for me as well, only this one is from the living room, the one that warmed Owen and me after we'd watched a movie, had fallen asleep together beside the fire.

Soon, there's a cup of sweet tea in my hand. I try to sip it, but my arm is shaking too much and it spills everywhere.

Dan and Cath tell me the police are on the way. In my mind, I see that detective woman coming back, picking apart my life, wondering why a man was murdered right above us as we chatted about Felix in my flat.

I want to go, run away, but Dan says I can't, that I'll have to give a statement.

After the police have been, when they have photographed and mapped the scene, when they have interviewed and questioned me as much as I am able to stand, written down every single word I've said and read it back to me, when I have signed the document and been ushered into the living room away from the body – away from Owen, who had done absolutely nothing wrong and didn't deserve this – I make a call.

'Answer, come on . . . *please* pick up . . .'

Bethany's phone goes to voicemail.

'Beth, hi, it's me, Isabel.' I try to keep my voice steady. 'I need a favour. I was wondering if I could come and stay for a few days. Nothing permanent, don't worry. Just until I get myself sorted. Call me back.'

I can't go to my parents' place, not if I don't have to. It's too risky.

'Love, is there anyone we can call?' a kind police officer asks, crouching down in front of me. 'Somewhere we can take you?'

'No,' I say quietly, shaking my head.

Then I see him – Owen, being carried out on a stretcher, hidden inside a black nylon body bag. I cover my face with my hands, unable to look. I'm certain it's all because of me.

31

It was meant to do her good, but Isabel didn't see it that way. Section 2 of the Mental Health Act, thanks to my vigilant observation and intervention, got her admitted to hospital for an assessment by her GP and a psychiatrist.

I told them she'd tried to kill me; that she'd tried to kill herself. I showed them bruises on my neck, and told them about the stash of pills beside her bed. I pleaded them to listen to me, finally made them understand how desperately worried I was about my Belle.

The treatment would be beneficial, I told her, though she fought and kicked against going in. But it kept her safe for the next twenty-eight days, out of harm's way, and I visited her on each and every one of them. I finally had my Belle out of that awful flat she'd rented, away from everything bad in her life. It hadn't done her any good at all – her skin was sallow, and she'd developed a cough.

The doctors observed and consulted with her, medicated and treated her, allowing me to spend afternoons in her company. Even when they told me what was wrong with her, what their diagnoses were, the medical words meant nothing to me.

In my eyes, Isabel was almost perfect, pretty much everything I'd been searching for. Still the best yet, and I wasn't about to let her go.

I was paying for a private establishment, of course, so it was a treat to sit with her in the lovely gardens, enjoying the spring sunshine, talking about old times, or walking with her through the wooded grounds. If it was raining or cold, we would go in the day room and play Scrabble together, lost in rarely used words and the silent thoughts floating between us.

Belle's *betray* crossed perfectly with my *love*.

'Triple letter score,' I said, laying down the word.

She spat on the floor and upturned the board.

The nurse, who was sitting nearby, glanced up. Her job was to trail Belle, logging her moves every fifteen minutes. She was present when she peed, washed, slept and ate, and made sure she didn't stab herself with a plastic fork at mealtimes. There was something growing inside her that made her want to self-destruct.

On a few occasions my visits overlapped with those of Isabel's parents, who came once a week to visit their daughter.

'Felix, oh *Felix*,' Ingrid said one day when we met in the car park. She rested her head on my chest, imploring me with dry eyes. 'Can't you *do* something to ease her pain?' She looked up at me, as if she knew more than she was letting on. 'Belle needs to feel special, be your one and only. You know what young women are like.'

I nodded, without confessing that I didn't. 'The mind works in mysterious ways,' I told her. 'Isabel will get well again. Then she'll get what she deserves.'

I smiled, and Ingrid nodded, believing me. She always referred to Sandy Acres as a 'rest home', as if Isabel was at a health farm, not a psychiatric unit. She took some small comfort from my words. A shame her daughter didn't adore me as much as she did.

One time I visited, Isabel's skin was the colour of cooked mushrooms, an even darker shade round her drooping eyes. They gave her medication from a trolley, but after they'd wheeled it away, she showed me her stash – a jingle of tablets in her pocket.

Isabel maintained there was nothing wrong with her, though she kept insisting they were coming to get her, whoever 'they' were. Her paranoia began to envelop her, keep her up at night, and the nurses reported her staying awake for three consecutive days and nights several times a week.

After that, I made sure they checked her more closely, ensured she took her pills. I wanted her to get well, though I can't deny it was wonderful having her there all for myself. But it wasn't a permanent solution.

Once she was released, she would live with me again. It was doctor's orders, and I couldn't wait.

Then she disappeared again.

'What do you mean, she's gone?' I said to the doctor

when I arrived one afternoon to visit. 'How can she be gone?' Didn't they realise she was mine, that she needed me? Hot rage flowed through me.

'She's allowed to leave,' she told me. 'What you must remember, Mr Darwin, is that for the last month or so, Miss Moore has been receiving treatment voluntarily. We can't stop her going.'

'I'm paying the bills, so surely it's up to me when she leaves?'

The doctor pursed her lips. My hands itched to slap her.

I left the hospital, furious, determined to find my Belle. I had done it once, I would do it again. She couldn't hide for long.

How wrong I was.

I began my search at her parents' house. I got to know that street and all its nasty middle-class goings-on well over a period of several weeks. It was no place for Mr Beefy to be holed up, hour after hour, day after day, staking out the movements of Ingrid and John Moore.

We spoke on the phone, of course, and they were as concerned as me.

'Not a single psychiatric condition with which to detain her,' I explained to Ingrid, my nerves in tatters from anger and frustration.

I imagined the woman's thin lips slashing out her reply as she sat on her faux mahogany telephone table seat in her beige hallway.

'Surely that's a good thing, Felix,' she said. 'At least it means she's better.'

I sprayed a laugh, knowing that, after everything, she would never be better. 'So where is she then?' My sweating hand gripped the handset, waiting for answers.

A pause before she replied. 'We don't know, Felix. Really we don't. Oh, please, she needs you. Find her, Felix. Please bring her home.'

In the following weeks, I spent much time in my flat, hunched over my desk, the lamp angled close to my precious pictures. It was all I had left.

I flicked open random pages of the album. Long gone were the days spent updating them, sorting and arranging, hunting and gathering. It was a big job, keeping everything in order, neatly organising details, logging and recording everything from shoe sizes, defining features and car registration numbers to favourite foods, dislikes, family names . . . the list was endless.

Then I saw Alexandra's pages – the first time I'd looked at her since I'd stuck in a newspaper cutting of her death back in February. They'd found her body in an alley, dressed up like a tart. She'd got what she deserved.

Next I hired a private investigator and set him searching for Belle.

One day, while washing my hands and breathing in the urine-stink of the men's service station toilets on a trip to my most northern branch, I stared into the mirror. Instead of me reflected back, I saw my father

339

– beer-and-burger-bellied, bald, and with a young woman clinging to his side, half naked, leering at me with a self-satisfied grimace.

And there, behind him in the shadows, was my mother – sweet and frail, as pale as death.

Vengeance would first take the form of not turning into him, hence selling off a few Mr Beefys. I had to pay for it all somehow, anyway. A plan was taking shape. Besides, I didn't want to spend my life selling burgers and fries when I could be enjoying it with Belle.

If only I could find her.

Three months later, I sacked the PI.

It was only when I visited one of my local Mr Beefys – one of my top performers as it happens – that things began to turn around.

The manager introduced me to his newest member of staff. I always drank tea with the most recent recruits, as was tradition. I liked to get to know my employees personally.

We hit it off. He seemed a decent sort, rather like me, and it turned out he was in a play. He gave me a ticket. I've always liked the theatre – and even more so now. It was afterwards, backstage, as he was introducing me to the rest of the cast, that I discovered some interesting news.

32

I spend the night fully clothed, shivering, curled up in a tight ball on the bed.

My backpack is beside me, and I have my phone in one hand, a kitchen knife in the other. The officer who took a statement from me, the one with the sour breath and the shabby uniform, said I was allowed back down to the flat, that it wasn't part of the official crime scene.

I force myself to stay awake, needing to keep alert, although I can't help dropping in and out of a fitful sleep. I reach for my phone, checking the time yet again, praying it's morning, even though it's still dark outside.

Five twenty-three a.m.

My head spins when I sit up, propping myself up against the bare wall with a couple of pillows. I cover my face with my hands.

Owen is *dead*.

As I sit here, alone and terrified, it feels as if everything is closing in on me, pushing down from above, forcing me to face all my worst nightmares. How can I have been so stupid? I'd fixed my life, patched up the holes well enough, managed some kind of existence in Delhi. Coming back has spun everything out of control again.

Worse still, I lied to the police. If I'm caught, it will be prison for sure. Yet how could I have told them the full truth when they took my statement? They would never have understood, never seen my side of things. Saying I was just Owen's lodger, that I didn't really know him very well, didn't feel right, but I didn't know what else to do in the heat of the moment. I didn't say we'd become lovers. My voice was brittle and fast, tripping over my fears as I explained how he'd let me stay in the flat as a favour. The officers were understanding, asked me to tell them my new address when I leave. I plan on going today, but I won't let them know where. Probably because I don't know either.

I drag myself out of bed, peering up to ground level and Owen's front steps. The crime-scene tape still flickers and twirls across the gate, glowing neon in the streetlight. The police guard, who was there all evening, seems to have gone now.

None of this makes sense. Why would anyone want to hurt Owen? Maybe it's something to do with his work, or involves someone I don't know. I mustn't assume it's to do with me; mustn't allow my fear of the past to mislead the police.

I make a cup of coffee, drinking it with shaking hands as I sit on the bed, knees drawn up to my chest, wondering if it's too early to call Bethany again. The messages I left for her last night grew more and more desperate, eventually begging her to let me come and stay. I didn't say why, that Owen had been killed. But she didn't call back.

By nine o'clock, when she still hasn't answered her phone, I grab my backpack, taking a last look around the flat. There's some food in the fridge, a couple of magazines and books on the coffee table, some scented candles I bought to disguise the lingering damp smell, and a few clothes draped over the back of the sofa. I can't take everything. They're only possessions, and I need to carry everything easily.

Finally, I head out, locking the door securely.

I'm tempted to push the key through Owen's letterbox, but, when I go out into the chilly morning air, my breath turning into white puffs of cloud, I'm met by the same officer standing guard on the steps again. I can't face talking to him in case I say the wrong thing, draw unwanted attention to myself, so when he lets me out through the tape I nod a brief thank you and head briskly up the road, wondering whether to take the bus or walk. In the end, I go on foot. I need to save every penny I have.

It takes me about twenty minutes to get there, and another twenty actually to get into Bethany's building, sneaking in through someone's held-open door as they come out.

I'm about to knock on her door, but I stop, exhaling in relief. The dull thud of a bass-line with Bethany's voice singing on top tells me she's home.

Thank God.

I knock loudly, waiting for her to answer.

'Bethany!' I call out when she doesn't come, rapping sharply again.

I don't want to disturb the neighbours, but thankfully the music goes off and, after more banging on the door, she finally opens it.

'Yes?' she says coldly, looking me up and down.

'I'm so glad you're home,' I say, folding from relief. 'You have no idea—'

I stop talking when I see the blank expression on her face. She stares at me, then closes the door a little. I press my palm against it.

'Beth, what are you doing? It's me,' I say with a laugh, although I don't feel in the least like being happy.

'I'm sorry?' she says. Her hair is wrapped in a towel and she's wearing a white robe. She holds the door open six inches. 'Do I know you?'

'What?' I laugh loudly now, a choked-up, almost hysterical croak. 'What do you mean, *do I know you*? I'm really not in the mood for jokes, Beth.' I put my hand on the door again, giving it a gentle push. 'Stop messing about. Just let me in, will you?'

She leans against the door, wedging her foot behind it. 'I have no idea who you are, but please get your hands off and go away.' Her face is cold and serious. 'You must have the wrong address.'

A chill rushes through me.

'Beth? Tell me you're not serious. I can deal with you

344

not wanting me to stay here, but for God's sake, just say so.'

My pack slips off my shoulder and on to the floor.

'Pretending you don't know me is mean. I've had a pretty lousy twenty-four hours and I really don't need this.'

My voice is trembling and I'm on the verge of tears.

'Beth, *please*?'

She shakes her head. 'I have no idea who you are. I want you to go away. If you don't, I'll call the police.' Her voice is iron-straight, unwavering. Her intense eyes pierce into me through the small gap.

I pause, staring at her, wondering if I noticed a flicker of recognition in her eye. If I did, it was fleeting. I break down and cry. This can't be happening.

'If this is some new part you're play-acting, I . . . I just can't take it today.'

I put my head against the wall to the side of her door, trying to stem the tears.

The door to her flat clicks shut.

I bang on it again, both fists hammering, my left foot kicking. 'Beth, don't do this to me. You're the only person I've got. Please listen.'

Then, in the silence that follows, it strikes me that she's *not* the only person I've got.

Not quite.

My stomach knots.

The realisation that Felix is close by, that he would help me in a heartbeat even from his hospital bed, fills me with dread and horror. How can I possibly turn to him after everything that's happened? But, mixed up with these feelings, there's something else, something I don't want to admit. It's almost relief – to know that if I'm at my very lowest, my most desperate, Felix will always pick me up and keep me safe.

I stand dead still, biting my lip, my face a contortion of anxiety.

Am I there yet? Is this my rock-bottom? How do you know if all is lost when you believe it has already gone?

In my mind, I hear Felix's voice, crooning, coaxing, drawing me back to him. He's a drug – always on my mind, however much I want to give him up.

I screw up my eyes, blocking him out. I must stay strong.

'Someone's been killed, Beth,' I whisper loudly through the door. 'I'm scared. I just need a place to stay for a day or two. Then I'll be gone, I promise.' I can't possibly tell her everything, but Beth's never been one to pry, to ask questions.

When there's no reply, I lean back against the wall, exhausted and confused. Nothing seems real any more. It reminds me of back then, when everything was out of control, when I did crazy things just to survive.

I thump the door, trying one last time. 'Beth, please! I was seeing this guy, Owen. We were lovers.' I'm speaking as loudly as I dare. 'And . . . and, Christ, now he's *dead*.' I bang again, letting out a frustrated scream. 'I'm not leaving until you open up!'

I hear the key turn, a chain slide into place. Slowly, the door opens a couple of inches and Beth is there again, staring directly at me.

'Listen to me, Beth, *please*. I found Owen dead on his kitchen floor. It's awful. I don't know what to do. He was so kind. We were good together. Stupidly, I thought things were finally going well.'

I wipe the back of my hand across my nose.

'Lovers?' Beth says coldly. 'You need to go. I don't know you.'

She flashes her phone at me by way of a threat, staring at me for a couple more seconds, making me wonder again if there's recognition in her eyes. Then the door shuts, and I hear the lock click again.

I feel as if I'm going to collapse, but somehow I drag myself and my pack down the stairs and out of the main door.

In the street, the cold air slaps me in the face. Everything seems tinged with grey and looks unreal. An old man walks past with his dog, stopping when he draws level with me.

'You all right, love?' he says.

He pauses, then shrugs and carries on when I don't reply.

I feel myself swaying and wobbling, my stomach knotting and cramping at the thought of everything. My heart gallops at a dangerous pace as I walk off, not knowing where to go.

I wish Mum was alive. She'd take care of me, comfort

me, tuck me up in my old bed and bring me a tray of soup and crackers. And I miss Dad terribly – his practical way of taking control, of making everything seem OK.

But because of me, they're both dead.

I feel so alone.

Although, not quite.

Something inside my heart shifts a gear – slowing it, speeding it, messing with the rhythm. It's a gear I never wanted to take again.

I turn in circles, fighting with my thoughts. It's as if no time has passed at all, as if I never even went to India, worked at Bestluck, or met Owen. Perhaps that's true. Perhaps if I go back to Felix's flat, everything will still be there as if I'd just popped out for milk. Him staring up at me from over the top of the newspaper, correcting me as I make our dinner the wrong way, upsetting him with my bad habits; me trying to get through each day without annoying him.

I love you, Belle he'd say last thing at night. If I didn't echo the same back, he'd make sure I didn't sleep, didn't get a moment's peace. Somehow he still managed to be fresh the next morning, in control. Normal.

Now, standing in the street, I can't help it when I turn and head towards Woodford Grange. Even though I know it's wrong. But where else is there?

I can't help it when my walk breaks into a slow run, despite the weight of my pack.

I can't help it that even though every part of me screams out to stay away, it's him I am drawn to.

It's not stupidity. It's not recklessness. It's lack of choice. It's fear. It's wondering what will happen if I don't.

33

There's a pattern of despair running through my time off work. It makes me wonder if I ever had a job or a career, blurring the last twenty years into a smudge of regret.

Was it all worth it, this long-term circus act of juggling family and work alongside my own sanity?

As I lie here in bed, I'm not sure how much longer I can keep it up.

I reach out for my pills. I shake the packet, finding it empty, although I know there are more downstairs.

Adam is suddenly standing in the bedroom doorway. He's holding a mug.

'How is it today?' he asks, pointing to my ankle.

It's propped up on two pillows, and has become the focus of our conversations these last few days.

'Sore.'

The truth is, it's the least of my problems. If I hadn't been driving and hobbling about on it, trying to keep up with Isabel Moore, it would be a whole lot better by now.

'But I'll live. Nothing another few days in bed won't sort.' I smile. A big, farcical one.

Adam looks sceptical. 'I made you this,' he says, placing the mug next to me. 'Camomile, to help you relax.'

He shifts awkwardly, turning to go, but then stops.

'Ray, you're not planning on . . .' He zips up his waterproof, indicating he's off out to work. He ruffles his hair nervously. 'You know, going out and about, are you?'

'Of course not,' I reply, much too quickly, sipping my tea and burning my mouth.

He shakes his head and stares at me, dark eyes burning into mine.

'Good,' he says with a nod, before walking off.

My ankle hurts more than ever when I press down on the pedal to drive. In the car park of Woodford Grange, I sit sideways, my legs poking out of the open door, pulling off my shoe and rolling up my black trousers to expose my leg. The skin is mottled and swollen, pulsing a purplish greeny-grey – the same colour as the low-hanging sky this morning.

I reach over to the passenger side and grab the Aircast boot, forcing it back on. Once I've pumped it up, it's instant relief. I can't stand the thought of dropping more painkillers, although I do, just to be sure. Within seconds, my stomach is burning again.

The receptionist stares at me, motionless for a moment, as if she's horrified to see me back so soon. The place doesn't exactly feel welcoming, with the woman coming

351

across as tight and unfriendly. But then I've not had much experience of private healthcare so wouldn't really know if it's normal.

'I'll see if the doctor's free,' she says reluctantly, disappearing down the corridor, leaving me standing in the waiting area.

She's gone a while, but eventually returns with a forced smile and a cup of strong tea. I eye it longingly.

'You're in luck,' she says, even though I swear I heard raised voices, some kind of argument. I imagined another refusal. 'But I'll need some ID from you.'

Reluctantly, I show her my warrant card, praying Bob doesn't get to hear about this.

'You can head on down to Mr Darwin's room. Third on the right. Dr Lambeth is expecting you.'

I thank her, walking off in the direction she's indicated.

The building is filled with beautiful period features – plaster mouldings, old doors with brass knobs, original floor tiles – although the fire exit signs and extinguishers dampen the ambience. Plus the smell of disinfectant is strong and nauseating, as if someone has just sprayed a bottle around for the hell of it.

'Hello, Dr Lambeth?' I knock on the door, pushing it open, hoping Darwin is there.

Inside, the smell is less pungent, and at least the window is open an inch or two. It faces out on to a lawned area at the back of the property – the garden of what would have once been a magnificent family home.

A man swings round.

For some reason, I expected someone wearing a white coat with a stethoscope draped around his neck, and approaching sixty. In reality, he's far from that, the only clue to his calling being the slightly lopsided Woodford Grange name badge he has pinned to the right of his tie.

'Good morning, Detective,' he says in a slightly embarrassing, overstated way.

In his late thirties, he's wearing dark trousers with a crisp blue and white striped shirt. He extends a tanned hand, indicating he's recently holidayed somewhere exotic. His hair is sea-spray blond to match.

'Sorry I couldn't see you last time you came. We're only a small facility and if there's something going on, we all know about it.' He laughs, flashing white teeth, like one of those celebrity television doctors.

'No problem,' I say. 'My name is Lorraine Fisher.' I purposefully leave off the Detective Inspector.

My eyes flick across to the bed. A frail-looking man, who I imagine was once attractive and full of life, is lying there, his body thin and wizened beneath the white sheet. It's almost as if he's a skeleton beneath his patterned hospital gown. He's awake, but not alert: his eyelids are drooping. Nothing apart from a few random face twitches indicates he's even alive.

'I was wondering if I could have a private word?'

All I want is to question the man in the bed, but there's no way that's going to happen without winning over the doctor first.

'Of course,' Dr Lambeth says, and calls a nurse to take

over what he was doing. He whispers something to her before leading me just outside the door.

'Mr Darwin's astounded us all,' he says proudly. 'Originally, the outlook was very depressing. He's not out of the woods, of course, and in terms of rehabilitation, I'm afraid his spinal injuries have rendered him paralysed from the waist down. It was a very bad accident.'

'So he'll never walk again?'

'No,' Dr Lambeth replies, pulling a remorseful face. 'But then, I'd never have imagined he'd regain consciousness either.'

He touches my elbow as if I'm a concerned relative.

'His early care had a lot to do with this remarkable outcome,' he continues. 'If the paramedics hadn't acted quickly, if the treatment at the QE hadn't been top notch, then it would be a different story.'

'When was the admission?' It's important I know.

Dr Lambeth nods obligingly, goes back in the room, and returns with a thick file. He flips through the papers, biting his lip.

'He was taken to the QE on the twenty-eighth of September, before being transferred here about a month later. I have the handover letter from the neurosurgeon, Mr Thomas.'

He angles the file to me and I glimpse the NHS Trust letterhead.

'Unfortunately, Mr Thomas's hopes were not high for this man.' His eyes flick down the report, skim-reading it. 'Mr Darwin was sent here because . . . well, because the outlook was so poor. I met Mr Thomas soon after to form a care plan, and it wasn't much more than a holding pattern.'

'Thank you, Doctor, that's helpful.' I make a mental note of the dates. 'Would it be possible to have a word with him now?' I'm pushing my luck, but I may not get another chance.

Dr Lambeth hesitates, then smiles. 'Sure. But not for long. It may even do him good to talk. He's re-learning all the time. Some of his words are tricky to understand.'

I nod, and follow him back in. As soon as I sit down, Felix opens his eyes. They are intense and staring, as if they're seeing the world for the very first time.

'Hello, Mr Darwin,' I say, feeling slightly unnerved by him. 'You've astounded the doctors, I hear.' I glance at the nurse, but she and Dr Lambeth are engrossed in one of the monitors.

He doesn't reply, just looks at me, his head bobbing slightly on the stalk of a very thin neck.

'I'm a police detective.'

I wait for his reaction, but there is none. I wonder if he can even hear me.

'I was hoping you'd be able to tell me about the accident.'

'Will . . . try,' he mumbles. His lips are dry and cracked, peeling apart when he speaks.

'Can you recall anything important about the twenty-eighth of September, the day of the crash?'

He is thoughtful for a while, his head dropping back

on to the pillow. His hand reaches for a controller, thumbing a button. The back of the bed rises slowly, making him more upright.

'Torrential rain,' he says. 'Skidding. Busy. Friday rush hour.' Felix gasps for air and closes his eyes for a moment. 'Late . . . for flight. Then nothing. Blackness.'

'I'm sorry if this is painful for you,' I say, jotting everything down. 'Can you tell me about Isabel Moore? When did you last see her before the accident?'

His eyes swell up as if they're waterlogged. 'Isabel,' he says softly. His fingers clench the sheet, knotting it into a white rose within his fist. He chokes down a dry sob.

'I think that's enough now, Detective,' Dr Lambeth says, seeing his patient getting upset. 'Mr Darwin tires easily.'

'Of course,' I say, thanking them both before leaving.

Once in the car, I prise off my Aircast boot in favour of my shoe. My ankle immediately starts throbbing again, but I can't possibly take more painkillers yet. Besides, I need a clear head to think about my next move. Something is bothering me about what Felix Darwin said, but I can't work out what. If I'm not careful, I'm going to run into Adam and his team at any moment, as I know we're only steps away from crossing paths. But for now, I need to keep going alone. Need to prove to myself, more than anyone, that I can do this.

34

The useless woman stands there, expecting answers. It makes me want to laugh, all the pathetic people on the payroll in this building, going back to their cosy little lives at the end of each day while I'm stuck here.

But we're only trying to help, they say.

I've been waiting for ever. No one understands what that feels like – to have a hole so huge in your heart, uncertain if it will ever be filled.

Then I check myself, put things into perspective. Things are actually going better than I'd expected.

I'm alive, aren't I?

'Penny . . . if that's what I should call you,' I say from my bed. I'm still getting used to their names. My voice is choked and clogged, but I force a smile through my tight jaw. 'How about, seeing as you're the receptionist, you play the part and deal with it?'

I shake my head, laughing at her ineptitude. It's not exactly been the best place to be holed up, what with that detective sniffing around, asking me stupid questions.

How does she expect me to remember those details? She'd been told about my injuries. Wasn't that enough? Anyway, I came across as tired and confused – what choice did I have, stuck like this? – and I don't reckon she'll be back.

'I've already told you, as well as everyone else in this damned place, that I would like to see Isabel whenever she comes. Day *or* night.' I pause. 'OK?'

I smile genuinely this time. I don't want to piss her off. She'll only go bad-mouthing me to the others, and then who knows what will happen then. For now, I need them all on side.

'If you're sure, Mr Darwin,' Penny says over-sweetly. 'I just wanted to check, that's all.'

She leaves, and I hear her heels clicking off down the corridor.

A minute later Isabel is standing in my doorway, a huge backpack looming behind her, as if someone's following her.

'I hope you don't mind me coming,' she says, briefly, breathlessly, then covers her face with her hands. A little habit of hers.

She smells of outside.

Saliva fills my mouth.

Last time she was here, I couldn't say much. I will be chattier now. She'll notice the difference in me. I'm getting better for you, Belle! Let's see if you're ready to begin again. Ready to be the lovely, beautiful woman you deserve to be, as well as the one I need.

'I was worried you wouldn't visit again,' I say croakily.

She shuffles into the room, lowering the pack off her stooped back, pushing it into the corner with her foot. Her eyes are heavy, red from crying. She stares at the floor.

'Sit down,' I say when she doesn't reply, patting the side of my bed.

She takes the chair instead, nervously lowering herself down. Looking at me through doe eyes. Then her head folds down on to her knees, her arms clamped over her neck. She doesn't stop crying for the next five minutes.

'Is everything OK, Mr Darwin?' Megan says, poking her head round the door. Her gaze switches between me and Isabel. Then she sees Isabel's backpack and frowns. It's in the way of the equipment, so she hoists it up. 'I'll just pop this out in the corridor,' she says, and I can't help wondering if she's thinking of riffling through the contents. I don't really trust her; don't really trust anyone here.

I raise my hand and nod, giving a little flicking motion with my fingers. They should learn when to butt out. She tells me to press the call button if there's a problem.

'What is it, Belle?'

I feel a fraud, lying here like this. Dr Lambeth told me Isabel is aware that nothing works from my waist down any more, that I won't walk again. A true test of love, if ever there was one. And surely harder for her to come to terms with than me.

She looks up. Her eyes are little sapphire jewels sunken in the puffy dough of her face. She's not been looking after herself.

'Felix, I'm in trouble and I don't know what to do.'

I salivate.

'Tell me.'

I try to sit up, but it's hard without being able to use my legs. I press the button on the bed controller, raising myself up.

'He's *dead*,' she says between quick, tight breaths. I can virtually see her chest clamping around her lungs and heart, forcing up her misery.

'Who is dead?'

'A guy. You don't know him.'

'A lover?' I ask. The 'v' makes my lips tingle.

She nods, making me want to kill her. Him.

'Your lover is dead.' My head falls back on to the soft pillow. Wallowing. Feathery mud. 'Lo-*ver*. Lover, lover, lover.' It bites the inside of my mouth. A bitter bee sting.

'The police think he was murdered.'

I stare at her, unable to miss her expression. 'That's terrible.'

I pass her a box of tissues from my bed table.

She looks at me, terrified.

'This lover,' I say, sipping on my water to stem the heat in my mouth, my head, my entire being. 'Did you . . . *love* him?'

Isabel gives me one of those pitiful female sniffles – half misery, half recovering joviality. 'I could have done given the chance.'

'I'm so sorry to hear this,' I say, stifling everything that wants to come out. No point scaring her off now that she's nearly mine again.

I reach out and take her hand, giving her my kindest smile.

She holds my hand back – a breakthrough moment.

'Thank you for being kind,' she says in reply, frowning at me suspiciously.

Then Megan is knock-knocking on the open door, coo-eeing her way in with a tray of tea. 'Thought you two could use a bit of refreshment,' she says, before retreating.

Isabel sips gratefully. Eyeing me.

'I didn't know where else to come,' she says while curling her hands around the little cup.

'It was me you ran away from, yet me you've run right back to.'

The irony is delicious – music to my ears. Almost an orchestra.

Isabel's hand, her beautiful porcelain hand, shakes as she places the cup back on the saucer. Only the finest china here at Woodford Grange.

'I tried to find you, you know.' I'd hate her to think I hadn't bothered.

'I'm sure you did.' Then she blows into three tissues. Her jaw clenches; her shoulders hunch. Tight and tense.

Did she think she would survive without me?

'How long will they keep you here?' she asks, narrowing her eyes.

She's no doubt thinking of logistics – how she'll care for me, where we will live, if we'll need a lift, ramps, special grab bars in the bathroom. She's imagining pushing me in a wheelchair, undressing me, washing me. Reading to me, and taking me on long walks.

Sliding on to my useless body to make love to me.

'A while.' I can tell she still loves me. 'I sensed you were near, Belle. Perhaps that's why I woke up.'

She likes this. Looks up and smiles. Some of the old warmth filtering back.

'You need a haircut,' I tell her. 'And some new clothes. What has become of you?'

She laughs, her light cinnamon hair dancing at her shoulders. Blue eyes gleaming. 'People change,' she says by way of excuse. Her lips pucker as if there's a drawstring. 'Like you have,' she lets slip, coyly looking away.

I imagine we're on our first date all over again.

I let pass a dramatic pause before saying, 'No. No, they generally don't.'

35

I need money. I have fourteen pounds and thirty-two pence in my purse and an expired debit card linked to a bank account with nothing in it. Then I remember the petty cash tin at Owen's office.

Even though I was owed money for my work, it doesn't seem right taking it, making a dead man pay his debts. But what choice do I have?

I feel in my bag for the office key. It's still there. Owen trusted me with it.

I head for Brandrick's with a heavy heart. It scares me to think that soon the police will be all over the place, scouring Owen's files and computers, searching for clues.

I kick up my pace. I just need to get in and get out before that cop comes back, asking her stupid questions, stirring everything up. What does she know about my life? What's done is done. She doesn't know the first thing about me and Felix, how it was. I just need to get out before it's too late, before I end up right back where I was to begin with.

For a second, I stop, wondering again if I ever really escaped. Whatever's happened, it's hard to forget that Felix has always been there for me.

He never really left me; was always in my thoughts.

I wipe away a tear, stumbling out on to a busy road. A car hoots me, making me jerk back. I feel dizzy, convinced I can hear Javesh's sing-song voice ringing in my ears. It's as if he's taunting me, circling me on his rusty bike. I try to catch sight of him, but all I see is a mother crossing the road, holding her kids tightly by the hands, giving me a wide berth as I stagger past.

I continue on, breathless and disorientated.

Maybe it was me; maybe he was right all along.

When I near the office, it's almost as if I'm lost.

Almost as if I've gone mad.

'That's odd,' I say, trying to locate a street sign. My vision goes blurry.

The terraced houses separating the main road from Brandrick's quiet street all look similar. I must have come down the wrong one, so I back-track a couple of blocks, trying to get my bearings. I head off down another similar-looking street.

'Excuse me,' I say to a man carrying a bicycle down his front steps. 'Do you know where Knowle Street is?'

He points down the hill and tells me it's a couple of roads across. I follow his directions, ending up back where I started by the familiar row of lime trees. And yes, there's the postbox and the corner shop where I used to buy coffee and biscuits. I take the key from my bag, stopping sharply as I finally reach the small façade of Owen's office.

A lump swells in my throat. Something is wrong.

I step back from the white frontage, staring at it, pushing my hands through my hair in frustration, looking left and right, up and down the car-lined street, to check I haven't got the wrong place. Two women with pushchairs veer either side of me, tutting and glaring because I'm in their way.

'Starline Minicabs' is painted on a sign in black lettering above Owen's office window. The plaque at the door with Brandrick's name and details is gone; there aren't even any holes where it once was. I don't know whether to go inside and ask whoever's in there what the hell's going on, or search down another street. I must have made a mistake.

With my pack on my back, I jog down the road as best I can, turn left, then pace up and down the parallel street. I do the same the other side, then I begin again at the top of Knowle Street, identifying the street sign, emblazoning it on my mind so there's no mistake.

'There's the postbox, the lime trees . . .' I say to myself, screwing up my eyes as I approach where Owen's office should be.

When I open them, Starline Minicabs is still there. An Asian man, about thirty, is standing in the doorway smoking a cigarette. He's wearing grubby low-slung jeans and a grey, unzipped hoodie with a T-shirt beneath.

'Need a cab?' he asks, eyeing my backpack. He blows smoke my way.

I stare up at the sign. It doesn't look particularly new. In fact there's weathering and flaking paint on the edges, as well as bird muck streaked down one side. I don't understand.

'Can I come in?' I say nervously.

The man drops his cigarette and stamps on it. A slow smile forms and his tongue pokes out between rough lips. I feel sick and scared, but I need to find out.

'Be my guest,' he says, gesturing me in with his hand. 'We welcome nice young ladies.' His accent is Birmingham mixed with something forced.

He gives me the creeps, but I go inside anyway.

'Derek, we got a visitor,' he says to a man sitting at a desk with several phones and a dusty computer that looks as if it's been there for years.

I stare around the room, taking it all in. I'm certain it's the same office, the same shape and size, but . . . but the leather sofa has gone, and so has Owen's drafting desk, and my small desk in the window. And there are no pictures on the walls or bright rug by the door. Instead, piles of boxes and general junk are stacked up around the office and the whole place seems dark and dingy, as if it's been neglected for years. There are a couple of other desks, but they're old and battered and I don't recognise them. The once-fresh walls are grimy, and the tall plant I watered for Owen has gone. The kitchenette looks vaguely the same, but none of the smart caddies are on the work surface, and the kettle is missing, a dirty plastic one in its place. The cream Smeg fridge has disappeared too, while the glossy-fronted cupboards are dull and stained with drip marks.

'I . . . I don't understand,' I say, wondering if I'd be able to sit down.

'You wanna cab, or what?' the man at the desk says, not noticing my distress. He turns back to his phones, clicking away at his computer, talking to a driver through his headset.

'No, I don't want a cab,' I say. 'How long have you been in this office?'

'Too bloody long,' he says, glancing at his watch. 'I got a fifteen-hour shift today and it's not even halfway through.'

'No, I mean how long have you occupied this building?'

'About six years, maybe more,' the Asian man says. 'My dad started the business, but he died and Derek came to help me out. Derek is my dad's mate's—'

'So you haven't moved in recently?' I don't care about his family history. 'As in yesterday?'

'No,' he laughs. 'Why are you asking all these crazy questions?'

My fingers are in my mouth. I gnaw nervously at my nails. *Stay calm, stay calm.* I force myself to think.

'I . . . I'm sorry. I must be in the wrong place. I'm looking for Brandrick's, the architect's office on Knowle Street.'

'Yeah, this is Knowle Street, but I don't know no architect or whatever. What number is it?'

The man hitches up his jeans, but they slip down again.

'Thirty-four,' I say quietly. But I already know that this

building is thirty-four. The sign above the window had the full address and the phone number on it.

'Yeah, this is thirty-four, chick, but as you can see, we is a minicab business.' He laughs and pulls his phone from his pocket, suddenly disinterested.

I creep slowly back into the tiny entrance hall. The door at the back to the toilet is still there, so I pull it open, stepping inside the small washbasin area, then on into the cubicle. It's basically the same, but a lot dirtier, and it smells revolting. The lilac hand towel and air freshener I bought for it are gone. Paper towels are stacked on the side of the sink.

'Did you actually want something, love, or are you just here for a piss?'

The door swings open. I turn, startled. It's the older man, Derek. He is almost too fat to fit through the narrow doorway, although I now know where the sour stench of stale sweat is coming from.

'Sorry,' I say, looking beyond him, feeling trapped. 'There's been a mistake. Yesterday, this was an architect's office. I worked here. I don't know what's going on. Do you know?' My voice doesn't sound like mine.

The man laughs, exposing rotten teeth and a waft of bad breath. His checked shirt strains around his huge belly.

'You on something, love?' he says cruelly. 'We've been here for years.'

He shakes his head and goes back to his desk, towards an office chair that neither Owen nor I used.

'Please,' I say desperately, running into the main office behind him. 'The architect, Owen Brandrick, has been killed, and now his office has vanished. You must know something.'

My voice squeaks and cracks as I stifle the tears. I try to keep control, but I have no idea what to do. I so desperately want to call that detective who came to see me, Lorraine Fisher, but she won't believe me – just like the others didn't before. She'll think I'm losing it, that I'm mad, that I need professional help, and then they'll put me back in that place. She seemed trustworthy, but if I get in touch, I'm risking so much. What if she's not on my side after all?

I clear my throat. I need to keep calm. 'I came to get some money,' I tell Derek. 'I have none, you see, and there was petty cash, and Owen was due to pay me, but then I found him covered in blood on his kitchen floor. He'd been stabbed and . . .'

I feel as if I'm going to faint – the ringing in my ears, the light-headedness, my legs going weak beneath me.

Derek stares at me incredulously. 'Look, love, I ain't got time for no shenanigans, and we ain't giving you no money. This is a minicab business not a bank, so either you're high on something or you've just escaped from the local nut house. Either way, if you wouldn't mind pissing off, it would be much appreciated. Jez?'

The younger Asian guy takes a few steps towards me.

I back away towards the door, grabbing my pack, raising my hands, showing them I'm going.

I stumble out on to the street. Hot tears stream down my face as I rush back up the road, heading for Owen's house and the flat. I don't know where else to go.

But when I get back, breathless and hysterical, when I reach the steps leading up to his front door, I stop suddenly. I inhale so sharply I almost drown on the icy air.

The last thing I see before my head hits the pavement is a beautiful woman with two young kids letting herself into Owen's house. There's no sign of the police or the crime-scene tape at all.

36

'Where am I?'

I hear a voice floating around me, then I realise it's mine. The sky is bright overhead, shadowed by a woman's face. She is beautiful, her blonde hair cascading above me as she strokes my forehead. She's frowning, looking concerned.

'You fainted,' she tells me. 'I think you hit your head. I'm going to call an ambulance.'

Two kids are holding tightly on to my ankles, propping up my legs on their shoulders. I try to wriggle free, but I'm too weak.

'Please, stay still,' the woman insists. 'You need to get the blood back to your brain.'

I turn my head sideways, the rough pavement grinding against my skull. I stare up at Owen's front door.

'Who are you?' I ask, gradually remembering what happened. 'What are you doing in Owen's house? Don't you know he's been killed?' I feel the panic welling in my chest again.

'Owen?' she says with a kind smile. 'I'm sorry, I don't know anyone called Owen. This is my house.' She turns to her children, equally blonde and beautiful. 'Good work, kids. Can you hold them up a bit longer?'

They both nod their heads, clearly happy to help.

'You don't understand,' I say, not sure how to explain everything that's happened. And I certainly don't want to be going off in an ambulance.

I kick my legs free from the children's grip and roll on to my side, ending up on all-fours like a dog. My head reels and my back arches. I think I'm going to be sick.

'I really wouldn't move if I were you,' the woman says, her voice holding kind, even though I've just shoved her children.

She ushers them up the front steps, telling them to go inside and put the television on.

'But Owen and I watched TV in there,' I whisper, remembering the cosy evenings we had together. I struggle to my feet, staggering and squinting from the pain in my head. 'He died in the kitchen.'

I can see by the woman's expression that she thinks I'm crazy. My coat has mud down one side and my pack has come undone, spilling out a load of my things.

'Look, I'm sorry, but you have to believe me. My name is Isabel. I met this guy called Owen, and I've been staying in his basement flat. He's an architect, and he gave me a job, and we . . . well, we got on well together, and then he . . . he . . . oh my God, he was killed, and I don't know what the hell's going on, or what you're doing in his house . . .'

My voice collapses and hot tears pour down my cheeks. I cradle my head, trying to ease the pain.

'I don't know who you are, but Owen never told me about a wife and kids.'

I squint at her. The light hurts my eyes so much.

'So I . . . I just don't know what to do.'

The sobs echo inside my head. Maybe that detective Lorraine would vouch for me, that I really was living in the flat. Then the familiar pang of anxiety comes as I worry about the consequences, fearful of Felix's reaction. But, finally deciding it's what I must do, I rummage in my pack for her number. It's not where I put it. More stuff falls out as I tear through my meagre belongings searching for it. It's gone.

The woman has stayed with me.

'I know a detective,' I explain to her, desperately. 'She interviewed me here. She'll help me.'

'A detective?' the woman says, frowning. 'I think it's a doctor you need to see. You don't look well. Would you like a glass of water? Come and sit on the steps. I'll call an ambulance.'

She's right. I'm not well. There's ringing in my ears, and my heart is pounding so fast it's making me breathless.

'No,' I say, sniffing. My eyes flick nervously up and down the street. She probably thinks I'm homeless and has alerted the police already. 'I don't want an ambulance.'

The woman is shaking her head, her phone in her hand.

'Look, the cops were here earlier,' I insist. 'There was crime-scene tape and a police guard. It was serious.' I point at the house frontage. 'If you let me show you where it happened, then . . . then I'll go. There are bound to be blood stains on the kitchen floor.' I beg her with my eyes. '*Please*?'

The woman stares at me, squinting.

'OK,' she says, quietly. 'Then you must leave. I don't know what you're talking about, but you do seem very upset.'

'Thank you, *thank* you.' More than anything, I want to prove I'm not going mad.

We head up the front steps, and she gives a little wave to the two pale faces at the front window to the left of the door. 'Just don't make a fuss,' she tells me. 'I don't want the kids upset.'

'Of course,' I reply, trying to stay calm.

But when she leads me in through the front door, my heart hammers inside my chest even harder, making me want to retch.

'It doesn't look right,' I say, staring around at all the various-sized coats hung haphazardly on hooks. And all the shoes, kids' and adults', arranged on wooden racks beneath. There are paintings on the walls that I swear Owen didn't have, and the place smells different now – of cooking and family, perhaps a dog.

'Come through,' the woman says patiently, still with her phone clutched in her hand, ready to dial. 'Maybe you'll feel better if you just take a look.'

Once inside Owen's big kitchen, nervous and frightened because this was where he died, I look around. I feel disorientated, unreal, as if someone is going to jump out from behind a screen and tell me I'm on some crazy TV show.

'Where's all Owen's stuff?'

Some of his furniture is here – the sofa, the pine table and chairs – but it's all the extra belongings, or rather the lack of his, that's worrying me.

For a start, the fridge is covered in kids' paintings stuck on with alphabet magnets, and the rug beside the table is littered with crayons and toy cars. There's so much clutter on the worktops, where before there was barely anything. It's as if I've walked into an entirely different home. I wouldn't have recognised it.

'Can I take a look?' I ask with my hand positioned on the pantry cupboard door.

The woman looks sceptical, glances back to the door nervously, but indicates for me to go ahead.

When I open it, instead of finding Owen's meagre supplies, I see it's stuffed full of typical family groceries, from giant cereal boxes and tins of soup to kids' plastic lunch boxes and stacked-up cartons of orange juice. Biscuits and jars of coffee and hot chocolate as well as a dozen different herbal teas line one shelf alone.

I put my hand to my forehead.

'Are you OK?' she says. 'You mentioned that there was blood.'

Her voice is tentative, worried, as if she's about to throw me out at any moment. Instead, she runs the tap and hands me a glass of water. I sip it gratefully.

That's when I see the mat, right where Owen was lying on the floor. It definitely wasn't there before.

'Yes, under there,' I say quickly, excited that I will be proved right. Someone has obviously tried to cover up the stain.

I drop to my knees and pull back the grey and blue rug – a magician at the final reveal.

Except nothing is revealed.

I whip back the other side, but it's concealing nothing. 'I don't understand . . .'

I scour the rest of the wooden floor, my eyes trawling up and down each sanded board.

'It was terrible, like a butcher's shop,' I tell her, concentrating on finding the stain. 'The ambulance crew will confirm it.'

'I think you've had a nasty fall. You're confused,' the woman says, her patience breaking. 'If you don't want an ambulance, I think you'd better leave now. My husband's upstairs. I can call him down.'

'Please believe me,' I say, almost bending double with frustration.

Then it occurs to me.

'My stuff! I left some things in the flat downstairs. I'll show you.'

I fumble around in my pocket for the key, then in my handbag, then in each compartment of my pack, but it's not there either. It must have fallen out along with the phone number.

'Just let me in and I can prove I lived there.'

'I don't think that's a good idea,' she says. 'Besides, the flat's been empty for a while. We're going to redecorate then rent it out.'

'Let's just look through the window then. I left some of my stuff on the coffee table and sofa. That's all I ask, then I'll go.'

The depth of sadness in my eyes must have tugged at something inside her, because she leads me back through the hall, outside, and down the steps to the basement. We both peer in through the grubby window.

A sharp pain folds up my stomach.

Apart from the sparse furnishings, there's nothing to be seen – no DVDs or clothes, no scented candles or magazines. It's all gone.

I leave the property, gathering my pack as I go. I head off down the street, glancing back over my shoulder. I have no idea what to do.

37

'Grace!' I call out, limping into the hall, taking hold of her arm before she leaves.

She's decided that going to work is a necessity if she's to save up for her travels, but not without asking a lad she works with to pick her up in his car. She's still frightened of someone lurking or breaking in, and Stella isn't much better thanks to me. But Adam has had a word with them. Told them that I'm under a lot of pressure and tried to reassure them. It almost kills me it's come to this.

'What, Mum?' she says, checking her watch and slinging on a jacket over her black trousers and white shirt.

'Remember at the end of September when you had loads of netball matches all in one weekend? Can you recall when they were exactly and what the weather was like?'

Grace's face crumples into annoyed lines that make her look briefly older. 'How and *why* would I remember that?'

'It's important, love. Can you think?'

Something's been nagging at me since I spoke to Felix Darwin, something that doesn't add up.

Grace peers out of the hall window, looking up and down the street. Finally, she pulls out her phone and flicks the screen on to her calendar.

'It was the last weekend of the month, according to this. I had two matches on Friday evening the twenty-sixth, then two others on Saturday and Sunday, the twenty-seventh and -eighth. And actually, now you mention it, I do remember the weather because we were all sweltering and coach was going on about an Indian summer and how we had to stay hydrated. She brought out a load of sports drinks because we were all so parched.'

'Hang on, you mean Friday the twenty-eighth?' I take my own phone from my pocket to check the calendar. I can see that Grace is right before she even replies.

So Felix's crash must have been on the Sunday, not the Friday. Or he got the date wrong, and it was the twenty-sixth, not the twenty-eighth. A likely mistake for someone who's been in a coma for weeks.

'And you're sure about the weather? Hot and dry all weekend, not raining?'

'Without a doubt, Mum. What's with the meteorology?' She looks out of the window again.

I stumble over a reply, but the toot of a car horn saves me.

'Gotta go,' she says, grabbing her bag. She stops, turning back. 'I remember that Emma got a sunburnt nose. It was definitely a scorcher.'

379

I lean forward to kiss her, but only manage to skim her cheek as she disappears out of the front door.

After she's gone, I head for my laptop to confirm the weather. Torrential rain, Felix Darwin had said, skidding. He seemed pretty sure even for someone with head injuries.

I make a coffee, listening out for the front door in case Adam comes back. I run a search for historical weather reports, soon finding a site that tells me all I need to know. There was no precipitation in Birmingham that weekend, and it shows the maximum temperature to have been twenty-five degrees Celsius and sunny.

To be sure, I take a look at the few days either side of that weekend: there was a warm dry spell for at least a week. In fact, I remember it. I was working on a case involving illegal immigrants and thought how unbearably hot the office had become, which is why Felix's recollection jarred with me.

'Hi, love,' I say to Adam when he answers his phone on the first ring. 'Just wondering what time you'll be home later.' I listen, holding my breath. 'OK. I'll save you some supper.'

I hang up with a small smile. Things need to be done. I know for a fact Bob is at a meeting in Manchester for two days, so it should be easy to slip into the office. I really should tell Adam about all this, but for now something makes me hold off. Deep down, I know it's pride.

*

The department is busy, but it turns out that this is a good thing. None of my team are about, thankfully, and no one else notices me arriving, sliding into my chair and logging into my computer. An old coffee cup sits exactly where I left it on the wooden mat Stella made in DT at school. A picture of the girls has been knocked out of place so I straighten it. Most of my pens have gone missing from my drawer.

I quickly log into the system and run a search for traffic accidents in Birmingham on the twenty-eighth of September. None of the RTAs recorded involve Felix Darwin or Isabel Moore's parents. I check again, changing the date to Friday the twenty-sixth, then the Saturday, but the story is the same. I can't find anything linked to the alleged accident. I change the search criteria, adding in every possible permutation to make sure I'm not missing something obvious, including different dates, areas, and even months in case someone was mistaken.

Half an hour later, I give up. As far as I'm concerned, no one called Felix Darwin has ever been in a car accident in Birmingham, nor anyone called John and Ingrid Moore; neither were there any fatalities during the period. I wonder if Adam and the team have already flagged this, though I'm not sure I would know if this was their line of enquiry. He's not been saying much about the case, not wanting to bother me by bringing work home, but it makes me sad I'm being excluded.

I head for the lift, trying not to make a spectacle of myself on crutches. A couple of colleagues look up as I pass, one raising a hand. The other calls out to me, wanting to talk, but I tap my watch, indicating I'm in a rush – as much of a rush as I can be like this.

I press the button for the lift, jabbing it several times when it doesn't come. Several other officers join me, asking how I'm doing, when I'll be back full-time. I reply vaguely, keeping my head down until the lift arrives, pondering what I've just found out. I can only hope that no one mentions my presence to Adam or Bob.

Adam is home an hour earlier than he'd led me to believe. No doubt trying to catch me out. But I'm way ahead of him. I even have a chicken, tomato and olive dish ready when he walks in, exhausted and soaking from the sudden downpour.

My stomach churns with a roll of deceit.

'Oh, love, look at you. You're soaking.'

'What's with all this?' he says, frowning at the kitchen table. Earlier, I put out a cloth, a couple of wine glasses, even the nice mats Jo, my sister, gave us for Christmas.

'What's with all what?' I say, placing a steaming terracotta casserole dish in the centre of the table. 'Grace is eating supper in her break at work, and Stella's already had food at her friend's. I thought I'd make something nice for us.'

I light the rarely used candle I've brought in from the dining room.

Adam stares at me suspiciously, narrowing his eyes, squinting at the table, then back at me. Then he rips off

a piece of kitchen paper and dabs his wet face and neck.
When he chucks it in the bin, he pauses longer than
necessary, staring down into the empty liner.

A little bleed of oneupmanship seeps through me. I
took the rubbish out earlier, with the Marks & Spencer
food boxes. He won't know it's not homemade.

'It's not like you to go to so much trouble,' he says,
pouring me a glass of Merlot and water for himself.

'Thanks,' I say. 'Now that I'm a Stepford Wife, there's
not much else to do.'

'Love—'

'No, no, Adam, stop.'

I take a green salad from the fridge, already decanted
into a wooden bowl from its plastic tray. I drizzle olive
oil on to the couscous.

'I've been pressured into taking this time off when I
don't want to, and I don't think it's right. I really need
to get back to work, Adam. There's nothing wrong with
me. I'm going crazy stuck at home.' I swallow guiltily.
'Look, I know I've come across as stressed and anxious,
and if Bob's going to escalate the complaints, then I'll
have to deal with them. But I just *need* to come back,
Adam.'

There's a pair of hands on my shoulders, guiding me
down into my seat.

'This looks delicious, Ray. Let's just enjoy the meal.'

He sits down opposite me, rubbing his large hands over
his tired face.

I stare at him, suddenly feeling selfish.

'Looks like I'm not the only one who needs a break,' I remark, serving him some chicken.

'Agreed,' he admits, picking up his fork. He jabs it into his food, but doesn't eat. 'It's not the same without you,' he confesses with a small smile. 'Did you get your prescriptions filled at the chemist?'

'Of course,' I lie, not having any intention of doing so. And I'm not going for the heart monitor either.

Adam nods, finally tucking into a piece of chicken. He makes an approving face. 'It's good,' he says, but then lays down his knife and fork, looking serious. 'We made an arrest today.'

I glug back a load of wine. 'Melanie?'

I suddenly feel chilled and pull my cardigan off the back of the chair, sliding it round my shoulders. They've been working forward at speed, and I've been in the dark.

Adam nods. Nothing else.

'I see,' I say, waiting for more information.

'I wanted to tell you, but felt it unfair to burden you with work while you're resting. He's an old boyfriend. Several leads from the appeal matched up. We're still getting things together for the CPS, but it's looking positive.'

'What about Alexandra?' My heart is thumping – weeks of work culminating without me.

He shakes his head.

'You still believe they're unrelated?'

'We're pretty certain he wasn't involved with Alexandra. He's got previous for domestic against Melanie, and we found traces of her blood in his car. The lab confirmed earlier it was Melanie's, although he claims it was old, from when he hit her during the summer.'

'Oh God,' I say, thinking what the poor girl must have gone through.

'Melanie came to Birmingham to get away from him, but he followed her down in a jealous rage, convinced she was seeing someone else. He was with her just a few hours before she died, and others in her university halls heard arguing, saw them drive off together. The CCTV confirms this – all the way to the city, in the direction of the canals. He claims he dropped her off in a back street as she asked because she wanted to walk, think about things. Unfortunately, there are no witnesses or further CCTV.'

I sigh, unable to believe what I'm hearing. So much has been going on without me, no doubt blowing my theories apart.

'I'll have his confession by morning. I'm leaving him to stew for a bit.'

'You're going back tonight?'

'The fucker's in a cell, not staying with us for a spa break.'

'Then I'm coming with you.'

I stand up, then sit down again. The small amount of wine has already gone to my head. I probably shouldn't have taken that codeine when I was cooking.

'No, love. Best you stay here.'

'And you're truly convinced he's got nothing to do with Alexandra?' I hear my voice shaking.

'Completely.'

'Adam . . .' I don't know how to put this without sounding mad, as if I've gone off at some desperate tangent just to win back Bob's favour. 'If you can just get me back on board for a couple of days, if you can hold off charging this man even for a few more hours, overnight, there are some other angles that could be worth investigating. God,' I add, hearing how desperate I sound, 'I wouldn't be saying this if I didn't think it was important. Then at least we'll know we've done everything.'

'We *have* done everything, love,' Adam says confidently.

I can't believe he doesn't see it. I'll never forget Alexandra's ankle when I was shown her body in the morgue. My own ankle throbs in sympathy in its boot. It was so similar to Melanie's wrist, the way the red welt was mottled with blood. And then there's Bethany and Isabel – their stories so similar, plus Felix and the mystery accident. I need help with this, but I can see convincing Adam is going to prove impossible. If I tell him what I know, all it will do is show that I'm still overwrought and in need of this break – not to mention that I've continued to pursue the case.

'What about the independent medical expert?' I ask. 'The dermatology report clearly stated that the wound on Alexandra's ankle was made post-mortem.'

'It *suggested* it might have been. The report was unable to be conclusive on that, Ray.'

'And Melanie's wrist. Did you get the report on that back?' My breathing quickens. 'And what about the other women who have reported similar harassments?' I'm sounding petulant now, desperate. 'Does that not mean *anything* to you?'

Adam sighs. 'Why not start afresh when you come back to work,' he says, placing a hand on my forearm. 'Just forget about this one, love. We've got it covered.'

Apart from Adam taking a couple of phone calls from the station, we eat the rest of our dinner in silence, me fighting with the mess in my head.

Later, when Adam has zipped up his jacket and headed back out into the night, I load the dishwasher, hobbling about the kitchen all alone. I pour another glass of wine to help my throbbing foot.

I pause, sipping my drink and staring out of the window into the dark and rainy back garden, wondering why Felix Darwin is lying in a hospital bed if he wasn't even in an accident.

'And where the hell are Isabel Moore's parents?' I say to myself as the pain finally begins to lift.

38

Finding a parking spot is tricky near the surgery. Adam's news last night knocked me sideways, filling my head with crazy thoughts about continuing the case alone. If I wasn't so stressed and anxious about everything, including fretting about Grace and Stella because now I've made them worried, I could perhaps find a way out of this cycle. Figure out a way to make Adam and Bob take me seriously. But while I'm like this, they're never going to listen to me. I've lost sight of the real me.

In any case, it's forced me to see if I can get a short-notice appointment with Dr Lewis. I'm hoping she may have some suggestions to get me back to work quickly.

I change into my boot and lock the car, shaking my head at the angle I've parked. It wasn't easy squeezing into the spot I found in a narrow street behind a row of shops, but at least it's near the surgery.

There's a noise – someone crying out, though only quietly, like a gasp of shock. Then I hear footsteps, perhaps someone running.

By the time I've figured out where they're coming from, there's no one in sight. The drizzle has started up again, and even though it's nine-thirty a.m., it might as well be the same time at night for the amount of light that's filtering through the low-hanging clouds.

'No, Lorraine,' I say firmly to myself, starting to walk, 'there's no one there. You are not being followed, and no one is watching you. You've been working too hard, you're in pain, and you've not been eating or sleeping properly. Your fitness levels are at an all-time low, you drink too much wine, and you take too many painkillers.'

I stop.

Another noise. The street is narrow and oppressive. I try to calm my racing heart by taking some deep breaths.

Yet another noise makes me swing round, one crutch raised at a right angle. If Adam could see me now, he'd have me locked up. Then I imagine him holed up in an interview room with a couple of other detectives, grilling the man they arrested, making progress on the case without me.

Even though my gut is telling me otherwise.

'And look where your gut's got you now,' I say angrily, though not loud enough for anyone to hear. 'Paranoid and desperate, and incapable of doing your job.'

I shake my head and walk on to the surgery.

My crutches fall from my grip as someone grabs my arm roughly from behind.

'Get *off*!' I shriek, kicking into self-defence mode before

I can even turn round. As I struggle, my hair comes loose, obscuring my view.

Then I hear a woman's cry, a pitiful sob.

'Oh my God, I'm so sorry,' she says, letting go, holding up her hands to show she's released me. 'I don't know what came over me. I called out to you, but you didn't hear.'

I take a deep breath and my heart slows. 'Isabel?' I say, wondering how she found me. She looks terrible – her face is pale and panicked, and there's real fear in her eyes.

She peers at me from beneath the mass of her fiery hair.

'You shouldn't have grabbed me like that. I'm a police officer, and I'm not exactly steady on my feet at the moment.'

I bend down to retrieve my dropped crutches. I want to tell her how much she frightened me, but don't. She's in a terrible state – shaking, gasping for air as if she's having an asthma attack. Her eyes are red and puffy as though she's been crying for several days.

'What's happened to you?'

Isabel shies away from me like a wary animal. Her clothes are dirty and her face is puckered with grief. She raises her hands. 'I'm sorry, you're right. I shouldn't have grabbed you. I was walking along and saw you turn down here in your car and . . . and I thought I should . . . There are some things you should know.' She touches her head, wobbling a little.

I move towards her. 'Are you ill?'

She tries to say something, but I can't tell what. Her

back is pressed against the wall of a building, one hand down by her side, her fingers clawing at the brick.

'I think I need help . . . I don't know. I . . . I'm confused. Someone . . . that woman . . . lots of women . . . and Felix . . .' She covers her face. 'Please . . . don't let him . . .'

I wonder if she's drunk, or on drugs. Nothing makes sense; no sentence is complete.

'OK, OK, take it steady. I will try to help you, Isabel. Would you like to sit in my car? It's warmer in there.'

Isabel nods and walks with me to the car, getting into the passenger seat when I beep it unlocked.

I start the engine.

'Tell me why you're so upset.'

'I don't know where to begin.'

Isabel's voice is quiet and breathy against the car's heating fan. I turn it down a notch. She turns sideways, looks me in the eye.

'Owen, the man who lived above me,' she says, her face scrunched up from worry. 'He was killed. Murdered. You must have heard about it at the police station. It was probably on the news, too.'

I swallow as the reality hits me. There's a lot at the office I haven't heard about, and I haven't caught the news in a few days. I've been too wrapped up in myself, to be honest, pursuing things I shouldn't have been.

'Actually, no.' I point down to my Aircast boot. 'I've been off work.'

'I found him lying in a pool of blood,' she whispers.

'He was stabbed. It must have happened around the time you came to my flat.'

I breathe in sharply. If she's right, and a man was murdered while I was in the vicinity, let alone in the same building, then I'm in more trouble than I can possibly imagine if it gets back to Bob.

'Did they give you the details of an officer to contact for support?' I ask. 'Who took your statement?' My mind races, wondering how I can find out more without raising suspicion.

Isabel looks vague, almost guarded, shrugging within the padded confines of her winter coat. 'I don't know. I was in shock. I didn't even think to ask. There were two officers, then another one came.'

'You shouldn't have had to ask.' I make a mental note to talk to someone about this. I certainly haven't heard anything about it. 'What about the crime scene? Who was in charge of that? Did forensics come?'

Isabel is shaking her head. 'I don't know,' she whispers shamefully. 'I left. They said I could go after I gave my statement. They had a police guard out there for ages.'

I think hard. I have no idea what this means, or what I should do. *Leave it up to Adam and Bob*, a small voice inside my head tells me. *They'll be all over anything relevant by now.*

'Since then, things have only got worse,' she tells me, barely able to speak. 'My best friend refuses to acknowledge me. Literally, as if she's never met me before. And when I went back to the flat because I didn't know where else to go, there was another family living in Owen's house. All the stuff I'd left downstairs had vanished, and . . . and . . .'

I raise my hand. 'OK, slow down,' I say, utterly confused. 'How about a coffee and you can tell me everything?'

Ten minutes later, we're sitting in a greasy-spoon-type place around the corner. The place stinks of all-day breakfasts and our table is coated in a layer of something sticky. Isabel refused anything except a glass of water, which she's barely touched, and I have a large black coffee and a couple more painkillers. The doctor's appointment will have to wait.

'Are you certain about all this, Isabel?' I say as kindly as I can. 'It's hard for an entire office to vanish, as well as a house.'

She shoves her glass, spilling some water. 'The buildings are still there,' she says through pursed lips, her eyes lit up with anger, 'but it's all *different*. Everything is all gone. My *life* is gone.' She looks away from me.

I sip some coffee. 'That is very strange.' I feel as if I'm humouring her. I'm beginning to wonder if she needs psychiatric assessment.

Isabel just stares into nowhere.

'How did you meet Owen . . .' I glance at my notes. 'Owen Brandrick? What do you know about him?'

'I met him in . . .' She hesitates. Her eyes grow wide. 'I'd gone away. Overseas. After everything went bad with Felix, after what he did, I . . . I needed to get away. I only came back because I found out my parents had been killed.' She bows her head.

'Where did you go, Isabel?'

'I went to Delhi.' There's a flicker of a smile, as if she's left a part of herself there. 'It's impossible not to lose yourself in Chandni Chowk.'

I feel sorry for her – she looks so dejected and alone. But there's something else about her, something I can't put my finger on.

'Owen was a rock to me,' she goes on. 'He was with me when I found out about Mum and Dad. He was amazing, helping me sort everything out. We became . . . well, you know. We got close. Apart from losing Mum and Dad, I thought things were finally looking up.'

Isabel stares pensively across the steamy café, twirling the glass in her hands. A tear collects in the corner of one eye.

'And your parents,' I say, gently swerving the conversation back to where I want it to be. 'Going to their funerals must have been a terrible ordeal. Did Owen go with you?'

'That's the awful thing,' she says. 'They were killed a month before I found out because no one could find me, so I missed their cremations and interments.'

'I'm sorry to hear that,' I say.

'When we got back, Owen helped me find their graves. He took me to visit them so I could say goodbye. I left flowers, although we didn't stay very long.'

Her hand shakes as she sips her water.

'Would you like to visit them again?' I suddenly ask, hoping she'll bite. 'It might help.' I glance at my watch purposefully. 'I have a little time right now. If you like, I could drive you.'

She stares at me for a few seconds, no doubt trying to fathom if I'm serious. I nod encouragingly, wondering what the hell's going on.

Bluebell Meadow burial ground is bleak and depressing in the drizzle and, at first glance, could be mistaken for a large suburban park with hillocks, young trees, and a few benches dotted around.

'Up this way,' Isabel says, leading me on through a gate.

Way ahead, at the far end of the meadow, there's a bright splash of someone's orange and yellow waterproof as they stoop over a grave. Otherwise we're pretty much the only ones visiting.

Isabel walks along the tarmac path at a brisk pace, but it's hard for me to keep up as the hill begins. I left the plastic boot in the car so I didn't slow us down too much, but my foot feels painful and swollen inside my regular black shoe.

'Their plots are easy to find,' she calls back. 'They're marked clearly, and I left flowers, but I suppose they'll be dead by now.'

There's excitement in her voice, as if bringing me here will somehow prove her unfathomable story. I'm just hoping it will prove mine.

'Is it much further?' I ask as we near the top of the hill.

The cemetery is bounded on two sides by a wood, and on the other by a busy road. The wind spreads traffic noise incongruously across the meadow.

'It's just up here and along the row to the end, 274a and b. They chose the plots themselves.'

There are tears in Isabel's eyes, though it could be from the wind. It's breezy up here, and feels as if there will be a storm soon.

Eventually, we drop down into a more sheltered area and head towards a wooded patch. As we reach the end of the row, she jogs on ahead.

'I should have brought more flowers,' she calls out, glancing back at me.

But then she stops abruptly. Her hand goes to her head and she darts back towards me, scanning the plaques.

Please don't make me walk any further, I think.

'That's odd,' she says. 'Hang on.'

She runs to the next row, and the next, stopping periodically to check the well-hidden numbers. The grass has grown knee-high over some graves, only the pathways between the rows having been lightly mown. There are no headstones to aid identification.

'It must be this row because, look . . .' Isabel points to the ground about ten metres before the woods begin. 'Here's plot 273. It's clear on the plaque, right?'

I finally catch up and take a methodical look at all the numbers. I'm about to suggest we check out another row, but suddenly she's sobbing uncontrollably.

She falls to her knees in the damp grass. 'Please, oh

please don't do this to me!' She stares up at the sky, as if she's talking to God.

'Isabel, calm down. You've obviously just made a mistake.'

I limp along another row, peeling back the overgrown weeds to see the markers.

'Are you sure you're right about the plot numbers?'

'One hundred per cent,' she sobs, staring up at me pale-faced, as if she's about to faint. 'They were right here, I swear it. I swear on my life!'

Then more inconsolable wailing as she falls forward on to the untouched and perfectly flat ground where her parents' graves were meant to have been. Her hair falls forward, exposing the back of her neck, and my heart pounds as I catch sight of her pale skin, the black tattoo standing out sharply on the nubs of her spine.

39

She's driven off, abandoned me as if I'm disposable, a nuisance. Chewing gum on her shoe.

She told me to go home. I don't know where that is.

But at least she genuinely wants to help me, said she'll follow up on some things. And she hasn't pried too much. I reckon it won't be long before she finds out what Felix is like, everything he's done. Then I pray it's just a matter of time before they arrest him. He can't hide in hospital for ever, not now he's woken up. I hardly dare hope there's a chance I will walk free from all this, never have to look over my shoulder again.

As she was talking in the cemetery, trying to calm me down, I felt a deep rage brewing inside me. I shouldn't have grabbed her again, but something flipped after I couldn't find the graves.

But the look on her face tempered me, made me get control of myself, and she almost appeared as weary and scared as I've become these last few days. I let go of her shoulders, apologising. I had to keep her on side.

'I'm so sorry,' I said, stepping back, fearful she was going to arrest me. 'I've been through so much this year.' I bowed my head.

'I understand, Isabel,' she said. 'The things you went through must have been very frightening. I'm sorry we weren't able to help more. And losing both your parents is unthinkable.'

I looked her in the eye then, hoping that she'd see the depth of my pain. I wasn't sure she did, so I took a breath and dared to mention it. I was so ashamed.

'My entire relationship with Felix was built around lies. He was never honest with me. In the end . . .' I paused. I was going to say *it drove me crazy*, but I didn't. She wouldn't have believed anything I said then. It's true what they say about the stigma. 'There were others,' I told her instead. 'Felix had other women in his life.' Not to mention his mother, I thought, but didn't say.

The detective nodded, looking interested.

'And he certainly had a type,' I added, hoping I'd said enough to set her thinking, though not enough for Felix to find out what I'd done.

'Thanks for being honest, Isabel,' she said, making my fear a little less.

'I actually went to see Felix,' she admitted as we walked back to her car. She was so slow, complaining about her ankle. 'It was odd. He seemed quite uncertain about details of the car accident.'

Felix has never been uncertain about anything, I wanted to tell her, but didn't. She wouldn't have understood.

It was actually simple when it came down to it. All he ever wanted was his mother back. He didn't really care how he got her, as long as no one stood in his way. For a while, I was his fix. In our own ways, we all were.

'I'm scared for my life,' I told her, suddenly wishing I hadn't. I'd grown so used to being careful about what I said, covering everything up, that it felt strange to tell her these things.

The detective nodded, seeming to understand.

Back in the car, she asked for my phone number. I gave it to her of course – with one digit changed. I'd done my bit. The rest was up to her. When she asked where I was going, I told her I wasn't sure.

'Your parents' house?' she suggested, concerned for me.

'Perhaps,' I said, shrugging. I'd helped her enough.

She took me back and dropped me off near Owen's place, making me promise that I'd get some food, look after myself. I agreed, then watched her drive off. After that, I walked around for ages, thinking, deciding what to do.

And now I'm here, in a bakery, the smell of soft doughy bread teasing my nostrils.

I edge forward in the queue.

'One bread roll, please,' I say to the woman behind the counter as I carefully count out some coins. I need to save my money.

'Just one?' she asks, looking me up and down.

'Can you spare a cup of tap water too?' I whisper.

She glances over to her boss, who is busy with another customer, and stuffs a paper bag with two filled rolls – egg and cress plus a ham and cheese. She charges me the forty pence she would have charged for the plain roll, and throws in a can of Coke too.

I stare at her warily, wondering what the catch is.

'Hurry up and get out of here,' she whispers across the counter, flicking her eyes back to her boss.

I see my gloved hand reach out and snatch the bag, concealing it within my coat. With my head down, my matted hair falling over my eyes, I hurry out of the shop.

All I ever wanted was to be loved, I think, darting between cars, weaving across the road. It's not my fault any of this happened, that I've ended up like this. I fight back the tears, trying to convince myself that I'm not to blame.

But it's hopeless. Tears stream hot down my cheeks as the sadness bites into me. I catch sight of myself in a shop window – dirty-faced, sunken-eyed, far from the wife and teacher and mother I once aspired to be.

Eventually, I come to a bus stop and sit down, cracking the can of Coke. I drink greedily. Then, guiltily, I take a small bite of the ham and cheese roll as if something as simple as a sandwich will sort out my life.

I close my eyes.

It tastes good.

I take another bite, then another, stuffing the rest of the roll into my mouth as fast as I can, shoving and pushing it in, chewing until my jaw aches, barely swallowing before the next mouthful.

I belch, drink more Coke, then set to work on the egg roll, feeling as if I'm about to explode. My head bulges with pain.

I can almost see the smug look on Felix's face. Hear his voice ringing in my ears, telling me to eat like a lady. All I ever wanted was to please him. To be a good wife.

Which is why I get up and head straight for Woodford Grange.

'I'm so sorry, but you can't see him right now.' Penny has her arms folded across her cardigan. Her expression is defiant.

'Why not?' I'm shaking and I look a mess. I haven't washed my hair in God knows how long, I've been wearing the same clothes for days, and my face has broken out from poor food and lack of sleep. Dark circles beneath my eyes frame the turmoil inside my mind.

'Because he's having some neurological tests. Anyway, it's not strictly visiting time.'

'But you've bent the rules before,' I say meekly.

My toes curl inside my trainers. I hate the way she's staring at me.

'I'm really sorry,' Penny says. I can tell she's trying to avoid looking me up and down, but her eyes have other ideas, sizing me up, reckoning she knows everything about me. 'The doctor wouldn't allow it.'

I don't know what to do. I feel helpless, let down. I

thought coming here was the right thing to do, but in reality, it's probably a sign. A sign that I should get away while I still can.

'I understand,' I say, trying not to sound desperate, even though I am. For some reason, I thought seeing Felix might help, might give me the courage I need.

I thank Penny and leave the nursing home, ending up in a cheap booze shop down the road. The girl with pink hair behind the counter barely looks up when I spend my last ten pounds on a bottle of value-brand vodka. It's the only thing that will get me through a night at my parents' house – the only place left for me to go.

With every step of the two-mile walk there, I count the ways in which my life has fallen apart.

Once, I was a school teacher with a class full of cocky adolescent kids. I went to staff meetings, assessed GCSE coursework, had a payslip every month, and a car that I owned. I rented a flat with a sofa, satellite television, a soft bed, and I had food in the fridge. Then there were my friends, none particularly close admittedly, but after school on a Friday afternoon we'd go to the Nag's Head and moan about Ofsted, parents' meetings and end-of-term reports.

Then I met Felix and that's when, piece by piece, my life fell apart. Even though I didn't see it until it was too late.

I twist the cap on the bottle of vodka, furtively swigging from it from within the cover of the plastic bag as I walk on.

He stole things from me, stripping me of everything I had. Then, when I was at my most vulnerable, he tried to change me into someone else. Into his mother. We spoke of her, of course, but he was always guarded, always cautious about what he revealed. I knew they'd been close; I understood he'd been devastated by her unexpected death – almost feeling responsible for it as a young boy.

When we started seeing each other, I genuinely believed he'd found what he was looking for in me – yes, a replacement for her, but also someone new, someone different and exciting. That's what I'd found in him, or so I thought. Despite everything, Felix had charmed me from the start with his quirky ways and zealous love.

If only it had just been me in our relationship.

The tears come at the thought of it all. A car hoots and swerves as my blurry eyes lead me dangerously across a busy road. By the time I reach Mum and Dad's, my pack weighing me down until my back is stooped, I feel as broken as I have ever been.

It was never meant to be like this.

It's dark when I unlock the door. Inside, the hall reeks of death, of sadness, of times long gone.

I go slowly from room to room catching sight of the ghosts. Felix is there, talking to my mother in the kitchen as she cooks the Sunday roast. Then he's admiring orchids with my father in the living room; pressing himself up against me in the downstairs toilet, telling me I am his for ever, his mouth coming down on my neck.

I see Mum and Dad waving us off on our first holiday together – a long weekend in a cottage near Padstow. Before things went really bad.

Felix had organised everything, from buying me a suitcase full of new clothes to a delivery of fresh lobster and champagne for our arrival at the beamy little clifftop place. I didn't know it then, but when I found the album, I recognised the cottage – photographs of Alexandra and Melanie also enjoying a weekend away.

Mum, of course, was delighted that things were getting serious between us, that I'd finally found someone.

Lying beside the fire that first night in the cottage, Felix gave me a small square box wrapped in shiny red paper. My heart stuttered at the thought of what was inside. I sat, not taking my eyes off him as he handed it over. Firelight sparked between us.

'Felix?' I said curiously. I couldn't help the grin.

'Open it.'

I pulled off the paper. Fingers shaking as I lifted the lid. Was this the moment?

'A locket?'

I pulled out the thin chain, trying not to look disappointed. A nugget of gold swung beneath.

'It was my mother's,' he said with a tear in his eye.

He took the chain and fastened it around my neck. In the distance, I heard the sea crashing against the cliffs, the wind dipping and diving around the cottage. Rattling the windows, shaking my heart. Warning me.

'I want you to have it.'

'It's beautiful,' I said, looking down as he picked it open with his nails.

'My mother's hair,' he told me, cupping the locket in his hands.

I held my breath, not sure what to make of the unpleasant bristly strands that were hanging around my neck. His mother was becoming a growing presence in our lives. I didn't realise it was some kind of test; should have taken it as another sign to end it while I could.

But I didn't have a chance to think more about it, because Felix's mouth was down upon mine, his moans tunnelling down my throat as resonant as the wind outside.

His mother was caught between us.

Watching on.

But I ignored the strange feeling, thinking instead that this was it, the night we would finally make love. I'd been waiting an age already – we'd been seeing each other for several months, after all. At first his reticence had been endearing, now it was simply frustrating. I thought he was ready to commit. Why else had he brought me here?

Instead, Felix pulled away and we eventually fell asleep beside the pulsing heat of the log fire.

Later, as dawn fingered its way through the curtains, he woke with a start, his body pained and tense, his muscles strung tight along his bones.

He stared right at me, as if gripped in the heart of a bad dream.

'Ellen?' he said, before dropping back into a disturbed sleep.

After realising it was just me.

Now, in my parents' house, I chuck cushions from the sofa on to the floor to make some kind of makeshift bed, and curl up with my vodka, necking it back greedily in the hope there'll be answers when I get to the bottom of the bottle.

40

The headache makes me feel sick – stabbed, wretched, as if I'm about to collapse. I stagger through to the kitchen, finding the remains of last night's dinner that I half cooked, but never ate. I turn on the tap and gulp down some water.

I spent most of the evening sobbing, finishing the vodka, going through old photograph albums, looking at pictures of Mum and Dad. Most were taken on caravanning trips, and some were of Dad with his precious blooms at flower shows. I dug out some older albums, finding pictures of myself as a child, a teen, and some more recent ones. But the one I couldn't take my eyes off was a picture Dad had captured of Felix and me in the garden, standing under the willow tree, peeking out together from behind the waterfall of leaves. The smile on my face said it all; the way Felix had his arms linked around me, staring into my eyes as Dad snapped.

After that, I couldn't help it that I tunnelled into the cushions and my own misery. I couldn't help it that I sobbed myself to sleep. I didn't wake until morning.

Now, in the cold light of day, I don't know what to do. I stare at the mess in the kitchen. There's food and washing up everywhere, and the whole house smells musty and unlived-in. Mum would hate it.

Selling the place feels even more insurmountable now. It's been empty for a while, and needs attention. No one will buy it like this.

Once, I would have asked Felix for help in deciding what to do. He was always good at sorting practical issues. But that was before everything went bad. *Really* bad. And now I can't even ask for Owen's help.

I sigh, letting out a little sob, and rummage in the cupboard for some paracetamol. My headache is terrible, and getting worse. It's as if the past is closing in on me, wrapping around me like a cloak. Or is it that I want to be shrouded by it, that I *have* to go back to him now he knows I'm here?

What we had was good once, wasn't it?

I tell myself it was, then try to shake Felix from my head. I get on with the washing up, boiling the kettle then pouring its contents into a bowl half full of cold soapy water. I plunge the dirty pans and plates into it. But I can't concentrate. I stare down the garden, looking at the willow tree. It's bare now, of course – its long, twiggy branches dropping down to the grass, revealing the place where Felix and I shared a kiss.

That was before I knew, before everything fell apart.

The memory makes me gasp. It's so painful.

Then, as if I'm being controlled by someone else, I

drop the pan I'm washing back into the water. A couple of tears fall into the bubbles, and I can't help it that I dry my hands, head out of the kitchen and upstairs. I know what I have to do – I don't want to, but I can't help it.

He's like a drug. A class A drug that insists I come back for more.

I'll never be able to leave him. I'll never be free from it all.

In the bathroom, something vile stares back from the cabinet mirror – a crazy-haired creature who's lost all her colour. 'He's not going to want you looking like this,' I say. Felix always preferred me at my best.

Tentatively, as if I'm going to let out a ghost, I open the mirrored bathroom cabinet door. Most of Mum's toiletries would have been packed up for Spain, and I have no idea what happened to their luggage. I find a can of body spray – just something cheap from the supermarket, but it'll do to help mask the stink that's coming from me. There's no time to shower, and the water will be freezing anyway.

I just need to get back to him, show him that everything will be OK – that *we'll* be OK. Tell him that I still love him, despite everything. That it's not too late to make it right.

In Mum and Dad's bedroom, I can hardly stand to look at the smoothed-out duvet and throw, all ready for when they came back from Spain. Mum was like that, neat and tidy.

I put my hand on the wardrobe knob, but I don't open it. It's the smell of her I'm most scared of – the subtle note of her sweet perfume. Anyway, her clothes are no use to me. Mum was much smaller.

Sitting on the dressing-table stool, I feel like her, getting ready for the day in her precise, exacting way. Mum rarely wore make-up, but there are a few cosmetics in the drawer. Perhaps I can transform myself back into the woman Felix loves and wants. It's probably my only hope now. Everything will fall apart otherwise.

'Not too much, Belle,' I hear him croon in my ear, his lips pushing through my hair. 'Don't want you overdoing it.'

I can almost feel the dig of his fingers into my shoulders as the ghost of him hovers behind me, scrutinising my appearance. He loved me in lipstick, but only the right shade. 'Anything red will clash with your hair,' he said, as if he was some kind of expert.

He was always trying to turn me into something, some*one*. To begin with, I was never sure who.

I find two old and dry lipsticks in the drawer, both scarlet. One is paler than the other, so that will have to do. I apply it to my chapped lips, my shaking hand making the edges smudge. I try to wipe it into a neater line, but I make it worse.

I draw a thick line of black kohl beneath my eyes, covering my lids in charcoal-coloured shadow. Mum's mascara is also dried up, but darkens my pale lashes enough.

I stare in the mirror, hoping Felix will approve.

'You're an undiscovered Rossetti painting,' he'd said on our trip to Paris. 'A pre-Raphaelite beauty.' Then he had me etched and marked as if I belonged to him. I didn't know anything back then.

I shake out my hair, attacking it with an old brush of Mum's I find in a bottom drawer. Her hairs are still in it, mingling with mine. Gradually, it springs back to life in an array of red and orange curls. Felix always loved me to wear it loose, freshly washed, and sprayed with rosewater.

'I hope you still want me back,' I say quietly while looking at myself in the full-length mirror. 'I hope it's not too late.'

Before I leave, I decide to honour Mum and Dad by opening the gift they left for me. Then, as I always did, I will write them a thank-you note to find on their return. It's just the way we did things.

Except this time, they won't be returning.

My eyes are filled with tears as I retrieve the little box from the back of Dad's desk cupboard and pull on the ribbon. Sitting in his leather chair, I try not to cry, not wanting to smudge my make-up.

Carefully, I take off the tissue paper, imagining Mum's slender hands wrapping it up before they went – a token left for their missing daughter. I stare at the contents, unable to move, but eventually I fasten the delicate silver bracelet around my wrist. I splutter a little cry of gratitude, so sad I won't ever see them again to say thank you.

It's a while before I can move, my heart filled with sadness.

Finally, I lock up the house and make my way back to Felix. Just as I always did.

By the time I arrive at Woodford Grange my make-up has smudged from my tears and the rain, and my hair is lank again. This time, Penny lets me in to see him.

'Belle, Belle, come and sit,' Felix says softly, patting the bed as I peek tentatively around the door.

He looks much better today. He's sitting up, and there are no tubes attached to him.

'I came to see you yesterday,' I tell him, trying to hide my anger. 'But they wouldn't let me in.'

'Well you're here now,' he says. 'And that makes me very happy.'

'It does?' I plump up my hair with my fingers, trying to restore some life into it.

Felix nods. 'More than you will ever know.'

I lower myself on to the bed beside him, careful not to press on his poor thin legs. How wizened they look beneath the sheet – useless skin and bone.

I fight back the tears.

Felix reaches out his hand, runs his forefinger beneath my left eye. 'And that's not like you,' he says. 'To cry.'

'No,' I say quietly.

When we were together, he didn't know about all the tears I shed – tears of pity, mostly. Stay or go? I became imprisoned by my own mind.

413

'You seem so sad, Belle.'

'I am,' I tell him, praying he'll know what to do. 'It's been a terrible time.'

If Felix was able to recoil, I think he would have done. As it is, he lies quite still, his hand twitching as if it wants to do something, but doesn't know what.

'You're safe now,' he croons.

I frown, giving him a look. He often used to say that, but my still heart sighs and my tight lungs draw in a breath at the sound of it.

'It was so upsetting,' I tell him. 'My best friend didn't even know me.' I explained what happened with Beth, and I tell him about having nowhere to live, how the place where I worked literally vanished into thin air, and how the paramedics tried to save Owen. It all sounds like a crazy dream.

My crazy nightmare.

Then there's something warm on me – Felix's soft palm, slowly stroking down my hair, over and over as if he's analysing every strand. I lean a little closer.

'Belle, do you not think . . .' He looks anxious. 'Maybe you're a little confused,' he says. 'Like you used to be.'

I stare at the bed sheet. The same stain is there from the last time I visited.

'Maybe,' I confess. The admission is a weight off my shoulders.

I drag my gaze up to him. I cover my mouth, stemming my sharp breaths.

'And what did you used to do when you were confused, Belle?' Felix tries to shift position, but winces.

'I used to come to you,' I say, feeling a spillage of warmth inside.

He tilts up my chin with his finger. 'And what did I do?'

'You kept me safe and helped me. You took care of me.'

'And what did you have to do in return?'

'Everything you asked,' I say.

Felix is nodding, his gaunt face looking bony and pleased. 'And that's what we're going to do now. I will take care of you. And you will be safe.'

I nod weakly. 'But everything is such a mess.'

He looks me up and down, smiling. 'And so are you. You need a wash, a change of clothes, you need feeding, and you need a comfortable place to stay. Things will feel better then.' He blinks slowly. 'You'll see.'

I nod gratefully, willing him to go on.

'Look in that drawer,' he instructs. 'Take two hundred pounds. Go and buy yourself some new clothes, some toiletries, and come back as quickly as you can. I will arrange with one of the senior staff for you to sleep in the relatives' room. You will be back where you belong, Belle. With me.'

He gives me the lightest of kisses on the cheek and flops back on to the pillow, exhausted.

I don't feel like going all the way into the city centre, so finding clothes that will please Felix is almost impossible.

I don't think he's going to like me in the grey sweatpants and T-shirt I buy in desperation from a discount clothing store not far from Woodford Grange, but at least they're clean and don't smell.

The chemist is a bit further on. I make a mental list of what I'll need – shampoo, soap, face cream, make-up. And maybe I'll buy a little gift for Felix to show my gratitude – perhaps a cologne, something to make him feel—

I stop dead still, blinking furiously in case I got it wrong.

'Owen?' I yell, standing on tip-toe to keep sight of his head. 'Oh my God, Owen, wait! It's me!'

People around me stare, cursing as I push between them, shoving my way through a cluster of shoppers outside the supermarket. My throat burns as I charge down the street after him, screaming for all I'm worth, tripping and stumbling along the pavement.

It was Owen! I *saw* him!

I run on, barrelling forward. I can't be far from him now.

But when I get to the corner, he's nowhere to be seen. I've lost him. I stop, panting, my arms dangling by my sides, clutching my bags of shopping. I stand on a bench, spinning round to see if I can spot him.

'Oh God, oh God, I don't understand . . .'

I'm crying again, wide-eyed and urgent. Everyone's staring at me, and a kid points at me.

'Are you OK?' an old lady asks, but I ignore her, pulling my phone from my pocket and dialling Owen's number.

It goes straight to his message service. The sound of his recorded voice makes me drop down off the bench and slump on to it, head in hands.

What the hell is happening to me? I *saw* him. I know I did. Owen's not dead.

But something tells me, as with everything else that's happened, that I must be mistaken; I must be confused.

I just need to get back to Felix.

41

Once again, I'm lying in bed waiting for Adam to leave for work. It goes against everything I stand for – the opposite of what I'm used to.

I feel terrible lying to him, but for now, it keeps him appeased. He's finally convinced I'm taking his and Bob's advice and resting. It's so frustrating, because together, I know we could crack this.

Anyway, since they arrested Melanie's alleged killer, he's had bigger things on his mind – like putting forward a case to the CPS before they run out of time.

It places me bottom of his pile of worries. But if they're forced to release the suspect, then I'm certain Adam's focus will shift right back to me. He'll want to know I've been sorting myself out, preparing to get back in the saddle. In return, he'll be my advocate to Bob, stop things going further. And that's exactly what I want, of course – I miss being part of the team terribly – but I know I won't rest if I don't follow this through.

Once the house is empty, I get up and shower. As I dry

myself, I notice that my ankle doesn't look quite so swollen today. Perhaps it's starting to get better.

Downstairs, the post on the doormat is filled with the usual – bills, bank statements and pizza delivery leaflets. There's a letter from the hospital, however, that I open with trepidation. It's the appointment for me to have the heart monitor fitted. I chuck it straight in the bin, feeling a pang of guilt. I'll phone later to cancel it officially.

I sit drinking coffee, tapping my pen frustratedly over a flow chart I've drawn up about stalkers and hospitals and accidents and Isabel and God knows what else in this mess of a case that I'm not even supposed to be working on, let alone botching.

My head falls into my hands when a text from Stella comes in, asking me to drop off her forgotten sports kit.

After I drive away from the High School and have filled up my car with petrol, I realise that the doctors' surgery is only a couple of streets away. My plans for an appointment yesterday were scuppered, so I decide to see if Dr Lewis can see me today. A letter from my GP stating that I'm fit and well will go a long way towards convincing Bob to take me back. One thing's for certain: my days can't continue like this. I'll end up going mad.

'Lorraine,' Dr Lewis says warmly, standing up as I come into her consulting room.

There was a cancellation. I'd only had to wait half an hour.

She pulls out the chair for me, glancing at my ankle as I try to hide my limp.

'I'm so glad you came back. How are you feeling?' She scans the computer monitor, keeping her attention half on me while reminding herself of my self-indulgent tale.

'That's the thing,' I say, as brightly as I can manage. 'I feel absolutely great. I don't know what you did for me, but it certainly worked.' I grin so widely it almost hurts.

Dr Lewis remains silent for a moment, still reading. 'I wasn't able to do very much, by the looks of it. You didn't really want the prescription I offered . . . and I referred you for a Holter monitor. Have you had that yet?' She looks up from the screen.

I shake my head vehemently. 'Absolutely no need. The appointment came, but I'm going to cancel it. I haven't had a single palpitation since I last saw you. I think the thought of it scared it into remission.' I pat my chest as if that will reinforce my case.

'I'm glad to hear that,' she says thoughtfully. 'How have you been sleeping?'

'Like a baby! It's incredible. After I left here, I decided to look into yoga, meditation, that kind of thing. It really helps with sleeping. It's actually changed my life. Better than any pills.'

'And your appetite? The anxiety?' she says, holding up her hands. 'Don't tell me, you're eating like a horse and don't have a care in the world, right?'

I know she's on my side, but she needs to believe me. I just need a clean bill of health, a letter to show Bob that

420

there's absolutely nothing wrong with me, to prove it once and for all.

I open my mouth, but nothing comes out.

'Lorraine, I've known you for aeons. Don't give me all this nonsense.' She leans back in her chair and takes off her glasses. 'Why did you come to see me today? Really.'

I shake my head, pretending to be incredulous. 'I don't know what you mean,' I say, frowning. 'Seriously, I'm eating well, sleeping well, and the anxiety is gone. I have the usual work stresses, but who doesn't?'

Kelly Lewis nods. 'So . . . you made an appointment to tell me you feel well. Most of my patients come to tell me the opposite.'

I pause, close my eyes for a beat. 'The thing is, there's this little hitch at work. It's nothing really, but it could all be sorted with a note from you saying that I'm fine and don't have any medical issues. Up here or otherwise.' I tap the side of my head.

'But I don't know you're fine, do I Lorraine, because you refused the test I referred you for. Your blood pressure was on the high side, and you had heart palpitations. They need checking out.'

I tilt my head back, congratulating myself on a brilliant own-goal.

'Like I said, there's nothing wrong with my heart, Kelly. Have another listen. Prod me and check me out as much as you like. You won't find anything wrong.'

Dr Lewis sits there staring at me, unnerving me because she doesn't seem to know what to do. When I leave her office five minutes later, it's without a letter from her, but very much with a grudging promise from me that I will attend the test she wants. I'll just have to find some other way to convince Bob and Adam that I'm absolutely fine.

At first, I don't think she's home, but Mrs Welland finally answers the door on the third ring of the bell. After she's explained that she was vacuuming, that she's got guests coming and that's why she didn't hear me, she ducks inside her house and retrieves a key. She dangles it at me, looking proud.

'She was here, you know,' she tells me in a low voice. 'Isabel Moore.' She glances next door. 'She didn't look well, mind. Look, why don't you take this, see if everything's OK in there.'

'That would be most helpful,' I say, plucking it from her hand and restraining myself from telling her that she could have told me she had a key last time I was here.

'I'm not sure she's there now, though. When I knocked, she didn't answer. But there were definitely strange goings-on in there,' she says, raising her eyebrows and folding her arms. 'Noises in the night. I said, Bill, do you think we should call the police? Bill said no, we shouldn't. So we didn't. But I'm glad you're here.'

'What kind of noises?' I ask, keen to get inside.

'Like a dog howling for its owner. Lots of crying. And doors were banging about until gone midnight. I went round to see what was going on, but couldn't get an answer at the door. I was going to use the key, but Bill told me to leave well alone. He said we could get into trouble. I feel very sorry for what happened to the Moores, but we're hoping for some nice neighbours soon.'

Then she closes her door, but not before reminding me to put the key through her letterbox when I'm finished.

The first thing I notice in the Moores' house is the stale smell. It hangs thickly in the hallway, probably because the place has been locked up for a while. I flick the switch, but the light doesn't come on. The door to my left – the living room, I assume – is slightly open so I push it with my foot.

'Hello, it's the police. Anyone home?'

I feel vulnerable. I am on my own, and no one knows where I am.

I carry on into the room. The curtains are closed and, even before my eyes grow accustomed to the dim light, I can see someone's been in here. It doesn't look neat and tidy, the way you'd expect it to be left if the owners were going away. All the big foam cushions from the sofas are dumped in a heap on the floor, and there are a couple of dirty plates and an empty bottle of vodka lying on the saggy sofa base. There's a backpack behind the door, spilling out some crumpled clothes. The room smells stale and musty. Of despair.

I pick my way through the mess and head into a small dining room, which appears untouched. The kitchen is a different story, however, with some dirty pans and plates in soupy water in the sink, packets and tins pulled from the cupboard, and the remains of a brown sludgy meal still in a saucepan on the stove. If I didn't know better, I'd think squatters had moved in.

'Hello?' I call out up the stairs, before spotting the door to my right.

Inside, there's a desk, a filing cabinet, a chair, a bookshelf, a dead plant, and other typical things found in a home study. I open the desk drawer and pull out some papers. The glossy brochures at the top of the pile are advertising villas in Marbella. Beneath that are what appear to be legal papers, but they're written in Spanish, so there's no chance of me understanding them.

Villa Paraíso Exótico appears to be a shiny new ex-pat community located around an elite golf course. It's not hard to spot that it's the same name on the legal document, which also contains the address. I'm obviously holding the retirement dream of Isabel's parents before they were killed.

If they were killed.

I tap the brochure, biting my lip, wondering if it's worth a shot.

'Hello, do you speak English?' I say, having decided it is.

'Sí, sí, how can I help you?'

I press my phone hard against my ear. It's a bad line.

'I'm trying to get in touch with a Mr John Moore who I believe owns apartment number twenty-eight in Hibiscus. Can you help me?'

'One moment,' says the heavily accented Spanish lady. 'I put you through to caretaker service.'

424

While I'm waiting, I walk back to the hallway and into the living room to check out the mess again, maybe poke through some of the belongings in the backpack, but someone comes on the line. Thankfully they also speak English.

'You not find Mr Moore here this afternoon, I sorry.' The man's voice is sincere and helpful, also thick with accent. He sounds friendly.

'You know Mr Moore?' I ask.

'Of course! Everyone know everyone here at Paraíso. I sorry, but he busy with the golf for a few hours. He be back by sunset. He can have a message from you, if you want.'

'Hang on,' I say. My heart's kicking up and I'm praying it's not going to skip off into some crazy rhythm. 'So John Moore is alive? And his wife Ingrid?'

'Sí, of course,' the man says incredulously. 'They are very much alive today.' He laughs. 'I don't know where is Mrs Moore, but maybe with her friends like the usual, or at the beach with her little dog.'

'So they're not dead?'

More laughter comes down the line as I try to establish that we're talking about the same John and Ingrid Moore.

'Not dead, very thankfully,' he says. 'I promise to pass on message, no problem,' he adds convincingly when I tell him I'm a detective, and that I will be involving the assistance of the local policía if I don't hear back from them soon.

After I hang up, my heart claps out an abnormal beat,

425

making my hospital appointment suddenly seem important. I'm certain I've hit on something, though I'm not sure yet if it has anything to do with Melanie or Alexandra's murders.

Either way, a non-existent car crash, two dead people who are still alive, and a man in a coma for no apparent reason, and it's time to get Adam involved. Even if he is going to absolutely kill me for not staying at home to rest.

42

'There was a murder,' I say, bracing myself for the back-lash. 'Apparently,' I add with an expression that I hope conveys my scepticism.

For a second, I view myself as they probably do – a woman who's meant to be at home resting, a woman who's hobbled into work without her crutches so she can appear normal, a woman whose face is burning with anticipation, and a woman who is spilling out information about a murder, a couple who were meant to be dead but aren't, and a car crash that never happened.

'Ray,' Adam says kindly, 'Bob and I are just going over some final details for the CPS. Can this wait?' He glances at the papers on the desk between them.

Bob stares at me wearily. 'No, let her speak, Adam.'

He gestures to a spare chair, indicating I should drag it over to his desk. Adam looks away, and I know what he's thinking: *don't blow it, Ray, don't ruin your chance of coming back.*

My ankle is hurting again, but I'm trying hard not to show it.

'A dead man – Claremont Road, Harborne,' I tell them.

'Yes, you've said that twice now,' Adam says, turning slightly and making a face at me he hopes Bob won't see.

'How come you know about this but I don't?' Bob says, surprisingly good-naturedly. He is being mild, humouring me.

'Exactly. Even *I* would know if there'd actually been a murder,' I say, shaking my head. 'I've been stuck at home all day with nothing to do but watch the telly. I'd have noticed it on the news if there'd really been one.'

'Can you hurry, love?' Adam says, glancing at his watch. 'The CPS are waiting for us.'

I know he has my best interests at heart, but I wish he would just hear me out. He was going to have a round of golf with Bob at the weekend, talk to him about me coming back off my 'holiday'. Adam said, given the advances they'd made in the Carter case, it would be timely, appropriate, that Bob would undoubtedly agree and no more would be said.

'I suppose I should add at this point that I didn't have to rest as much as I'd anticipated.'

I study Bob's expression carefully.

'What I'm trying to say is . . .' However I tell them, it's going to sound crazy. 'Look, I was sick of feeling useless, so I followed up on one or two of my hunches—'

'Hunches?' Adam says. He's about to put his hands over his face, but thinks better of it.

I nod, knowing he won't approve. It was a side effect of being *on holiday*, I think but don't say. 'It was the non-existent stalkers that bothered me most about the Stanford and Carter cases. So I checked into some similar reports, and followed up on one or two. Just in case.'

I give each of them a glance, but they don't say anything.

'Look, what I discovered needs looking into, even if it's got nothing to do with the murders.'

'Well you've got me hooked,' Bob says dourly.

'Like Alexandra and Melanie, a woman called Isabel Moore also complained of being stalked. She couldn't provide any evidence either.'

'I hope this gets better, Ray.'

'Oh, don't worry, it does. Isabel fled the UK earlier in the year to get away from a man called Felix Darwin. But she was forced to return when her parents were killed in a car crash.'

This is where I'm going to sound like a mad woman, chasing red herrings around Birmingham while Adam and Bob were following leads that actually led to an arrest.

'As you can imagine, Isabel was bereft and vulnerable, especially when she discovered that Felix Darwin was driving the car in which her parents were killed. He was taking them to the airport. They were off to start a new life in Spain by all accounts.'

'Tragic,' Bob says flatly.

'Indeed,' I say, slowing myself down so it comes out correctly. 'Felix Darwin survived the crash, but was in a coma. He recently regained consciousness and is being cared for in a private nursing home.

'Meantime, Isabel's intention was to sort out her parents' affairs, sell their house, and return to India where she has a job. She met a man called Owen Brandrick. He helped her out, took her in, let her stay at his place, and gave her some casual work in his office.'

'Don't tell me, they fell in love and there's a happy ending, right?' Adam steeples his fingers under his chin, giving me a pitying look that says *I tried to save you . . .*

'I would go and ask him, except he's dead. Stabbed in his own home, according to Isabel. She discovered him. The emergency services were called, but they couldn't revive him. He died right in front of her. Officers went out.'

Bob leans forward on his desk. 'A murder that I haven't heard about right in the middle of my city? Get to the point, Lorraine.'

'There was no car crash.'

I wait, watch their expressions. Both are blank and unimpressed.

'And actually, it turns out there was no murder, either.'

Still blank.

'There was no call made to emergency services from that address, or any mobile number registered or located there. Isabel has since discovered that Owen Brandrick's house is now occupied by a new family, and the architect's office where she worked has turned into a minicab business. Oh, and her best friend doesn't recognise her.'

Bob bellows out a deep laugh.

'You've passed this on to the mental health team, I take it?' Adam says. 'The woman clearly needs help.'

'I also should mention,' I say, ignoring him, 'that the QE Hospital have no record of ever treating a Felix Darwin.' I fold my arms. 'Oh, and Mr and Mrs Moore, Isabel's dead parents, are alive and well in Spain. I confirmed this today.'

Adam's eyes grow huge, and he gets to his feet.

'Fine,' he says, sliding the papers back to Bob. 'I'm happy with these alterations if you are. We can submit.' He gives a curt nod to Bob before leading me out of the office by the arm. He stops in the doorway, turning back. 'And don't worry, I'll sort this,' he adds, as if he's dealing with a naughty child.

I follow him to the lift, remaining silent, waiting for the outburst.

'One week, Ray,' he says, jabbing the button. 'One bloody week off work was all I wanted you to take.'

It's only when we are inside the lift and the doors slide shut that his arm slips around my waist, pulling me close. It's then that I know he believes me.

43

I don't know how long I've been gone – maybe two, three hours now. Sitting here, shell-shocked, I lost track of time. Felix will be angry, fuming in his hospital bed, pressing the nurses' call button, demanding they find out where I am. But I couldn't face going straight back.

He'll think I've left him again. If I tell him that I saw Owen alive after saying he was dead, he'll send me back to that place. I really want to confide, but I can't risk him thinking I'm ill again. Although perhaps being sectioned, being secreted away in a mental health institution, is the best thing for me.

How could everything have gone so wrong?

Slowly, feet dragging, I leave the park bench and head back to Felix. I simply don't know where else to go. The sight of Owen burns in my mind. Was it really him?

A van pulls out of the nursing home car park as I approach. I stop, looking up at the building, making sure I've got the correct one. I haven't been concentrating. The big properties all look similar down here – set back, with big driveways, concealed by trees and bushes – and for a moment I think I have the wrong entrance. Then I recognise the pots of winter cyclamen either side of the front door, spangles of bright pink and red in the murk.

I go up the steps to press the intercom buzzer.

It's not there.

I stand back, looking around again. It's definitely the right building. I go back out on to the street to check the sign, to make certain. I didn't notice it on the way in – probably because that workman's van was blocking it.

The sign isn't there either.

Stay calm, I tell myself. It's probably just being repainted or replaced. This isn't going to happen again.

I grip my shopping bag tightly and go back up to the door, trying the handle. Thankfully, it's open, so I let myself in, expecting to see Penny sitting behind her desk. But she isn't there. And neither is the desk, or the vase of lilies, and her computer is gone, too. There's not even the little brass bell for me to ring.

I spin round, eyes stretched wide. The waiting-room chairs are all missing, as well as the signs giving directions for the various rooms – Assessment Unit, Relatives' Room, Visitor Toilets, Staff Room.

All gone.

It looks more like someone's private house than a nursing home, making me feel I've walked into the wrong place. There's a plush circular rug at the bottom of the stairs behind where the desk once was, and other random items are strewn about – a newspaper, some unopened mail on a side table that wasn't there earlier, a couple of coats hanging by the door, and paintings I don't recognise. I've spent enough time here to know. The place even *smells* different.

I venture further inside, stepping across the threshold Penny usually guards.

Yes, the smell. As if someone is cooking.

I cup my hand over my mouth, partly to prevent a scream, and partly to stop myself throwing up. I have never felt so alone, so scared, as if my life is about to be turned upside-down. I should call Lorraine Fisher, but I don't have the guts to speak on my phone right now. It's as if my strings are being pulled, as if I just can't help walking into whatever this is. For my own sanity, I need to know what's going on.

The door to the office where I often heard staff chattering and working is ajar. I go up to it, and knock tentatively.

'Hello?' I say. 'Penny, are you in there?'

There's no reply, so I push the door open to reveal a small sitting room, not an office as I'd imagined. A marble fireplace takes up the far wall, with a couple of armchairs, an old television, a rug, a low table, and bookshelves arranged around the room.

There's nothing remarkable about the bland and slightly dated decor, except I can see immediately that it's not a workplace, and it certainly doesn't look remotely medical.

I think back, certain this was the room where I heard the voices. I even remember the whirr of a printer, the women talking about Christmas, organising the works party. The television is switched on, a movie playing on silent. The remote control is on the arm of the chair so I pick it up and press the volume button, curious. The women's voices on the film are the same as I heard, still talking about the same things.

My hand goes to my head as my breathing quickens, trying to dispel my disbelief. I feel the early warning signs of losing control slipping through me – dry mouth, blurry vision, dizziness.

I can't let it happen again.

I need to find Felix.

Back in the hall, I notice the pile of mail again, left on the small table beside the door. I pick up one of the letters, turning it over in my hand.

The print resolves slowly, my brain not assimilating it at first. But it's there, his full name, printed clearly above the address of this building on something official, perhaps a bill. I see it just at the same time he calls out my name.

'Belle!'

I swing round.

Felix is standing there, a knife in his hand.

'You've been gone *ages*,' he says, beaming.

He's wearing a butcher's apron.

I recoil, stumbling backwards, knocking into the table.

Something crashes to the floor, but I don't take my eyes off him or the knife.

'What's going on, Felix? Why are you out of bed? Why are you . . . why are you *walking*?' I can't believe it, but

take another step back nonetheless. 'Are you better? It's
. . . it's amazing.' My voice falters.

'Don't be afraid,' he says, approaching me, glancing at
the knife as if he doesn't quite know what to do with it.
'I'm making us a nice meal. Your favourite.'

I shake my head until my neck hurts. My back is pressed
up against the wall, my hands wringing together as a cold
sweat breaks out on my face. 'Please . . . please don't do
this to me, Felix. I came back to you, didn't I? Just as you
wanted.' I step back again. 'Everything I've done has been
for you. To *please* you.'

I try to quell the shaking in my voice as I glance about,
hoping someone will come.

'Where's Penny? And where's your doctor?'

He's only three feet away now, smiling, that faraway
look in his eyes telling me he doesn't know what he's
doing.

'What have you *done*, Felix?'

'Doctor?' he says. 'I don't need a doctor. I need *you*,
Belle. Beautiful Belle who finally came back to me.'

He stares at the knife, runs his thumb sideways across
it.

'Where's Dr Lambeth? You're not well. You were in
an accident. I don't know why you're even walking. It
must be a miracle, like when you woke from your coma.'

I realise how ridiculous I sound, but there's a chance I
can humour him, at least until I can get out. How could
I have been so *stupid*?

'Oh Belle, you poor confused thing. Come into my

kitchen and let me make you a cup of tea. Just the way you like it.'

He turns, beckoning me to follow him.

'No, Felix, I don't want tea, and I don't want to be here.'

I run to the front door and grasp the big handle.

Felix doesn't stop me. He just stands there, watching, a pitying look spreading across his face as I tug on the brass knob, screaming with frustration.

The door is firmly locked.

44

Beautiful submission shining on her face, just the way she's always liked it.

'When will you learn?' I say, taking her gently by the arm and leading her away from the door. She's still clutching her plastic shopping bag, her handbag slung over her shoulder. 'Why do you want to leave? The whole place is secure and locked anyway. You're with me now, back where you belong.'

Little kitten noises escape her mouth, and her eyes dart around the hall, searching for another escape route.

'Come,' I tell her, pulling her towards the kitchen. 'Let's have a cup of tea. I'm cooking something nice for later.'

'What have you *done*, Felix?' she keeps saying in a voice so frail I can hardly hear her. 'What has happened to the nursing home?' Spit bubbles at the corners of her mouth.

Her feet dig into the floor like a reluctant child, so I end up dragging her along.

In the kitchen, I put the knife in the sink. Frankly, it doesn't seem safe.

'What nursing home, Belle?'

'This one!' she says, her voice cracking into a sob.

'Anyone can see that it's not a nursing home, Belle.' I look at her pityingly. 'I think you need to calm down.' I press her gently on the shoulders, sitting her down. She shudders when I touch her. 'You're having one of your episodes, Belle. You need to listen to me – you were mistaken, OK?'

'No,' she says. 'No, I'm not mistaken and I'm not OK. Tell me what's going on, Felix, or I'll call the police!'

'You would do that?'

Isabel sinks in on herself, folding her shoulders together, thinking hard. Then, correctly, she shakes her head.

'No.'

'Now,' I say, sitting down beside her. There's a plate of biscuits between us, a brewing pot. 'Let's not overreact.'

I reach out to stroke her hand, but she swipes it away.

Isabel's eyes are as red hot as her hair, beating into mine with a pulse that sets my heart on fire.

'I'm so glad you're home,' I say truthfully. 'And I'm sorry it took all this to get you back.'

Belle remains silent.

'I know you want me back too.'

She looks at me – a cold shield of ice glazed over her flickering eyes. The carrier bag of new clothes is clutched on her lap beneath tightly folded arms.

439

'You put me in that place!' she screams. 'There was nothing wrong with me until I met you!'

She lashes out, but I catch her wrist, steadying her as if she's a wild mare. Her eyes bulge with realisation.

'Now stop, just stop—'

'It was *you*,' she says, panting out the words in a spray of spit. Her face is a beautiful breaking sunrise. 'It was you who lured me back here, you who killed Owen, and you who killed my parents. You're a murderer!'

I restrain the growl that winds its way up my throat.

'Not quite correct,' I say. 'But we can deal with the details later. First, I'd like to show you my – sorry, *our* house. Do you like it? I'm only renting it for now, of course, but the option is there to purchase it if we both love it. A bargain at three grand a month. It needs some work but—'

'You are *renting* this place?'

Isabel's face is awash with confusion, poor lamb.

I nod. 'It made a fine stage set, don't you think? And it will make an even finer home once we furnish it to our taste.' I watch for her reaction, but she can't speak. 'I take my hat off to Luke Manning and his band of willing players. A wonderful cast of actors, although there were one or two slip-ups, but nothing too noticeable. Thank God for desperate and starving artists.'

Belle remains silent.

'To them, it was simply a documentary in the making – a social experiment with hidden cameras for an extension to my PhD, hopefully being pitched to Channel Four to be aired next year. They were more than happy to play their parts for the right price and a bit of fame, and knew not to ask questions if they wanted paying.' I stifle a triumphant laugh. 'I swear I can make any*one* do any*thing*.'

'What are you talking about, Felix?' Isabel whispers, crying now – desperate little shots of self-pity. 'What PhD? And who is Luke Manning?'

'The one you agreed to participate in, my love. I told them that you'd joined a database of volunteers, willing to undertake any research project without knowing specifics, and I was using you as my subject. "The Impact of Grief on Rational Behaviour" or something like that. I spun it rather like one of those illusionist's TV shows. You have no idea you're on it, but I told them you were game and had signed up a while ago. They probably wouldn't have helped otherwise, even though they were just in it for the money, of course.'

She shakes her head, standing up again, but I slam her down into the chair, just the way she likes it.

'Anyway, even if they didn't believe me, or thought the whole project dubious, they didn't care. They got paid every two days in cash. Luke Manning – Owen Brandrick to you – has been my right-hand man throughout.' I wait for her to absorb this piece of news. 'Although it turned out his intentions weren't entirely honourable with you, were they? And after I'd paid him handsomely, too. I should have killed him off for real.'

'But Owen is dead!' Isabel wails pitifully. She tries to wriggle from my grip.

'Of course he's not dead. He's a highly trained actor, my love.'

'But the ambulance crew came, and the police. They took his body away.'

'Did they?'

My poor, poor baby. She cradles her head, dropping it down on to the table, muttering things about hallucinating, about seeing him.

'You're confused,' I say, crooning in her ear. 'But you're safe now. You belong to me again.'

She stares up at me, a tiny twinkle in her sad eye.

'I feel faint. I need some water.'

She spots the rack of glasses above the sink.

'Help yourself,' I tell her, keeping my eye on the route between her and the door. I know what she's like.

At the sink, she runs the tap then gulps greedily, her stooped back facing me. She leans forward, as if she's going to throw up, but instead she swings round, grappling with her shopping bag.

'You're lying!' she says, her hands and the bag dropping to her side. 'This is a nursing home and you've killed all the staff. You're a monster!'

Instead of disputing this, I show her around the property – all ten bedrooms of it. I keep a firm grip on her wrist, leading her from room to room. She trips over on her own reluctant and unstable feet, making unexpected noises at every turn.

'It used to be an old people's home,' I tell her. 'So there wasn't much to be done. The paintwork was suitably bland and chipped, the doors already laden with fire escape weights, and the carpets brown and worn. I decided to revamp the waiting area, make it seem welcoming and more like a private establishment. Besides, Penny was under orders to allow you only into certain areas. It all worked out rather well, I thought.'

'You're mad,' she says breathlessly, grappling with me until I am forced to restrain her.

When she is silent, I take her to my room.

'I've not had a chance to clear this out yet. While you were gone, the team came in to help transform the reception area into something resembling a family home. I felt the time was right, that you'd finally come back to me, wanted me in your life again. After all, you have nowhere else to go.'

'Family *home*?' she says bitterly. '*Accepted* you?' She turns away.

'It's the perfect house for children, don't you think?'

Belle doesn't reply.

'I'll resell all the medical equipment, of course. It was so easy to come by on the internet, and I got a good price given the quantity I bought. I didn't think much of the bed though.' I pat the plastic-covered mattress, glad to be free of its confines.

Isabel pulls away from me, walking slowly around my room. I let her go, standing guard at the door. She trails her fingers across the monitors, picking up the limp tubing from the ventilator that no one had a clue how to use. My mouth is still sore from where I taped it in place.

Isabel grabs my medical notes and shakes the file in my face. 'You fabricated everything?'

I nod.

For a moment, she is silent. 'And Owen's not dead?' she whispers weakly, as if the fight in her is finally waning.

I shake my head.

She shakes hers too, slowly and incredulously, squinting and focusing somewhere a long way away.

'But . . . but he was working in India. He brought me a letter from the High Commission about my parents.'

'Did he?' I say, waiting for the penny to drop. 'Even the worst news is real if you don't question it.'

Isabel goes ghostly white. All I want is for her to eat a good meal and take a shower. I hope she bought some decent clothes on her shopping spree.

'My parents . . .' she says. 'So . . . so they're not dead?' Her voice is hopeful and brittle. She touches her head as if it's aching.

'How else was I going to get you home?'

'You . . . you *bastard*!' She launches herself at me, grabbing for my throat. 'Where *are* they?'

I push her down on the bed, pinning her flat on her back. She thrashes her legs and arms, catching me on the cheek with her nails.

'You ran out on me, Belle, and that wasn't what we agreed, was it? Not part of the deal.' My face is inches above hers. 'Remember?' I'm so close, we're almost kissing.

Her head whips sideways and she bares her teeth, trying

444

to take a bite from my hand. Her breath is short and panicky, sitting high up in her chest. A wheezy sound comes out of her throat.

'But I saw news reports about the accident. I spoke to the coroner. Owen took me to the crash site.' She's crying now. 'I even left flowers at their graves!'

She tries to sit up, so this time I allow it. She leans forward and falls into my arms, sobbing against my shoulder. Just where she should be.

'Why did you do this to me, Felix? I loved you. I trusted you.'

'My dear Belle, don't weep.' I hold her tightly, kissing her head. 'Sometimes love is not enough. Sometimes we have to give up our entire self; become entirely self*less*.'

I stroke her beautiful red hair, pressing it to my face, searching for a whiff of Mother's scent. But it's become lost in the decades – as misplaced as me, her only son, left to grow up with a father who didn't care.

'I just don't understand why you would *do* this.' She remains wrapped in my arms.

'After you ran away, I had plenty of time on my hands to figure everything out. And plenty of money to pay willing participants.'

As far as Belle is concerned, I am still a pilot, though truth be known, my Mr Beefys are far more lucrative. Not half as alluring, though.

'Fake websites and news reports cached on Luke's – sorry, *Owen's* laptop, were easy to make up and link together on a local browser. The technology was simple thanks to online videos and forums, and it was rather enjoyable being a journalist. And I'm quite good with graphics now – manipulating photographs, putting my number plate on someone else's crash picture. Adding in a streak of dark green paint on an already-wrecked crash barrier, and a couple of mounds of earth in a cemetery, were child's play in the scheme of everything else.'

Isabel just sits there, taking it all in, frowning, not wanting to believe a word.

'It was a tightly orchestrated operation, relying heavily on the cast and good communication. I can't say it wasn't stressful at times. Swapping an architect's office back to a minicab business in such a short space of time was an incredible feat of teamwork, not to mention the cost of paying off the owners of the building, and to keep quiet.'

I wait, hoping for a reaction, but disappointingly she's stagnant from disbelief.

'Talking of children, little Rosie and Hugh were good, weren't they? I hear their first aid skills are excellent. It wasn't their house, of course, but the woman was their real mum – single, and desperately in need of the money. Another of Luke's recruits. In fact, pretty much everyone you've spoken to since your return was part of the cast, from doctors to coroners to paramedics. My very own little theatre company.'

Isabel's breathing quickens, making her shoulders rise and fall. It's a lot to take in, but I can't help the low laugh.

'And I especially enjoyed the footage from the fake alarm sensor cameras in Owen's house. Sorry, not Owen's house exactly, rather the place I'd promised to house-sit for an old friend. It was most entertaining to watch you both, although I admit that's why I had him killed off – well, killed off as far as you were concerned. Fucking you wasn't in the script.'

Isabel tenses and pushes away from me, making bleating noises and thumping her fists against my chest. She almost reaches my heart through my wasted muscles. I ate nothing but half a cup of rice a day for three months to lose weight for my comatose self.

'The thing is, Belle, you left me and I had to be certain you wouldn't do it again. What better way than to make your new life come crashing down around you? It brought you right back to me, where you belong.'

She doesn't reply.

'I've been searching for you since I was eight years old, Belle. I'm not letting you go now.'

Isabel takes the handkerchief I give her and wipes her eyes.

I can tell she's almost there now; almost given up and relinquished herself to me.

'Be good now and tell me that you love me.'

I shift closer to her.

'No,' she says. 'I . . . I can't. I don't.'

'Don't say that, Belle. You know that's not true. You do love me. You told me enough times.'

'I told you when things were good,' she snivels. 'But that's a long time ago now. I don't know who's the maddest, me or you.'

447

'We're both mad, Belle. Mad for each other.'

I hold her tightly, squeezing round her ribs until I hear her breathing slow. The shopping bag, still around her wrist, rustles between us. Then we stare into each other's eyes, holding the magic for what seems a lifetime. I tell her how sorry I am, how things should never have come to this, that all I wanted was for us to be happy.

And then she's crying again, choking out hot tears as our mouths coyly brush close, a kiss she will never forget, joining us for ever, me whispering down her salty throat. Our arms wrap tightly around each other's backs, embracing for ever, never letting go, holding on to everything.

It's only when I look down that I see the blood dripping on to the floor. I smile at her – a blooming grin offset against the look of terror on her face.

45

'Ray, you've got me for one hour then I'm back at the office.'

Adam drums his fingers on the wheel of his car, driving slowly through the traffic. He keeps glancing sideways at me, unnerving me, making me feel as if I'm playing truant from school.

'Thanks,' I say, as confidently as I can manage. I knew, when it came down to it, I'd be able to rely on him. 'I really appreciate this, Adam, just so you know.' I reach over and touch his hand, silently praying I'm not wrong. 'Let's go back to Woodford Grange. I want to speak to the doctor again, look deeper into Darwin's medical history. And I want to find Isabel Moore. To be honest, I'm really worried for her safety.'

Adam nods, following my directions to the nursing home. Once we're in the street, the building is harder to find than last time. We have to turn round twice until I spot it set back behind a wall and trees.

'I'm sure there was a sign here before,' I say as we get out and lock up.

We walk up to the door, but Adam has stopped on the gravel. He's staring up at the building.

'Wasn't this the place in the paper?' he says.

'What do you mean?'

'You remember, when we were thinking of moving house not so long ago, we had a laugh at the price of property. I swear there was a feature on this house in the paper. We commented on it. It was several thousand a month to rent and the price tag was well over a million.'

'Oh yeah, that's right. The one I put an offer on,' I say, rolling my eyes and smiling inwardly.

I go up to the door to ring the intercom. But the bell isn't there, so I knock. Then I knock again, much louder this time. When I try the handle, it's locked.

I hug my arms around my body and inadvertently stamp my feet. Pain shoots up my bad ankle. In the interests of looking normal for Bob, I didn't wear my support boot.

'This is really odd,' I say. 'I'm sure there was a buzzer on the wall last time I came.'

I knock again, but still no one comes. We both step back, inspecting the front façade.

'You're sure we're in the right place?' Adam asks, giving me a look.

'Certain,' I say, wondering if he could be right. 'I parked over there last time I came,' I say, pointing to a bush. I remember because I couldn't open the door properly.

I go back down the steps. Adam follows, taking my elbow when he sees me limping.

'Shall we try the back?' I say, and he agrees.

Thankfully the side gate is unlocked. I didn't fancy the thought of Adam hitching me over it. At the rear of the property I try to peer in through the windows, but they're too high, the ground levels being different to the front.

'I can't see much, can you?' I ask, standing on tip-toe. My ankle is throbbing now.

'It looks like a staff room or something,' Adam says, cupping his hands to the glass, just able to reach.

'It might be Felix Darwin's room, or maybe it's the next window along. Crouch down and let me get on your back for a proper look.'

This is the last thing I expected to be doing today.

'Ray, you'll hurt yourself.'

'Just do it, Adam,' I say, pointing to the spot.

He fixes himself in place against the wall and I use my good leg to lever myself up. At first I don't see much, but then my eyes grow used to the dim light in the room. I get down off Adam's back, yelping as I land.

'Felix Darwin is in his hospital bed just like last time,' I say in a low voice, wondering what the hell can be wrong with a man who was never even in an accident. 'He's alone and looks asleep. No nurses visible. Let's try the front again. Someone must be in there.'

We go back round to the main entrance. This time, the front door is wide open. We look at each other and nod, staying silent, each of us switching into a different mode.

Adam goes in first, given that I can barely walk, let alone run or give chase if need be.

'It all looks different,' I whisper as we step inside the hallway.

Adam nods, beckoning me close.

'Hello, anyone here?' he calls out. 'Police! Show yourselves.'

I almost expect Dr Lambeth to come striding out of one of the patient's rooms, chastising us for making a scene, but deep down I know that's not going to happen.

'Darwin's room is down that way,' I say, pointing to the corridor. 'Third on the right.'

Adam nods and walks on. There's no one to be seen, and no reply to his call. Slowly, he pushes the door open. Felix Darwin is still asleep.

'Mr Darwin?' I say.

Adam walks over and taps his shoulder. I mouth *be careful* when he glances back at me.

'Are you awake, Mr Darwin? We need to speak to you.'

The room looks exactly the same as last time, just without the staff. I keep guard by the door, half in and half out. I don't know what's going on, but I don't like it.

'Mr Darwin,' Adam says more loudly, 'can you hear me?'

'He was conscious the other day,' I say. 'And I saw his doctor.'

'She's gone,' says a desolate voice.

It takes a second for me to realise that it's Felix Darwin

452

talking. His eyes are wide open, staring at the ceiling. His face is ashen as if he's been drained of all blood.

'What do you mean?' Adam says, standing beside him.

Tentatively, I walk over to him. 'It's important you tell us what's going on, Mr Darwin,' I say. 'Who's gone?'

He fixes his eyes on the ceiling as if he's in some kind of semi-conscious state.

'Belle,' he whispers, though it's hard to make out.

'Adam, we should find a doctor,' I say. 'Or maybe call an ambulance.'

'I never meant to hurt her,' Felix says weakly.

'Who have you hurt?' I ask, wondering if he means Isabel. I turn to Adam. 'Search the building, see if there are any casualties. I'll keep him talking.'

Adam hesitates for a beat. 'Ray, I don't think—'

'Go, I'll be fine,' I tell him, reaching inside my jacket pocket and retrieving my pepper spray.

Adam nods and leaves the room. A paralysed man is hardly a threat, I tell myself, although I'm not so certain he's truly bedridden. I hear Adam's footsteps running up the stairs to search the rooms above us. I pray he's quick.

'I know there was no car crash, Mr Darwin, and I know Isabel's parents are alive, even though you told her they were dead. Is it Isabel you've hurt, Felix?'

He makes a barely perceptible nod.

'Where is she now? Did you hurt Alexandra Stanford and Melanie Carter too? Did you kill them, Felix?'

Nothing. He just stares at the ceiling, his eyes looking the saddest I've ever seen on a human.

453

'It's important you keep talking to me, Felix. Where is your doctor?'

He doesn't reply. I hear Adam upstairs, calling out, opening and shutting doors. It doesn't sound as if he's found anyone else in the building, confirming that this is no hospital.

I go round the other side of the bed and sit down, taking the weight off my sore ankle while I wait for Adam to return. Felix doesn't look as if he's about to leap up and attack me.

And that's when I see the pool of blood on the sheet, dripping on to the floor in a steady tick-tick of congealed red. It's coming from his back.

46

The drive to Isabel's parents' house takes longer than it should. Adam mounts a couple of pavements where necessary, cuts through some lights, blares his horn at an old man who's stepped out on to a crossing, and nearly hits a parked car. We have no idea what we'll find when we get there, only that before he died, Felix told us in an expiring, wheezy voice that he thought that's where Isabel was going, that she was heading home. I just hope it's not too late.

'Next left,' I say, holding on to the door handle as we corner sharply. We turn into the quiet close and scream down to the end. 'That house there, the overgrown garden.'

He skid-parks sideways across the drive, making me bump my head on the window. He's straight out of the car and at the door, hammering on it, rattling the locked handle, before I've even got out. I limp up the path to his side.

'This any use?' I say, handing him the key Mrs Welland gave me. I didn't give it back.

Adam shoves it in the lock and we barge inside, ready for anything.

In the distance, I hear the wail of sirens – presumably the back-up we called.

We go into the living room, stepping over the mess.

'Damn, I think she's left already,' I say breathlessly.

I kick a few cushions out of the way with my good foot, despairing, not knowing what I'm looking for. The carpet is strewn with old socks, tissues, that empty bottle of vodka – nothing helpful. Nothing that will lead us to Isabel.

'Felix definitely said she was heading home,' I say, following Adam into the dining room, then on into the kitchen.

He screws up his face at the mess.

'But that doesn't necessarily mean here,' I continue.

It's bugging me. As he slipped away, Felix was difficult to understand. I listened intently to what he was trying to tell us, but his voice was a crackled, bubbling whisper.

Back in the living room, Adam's eyes scan the scene.

'I'm certain he mentioned a hotel,' he says. 'And he kept wishing her the best of luck too. Very strange, given what happened.'

I shake my head. By now, officers should be at Woodford Grange. Hopefully they will turn something up at the scene. Apart from that, we don't have much else to go on.

Adam checks the rest of downstairs before going up to the bedrooms, while I wait in the hallway, giving me a chance to tap the words Felix said into Google, to see if there's an expression or meaning I'm missing. It's clutching at straws, but I'm certain he was trying to tell us something.

The search throws up millions of hits for 'best of luck'. Then I type it all as one word, which is what it actually sounded like when Felix spoke it, but that doesn't bring up anything that seems useful either. I then type in 'best', 'luck' and 'hotel', expecting to be presented with a string of guesthouses across the English-speaking world. To my surprise, top of the list is a website for a Bestluck Hotel in India. I click on it. It takes a while to download, but when it does, it shows a shabby but quaint-looking place with Chandni Chowk in the address.

Of course! Isabel mentioned this street name when we were in the café together. It was clear to me then from the expression on her face that after her stay in India she'd left a part of herself there.

I pause, thinking, frowning, staring at my phone screen. Adam comes back downstairs and goes into the living room, snapping on a pair of gloves, saying he's going to search through Isabel's backpack. I'm surprised it's still here.

I follow him in. 'Adam, I think I might know where she's heading.'

Adam stands up from Isabel's pack, giving me his attention. He's holding a couple of things down by his side. His expression is tense yet unreadable.

'She could well be heading to the airport, if she's not there already,' I say, wondering what he's found.

Adam looks curious, narrowing his eyes.

'When Felix said she's going home, I think this is where he meant. Look.' I show him the hotel website on my phone, briefly explaining the connection.

Adam nods sourly, a look of remorse spreading across his face. 'And I think I know why she went there in the first place,' he says. He holds up a little maroon book. 'She must have dropped it.'

He opens it, showing it to me.

'Christ,' I say.

'Christ indeed.' He sighs heavily, knowing what's coming next. Briefly, he takes hold of my hand. 'Ray, I'm sorry for doubting you,' he says warmly. 'You were right to pursue this.'

I give him a brief nod, squeezing his hand back. 'Come on,' I say, 'we've got a case to wrap up.'

Yet for some reason, as we dash out to the car, explaining to the incoming officers that they must preserve the scene at all costs, I find myself praying that we're wrong.

47

Poor, poor Felix. My baby. My love. My never-quite-lover.

Goodbye to you for ever.

I will miss you.

You were right. I did love you once. In fact, you were my life – until you broke me.

And did you know that, for a long while, every single one of my days revolved around waiting for the three-fifteen end-of-school bell so that I could rush home and make myself beautiful, just the way you liked me to look, ready for our evening together?

Before you, all I had was my slightly dull job. You coloured in my monochrome life, Felix. An ironic statement for an art teacher, I realise.

You made me feel special. You recalibrated my life, and turned me into something I wasn't. At first I liked it, but then you became a disease, winding your way insidiously, sickly, through my veins. I didn't realise until it was too late; until I'd become yours. None of me belonged to *me* in the end.

I laugh out loud, making the passenger in front of me turn round and stare.

And just so you know, Felix, just so you're aware, when I discovered your stash of photographs hidden away in your spare bedroom, I briefly felt good, that I was The One, as you'd written. Special. Perfect.

Only I wasn't, was I?

I wasn't really special at all. Because you had others, all lined up and ready to go if I should let you down.

And I did let you down, didn't I?

I shuffle forward in the queue. A monotonous announcement is made for the hundredth time about not leaving luggage, that it will be removed. My small bag is on my shoulder – light, just like last time.

When I went back to the house, I didn't dare risk even ten minutes to pack everything properly, which I probably should have done. I grabbed the essentials and got out fast, abandoning the remains of my life in England entirely.

Once I got to the airport, I went straight to check-in. But as I went to get the ticket and my passport from my bag, I ended up dropping to my knees, panicking, rummaging through the contents of the saggy cloth bag. *No, no, no* I said over and over in my head, the people behind me growing impatient. *Dear God, no* . . .

I didn't know what to do.

Slowly, I stood up, thinking hard. Finally, as I neared the front, I left the check-in queue, went up to the airline's ticket counter and made my request, feeling sick, sliding the cash I'd come across in Dad's study and the passport across the counter. There was just enough money to cover it.

Now I'm trying not to look upset as I stand back in line at the Air India check-in desk, praying I pass for any other weary and disorganised traveller. The way I'm dressed – ripped combat trousers, an oversized cardigan, beaded sandals – I certainly fit the backpacking profile, if a little older than several other gap-year-type travellers I've spotted. I look around me, staring down the queue as it moves forward painfully slowly. I take deep breaths, trying to calm my heart.

When I reach the front, the check-in clerk barely looks up.

'Hi,' I say, handing him my passport and a printout of the details I just got from the airline's desk.

'Good afternoon, Miss.' He nods, giving me a quick glance.

I like the Miss. It's almost as if he knows how close I came to marrying you. It was Mum's dream to organise our wedding. A pang of sadness shoots through me at the irony. Even though they're not dead, I'm never going to see them again. At least I've already begun the grieving process, I tell myself, closely watching the clerk as he taps into his computer.

How I'd love to tell him! How I'd love to shout out to the whole airport that you didn't get me, that I'm the lucky one who got away unscathed. Out of habit, I glance over my shoulder. Of course, there's no sign of you anywhere.

The check-in clerk looks at my passport, flicking through the many visas and stamps it contains. 'Off duty?' he comments.

I smile, give him a little nod, praying it's all in order.

He holds the passport open, tapping at his computer, and asks me to put my bag on the scales. It only weighs five kilograms.

'Travelling light?' he says with a smile.

'I'm used to flying that way,' I tell him, remembering. He seems satisfied.

The clerk asks me if I packed my bag by myself. I confirm that I did, and that I don't have anything dangerous in my luggage or on my person.

Only the memories.

'May I have an aisle seat?' I ask, hating the feeling of being trapped, hemmed in. I never used to mind.

He nods, and finally prints out my boarding pass. He slides it into the photograph page of the passport, giving it one more glance.

The photograph is a good one. Red hair and blue eyes are rare, as you told me countless times.

The check-in clerk smiles, handing me back the documents. 'Have a good flight, Miss,' he says, before calling the next person up to the desk.

'Thank you,' I say, turning to leave, keeping my head down.

Then, with a brisk pace, I head for the departures lounge.

Finally, I am free.

48

We're hedging our bets, could still be way off the mark, but I insist on following my instincts. Adam agrees.

Once the necessary calls have been made, the duty team back at the station briefed, we get moving. Having checked likely flights that Isabel could be taking, we head for Birmingham Airport. There's a flight to Delhi due to leave in less than an hour.

'I hope we're not too late,' I say, hanging up from requesting border control alerts. It's out of my hands now, although bringing an airport to a standstill is no mean feat. 'And let's not call Bob yet,' I say as Adam speeds through the gears.

He gives me a silent nod. Even though Bob will have got wind of things by now, I need to make sure I'm completely right before he finds out the full story. It could mean the end of my career otherwise.

The airport has never seemed so far away, but when we finally arrive we get immediate clearance through the barriers. We leave the car in a high-security area right outside the plate-glass windows of Departures and are met by a special escort team.

'Alan Jenson, head of airport security,' a stocky man in his fifties says, briefly shaking our hands. Dressed in a suit and high-vis wear, he updates us on intelligence gained in the last few minutes. He's flanked by three armed and uniformed officers.

'This way,' the younger officer says when instructed to lead us on by Jenson. His Heckler and Koch semi-automatic hangs diagonally across his front, looking nonchalant, yet ready for action within a split second.

My mouth dries up and my heart kicks off its ridiculous rhythm again as we follow.

What if I'm wrong?

A stressed-looking suited woman rushes up to our group as we forge ahead, striding down the long tiled concourse.

'Here you go, sir,' she says, handing Jenson a folder.

Jenson nods and takes it, giving it a quick once-over as we continue along. He passes it to me.

'The passenger list for flight AI114. It's a Boeing 787 Dreamliner at full capacity – two hundred and thirty-four. Six no-shows so far.' He glances at his watch.

I scan the list as fast as my eyes will allow, conscious of the time.

'Adam,' I say suddenly, gripping his arm, bringing us to a halt.

The airport noise momentarily silences as I focus on the name. I hold out the list, pointing to the relevant line.

'How the hell did that happen?' he says, glaring at me then the others.

I don't know what to say. I close my eyes for a few seconds and shake my head.

'Can we get to the departures lounge?' I ask. 'The flight's being held, I presume?'

'Clearance confirmed,' Jenson says as we head off again at a brisk pace. 'And no, the flight is not being held. I haven't yet received official instructions. At best I can delay, but unless we're talking about a security risk here, there are protocols I need to follow.'

He lags behind as Adam and I overtake families and pushchairs, weave between single travellers with pull-along bags, and avoid a beeping special-assistance cart. Again I check my watch then cast a glance at a departures board. Flight AI114 is now at the top with 'Last call for boarding – Gate 17' flashing beside it.

'It's leaving on time, we need to hurry,' I tell Adam, clamping my teeth against the pain in my ankle.

From experience, I know that once the aircraft doors are shut we'll have one hell of a battle to do anything about it. I hadn't bargained on taking a trip to India any time soon.

'Let's go then,' Adam says, kicking up the pace into a run.

The armed guards follow us as we break further away from Jenson.

The concourse seems never-ending, with long queues of passengers waiting to board at the various gates. I nearly trip on a grizzling toddler, then a large group of foreign students slows us for a second or two. Each gate seems further apart than the last, but finally number seventeen comes into sight.

There's a large cluster of passengers still waiting in line to board, although from this distance I can't make out Isabel among them.

'Adam, wait,' I say, catching my breath. 'I've dealt with her. If she's here, let me approach her first.'

He proffers a reluctant nod, slowing down to my pace as we reach the back end of the queue. No one pays us any attention until we're flanked by the guards and Jenson.

We scan the line, which is now moving forward at a steady pace as the Air India staff check boarding passes. I get annoyed looks from several passengers as if I'm about to push in. Many are Indian, some in large family groups, and there's a group of twelve or so lads clearly part of a sports team judging by their uniforms.

I scan for a lone white female, praying she's not already gone through.

'It's no good,' I say to Adam, stopping and pushing my fingers through my hair in exasperation. 'She's not here.'

'Are you certain?'

I nod. 'We'll need to do something else.' I turn to Alan Jenson. 'Can you find out if she's boarded already?' I point to the name on the list again. 'We need to delay—'

I stop speaking abruptly, staring at a row of seats about fifty feet away. I turn to Adam, shielding one side of my face as best I can.

'Drop back now,' I instruct him and the officers.

They nod, understanding immediately, casually falling into line beside Jenson as if they're on a routine patrol.

An announcement rings out for all remaining passengers for flight AI114 to make their way to gate seventeen, final call.

'She's sitting over there,' I say to Adam, gripping the thick padding of his jacket sleeve. 'Look, she's about to come over to the gate.'

My ears whoosh as adrenalin pumps through me. I keep my eyes on Isabel as she joins the back of the shortening queue, a small embroidered bag slung over her shoulder. She clutches her passport and boarding pass in her right hand.

'Let's go,' I tell Adam, circling round to the end of the line in a wide sweep.

I'm feet away from her, approaching from behind, watching as my hand comes out and settles on her shoulder. Her hair is unkempt and her clothes dirty, as if she's been in them for days. I know she probably has.

'Excuse me,' I say firmly yet as inconspicuously as I can. Several other passengers turn round before she does. 'May I check your passport?'

I'm beside her now, my hand having slipped down to her elbow. She's still holding the passport, ready to show the airline staff. Adam flanks her on the other side, while Jenson and the guards have drawn close.

Isabel swings round. Her face blanches when she sees me.

'What?'

'I'd like to check your passport please.'

She glares at me, the fire in her dead eyes flickering hopelessly.

'You can't do that,' she says, shrugging away from me, trying to get closer to the front of the queue.

Adam steps forward, making his presence known.

Gently, I ease the passport from her fingers. Reluctantly, her grip loosens, and her eyes slowly drag up to Adam, then me, her lips mouthing unintelligible, slow-motion words.

I open the passport to the photograph page.

At first glance I think I've made a terrible mistake. Isabel Moore's photograph stares back at me. But then I read the name, and the familiar, haunting expression of Alexandra Stanford resolves, her half-formed smile belying her fate. The similarity between the women is undeniable.

Adam has Melanie Carter's passport, which he found at the Moores' house, safe in an evidence bag, along with Isabel's own passport. She'd obviously picked up the wrong one.

I swallow down the lump in my throat.

'Isabel Moore, I am arresting you on suspicion of the murders of Alexandra Stanford, Melanie Carter and Felix Darwin. You do not have to say anything, but it may harm your defence if you fail to mention when questioned something which you later rely on in court.'

I hear myself speaking automatically as I watch the remaining blood drain from Isabel's face. The armed officers surround her, removing her bag and handcuffing her. In the background, I'm aware of more airport security staff clearing the area, people with children first.

Isabel doesn't resist. She stares at the floor, her gaze dropping lower and lower until I'm concerned she's going to faint.

A commotion breaks out around us as the passengers are ushered away, as they hear that there's a murderer in the vicinity. A woman grabs her child and scampers away, making several others follow suit until Adam calls for calm, announcing that there's no need for concern. Eventually, security brings the crowd under control.

I take Isabel's arm. 'Follow me,' I say, urging her on, willing myself to overcome the pain in my leg as I'm faced with the long walk again.

For a moment, she's frozen, unmovable, and our eyes lock. I try to work it out, pick apart why she did it; why she took their passports, ground off their tattoos, stole their young lives. My gut tells me jealousy, that Darwin drove her to it with his unrelenting quest for the perfect woman, but time will tell me more. In this line of work, answers are often only revealed once the puzzle is solved.

'Let's go,' I say, tugging on her arm.

Finally, she moves. As I escort her away with Adam and the three guards flanking us, she turns and whispers something to me. Her lips brush against my ear, wrong-footing me, making me stumble.

'Love cancer,' she breathes.

Her eyes are aglow, too intense to look at, and she gives

an insane laugh, throwing back her head so that her hair catches in the wall of light spreading in through the huge windows.

I pull away, shocked, but still holding her in a vice-like grip.

A woman driven to madness, I tell myself, fixing my gaze firmly on the end of the long concourse.

A place I refuse to go.

49

Half an hour after registering at the clinic reception, I still haven't been called. Adam sits beside me. He taps furiously on his Blackberry. In the midst of everything, we can barely spare the time for this, but he insisted I come; said he'd come too.

'Sorry,' I say, nudging him, wondering how to make it up to him. He has no idea how grateful I am that he's here with me. If I'd cancelled, they said I'd have to wait until after Christmas for a new appointment.

Adam frowns and smiles at the same time, slipping his hand on top of mine. He clenches my fist, trying to stop the tremor.

'I wouldn't be anywhere else,' he tells me. 'Anyway, you're not exactly having a heart transplant,' he adds, winking.

'Thanks, Adam.'

Sympathy from him is hard-won, although for some reason his wry comment reminds me of Isabel – of her torn and tattered heart; of how she wrestled love and infatuation, neediness and obsession, only for it to end in tragedy.

Following a comprehensive psychiatric assessment, she's being held in a secure unit, though I don't imagine a jury will be so accommodating when her case reaches court.

'There's absolutely nothing wrong with me,' I say, feeling a fraud, sitting in a waiting room full of people who are probably far sicker than me.

'Let the doctor be the judge of that.'

'Too much caffeine and not enough sleep,' I say, getting up as my name is finally called.

Adam squeezes my hand. 'Remember, it's just a few sticky pads, a couple of wires and a pack round your waist.'

Our fingers pull apart as I walk off. I glance back over my shoulder, smiling and rolling my eyes as the nurse leads me to a small room.

Fifteen minutes later, Adam and I are on our way and my nerves have subsided. I'm barely aware of the monitor.

'Will you drop me at the office?' I ask as we leave the car park.

'You need to let this go now, Ray,' he tells me, sighing, but swings the car round anyway. 'Don't dilute the charges we have.'

He means Isabel's inevitable insanity plea. The more people who are seen to have messed with her head, the more of a case she'll have.

'Don't you think Bethany Adams and Owen – sorry, Luke Manning should pay their dues?'

'Ultimately, of course. But let the defence lawyers deal with it, if they see fit. Pounding a fraud case that's technically a civil matter is a waste of your time, not when we need to focus on Isabel Moore. Bob's not going to—'

'Let me draft the charges, then I'll clear it with Bob,' I say. 'I'm going down the obtaining services dishonestly route. Isabel worked for Ow— for Luke, after all. She claims she was owed money. It could carry weight. One more afternoon, Adam, that's all I need.'

I pray he doesn't notice the quiver in my voice, or how insubstantial my proposed charges seem. Or even that, somewhere deep inside, I carry an ounce of sympathy for Isabel. I just want justice, the same as all of us.

It makes me wonder: is it easier to convince someone that you *are* mad, or persuade them that you're not?

Last night, I had a team sift through Felix Darwin's personal affairs. Twenty-three aliases later, we established that he was in fact called George Baum, owner of a chain of fast-food restaurants. Squeaky clean on all counts – apart from maintaining a sick and comprehensive log of a number of disturbingly similar-looking women that he systematically stalked and harassed over several decades. We've already ascertained from speaking to colleagues and estranged family members that he'd been a loner since his mother died when he was a kid. The profiler already believes he had a psychological condition based around her, that he was trying to replace her.

'Thank God there are services in place these days to snag people like him before it gets too late,' I say to Adam, though we both know it's not an infallible science. 'Services to help kids like Baum,' I go on to explain when Adam looks perplexed. Too many still slip through the net, often right under our noses. 'His father found his way on to the sex offenders' register for a start.'

'That's all ancient history, love,' Adam says, wrenching on the handbrake. 'You sure you don't just want to come home?' He squeezes my leg as we pull up outside the office.

'But ancient history makes the present,' I tell him, catching the thoughtful look in his eye. 'And no, this is a good chance for me to catch up. On *my* time,' I add before he berates me again.

Adam leans over and gives me a kiss, waving a quick salute as he drives off. I head into the building.

'Ma'am,' DC Rowlands says as I go into the department, trying to conceal my limp – a vestige of my once-paranoid state. 'Good to have you back.'

'Good to be back, Ed,' I say. I'm about to walk past his desk, but I stop, composing myself. 'Thanks for your help with everything.' He's always been loyal to me, shown his integrity. 'It's officers like you who hold this unit together,' I add, feeling the flush in my cheeks.

'Thank you, ma'am,' he says, giving me an appreciative look.

Before I leave, I catch the eye of the officer next to him, a serious, rather aloof DC who's not been here long. He gives me a tight nod before looking away, making me wonder about him. I suppose I'll never know for certain who complained, though it won't stop me second-guessing. Perhaps they did me a favour, I think, heading off to reclaim my desk.

I settle down, logging in at my terminal. Usually around this time my heart would set out on an hour-long run of skips and palpitations. I sit and wait for them to kick off – but, strangely, there's nothing.

Earlier, Dr Lewis gave me a prescription for anti-inflammatory pills that dealt with my ankle swelling almost immediately. Perhaps the reduction in pain and knowing I'm finally back at work unconditionally is enough to settle things for now. That and the fact that Bob informed me the complaints have been withdrawn. I show my gratitude by beginning the day with the references I promised the young constable who recently sat his exams. I heard he did well.

Dr Lewis, aside from all her other help, also left a note for me at the surgery reception suggesting I regularly schedule in some holiday, and actually do the fitness classes I bragged to her about. So far I've ordered a yoga mat online, have Christmas Eve booked off, and I'm considering a week's holiday in the New Year. But I don't want to get ahead of myself.

'Any news from the CPS?' I ask Ed as he follows me back to my desk from the coffee machine. The call should come any time now.

'All quiet so far,' he says. 'But a young lady hand-delivered something for you earlier. Rachel brought it up, said it was important.'

I sit down at my desk, straightening up the picture of my girls, and pick up the envelope. I open it, watching as Ed retreats to his desk. Inside are two tickets and an information leaflet for a play at the Little Theatre. Reading that Bethany Adams is playing one of the lead roles, I take out the handwritten note.

It simply states *Sorry*.

I lean back in my chair, tickets in hand. I stare out of the window, taking it all in, thinking what it means.

'Ed,' I call out. He comes over immediately. 'Is that charity raffle you organised still going?'

'Yes, ma'am,' he says. 'We've raised nearly a thousand pounds so far.'

'Jolly good,' I say. 'Then add these tickets to the prize list.'

DC Rowlands takes them and turns to go, puzzled, but grateful for the donation.

'And do me a favour, Ed.'

He stops, looks back.

'Don't say you got them from me.'

When I get home, I find that Grace has cooked a meal. Standing in the doorway, I stare at the kitchen, sizing up which is more amazing – the fact that she's done this, or that she's used every single saucepan and utensil we own.

'I had to,' she says, scowling and shrugging at the same

time. She heaves a huge lidded casserole pot from the oven. 'There was nothing to eat. Just ingredients.'

I can't help the inner smile.

'No microwave meals, you mean,' Adam says, coming in shortly after me and catching the tail end of the conversation. His face glows from fresh air, from a few hours off, from relief.

'What meat is it?' Stella chimes, sliding into her space at the table.

Grace dollops huge spillages of food on to our plates, passing them round. She pauses, staring at her sister. 'No idea. Just meat I found in the freezer.'

'It's actually really good, love,' I tell her, trying some. 'And I think it's pork.'

I spoon the lumpy mash out for everyone.

'Did you nail the charges against Bethany and Luke?' Adam asks me quietly as we all tuck in.

I cast him a look, nodding, though still feeling concerned that they won't stick. 'Anyway, no talking shop at the table.'

The truth is I left the office shortly after I'd given Ed the tickets. I went shopping instead, mulling over everything that had happened. I was sold some silly face cream for an equally silly amount of money in a department store, bought some new pyjamas, some fruit from the market, and a new shirt for Adam.

'Sorry. And look, you two,' he says to Grace and Stella, slapping a couple of glossy holiday brochures on the table. 'I found these on the hall table.' He winks at our daughters.

'I picked them up when I was in the city,' I say, horrified he's found them. 'It was just in case,' I add, trying hard to cancel out Adam's enthusiasm. 'I'm not certain I can take the time off yet.'

'*Flor*ida!' Stella exclaims, swiping up one brochure.

'I'd rather go to India,' Grace says, squirting a load of tomato sauce on her stew. 'Rosie's going in a couple of months as part of her gap year and . . .'

I pause, my fork halfway to my mouth, as Grace tells us about her friend's adventures. It sets me thinking about Isabel again, and how she ran away to Delhi and scratched a living as a maid in a hotel. She told me all about it while she was curled up on a plastic stacking chair in the interview room during one of our many chats. She chewed on her sleeves, rocked, and scratched at the table until her nails broke. Adam and another officer sat quietly in the room, listening.

'It was all because of him,' she said over and over, her voice becoming increasingly edgy.

While she hadn't confessed to murdering Alexandra and Melanie at that point, she hadn't denied it either. The forensic evidence was being fast-tracked through the lab, and, of course, predictably she claimed her attack on Felix was self-defence.

Before he died, Felix managed to tell both Adam and me that she'd pre-meditated stabbing him by concealing the knife in her shopping bag, pushing it into his back when they were embracing. The angle and depth of the wound on the body corroborated this, and fitted with scene evidence and blood patterns found there and on Isabel. Felix also told us where he'd watched her dispose of the kitchen knife – in the sharps disposal bin, as she'd waited for him to die. That wasn't long before we turned up.

It was more information than we'd had to go on in months, and I didn't believe any amount of denial from Isabel was going to untangle her from our forensic net.

She was a pathetic sight – a fearful, damaged woman who had reverted to a childlike state. She maintained it was all because of him.

'You hear something from someone for so long, so often and so convincingly, that in the end, you believe it,' she told me nervously. She was staring at the wall as if it was a cinema screen playing out the story of her life. 'I was *his*,' she told me. 'All his, for so long.' She rocked and cried some more, her story trickling out in sputtering bursts. 'I was the one,' she said. 'His only one. Do you know what that feels like?'

I didn't reply, just waited for her to continue, which I knew she would.

'It feels even worse when you find out you're not.' She took a sip of water, clearing her throat. 'When I discovered all the others, I didn't know what it meant at first. It never occurred to me that he'd been *lying* to me. If someone tells you they adore you, if they go out of their way to keep you at all costs, you never expect that.'

Isabel stood up then, even though the newly qualified social worker, Michael, who'd been summoned as her appropriate adult, encouraged her to sit down, to stay calm.

'How *could* he?' she asked no one in particular. She narrowed her startling eyes, searching for the right words. Her head bowed. 'I truly thought he loved me,' she whispered. 'And when I realised he didn't, something in me ignited. My reality had been turned on its head. What I'd believed all along, what I'd *suffered* for, simply wasn't the reality.'

'And how did that make you feel, Isabel?' I asked. 'What did those feelings make you do?'

She shook her head then, beginning a long smile that took the next few moments to spread. But I still needed to hear it.

'At first, after I discovered that book, I just wanted to die. It was his life's work. Pages and pages filled from way back with the details of women he'd become obsessed with. They all had to resemble his mother, of course.' Isabel gave a laugh. 'Turns out I was the closest.' She stared into nowhere again, tuning into another place. Her next words came out as a whisper. 'I had to put things right.' She was shaking, every cell in her body dancing.

'Did you kill Alexandra Stanford and Melanie Carter out of jealousy, Isabel? Do you confess to their murders?'

She began by nodding – a little flicker of her chin, her neck, her forehead. 'Afterwards, I got their keys, went into their homes, you know. Took their stuff.' She looked up at me. 'Jewellery, passports, bank details . . . I just grabbed anything. I wanted to feel as if they'd been stripped, violated, betrayed. Like I had been.'

'Whose homes did you go into, Isabel? Can you be more specific?' I asked. I didn't feel I was getting through to her though. She was in a dreamlike state.

'I would have worked my way through all the others had he not found out,' she said with bitterness in her eyes and a slow shake of her head. 'Even though I'd left him, got my own place, I was never really alone. Once he found out where I lived, he was always there, following me, watching me.' She seemed to be losing her grasp on reality, her eyes growing cloudy, her body swaying in a circle.

'Are you referring to Felix Darwin?' I asked.

She nodded. 'But I didn't know he was following me when . . . I . . . I thought I was alone. I just wanted to make them not his.'

She looked down, touching the back of her neck.

I knew what was there.

'Isabel Moore, I'll ask again. Did you kill Alexandra Stanford and Melanie Carter?'

'Yes,' she said, finally, without emotion. 'Yes, I killed them both. I wanted to take away everything they'd taken from me. My life had been stripped bare by Felix, scraped back to the raw elements of existence. As long as they were alive, I didn't have a purpose. I believed Felix, you know. I truly believed I was his.'

'So Felix Darwin knew you'd killed Alexandra and Melanie?' I asked.

She was already nodding, almost proud of their complicity.

She gave a bitter laugh. 'Felix following me, following those girls. They didn't know, and I didn't know.' She tipped back her head, her hair catching in the light.

I gave Adam and my colleague a glance. They remained stony-faced.

'Afterwards he promised that he loved me still, that he wouldn't turn me in. Not if I went for treatment. I didn't want to go into hospital, though. In fact, a part of me wanted to be caught, thrown into prison. At least I'd have been free. Safe.' Isabel took a moment, sipped her water. 'But he had me sectioned, convincing me we had a future together when I got better. He made me promise that I'd stay with him for ever. In return, he said he'd never tell, that he'd burn the book.'

For a while after that, Isabel just sat there, shaking her head, staring at the wall, rocking gently. Her skin looked almost see-through, showing crazy maps of veins on her inner wrists, along the length of her neck.

'He was always trying to help me,' she said suddenly, reignited. 'Make me his; make me better than I was.' She gripped the edge of the table, spilling some of the water. Then she laughed – a cackle far too old-sounding to have come from her. 'He broke me.'

Her warped grin sent a chill through me.

The medical reports stated she'd been admitted to the psychiatric unit against her will, sectioned for being a danger to herself and others. She'd even threatened violence against her parents. Even though she stayed in Sandy Acres longer than her initial treatment required, the reports showed her suddenly disappearing without discharging herself.

'Did you go to India to get away from Felix?'

She shrugged, but then nodded. 'I had time to think in hospital. I actually started to feel better. Though perhaps I was running away from myself, too. From what I'd done. Either way, I knew I couldn't go through with his deal.'

Soon after that, we called it a day, knowing we had enough evidence to charge her with all three murders. As far as I was concerned, forensics were a necessity, but ultimately a formality.

The team assembled in the department, and Bob congratulated me in his own slightly dour way. We were having a celebratory drink when Rowlands presented me with the news. A team had been into Felix's flat, taken it to pieces. I've only seen photographs of the album so far, and then only a dozen or so pages and what they contained. Apparently there were many, many more, but it made me stop and think; made me consider just for a moment what it was like for all those young women who lived under the fear of him: Alexandra, Melanie, and Isabel – all casualties of Felix Darwin's obsession.

Standing around our desks, looking around our shabby, slightly chaotic office where colleagues – some as close as family to me – were still hard at work, I felt glad to be back; glad to be part of the team again.

I raised my drink silently, in honour of the two dead

girls, who were not much older than my Grace. Bob and Adam automatically chinked my glass, not realising who it was I was remembering with the silent prayer in my head. I gave a sad nod and smile, knowing I wouldn't be seeing Alexandra at night ever again.

'Mum . . . Mum?'

The room comes back into focus.

'What's wrong with your dinner?' Grace asks.

'It's delicious,' I tell her, trying not to sound vague.

'Mum's got a lot on her mind at the moment,' Adam says. 'It's a busy time for her going back to work after injuring her ankle.'

I like it that he's covering for me, but it's time for the truth.

'Stella, Grace, my ankle wasn't the reason I took time off work.'

They look up from their food.

'I was stressed and anxious. I wasn't sleeping or eating properly, and I think I was verging on depression.' I lay down my knife and fork. 'That's why I took time off. Actually, I was *asked* to take time off. To sort things out.'

They don't say anything.

'I had to tell you the truth. What if one of you feels that way in the future?'

'Fair enough,' Grace says in her matter-of-fact way.

Stella's soaking it all up in her usual watchful fashion.

I nod, putting one hand on each of my girls' hands.

'Anxiety plays cruel games if you let it,' I tell them, not wanting to trivialise the condition.

I look at my lovely daughters, knowing I'd do anything to ensure their happiness.

What parent wouldn't?

My phone rings over on the counter, vibrating against the work surface.

'I should take it,' I say, standing up, knocking against the table.

Adam's hand is round my wrist. 'No work at dinner, remember?'

'Adam, stop it,' I say, pulling out of his grip and dashing across the kitchen.

Forensics have been all over the Moores' house today, sifting through the wreckage Isabel left behind. They promised me an update.

I answer it, retreating into the hallway so as not to disturb the others.

When I come back into the kitchen ten minutes later, I'm wearing my coat and have my bag slung over my shoulder. The disappointment on Grace and Stella's faces eats into my heart.

'This had better be important,' Adam says, shovelling in a mouthful of stew.

I open my mouth to speak, but nothing much comes out. My mind is still a jumble of what I've just been told. There's so much to get to work on.

'Ray, where are you going?' Adam asks, laying down his knife and fork.

'Actually,' I say calmly, looking at my family and taking off my coat again, 'I'm going nowhere.' There's nothing I can do tonight.

Adam smiles, putting his arm round me as I sit back down at the table.

'Now, how about we choose somewhere from these brochures?' I say, spreading them out.

'Really, Mum?' Stella says with a loud whoop. She punches the air.

'When?' Grace asks, looking at me cautiously, as if I'll change my mind at any moment. There's an imperceptible glimmer of excitement in her eye.

'Soon,' I say, silently promising not to let them down. 'How about very, very soon?'